"You've forgotten what it's like to be young and in lust."

"Bebe and Aldo are *in love*," Cydney said hotly, glaring at Angus. "I'm not sure you know the difference."

"Between love and lust? Sure I do. I can prove it right here."

"Can you?" She raised an eyebrow. "I'd like to see that."

"Then keep your eyes open," he said, and kissed her.

Hard and swift, like he'd been aching to all night, expecting her to push him away and ready to release her the second she did, but her lips parted—stunning him and thrilling him—drawing him deep into the sweetness of her mouth. Gus groaned and lifted her, pressing himself between her legs, and swung her onto the counter. . . .

MOTHER OF THE BRIDE

Lynn Michaels

IVY BOOKS • NEW YORK

With love for John and Teri Lea Chandler Purcell,
and Mother Jean Chandler

An Ivy Book
Published by The Ballantine Publishing Group
Copyright © 2002 by Lynne Smith
Excerpt from *Star Struck* by Lynn Michaels copyright © 2002 by Lynne Smith

ISBN 0-7394-2483-1

Manufactured in the United States of America

chapter
one

The worst day of Cydney Parrish's life was a Monday. The last Monday in October. It began when she woke with a start at 7:12 A.M. Her clock radio should have wakened her at six, but the alarm was set on P.M. instead of A.M. She'd forgotten to check it at 2 A.M. Sunday when she turned the clocks back an hour from daylight savings time.

Cydney was particular about things like that. Obsessive, her sister Gwen said, but if the *Kansas City Star* said set your clocks at 2 A.M., Cydney set her clocks at 2 A.M. Who cares when you set the damn clock, Gwen argued, so long as you set it? Cydney cared, that's who, and Cydney sprang forward and fell back exactly at 2 A.M. every April and October.

When she saw how late it was, she wanted to fall back under the covers, but she sprang forward—into the shower, into her clothes, into her office to grab her briefcase, her portfolio and her camera case. She stopped just long enough to pound on her niece Bebe's bedroom door and yell at her to get moving or she'd miss her first class.

Cydney was late for her first appointment. She dropped into a chair in the lobby of Stellar Publications, one of her biggest and best accounts, breathless and annoyed. She was always on time, always. Unlike Gwen, whose tardiness on photo shoots was legendary.

"They can't start without me," she'd say. "I've got the camera."

And an ego to match her genius with a 35mm Nikon in her hands. Gwen Parrish had two Pulitzer Prizes. Cydney had a mortgage and Bebe, Gwen's nineteen-year-old daughter from her first marriage. And spider veins, she thought sourly, rubbing the thready little red spot she'd found on the back of her knee in the shower. She hoped it was just a bruise. Thirty-two was too young for spider veins.

It was also too young to be hit on by Wendell Pickering, art director of *Bloom and Bulb* magazine, a lanky man with thinning hair and pale eyes. He made the pass once he finished nitpicking the six-page spread on perennial borders Cydney had stayed up until 3 A.M. to finish.

"I'm afraid I can't approve this," he said. "I might be able to over dinner this evening if you think you can make the corrections by seven-thirty."

Then he smiled and laid his hand on her tush.

It was now 2:30 in the afternoon. Cydney had a parking ticket in her purse, a headache and no Tylenol, a notebook computer with a blown graphics card that thought it was an Etch A Sketch, a roll of film a client had accidentally exposed and would have to be reshot, a broken heel on her best pumps, and now a man with a neck like a chicken who actually thought she'd go out with him to salvage a $2500 photo layout.

"I'm busy tonight, Wendell," Cydney said in her iciest voice. Sticking my head in the oven, she thought. "Now take your hand off me while you still can."

He did. Quicker than you can say "sexual harassment."

Cydney shoved the layout in her portfolio, told Pickering she'd deliver the corrections to his secretary in the morning and flapped out of *Bloom and Bulb* in the old pair of loafers she'd dug out of the back of her blue Jeep Cherokee when she broke her heel. The loose nail in the left sole scraped the sidewalk and made her teeth clench as she slid behind the wheel and slammed the door hard enough to rock the truck.

Gwen was in Moscow interviewing Vladimir Putin for *Newsweek*. She was in Kansas City, Missouri, fending off Wendell Pickering. What was wrong with this picture?

I'm glad you asked, said the little voice that occasionally made itself heard from the depths of her psyche. *I've been waiting for years to tell you.*

"It's a rhetorical question," Cydney muttered, rubbing the throbbing bridge of her nose. "I love my life."

And she did. She really did. She loved her family and she was proud of Sunflower Photo, the freelance photography and graphics studio she'd built without any help from Gwen or their parents. It was a rotten day, that's all. A thoroughly rotten day. Throwing in the towel wasn't in Cydney's nature, but she'd simply had enough. She dug her cell phone out of her briefcase, postponed her last two appointments of the day till Tuesday, and drove to the grocery store.

In the produce aisle she slipped on a grape and wrenched her left ankle. She didn't realize she was out of checks and had only twenty bucks in her wallet—and no credit or ATM cards—until the checker rang up $34.17. The people in line behind her shifted and muttered while she gave back fourteen dollars and seventeen cents' worth of stuff.

"I'm going home." Cydney gritted her teeth as she limped the groceries out to her truck. "I'm going home and I'm going to scream."

And that's exactly what she did, once she dumped the two paper sacks on the kitchen table, walked down the hall, opened Bebe's door and saw her niece naked on the bed underneath a young man with long blond hair. Bebe screamed, too. So did the young man on top of her.

Cydney slammed the door and went back to the kitchen, cheeks burning, hands shaking, brain reeling. She put the milk away, took a dozen eggs out of a sack and dropped them when Bebe came pelting through the doorway wrapped in the sheet that moments before had been tangled around her ankles. Her throat was flushed, her face shining as she thrust the diamond ring flashing on the third finger of her left hand in Cydney's face.

"Look, Uncle Cyd!" she squealed. "I'm engaged!"

Egg yolk dripped into Cydney's shoes. Dread dripped into her heart. Sweet little Bebe, who didn't have sense enough to think her way halfway around a BB, was engaged.

Her niece's smile faded and she bit her lip. "You don't look happy for me, Uncle Cyd."

"This isn't a good time to call me Uncle Cyd," Cydney warned. "This is a good time to call me long distance."

"Because you caught us in bed?" Bebe thrust her hands on her hips. Wisps of red hair worked loose from her long single braid and curled around her face. "Really, Aunt Cydney. Aldo and I are *engaged*! I called Mother in Moscow. *She* is delighted. She told us to celebrate our love!"

"Of course she did! She's ten thousand miles away! She doesn't have to deal with this!" Cydney clapped her hand over her mouth and the frustrated "I do!" she wanted to shriek at Bebe. Instead she drew a breath and forced herself to smile. "I'm sorry, Bebe. I've had a bad day, that's all." She held out her arms. "C'mere, Red. I'm happy for you."

I think, Cydney thought, until an awful possibility struck her. "You don't *have* to get married, do you?"

"No, Uncle Cyd." Bebe laughed and pulled out of her embrace. "We want to get married."

"For God's sake, why?"

"That's what Grampa Fletch said."

"You called him, too?" Wonderful, Cydney thought. A long distance call to her father in Cannes to add to the one to Gwen in Moscow. "Did you call Gramma George?"

Bebe bit her lip and lowered her big brown eyes. "Uh—no."

Of course not. Georgette Parrish, Cydney and Gwen's mother and Fletcher Parrish's first wife, was a local call.

"I'll do it," Cydney said. As usual, she thought, lifting her right foot out of a pool of egg yolk. "I suggest you and— what's his name?"

"Aldo." Bebe beamed. "Aldo Munroe."

"Right. Aldo." The name Munroe rang a bell, but Cydney was too rattled to think why. She kicked off her loafer and made a face at the egg dripping off her stockinged toes. "You and Aldo get dressed and we'll talk."

"Sure thing." Bebe turned to leave, but spun back, her eyes wide. "Oh, I almost forgot! Guess what? Mother is getting married, too!"

"I'll call a press conference," Cydney shot back, ripping a paper towel off the roll and stuffing it in her shoe.

"That's really sweet of you, Uncle Cyd, but Mother said she'd do it herself when she gets home from Moscow."

And away Bebe went, twirling out of the kitchen like a lithe young goddess. She had Gwen's innate grace and her grandfather's knack for looking drop-dead delicious in anything. Or nothing.

On the inside of Bebe's closet door hung a blowup of the seminude *Playgirl* centerfold that Cydney and Gwen's father, Fletcher Parrish, *New York Times* best-selling author of umpteen-jillion spy novels, had posed for when Bebe was two years old. He'd done it as a birthday surprise for his Nymphet Wife Number Three. Gwen had taken the photo and given the poster to Bebe on her fourteenth birthday. Cydney thought Bebe hanging the poster in her room—even on the inside of the closet door—was creepy. Bebe thought it was a hoot.

So why was she surprised, Cydney wondered, that she'd come home in the middle of the day and found Bebe in bed with a boy? Despite Gwen's claim that she wanted a solid and stable upbringing for her daughter, she'd spent the last fifteen years that Bebe had been in Georgette and Cydney's care undermining the values she said she wanted for her child. The poster, the birth control pills when Bebe was sixteen—for which Cydney was suddenly grateful—the red Mustang convertible, whirlwind shopping sprees to New York to buy designer school clothes.

Why, indeed, was Cydney surprised? And why was she standing in a puddle of broken eggs watching the peppermint stick ice cream she'd bought melt through the bottom of the grocery sack and drip off the edge of the table?

Because Gwen was getting married, that's why—for the fifth time—and because Wendell Pickering was the best offer Cydney had had since the last time Gwen had called a press conference to tell the world she was getting married.

"Gwen is so much like Fletch," Georgette was fond of saying. "So focused and yet so carefree and impetuous. And what charisma!"

What horse-hockey, Cydney's little voice said, but she ignored it and shoved the half-melted ice cream into the freezer.

Gwen and Fletcher Parrish were driven and ruthless—*People* magazine said so—their stunning successes and stellar careers nothing more than overcompensation for failed personal lives. Cydney had been so incensed by *People*'s Father's Day cover story—"Like Father, Like Daughter"—that she'd canceled her subscription.

She'd also sent a blistering letter to *People*'s mail column. She was Fletcher Parrish's daughter, too, and she wasn't a failed anything. She owned her own home and her own business, had lots of friends and a full social life. So what if she wasn't rich and famous like her sister Gwen? What did wealth have to do with success?

"Oh, nothing much, honey," her father said to Cydney on the phone when he'd read her letter to the magazine. "Just everything." And then he'd laughed.

"How many times, Cydney," Georgette said, "have I told you to look before you leap?"

"If I'd known you felt so left out," Gwen said, "I would have insisted that you be included in the article."

Well why wasn't I? her little voice had demanded, but not Cydney. She'd been too mortified to admit how hurt she'd felt at being left out. Bebe was included. After all, she was Gwen Parrish's daughter. So was Georgette, who was Gwen's mother and a nationally syndicated etiquette columnist ranked right up there with Miss Manners. *People* had even sent a photographer.

The thing that hurt the most, besides the photographer asking Cydney to drive him to the airport, was that her family didn't understand about the letter. Her point was that fame and money were only two tiny little inches on the ruler of success. There were lots of other inches, like self-reliance and self-respect, being a giver and not just a taker. Like being loved for your own sake, not for who or what you are.

Cydney wiped the last of the eggshells off the floor and threw the paper towel away. While she washed her hands, she gazed out the window at the big maple tree shedding vivid red leaves over the brick patio.

"I think I'll go outside," she said, "come back in and try that screaming thing again."

Go ahead, her little voice said, *but it won't change a thing.*

chapter
two

And it didn't. Things were just as bad when Cydney went back into the house and found Bebe's beloved on the white wall phone in the kitchen. Long distance, naturally, which Bebe indicated by slowly drawing her arms wide apart.

She opened her mouth to try that screaming thing again, but snapped it shut when Aldo said: "C'mon, Uncle Angus. Cut me some slack."

The bell she'd heard earlier rang again in Cydney's head. Clanged and banged and so did her heart. Uncle Angus couldn't possibly be Angus Munroe, could he? World-famous mystery author, who Cydney wanted to be when she grew up? Once Bebe was through college and she finally had time to finish the book she'd been writing for—Gosh, how long was it? Three years?

Five, her little voice said, *but who's keeping track?*

"Yes, I *am* old enough to know what I'm doing," Aldo said hotly. "I turned twenty-one yesterday, Uncle Gus."

Surely there had to be another Angus Munroe in the world to be this long, tall drink of water's Uncle Gus. And if Aldo was twenty-one, then Bebe was a rocket scientist. His hair was nearly as long as hers, too, a shoulder-length palomino mane. He made a face at whatever his Uncle Gus was saying, caught Cydney sizing him up and turned as red as the maple tree outside the window.

"Twelve thousand dollars is not too much to spend on an engagement ring," he said angrily. "Just wait till you meet Bebe. She's worth her weight in diamonds."

Aldo caught Bebe's left hand, where the rock under discussion—big enough to make Liz Taylor drool—flashed like a laser. He gave his intended a look so overbrimming with love that Cydney felt a lump swell in her throat—and any doubts she had about Bebe marrying this boy vanish.

This was it. This was being loved for your own sake, not for who or what you are. Cydney couldn't imagine what it must feel like to be the object of such open adoration. She just hoped she'd get a chance to find out in her lifetime.

But not, her little voice said, *with Wendell Pickering.*

"Amen," Cydney agreed, unaware that she'd said it out loud until Bebe blinked at her and said, "What?"

"I said—" Cydney thought fast, bent her left wrist and tapped the face of her watch "—ahem."

Bebe whispered in Aldo's ear. In mid okay-okay nod, his jaw clenched and his face flamed again.

"No, Uncle Gus. I will not listen to the benefit of your experience. Why not? Because you don't have any! You've never been married and you haven't stuck your nose out of Crooked Possum in ten years except to—" Aldo broke off and rolled his eyes. "Oh, pardon me. Eight years."

Oh God. It *was* him. Angus Munroe. The man nearly as famous for being a recluse as he was for his string of best-selling mysteries. Eleven and counting. Not to mention his drop-dead-gorgeous looks. Cydney should know. She had a wall full of Angus Munroe pinups in the locked room over her garage where she spent her weekends writing.

Most of the photos were years old and clipped from magazines, shots of Angus Munroe's back and angry, over-the-shoulder, go-away glares. The prize of her collection, cut from the jacket of his latest book—the first publicity photo he'd posed for in ten years—showed him leaning against a rangy pine tree on his retreat in Crooked Possum, Missouri, deep in the heart of the Ozark Mountains. In hiking boots and tight, faded jeans, arms folded across his plaid-flanneled chest. A day's growth of beard on his jaw, a lock of dark hair drooping over his forehead. A pulse-pounding Heathcliff scowl on his face.

"Pretty boy," Fletcher Parrish sniffed on the phone when

Cydney asked him if he'd read Munroe's new book. "Can't write his way out of a sentence."

A slow smile spread across Cydney's face. Well. Maybe this wasn't such a rotten day after all.

"I'm hanging up now," Aldo said loudly into the phone. "Bebe's Uncle Cyd wants to talk to me."

He took the receiver away from his ear, but Angus Munroe kept talking. Make that haranguing, his voice raised and angry enough that Cydney could hear him. Aldo shot her a helpless look; she gave him a that's-okay shrug. He sighed and put the phone back to his ear. Cydney grabbed Bebe and towed her into the living room.

"Redhead," she said, keeping her voice low. "Did you tell Grampa Fletch who Aldo's Uncle Gus is?"

"Sure." Bebe blinked at her. "He's Aldo's guardian. At least he was until yesterday, when Aldo turned twenty-one. That's why we couldn't get engaged until today, 'cause his Uncle Gus is real protective—like you, Uncle Cyd—and Aldo knew he'd throw a fit."

"Is that why you didn't bring Aldo home before now? Why I didn't even know you were dating someone seriously?"

"Don't be mad, Uncle Cyd. It wasn't because of you. It was because of Aldo's Uncle Gus. Aldo was afraid he'd do something."

"I'm not mad, Bebe. Did you tell Grampa Fletch that Aldo's Uncle Gus is the same Angus Munroe who wrote *Paid in Full*?"

Bebe's eyes flew wide open. "He *is*?" she squealed.

Cydney nodded. Slowly, so Bebe wouldn't miss it.

"Wow, Uncle Cyd!" Her niece's voice throbbed with admiration. "How do you know all this stuff?"

"I'm psychic," Cydney said simply. "What did you tell your mother?"

"Just what I told Gramps. That Aldo's Uncle Gus is his guardian."

Y-e-e-s-s! Cydney exulted. One up at last on the Dynamic Duo. She figured she deserved one after the letter to *People*.

She could see it now. Gwen, stunned and speechless that

her "dear little dimwit"—her sister's pet name for Bebe—had bagged the nephew of someone even more famous than she was. And Fletcher Parrish, fuming that his granddaughter was marrying into the family of the "Pretty Boy" who'd knocked him out of first place on *The New York Times* List. And in the middle of it all, there she'd be, little Cydney the Nobody, smiling and saying serenely, "Well of course *I* knew."

Personally, her little voice said, *I like "nah-nah-nah-nah-nah."*
So did Cydney. Too bad it was s-o-o-o childish.

Almost as childlike as the wide-eyed wonder on Bebe's face as she raised her hand and watched the diamond in her engagement ring flash in the sunlight slanting through the open miniblinds on the living room windows. Where, Cydney thought, did a twenty-one-year-old kid get twelve thousand bucks for a rock the size of Gibraltar?

"I'm sorry, Miss Parrish." Aldo appeared in the doorway between the kitchen and the living room. "Uncle Gus gets wound up sometimes. I'll pay for the call."

"Never mind, Aldo." Cydney pointed at Bebe's ring. "So long as you can pay for that, I'll be happy."

"Oh no problem, Miss Parrish. I've got a trust fund."

"So do I!" Bebe squealed, clapping her hands delightedly under her chin. "Isn't it amazing how much we have in common?"

"It isn't amazing." Aldo stepped out of the doorway and opened his arms to Bebe. "It's kismet."

"Oh Aldo," she sighed, drifting toward him starry-eyed.

"Oh no." Cydney caught her niece's elbow and swung her around. She'd seen enough of unbridled passion and Aldo's backside for one day. "You sit over there, Aldo."

Cydney parked Bebe on the pillow-backed mauve sofa and Aldo on the matching love seat. And herself, for good measure, between them on the corner of the square oak coffee table.

"Start at the beginning," she said. "Where did you meet?"

At UMKC, the University of Missouri at Kansas City, at the

end of the spring semester. They'd been dating for six months, on the Q.T. because of Aldo's overprotective Uncle Gus.

"He's got this thing about my money," Aldo explained. "He thinks I'm gonna piss it all off, though I keep telling him I couldn't possibly. Do you know how fast interest compounds on fifteen million dollars, Miss Parrish?"

"Um—no," Cydney said, and gulped.

"My parents were killed in a plane crash when I was four. That's where the principal came from, their life insurance and the settlement from the airline. I don't have to work, but I've always wanted to go to college, 'cause I want to be an architect. I'm gonna build this really cool house for me and Bebe."

"When exactly," Cydney asked, "do you plan to get married?"

"I thought tomorrow at City Hall, so Uncle Gus can't try to stop us. But Bebe wants to wait until her mother gets back from Russia."

Gwen was due home in a week. That was awful damn quick.

"What's the rush?" Cydney asked Bebe.

"Just once," she said, "I'd like my mother to be here for something special, and you know how she is, Uncle Cyd."

Her niece's chin quavered and her eyes filled with tears. So did Cydney's, sympathetically, remembering Bebe's first prom, the day she made cheerleader, her first C in English, her high school graduation. Cydney had been there to pin on corsages, take pictures and give hugs, but not Gwen.

"I want to pick Mother up at the airport and take her straight to the church," Bebe said. "If I don't, some magazine editor will call and she'll be gone again."

"Oh, fine then," Cydney said facetiously. "For a second there I thought you wanted to get married on the runway."

"I don't think they'd let us, do you?"

"No, Bebe," Cydney said gently. "The FAA has rules against weddings on runways."

"Oh," she said disappointedly.

Sadly, Bebe wasn't kidding. About getting married on a

runway or about how quick Gwen could—and probably would—be gone again.

"Call Gramma George," Cydney told Bebe. "Don't tell her anything, just invite her to supper."

"You said you'd call her."

"I want to talk to Aldo alone, Bebe."

"Oh. Okay," she said happily, and headed for the kitchen.

"Your Uncle Gus," Cydney said to Aldo, "is Angus Munroe the mystery writer, isn't he?"

"Yes, Miss Parrish. Have you read any of his books?"

"One or two," Cydney lied.

She owned them all in hardcover, kept them in a glass-fronted bookcase in her room over the garage. She kept several copies of the paperback editions in the house for reading. Over and over, studying his style, soaking up his voice. She'd memorized whole passages of *Dead Soup*, his first book and his first best-seller.

"Read them all, Miss Parrish. He writes about this private detective named Max Stone. If you know Max Stone, you know my Uncle Gus. Max doesn't trust people, especially women, and neither does my Uncle Gus. He's a really good-looking guy, see, and women crawl all over him. He thinks it's because he's a famous writer and has lots of money. I tell him it's because of his face but he doesn't believe me. I'm just a kid and I don't know squat."

"That's very perceptive of you, Aldo." If he was telling the truth, and Cydney felt that Aldo was—from his perspective, anyway.

"Uncle Gus was only twenty-five when he hit it big. All the publicity and hype and women drooling all over him at book signings really got to him. That's why he moved us to the Ozarks. Believe me, Miss Parrish, nobody can find Crooked Possum or my Uncle Gus unless he wants them to."

"Is that so?" Cydney fanned the flush creeping up her neck with the *TV Guide* she'd snatched off the table.

Because she'd tried to find it herself, Cydney knew Crooked Possum wasn't on any Missouri road map. She'd spent hours looking for it last summer while she was in Branson—the nearest point of civilization as well as the upstart Mecca of country music—shooting a photo spread for a travel magazine. She'd wandered over hill and dale and never found the place, but she'd gotten some breathtaking shots of soaring ridges and shady hollows she'd sold for a nice chunk of change to a calendar company.

"Since you're twenty-one now, I don't see how your uncle can stop you and Bebe from getting married," Cydney said. "Especially if he never sets foot out of the Ozarks."

"This just might bring him out," Aldo said worriedly. "And Uncle Gus can be damn hard to get along with when he makes up his mind to be difficult."

"Don't worry, Aldo," Cydney said firmly. "So can I."

Oh please, her little voice said. *You have trouble making up the bed.*

"Uncle Cyd!" Bebe let out a shriek and came pelting out of the kitchen. "Guess what, Uncle Cyd! Guess what?" She was jumping up and down, her braid bouncing and her eyes shining. "Gramma George is getting married, too!"

chapter
three

Nothing could have surprised Cydney more. Except hearing, maybe, that her mother planned to butch her perfectly coiffed champagne-blond hair, dye it pink, pierce her nose and join a metal band. Which didn't sound like a bad idea.

By the time supper was over, a melt-on-your-fork pot roast provided by Georgette and her Crock-Pot, Cydney was beginning to consider it. Or maybe a Tibetan nunnery. Anything to escape the oohing and ahhing Bebe and Georgette were doing over the latest issue of *Bride* magazine.

She could hear them in the living room while she loaded the dishwasher, wiped the counters, the refrigerator door—Gosh, where did all those fingerprints come from?—the canisters, the bread box, the microwave. She polished the ceramic-tile tabletop and had just started on the range hood when the brides came trooping into the kitchen with Aldo.

"Coffee break," Georgette said, nudging Cydney aside to put the stainless steel kettle on the electric burner.

"I'm going to take Aldo back to his apartment," Bebe said, snuggling under the arm he'd draped over her shoulders.

"Do you have a roommate, Aldo?" Cydney asked.

"Uh, no," he said, flushing to the roots of his hair.

Cydney ignored Bebe's muttered "You should've said yes," and handed her the pencil and notepad she kept by the telephone. "Phone number and address. If you aren't home by eleven, I'm calling. If you aren't home by eleven-thirty—"

"I know." Bebe finished writing and handed the pad back to Cydney. "You'll be knocking at the front door."

"My Uncle Gus will love you, Miss Parrish." Aldo grinned

at her over his shoulder as Bebe tugged him out of the kitchen
and into the dining room, where a pair of French doors led
outside onto the patio. "Don't worry. Bebe will be home on
time. She has classes in the morning and so do I."

"I'll be home late tomorrow, Uncle Cyd." Bebe opened the
right-hand door and turned to face her. "We're picking up
Aldo's car."

"Is it being repaired?"

"Nope," Aldo said. "It's my birthday present to me. A
Jaguar XJ8."

"How nice." Cydney had no idea what a Jag went for, but
with Bebe's ring she figured Aldo must've put a huge dent in
his trust fund. "By the way, Aldo. Happy birthday."

"Thanks, Uncle Cyd." He grinned as Bebe tugged him out
of the house. "I'll make sure Bebe's home on time."

The door clicked shut behind them and Cydney frowned.
Maybe Angus Munroe was right to be worried. She trailed
Bebe and Aldo to the French doors and flipped the wall
switch that turned on the outside lights—the carriage lamps
on the patio wall, the yard light in the middle of the lawn,
and the security flood on the detached two-car garage.

This time yesterday it had been dusk, now it was dark. The
maple tree's fiery leaves looked as dull and brown as the brick
walls of the house and the garage, as faded and lifeless as
Cydney felt watching Bebe and Aldo splash through them.

"Aldo seems like a very responsible young man," Georgette
said over the shriek of the kettle, but Cydney didn't answer.

She stood at the French doors with her arms folded and
tears pricking her eyes as the garage door went up and Bebe's
red Mustang backed down the driveway. As soon as Gwen got
home from Russia, Bebe would be married and gone. Cydney
was happy for her—she truly was—but she couldn't help wondering what she was supposed to do with the empty room in
her house and the hole in her life. Get a cat?

She waited to make sure Bebe remembered to push the remote to shut the garage door, then turned into the kitchen
and sighed. So did the kettle as her mother took it off the
burner and made her coffee.

Cydney drank tea, but she kept instant decaf for Georgette. In a silver caddy with a spoon clipped to the side that her mother had given her to put on the Lazy Susan in the middle of the kitchen table because the coffee jar sitting there looked s-o-o-o tacky. Cydney didn't think so, but Cydney hadn't said so. She'd said thank you and polished the damn thing every month or so, so it wouldn't tarnish.

"You were a little heavy-handed with Bebe, don't you think?" Georgette stirred Sweet 'N Low into her coffee and glanced at Cydney. "She's nineteen years old and engaged to be married."

"So I should suspend the rules?"

"A girl only gets engaged once."

Oh really? Cydney wanted to snap. This is your second engagement and Gwen's fifth. Which had nothing to do with the fact that Cydney had never even been asked to go steady. Nothing at all.

"Even more reason," she said, shuddering at the memory of Bebe and Aldo tangled in the bedsheets, "to enforce the rules."

"I can see my face in the countertop." Georgette turned away from the gleaming butcher block. "Would you like me to don my white glove? Or would you rather tell me what's bothering you?"

"Truthfully," Cydney said bluntly, "I don't believe for two seconds that you actually intend to marry Herb Baker."

"But of course I do." Georgette carried her cup and saucer and cloth napkin—she broke out in hives at the mere thought of paper ones—to the table and sat down. "In a candlelight ceremony on December twenty-fourth at eight P.M. Just as I wrote in the engagement announcement I'm going to fax to your father as soon as I get home."

"I rest my case." Cydney gave a triumphant smile and sat down across the table from her mother. "You're still trying to make Dad jealous."

Georgette's eyebrow arched again. "I also plan to fax it to the society editor at the *Star* for inclusion in this Sunday's column."

"Considering the time difference between Kansas City and Cannes," Cydney went on, unconvinced, "your fax will be the first thing Dad sees when he walks into his office tomorrow."

"Of course it will be. I planned it that way."

"Hoping, of course, to ruin his day."

"On the contrary. I'm sure it will make his day." Georgette sipped her coffee and smiled. "No more alimony."

"So that's your story and you're sticking to it?"

"It's the way things are, Cydney." Georgette reached across the table and squeezed her hand. "I know the divorce was difficult for you, but you're a grown woman now. It's time you realize your father isn't coming home to us."

"I know that, Mother." Cydney jerked her hand away. "You're the one who's been saying for the last eighteen years that someday Fletch will get tired of all those voluptuous young bodies and come crawling back to you. You're the one who cross-stitched it on a sampler."

"It's not a sampler, it was a pillowcase. It was part of my Coping with Divorce therapy and I threw it away ages ago."

"I should hope so, Mother. I'm sure it was threadbare."

"So is my patience, Cydney. That's why I said yes on Sunday when Herb asked me again to marry him. I'm not getting any younger."

"You're only fifty-eight," Cydney said, trying to be encouraging. "I'll bet you don't even have spider veins."

"Of course I don't. I exercise to keep my metabolism up and my circulation going."

Cydney belonged to a gym but rarely had time to go. She hadn't had time for much of anything since Bebe had moved in with her five years ago, when Georgette's book, *Etiquette for All Occasions,* came out and her column really started to take off.

"If you could keep Bebe for just a while," her mother had cajoled. "Until I get all these damn TV shows and book signings out of my hair."

Of course Cydney said yes. She loved Bebe, and her niece spent most weekends with her anyway, so Georgette would have time to write. A fourteen-year-old, Cydney soon discovered, took a lot of time. So did a fifteen-year-old, a sixteen-year-old and so on.

Cydney didn't have time for the gym, but Georgette had time to exercise two hours a day, beginning with a morning jog and laps in the indoor pool Fletcher Parrish's alimony paid for. In the afternoon she dictated her column to her secretary while she did the Stairmaster with nary a huff or a puff.

In the last five years, Georgette had published two updates to *Etiquette for All Occasions*, while Cydney's book was unfinished. Georgette still had time for TV appearances and book signings. Cydney didn't have time to wind her watch. She had spider veins and her mother didn't.

There's a word for what you are, her little voice said.

"Chump," Cydney said. Georgette shot her a sharp glance over her cup, put it down and asked, "What did you say?"

" 'Chump,' Mother," she said fiercely. "I said 'chump.' "

"That's no way to talk about your father, Cydney."

I'm not talking about Dad, Cydney wanted to shriek, I'm talking about me! But she didn't. As usual. She just sat gritting her teeth and watching her mother sip her coffee. Was she the chump of the century or was she just feeling sorry for herself?

Always the bridesmaid and never the bride. Not that she wanted to get married. She loved her life. She really did. Cydney hadn't a clue why she suddenly felt so angry and abused.

"I should be off." Georgette carried her cup and saucer to the sink, rinsed them and turned to face Cydney. "Remind Bebe to call me tomorrow when she gets home. We're going shopping for her wedding dress."

"Are you sure you have the time?"

The words were out before Cydney knew it, in a nasty, waspish snap that surprised her and jerked her out of her chair. Georgette tucked the Crock-Pot Cydney had washed and shined with Windex under her arm, turned away from the counter and arched an eyebrow.

"What's the matter, darling? Feeling put-upon?"

Cydney faked a laugh. "Who, me?"

"You'd be a fool if you didn't."

Cydney blinked. "I would?"

"Of course you would." Georgette unhooked her purse from the back of her chair and looped it over her shoulder. "We all take shameless advantage of you."

"Well." Cydney shrugged. "I wouldn't say shameless exactly."

"You would if I weren't standing here." Georgette laughed. "And you'd be absolutely right. I've been feeling very guilty about it lately. I'm as happy for you as I am for Bebe that she's getting married. Now you'll have all the time in the world to finish that book you've been writing for the past ten years."

"Five years," Cydney corrected her. "It's only five years, Mother."

"No more using Bebe as an excuse for not having time to write." Georgette wagged a finger at Cydney, then gently caught her chin. "Don't be so afraid of failing, darling, that you never try."

Then she dropped a kiss on Cydney's cheek and sailed through the dining room, her car keys jangling as she fished them out of her purse. "Don't forget to remind Bebe to call me when she gets home!"

The French doors slammed shut and Cydney's mouth fell open. She stood in the middle of her kitchen, slack-jawed and stunned at her mother's perceptiveness.

How had Georgette known? How had she given herself away? How come she couldn't have been born an orphan?

Well, you know what they say, her little voice said. *If it isn't one thing, it's your mother.*

chapter
four

It wasn't fear of failure that frightened Cydney, it was fear of success. A little niggle of worry that if her book sold and did well, she'd wake up some morning and discover she'd turned into Gwen. Cydney loved her sister, she really did, but she had no illusions about her. Which, of course, she could never tell their mother.

Why not? her little voice asked. *Gwen is ruthless and driven.* People *magazine says so. Maybe Georgette won't admit it, but I'll bet she knows it. She's got your number, doesn't she?*

Cydney still couldn't figure out when Georgette had come out of her self-absorbed fog long enough to nail her deepest fear right on the head. Maybe it was a Mother Thing. Like always knowing, when she was little and Georgette was in the kitchen, that Cydney had her feet on the couch. Every time without fail, her mother would holler: "Get your shoes off my sofa, young lady!"

Even Gwen, who most of the time made Joan Crawford look like Donna Reed, possessed a sixth sense about Bebe. Whenever she was sick or unhappy the phone would ring and it would be Gwen. Scary people, mothers.

It was 9 P.M. and Cydney was in her office; it was the sunporch when she'd bought the house eight years ago. She was finishing the changes on the perennial border spread for *Bloom and Bulb*. She put her T square down and smiled. Perfect. If Wendell Pickering nitpicked this, she'd tell him to take his twenty-five hundred bucks and go get a hair transplant.

Cydney didn't need the money. She had a trust fund of her

own, courtesy of her father. A nice little chunk she added to when she could and planned to never touch. Worst-case scenario, she figured it would keep her, or Bebe, who was the beneficiary, from ending up a bag lady.

So far as Cydney knew, Gwen had made no provisions for Bebe's future. They'd had a rip-snorting phone fight about it when Bebe graduated from high school.

"Only you," Gwen said, "would give an eighteen-year-old girl a one-thousand dollar savings bond."

"She can use it for college," Cydney retorted, affronted. "What's she supposed to do with a trunk full of silk lingerie?"

"Catch a man," Gwen replied bluntly. "Preferably one with a degree in something that will earn a nice living. Why do you think I'm sending her to college? I just hope she lands a pre-med or a pre-law student before she flunks out!"

In Aldo Munroe Gwen had gotten her wish and then some.

Her writing room over the garage had once been a studio apartment. Cydney rubbed her right temple where her headache still pulsed and gazed at the glare of the security light on the apartment's dark windows. How many weekends had it been since she'd climbed the stairs and turned on her spare PC? Two?

Three, her little voice said, *but who's counting?*

A breath of cool autumn evening drifted through the two jalousie windows Cydney had cranked open, rustling the box hedge she kept clipped even with the brick half walls of the sunporch. Leaves skittered across the patio. She shivered and rubbed her arms. Wednesday was Halloween, Thursday the first of November.

What would she do for the holidays without Bebe? Georgette went skiing on Thanksgiving and took a cruise over Christmas. A wedding cruise this year if things got that far, which Cydney still didn't believe. Her father would be in Cannes with Nymphet Wife Number Six, and Gwen who-knew-where with her new husband. Cydney hadn't asked Bebe who Gwen was marrying because it didn't matter. Like father, like daughter, it wouldn't last. Cydney figured she'd discover the name of Gwen's intended on the front page of

The National Enquirer the next time she went to the grocery store.

Which reminded her—she was out of checks. Cydney got up from her drawing table and started up the two brick steps that led to the dining room, stopped and stared at the dark windows of her writing room again. Was it really three weeks since she'd been up there?

The desk clock beside the lamp said it was 9:15. Two hours until Bebe was due home. Cydney didn't feel like writing. Her late night and rotten day were catching up with her. She ached all over, especially behind her right knee, where she just *knew* that damn bruise was blossoming into a spider vein, but two hours were better than nothing. She hadn't turned on the wall furnace in the apartment yet. She'd need a sweater and a cup of tea to keep her warm while she lit the pilot.

Ten minutes later, with matches and the key in the pocket of an old snagged navy cardigan and a tea bag steeping in a mug, Cydney climbed the stairs, unlocked the door and groped for the light switch. She meant to turn on just the lights, not the ceiling fan, too, but accidentally flipped both switches.

The blades whipped to life on high, raising a cloud of dust thick enough to be called a sandstorm in the Sahara. A sheaf of manuscript pages on the desk took flight, three of her Angus Munroe pinups spun off her corkboard onto the floor.

Cydney sneezed, turned off the fan and set her cup on the Formica bar that separated the rest of the small, one-room apartment from the even smaller kitchenette. Batting dust out of her face, she made her way to the windows and opened them a couple inches to let in some fresh air, then dropped to her knees to pick up the pictures.

The pine tree pose from the jacket of *Paid in Full* had landed on the seat of her old office chair, one of the over the shoulder, go-away glares on the floor next to it and the other facedown under the desk. She whacked her head retrieving that one, hard enough to see stars and send her headache soaring. She sat back on her heels and rubbed her stinging, pounding head as she turned the picture over and looked at it.

She couldn't remember which magazine she'd cut this one from. It was black and white and showed Angus Munroe in a cable-knit sweater against a foggy shoreline dotted with pine trees. His arms were folded, his dark hair lifting off his forehead. He looked like a baby in this picture. And he didn't look happy.

Cydney picked up the color book jacket photo and compared it to the black and white. Same scowl, same crossed-arm pose. A fiercely private man, she guessed, and very protective of Aldo, Bebe said. If he came to the wedding, would he eat cake, drink punch and kiss the bride? Or would he just sit in a pew scowling with his arms folded? It was hard to picture him doing anything else since that's all she'd ever seen him do.

It struck Cydney that until today, until she'd met Aldo and heard his angry voice on the phone, Angus Munroe hadn't seemed real. Now he seemed so real that her breath caught as she studied the photos and noted the resemblance between uncle and nephew—the shape of Angus Munroe's jaw, the length of his nose. So much like Aldo's it was scary.

So was the thought of meeting him at the wedding. Panic clutched Cydney's stomach. How much weight could she lose in a week? What would she wear? What would she say to him?

"Hello, Mr. Munroe." She put on her best smile and offered her hand to the book jacket photo. "It's a pleasure to meet you."

Her voice sounded funny over the tinny ring in her ears from the whack she'd taken on the head. It throbbed with every beat of her heart and made the deep voice that answered—from the depths of her imagination, Cydney thought—sound like it was coming from the bottom of an empty fifty-five-gallon drum.

"Nice to meet you, too, Miss—?"

"Parrish. Cydney Parrish. I'm Bebe's aunt."

"I thought she had an Uncle Sid?"

"That's Bebe's nickname for me, Uncle Cyd." Cydney

laughed, pretending. Hey, this was fun. She ought to whack herself on the head more often. "I've read all your books, Mr. Munroe."

"So I see," the deep voice answered. It didn't sound hollow anymore. It sounded like Angus Munroe was really in the room, standing behind her, eyeing his books lined up inside the barrister bookcase. "Are all those pictures of me?"

"Pictures?" Cydney laughed again, charming the scowl off his face. "What pictures, Mr. Munroe?"

"The ones in your lap," the voice snapped, sharp and edgy and very close. "The ones on the wall over the desk."

Cydney not only heard the floor creak as if someone were walking across it, she felt it. Her heart seized as she shot up on her knees and whirled around. Angus Munroe—tall, dark and drop-dead handsome in indigo jeans, hiking boots and a navy suede bomber jacket—jammed a pair of wire-framed half glasses over a nose shaped just like Aldo's. He grasped the back of her old desk chair and leaned over it to take a closer look at the photos on her corkboard.

"My God. They *are* pictures of me. They're *all* pictures of me." Angus Munroe, Cydney's idol, the man of her dreams, yanked off his glasses and whipped his head toward her. "What kind of a nut are you?"

chapter
five

A very fetching nut, Gus could see, now that she stood on her knees facing him. Even with her mouth open, gaping at him like a freshly landed fish. A rainbow trout, he thought, watching her face turn every shade of red known to Crayola.

It wasn't a beautiful face. Her mouth was too big and her nose too pert, but she had lovely, almond-brown eyes tipped up at the corners and oddly dark brows for someone with such silvery blond hair. A gamine face, the face of a pixie.

The face of a nut, Gus reminded himself. Probably harmless, but still a nut. He shoved his glasses in his jacket, gripped the loose back of the old posture chair with both hands and gave her his best scowl.

"Which variety of nut are you, Miss Parrish? My biggest fan or Glenn Close?"

His allusion to the movie *Fatal Attraction* shot a fresh wash of red up her throat. She sank on her heels and ducked her chin.

"How about," she said in a mortified voice, "the kind of nut who has no idea how to explain this and wishes she were dead?"

One hand crept up and brushed a wisp of dust out of her silver curls. She looked so waifish and woebegone Gus almost said, "Aww," until it hit him that maybe she wasn't being charmingly coy but coolly calculating.

You make me sick, Munroe, said the voice that occasionally spoke up from somewhere inside him. Gus wasn't sure if it was his conscience or his muse, but it was definitely a butinski. *Like she knew you were coming and planned this.*

Like all the women you think are after you because you're a rich, famous writer lay awake nights dreaming up screwball scenarios like this to get your attention.

"Hey, it could happen," Gus said, unaware that he'd blurted it out until Cydney Parrish blinked up at him and asked, "What did you say?"

"I said—" Gus shifted his gaze to the papers scattered across the desk. He picked up a handful to straighten them and asked, "What happened? Looks like a tornado went through here."

"One did, sort of." Cydney Parrish scooped up the pictures that had fallen out of her lap, slapped them facedown on the desk and got to her feet. "I turned on the fan when I turned on the lights and everything just—went with the wind."

She made an awkward sweep with one arm. Gus glanced at the typed pages he held and realized they were part of a manuscript, which was no surprise since she was Fletcher Parrish's daughter. He read the title in the upper right-hand corner, *Stone Dead*, before she snatched the pages out of his hand and put them on the desk.

"Sorry for barging in," Gus said. "When no one answered the doorbell, I walked around back, saw the lights and—"

"Caught me making a fool of myself." She ducked her head again. "I've read all your books and really enjoyed them, Mr. Munroe."

Gus wanted to like Cydney Parrish. If he hadn't spent half his life idolizing her father, reading and studying and learning from Fletcher Parrish's books, and if only the mean-spirited old bastard hadn't cut him dead the only time he'd ventured out of Crooked Possum to meet Fletcher Parrish at a mystery writers' conference, he might've managed it. But he couldn't—and he wouldn't—let his guard down until he found out just exactly what was going on between Aldo and Parrish's granddaughter.

"Thank you, Miss Parrish. But do you really think my nephew and your niece should get married?"

She glanced up warily. "Why shouldn't they?"

"I think they're too young. And I don't think they've known each other long enough."

"You're entitled to your opinion, but Bebe and Aldo are both of legal age. They don't need your permission or anyone else's to marry."

"My permission, no. My approval, yes."

Cydney Parrish's chin shot up. "What do you mean?"

"My brother, Arthur, was a very cautious man." Gus withdrew from his jacket a copy of the codicil to his brother's will he'd had his lawyer fax him—just in case—after he talked to Aldo. "The terms of Aldo's trust state that if I judge his behavior to be irresponsible or imprudent I can extend my guardianship and control of his trust for another five years."

"I see." Cydney Parrish folded the fax into her sweater pocket without looking at it. "So if Bebe doesn't meet with your approval this could be a very long engagement."

"I wouldn't put it that baldly, but yes, I suppose so."

"Is Aldo aware of this?"

"I came to explain it to him. And to meet your niece."

"Bebe isn't here. She's with Aldo."

"They aren't at his apartment. I went there first. Aldo gave me your address on the phone, so I thought they might be here."

"I have no idea where they are. Bebe's curfew is eleven-thirty. You're welcome to wait, if you'd like."

Gus glanced at his watch—10:15. "I won't be keeping you up?"

"I always wait up for Bebe. I can give you a cup of coffee if you don't mind instant decaf."

"Decaf would be fine, thanks."

"After you." She swept her arm toward the door.

Gus waited on the wooden landing while she turned off the lights and locked the door. He could hear the whine of traffic from Ward Parkway, a few blocks to the east, one of Kansas City's grander boulevards sweeping south in a wide and affluent arc from the Country Club Plaza. A dog barked a couple houses away. The still and damp night air smelled pleasantly of dying leaves and wood smoke.

Cydney Parrish, he noticed, as she ducked past him on the landing and led the way down the steps, smelled faintly of . . . lilacs? Or was it Windex? She stopped when they reached the blacktop driveway and she saw his car. The long, sleek British racing green hood gleamed black in the wash of the security lights.

"Is that a Jaguar?" she asked.

"Yes."

"What model?"

"An XJ8 coupe."

"Very nice," she said thoughtfully, looking the car over.

One of the fuzzy moths darting around the lights took a dive into her hair. Gus reached up to pluck it out, caught himself and lowered his hand. She brushed the moth away, led him through a gate in the chain-link fence and across the backyard.

"Watch out for wickets," she said over her shoulder. "I was one short when I pulled them up yesterday."

Cydney Parrish wrote in secret—the locked door and the way she'd snatched her manuscript out of his hand told him so—and played croquet. Gus hadn't played since he was a kid, growing up in a house very much like this one with its ivy-covered brown brick walls and half-beamed stucco gables.

It had been a long time since he'd sent his brother Artie's battered croquet ball hurtling into their mother's flower beds. They'd played badminton, too. Gus looked over his shoulder, saw a privacy fence on the back property line and a sagging net suspended between thin metal poles. He and Artie had played with their parents' tennis rackets, which had sent the shuttlecock whizzing over the net at light speed.

The memory gave Gus a sharp stab of nostalgia, loss and a twinge of unease. No matter how it looked, he wasn't behaving like a Victorian patriarch. He didn't give a damn about the money. He cared about Aldo. His tall, lanky, goofy nephew was all the family he had left, and Artie had trusted him—little Gus the geek, who'd used to pretend he was John McEnroe charging the net at Wimbledon—to take care of his son.

"I'll bet your missing wicket is buried in leaves," Gus said, crunching through leaves the size of his hand shed by the maple tree soaring over the roof of the house.

"Probably. But I love to watch the leaves blow around."

So did Gus. He liked birdbaths, too. Cydney Parrish had one on the front lawn and one here in back. Birdfeeders hung from the maple tree and sat on the brick wall lit by carriage lamps that enclosed the patio. Evening dew sparkled on the redwood furniture, chairs and a table with benches. No umbrella and no drapes on the French doors that led into the house, into the dining room. Cydney Parrish must like the sun.

"Have a seat." She opened the right-hand door, stepped inside and gestured him toward an oval oak table. "I'll put the kettle on."

Gus followed her, shut the door and took off his jacket. She turned left into the kitchen, through a doorway between half walls with spindles. He hung his jacket on the back of a ladder-back chair padded in mauve corduroy that faced the kitchen and creaked when he sat down. He smelled furniture polish and roses, looked behind him and saw a basket brimming with potpourri on a hutch with glass doors. An open doorway next to the hutch led into a sunporch with jalousie windows, an artist's drawing board and a banker's lamp burning on a desk.

Gus turned around and watched Cydney Parrish open a drawer for spoons, a cabinet for mugs and pluck a tea bag from a canister. He didn't know what to make of her. Until half an hour ago he'd thought she was a man. Until Aldo floored him with the news that he was marrying Fletcher Parrish's granddaughter, he'd thought the old bounder had only one child, Gwen. The mother of the bride, soon to be a bride herself.

He'd seen the headline—GLAMOROUS GWEN TO MARRY RUSSIAN PRINCE—on the front page of a tabloid in the convenience store where he'd stopped for gas. He'd bought a copy and read the article. This was Gwen Parrish's fifth marriage, to an honest-to-God Romanov, a very distant cousin of Czar Nicholas. She'd been widowed the first time—Aldo told him

Bebe's father was dead—and divorced the rest. Her father was on wife number six. Gwen Parrish lived out of a suitcase, which was, Gus suspected, the reason her daughter lived in Kansas City with her aunt.

Cydney didn't fit in the same picture with Fletcher and Gwen Parrish. She didn't look anything like her sister—a Candice Bergen ringer with a Kathleen Turner voice he'd seen on *60 Minutes*—or her larger-than-life father. Except for talking to pictures of him cut out of magazines, she seemed perfectly normal.

"Help yourself." She brought a tray into the dining room and put it down in the center of the table. "I'll be right back. I have something to show you."

She cut through the kitchen and vanished down a dark hallway. Gus hoped she wouldn't reappear in a negligee.

Speak for yourself, Munroe, his inner voice said, which surprised Gus. Cydney Parrish wasn't his type.

A plate of macaroons, homemade by their lopsided shapes, sat on the tray next to the coffee. They were good. Gus was midway through a second one when Cydney came back with a brown Kraft envelope. Uh-oh. Manuscript size. Gus swallowed and took a swig of coffee.

"I don't read manuscripts by aspiring writers, Miss Parrish. It's nothing personal. Just my rule."

"Don't worry." She nudged the tray aside, undid the clasp on the flap and upended the envelope. "This isn't a manuscript."

Several smaller envelopes tumbled out onto the table, all labeled in magenta ink and a neat, boxy script. One said "IRAs," another "Stock Portfolio" and a third "Trust Fund from Dad." She opened this last one, unfolded a sheet that said "Quarterly Summary" at the top, laid it in front of him and pointed to a bottom line that made him gulp. Gus glanced up at Cydney Parrish, her hands spread on the table and fire in her eyes.

"My niece has a name, Mr. Munroe. It's Bebe. Short for Beatrice, which is Latin for 'she who makes others happy.' She makes Aldo happy, he makes her happy, and that's all I care about. I love Bebe and I will not let you break her heart.

I have enough money to support her and Aldo and put them through college, so why don't you take this—" she pulled the faxed codicil out of her pocket and smoothed it flat on the table in front of him "—and Aldo's fifteen million dollars and shove them where the sun doesn't shine."

"Uncle Gus!" The French doors banged open and Aldo burst into the dining room. "What are you doing here?"

His nephew raked back his shoulder-length hair—which Gus hated—and glared at him. His jaw twitched and two bright angry spots burned in his cheeks. Gus shifted in his chair to face him.

"I'm having coffee, Aldo, and being put in my place by—"

A goddess. A tall, lithe young goddess with a flaming braid, a face by Rubens and a body by *Playboy* stepped into the house behind Aldo. A diamond solitaire big enough to choke a horse flashed on her left hand. Bebe. Worth her weight in diamonds. She who makes others happy. Just by breathing.

She flicked Gus a nervous glance with the biggest, dewiest brown eyes he'd ever seen, then dropped her gaze to the table. She blinked and lifted a startled, worried frown to Cydney Parrish.

"What's going on, Uncle Cyd? This is your God-Save-Me-and-Bebe-from-Living-in-a-Refrigerator-Crate-and-Eating-Cat-Food Fund. Why are you showing it to Mr. Munroe?"

"Yeah, Uncle Gus." Aldo flung himself hands first onto the table and into Gus' face. "What are you trying to pull?"

"Nothing. I just drove up to meet your fiancée and—"

The dazzling Bebe reached for the faxed codicil. Gus made a grab for it and so did Cydney. They both missed and ended up slapping hands in the middle of the table. Bebe raised the fax to her nose and read it, her lips moving, a frown puckering her flawless brow.

"What is it, Bebe?" Aldo peered over her shoulder.

"Read it." She handed him the fax and turned her big, brown bedroom eyes on Gus. "I'm not very smart, Mr. Munroe, but I understand enough of what's on that paper and I know my Aunt Cydney well enough to figure out what it means."

Aldo looked up from the codicil, bewildered. "You do?"

"It means your uncle doesn't like me and he's going to keep your money until you're twenty-five, but Uncle Cyd is going to cash in her God-Save-Me-and-Bebe Fund so we can get married."

Her full, perfect lips trembled and tears formed on her incredibly long lashes. Gus felt like a heel, a jerk. A Victorian patriarch.

"That's what it says." He got quickly to his feet and came around the table. "But that's not necessarily what I plan to do."

"Isn't it?" Cydney snatched the fax from Aldo and threw it, a crumpled-up little ball of thermal paper, at Gus' chest. "Then why did you barge into my house and shove that under my nose?"

"Good question, Miss Parrish. Glad you asked it. The truth is—"

The truth was, he'd seen red when he'd heard the name Fletcher Parrish. It was also true that he'd felt old and alone and left out, but his pride wouldn't let him admit that.

"The truth is—" Gus drew a deep breath and let it go. "I feel like a horse's ass and I wish somebody would kick me."

"How 'bout a punch in the nose?" Cydney asked darkly.

"Why not?" Gus smiled sheepishly. "I think I deserve it."

"Okay," the beautiful Bebe said, and then she slugged him.

chapter
six

Gus woke up surrounded by flowers, baskets and vases heaped with blooms in every color and variety known to horticulture. Panic shot through him and his heart seized. I'm dead, he thought. Dead and laid out in a funeral parlor. Then he blinked and his eyes focused on a plastic glass full of ice chips on the narrow, laminated table that was pushed up against his chest.

Hospital room, he realized. I'm in a hospital room. How in hell did I get here? He'd never been able to take a punch, but this was ridiculous.

Gus pushed himself up against a rock-hard pillow. The mattress beneath him rasped and felt like it was stuffed with corn husks. The hiss it made, like a tire losing air, brought Cydney Parrish to his bedside.

"How do you feel, Mr. Munroe?" She leaned toward him, peering anxiously into his face. "Can I get you anything?"

Now that he was semiupright, Gus felt the slow, sick thud in his head and a wash of dizziness. He raised his hand to cover his eyes until the room stopped spinning, just as Cydney Parrish raised hers to tug the cement pillow up behind him. Her hand smacked his nose. Gus howled.

"*Oh I'm sorry!*" she cried. "Oh Mr. Munroe! Let me—" She reached for him again and Gus clapped his hands over his nose.

"No!" he said, only it sounded like "Dough!" He lay back against the pillow and closed his eyes. "I'm okay." Gus swallowed the foul taste in his mouth and felt his stomach lurch. "I think."

He heard a screech and cracked one eye. Cydney Parrish pulled a high-backed, lime-green chair close to his bed and sat down. The vertical blind on the window behind her was closed, but the thin line of sunlight that edged the slats— Sunlight? Jesus. He'd been out all night!—blazed like a klieg light. Gus winced and shut his eye.

"Why am I in the hospital?"

"Bebe hit you. Do you remember?"

You bet he remembered. The beautiful Bebe. She who makes others happy and packs a punch like Evander Holyfield. He remembered the crunch of her fist against his nose but he didn't remember hitting the floor. Or what happened after that. Like how in hell he'd ended up here.

"Is my nose broken?" It felt like it was, throbbing like a stubbed toe in the middle of his face.

"No. The cartilage is just cracked."

"Then why do I feel like somebody dropped an anvil on my head?"

"Uh, well. I—um—I imagine it's the concussion."

Gus opened his eyes. Slowly, avoiding the window, focusing on Cydney Parrish. She sat jiggling nervously in the chair, her knees crossed and her fingers clasped around them. He'd last seen her in jeans, a sweatshirt and a droopy navy blue cardigan. Now she wore tan trousers and a creamy turtleneck. A beige and brown and orange tartan shawl lay over the arm of the chair. She didn't look waifish and woebegone. She looked well tailored and well heeled. A very fetching nut, if you liked petite blondes with tiny noses and big brown eyes, which Gus didn't.

"How did I end up with a concussion, Miss Parrish?"

"We didn't mean to drop you, Mr. Munroe." She edged forward in the chair. Earnestly, Gus thought, beseechingly, her fingers so tightly clenched on her knees that her knuckles were white. "We tried to wake you up, but we couldn't, and Bebe was getting hysterical. She thought she'd killed you. Aldo and I were trying to get you off the floor."

He remembered now. Sort of. A hazy recollection of

thumps and shrieks and tears. "And that's when you dropped me?"

"No. We dropped you in the backyard. We were trying to get you into my truck so we could take you to the hospital. I had your feet, Aldo your shoulders. Bebe was walking beside you holding your hand. Everything was fine until she tripped over the wicket."

What wicket? Gus almost asked, then remembered trailing Cydney from the garage to the house, the leaves crunching under his feet . . . their smoky scent and the memories of Artie they'd stirred . . . the shapely curve of Cydney Parrish's silhouette in the wash of the patio lights. When had he noticed that? Gus couldn't remember and it made him scowl.

"The wicket you couldn't find because it was buried in leaves?"

"That's the one." She nodded miserably. "Bebe fell flat on her face and Aldo let go of you to help her up. The resident in ER last night thought she'd broken her ankle. So did I. It was so swollen and Aldo was frantic. They took an X ray. It's just a bad sprain. A double sprain."

Cydney Parrish rattled on about ice packs and air boots. Gus listened, wondering where he'd been while the entire emergency room staff, or so it seemed hearing her Uncle Cyd tell it, devoted themselves to Bebe and her sprained ankle. He could see himself lying unconscious on a gurney pushed out into the hall, nurses flitting past him like he was a stiff waiting to be wheeled off to the morgue.

It hadn't been that way at all. Someone had taken the time to determine his nose was only cracked, not broken, his skull only concussed, not fractured—but that's how Gus felt. Pushed off and forgotten. Dropped like an afterthought—or a crabby old Victorian patriarch with a glass jaw—when the beautiful Bebe tripped over the wicket.

Cydney Parrish ran down finally, like a wound-too-tight music box. She had a lovely voice. Clear and smooth. Perfect for distracting him from his cracked nose and concussion and the fact that she was here and not Aldo. He wondered what it meant. Probably that his nephew was still pissed at him.

"How long will Bebe have to wear this air boot?" he asked.

"A week, at least. Maybe ten days."

"Well then." Gus smiled. "The wedding will have to wait."

"No it won't. Bebe wants her mother here—my sister, Gwen. She'll be home from Moscow next Thursday, so we've scheduled the wedding for the following Saturday. That's twelve days, which is more than enough time for Bebe's ankle to heal."

"Why the rush? This isn't a have-to wedding, is it?"

"No, Mr. Munroe. Gwen is a photojournalist and she has a very busy schedule, so we're simply trying to fit the wedding in around her schedule."

"That's backwards, Miss Parrish. I know who your sister is, and I'd think she'd want to make sure Aldo and Bebe are certain of their feelings before they leap into marriage. I know I do. Surely if she has, say, six months to plan for it, your sister can find a few days in her schedule to attend her daughter's wedding."

Gus would. In his head, in fact, he was already planning around the May first deadline for his next Max Stone mystery. How many more pages he'd have to write per day, how many more hours he'd have to spend at the PC to finish the book and still have time to play father of the groom.

"I'm sure it does seem backwards to you," Cydney replied, not quite meeting his gaze. "But my mother and Bebe and I are so used to arranging family events around Gwen's schedule that it's second nature."

So was covering for her sister, Gus surmised. Like father, like daughter. He'd read an article in *People* magazine that said Gwen Parrish was every bit as driven as her father. A not-so-nice euphemism for selfish as hell.

"Aldo put you up to this, didn't he?" Gus asked.

"What do you mean?" Cydney blinked at him, the picture of innocence. "Put me up to what?"

"Coming in here to con me, bribe me, beg me—whatever it takes to keep me from putting the kibosh on this wedding."

"Aldo did no such thing. We drew straws and I—I mean, I

volunteered. I wanted to give you this." She unzipped her brown leather purse, withdrew a business card and handed it to him. "My attorney. I told him to expect your call. I should've gotten out the leaf blower and found that wicket. I didn't. I was negligent. Sue me, Mr. Munroe. Don't use this to ruin the wedding."

Gus was stunned. What a perfectly brilliant idea. Why hadn't he thought of it? And why was Cydney Parrish looking at him like she expected him to sprout horns and fangs? Where had she gotten the idea he was such an ogre?

Can't imagine, Munroe, his inner voice said. *Maybe you barging into her house waving Artie's will had something to do with it.*

"I wouldn't dream of suing family, Miss Parrish." Gus tossed the card on the table. "I'm offended that you think I would."

"Perhaps I got the wrong impression, Mr. Munroe."

She plucked the codicil to Artie's will out of her bag, unfolded it and smoothed it on the table in front of him. She had to get out of her chair to do it, which brought her close enough that Gus could see how amazingly dark her eyebrows were, how long and thick her lashes. He drew a breath of her perfume, a light, flowery scent that soothed the throb in his nose. The faxed codicil was a crushed and wrinkled mess. Gus had last seen it wadded into a ball in Cydney Parrish's hand and flung at his chest.

"If I jumped to conclusions," she said, settling back in her chair and nodding at the codicil, "that's why."

See? his inner voice said. *Told you so.*

"Oh shut up," Gus snapped. "I hate it when you're right."

Cydney Parrish went stiff in her chair. "What did you say?"

"I said—" Gus snatched up the codicil, crumpled it and tossed it into the trash can beside the bed. "I'd like a chance to make things right. We got off on the wrong foot last night. It was entirely my fault and I apologize. Care to start over?"

Cydney's chin took a swift, dubious jerk to one side.

"I'm Aldo's uncle, Angus Munroe." Gus stuck his right

hand through the bars on the bed rail. "Pleased to meet you, Miss—?"

He threw in a smile. A rusty, rarely used one. Cydney Parrish didn't return it, but she inched forward in her chair and slipped her hand into his.

"Parrish," she said warily. "Cydney Parrish. Bebe's aunt."

"Is Aldo here, by any chance?"

"No. He and Bebe had classes this morning. He left you a note and your keys. Your car is in the parking lot."

She took her hand back and dipped into her bag, pulled out a folded sheet of white paper, his glasses and his keys and gave them to him.

"Thank you." Gus put his keys on the table, his half lenses gingerly and crookedly on the tip of his swollen nose, unfolded the note and read:

Uncle Gus. This is a warning. You do anything—and I mean *anything*—to cause trouble for Bebe and me or to screw up our wedding and I'll never talk to you again. I mean it. I'm twenty-one and I can get married if I want. If you're so worried about my money, you keep it. It'll be mine when I'm twenty-five. I can work for the next four years and so can Bebe. I'll be at her Uncle Cyd's house around five if you want to talk to me before you go back to Crooked Possum.

—Aldo

P.S. You behaved like a jerk last night and you owe Miss Parrish an apology.

Gus' temper and the dull, sick throb in his head soared. He put his head back against the rock disguised as a pillow and shut his eyes. He wanted to crush the note in his fist and make Aldo eat it. Or eat it himself along with the codicil. He'd behaved like a jackass and he knew it. He didn't need Aldo to remind him.

"Mr. Munroe? Are you all right?"

Cydney Parrish laid a hand on his shoulder, a light, gentle touch Gus felt through the thin blue hospital gown he wore.

He opened his eyes and saw her leaning forward in her chair, her arm slipped through the bed rail to reach him. What lovely eyes she had, almond-shaped and almond-colored with amber-flecked irises. Peach-kissed skin and a mouth to match.

"Can I get you anything?" she asked.

How 'bout a kiss? his inner voice suggested.

"A mirror," Gus said. "I'd like a mirror."

She bit her lower lip—the one he was fantasizing about nibbling—dug a gold compact out of her purse, opened it and passed it to him. Gus raised the round mirror in the lid and surveyed the damage. He looked like he'd run face first into a brick wall. Both eyes were turning black, he had scratches on his chin and his jaw and W. C. Fields' nose.

"The swelling should go down in a couple of days," Cydney said. "Sooner, the doctor said, if you use ice packs."

Gus shut the compact and passed it back to her. "Aldo said I could see him at your place around five. D'you mind?"

"Not at all. You're welcome to stay for dinner if you'd like."

"Thank you, Miss Parrish, but Crooked Possum is a long drive. Perhaps another time. Thank you for coming this morning."

"You're welcome, Mr. Munroe." She rose from the chair and looped her purse over her shoulder. "I brought you some toiletries and your clothes. I washed them and put them in the closet."

"And the flowers, Miss Parrish? Did you bring those?"

"No. They were here when I—" She broke off, an affronted blaze flaming across her cheeks. "I'm not trying to bribe you with flowers and a home-cooked meal, Mr. Munroe. I didn't come here to con you. I came to talk about Bebe and Aldo. I hoped we could discuss the wedding like adults and come to an agreement."

"I came to Kansas City for the same reason, Miss Parrish. No offense, but I didn't come to talk to you. I came to talk to Aldo. He thinks I'm in a twist over his trust fund, but he's wrong. I couldn't care less about the money, but I care a great deal about my nephew."

"What about Bebe?" she demanded.

"Bebe isn't my responsibility. Aldo is. It's up to him to convince me that he knows what he's doing."

"I see." Cydney Parrish snatched up her shawl and stalked toward the door. She caught the handle and flung a look at him over her shoulder. "How about you, Mr. Munroe? Do *you* know what you're doing?"

chapter
seven

Did he know what he was doing? What kind of question was that? And who did Cydney Parrish think she was to ask it? Gus *always* knew what he was doing. Every minute, every second, every hour of every day.

He sat up on the side of the bed, fuming over the cheeky question. The door opened and a nurse came in pushing a cart.

"Doctor will be in soon. You can get up and get dressed if you feel like it. Sorry about these." She smiled as she loaded the floral bouquets on the cart. "Delivered to the wrong room."

Oh swell. Another apology he owed Cydney Parrish.

Gus wobbled into the bathroom with the disposable razors and shaving cream she'd brought him, leaned one hand on the sink, probed the back of his head with the other and found the lump in his skull. Just grazing it with his fingertips made him gasp and spots dance before his eyes. What the hell had he landed on when Aldo dropped him?

"Grazed the edge of a concrete birdbath," the doctor told him. "Lucky you've got a hard head."

Oh, the tales I could tell, his inner voice said wearily.

The doctor, a crusty old coot in a rumpled white lab coat, came in just as Gus was getting out of the shower, feeling steadier and a whole lot better. He checked Gus' reflexes, shined a penlight in his eyes that damn near blinded him and gave him a flash of memory—a dazzling overhead light and fingers poking the back of his head. Last night in the emergency room, Gus guessed, and asked the doctor why he couldn't remember more.

" 'Cause you've got a concussion. Mild, thanks to that rock you've got for a noggin. Memory gaps are normal. Nothing to worry about. We kept you overnight just as a precaution."

The doctor wrote him a prescription for the headache, told him to take it easy for a couple days, lay off booze for a while, and said he could get dressed and leave. Gus did, in the clothes he'd worn the day before, freshly laundered by Cydney Parrish.

He sniffed the sleeve of his gray sweater on his way to the elevator and smelled fabric softener. Liquid or dryer sheet? he wondered, and decided Cydney Parrish was the liquid type. She'd ironed his jeans, too, and brushed his gray suede hiking boots.

It's nice to have a woman around the house, Munroe, his inner voice said, but Gus pretended not to hear.

After he signed his release forms, Gus filled the prescription at the pharmacy in the hospital lobby, bought one of those blue chemical ice bags already frozen and went in search of his Jaguar. Aldo hadn't set the alarm, but he'd parked the sleek, British racing green coupe diagonally across three spaces in the back of the lot. Well. Maybe he'd only make Aldo eat half of his smart-aleck note.

Gus headed for the Country Club Plaza, the swankiest chunk of real estate in Kansas City. One of the first shopping areas in the country, dotted with fountains and statuary, its architecture modeled after Seville, Spain, with towers and grillwork and names like Gucci scrolled over shop doors. Gus hated city traffic and took the back streets, confident that he could find his way.

An hour later he was lost, wandering like a rat in the maze of one-way streets on the north side of the Plaza, the chemical ice bag turning to blue goo on the tan leather seat beside him. The streets that refused to go where he wanted them to were lined with stately homes and soaring trees that had been shedding leaves here, vivid gold and blazing red, since the pioneers headed west in their ox-drawn wagons.

The fourth time he passed the Nelson-Atkins Museum of

Art, Gus pulled into the parking lot to check his road map. He didn't always leave home with his American Express card, but he always left home with a road map. Except this time. He could've sworn—but he couldn't remember—having a road map last night. It wasn't in the glove compartment, between the seats, under the seats or in the trunk.

He decided to hell with it, locked the car and set the alarm and walked the mile or so to the Plaza. Slowly, taking his time since it was barely one o'clock and he had four hours to kill until he met Aldo at Cydney Parrish's house. He hoped he could find the place. He couldn't remember how he'd found it last night without a road map.

He ate lunch and took a pain pill, then strolled into Barnes & Noble. His heart in his mouth, his hands sweaty in his jacket pockets, but no one recognized him. With his bruised eyes hidden behind his Ray-Bans—he had to spread the nose pads to get them on—and a navy wool ball cap tugged over his forehead, he figured even the sharpest-eyed clerk would need his dental records to identify him.

What a joy it was to wander the stacks unmolested. Online bookstores were the best invention since unlisted phone numbers for a confirmed recluse, but there was no smell on earth as sweet as the smell of books. *How about Cydney Parrish's perfume?* his inner voice asked, but again Gus played deaf.

His ego, which felt damn near as beat up as his face, got the best of him in Mass-Market Fiction. While the clerk talked to his girlfriend on the phone, Gus turned *his* backlist titles face out, spined Fletcher Parrish's, and stood back grinning at his handiwork. Served the old bugger right for cutting him dead. All he'd wanted was Parrish's autograph, a chance to tell him how much his books meant to him. *Well,* said his inner voice. *This is a nice way to show your appreciation.*

Gus frowned, put the shelves back the way he'd found them and headed for the car. His legs felt like Jell-O, the top of his head like it was going to blow off by the time he reached the museum. He cut through the outdoor sculpture garden, found a bench that gave him a view of the south lawn and sat down. On the still summer-green grass lay two sculptures of giant shuttlecocks.

"Hey, little bro," he could almost hear Artie say with a wink and an elbow in the ribs. "Let's see you hit one of those over the net."

Gus smiled in spite of the ache in his throat. Artie had written his will expecting Gus would be a lot older if something happened to him and Beth. He hadn't planned on Gus being nineteen and left with a four-year-old to raise, but that's what had happened.

Of course he knew what he was doing. What a stupid question. You couldn't raise a child on a wing and a prayer. You had to have a plan and Gus had written one—a plan for his life and one for Aldo's—the day after Artie and Beth's funeral. He'd set goals and he'd achieved them. He'd worked full time while he finished college and Aunt Phoebe, his father's sister—dead now, bless her heart—took care of Aldo, fed him and read to him and taught him his letters and numbers. Gus earned a degree in English and got a job teaching to support the three of them.

He taught for three years, broke his leg in two places showing Aldo how to slide into second and wrote the first Max Stone while he was in the cast. He sold it, got an agent and a contract for two more books and sent Aunt Phoebe on a cruise. He thought he'd written a pretty good little detective story. So did his publisher until *Dead Soup* hit number three on *The New York Times* List. He still had nightmares about the thrown-together book tour, the print and radio interviews, the photographers and the readers—mostly women who drooled over him and Max Stone—lined up for his autograph and his phone number at book signings.

He'd been an unmarried, twenty-five-year-old English teacher who lived in Joplin, Missouri, with his orphaned nephew and his maiden aunt. A great publicity angle. The press agent assigned to him by his publisher played it for all it was worth. Gus handled it—he hadn't liked it but he'd handled it—until the day Aunt Phoebe came home with one hand clutching her heart and the other a supermarket tabloid.

The headline and supposedly the actress cast to play Max Stone's faithful secretary, Thelma, in the movie version of *Dead Soup* claimed GORGEOUS GUS ASKED ME TO BE ALDO'S MOMMY. The accompanying photo showed Aldo riding his bike on the street in front of Aunt Phoebe's house in Joplin.

Within an hour, the house was up for sale and Gus and Aunt Phoebe were on the road with Aldo, looking for a place to keep the bright and happy towheaded ten-year-old safe from prying reporters and photographers. They'd gotten lost in the Ozarks—even with a road map—found Crooked Possum purely by accident and stayed there.

Becoming a mega-best-selling author hadn't been in the Life Plan Gus had written for himself. Bebe Parrish wasn't part of the plan he'd written for Aldo, either, and that was the problem. It was Aldo's life to plan, Aldo's life to live and Aldo's life to screw up. It didn't matter that Aldo was all he had left of Artie, all he had left of Aunt Phoebe and his family. It was time for Uncle Gus to butt out.

And do what? he wondered with a heavy sigh. Get a dog?

Gus glanced at his watch, saw that it was almost four and rose from the bench. He stretched, felt his stiff neck muscles grind and took a last, long look at the giant shuttlecocks on the grass.

"Damn it," he said unhappily. "I *don't* know what I'm doing."

He didn't have a plan or a road map. No outline to follow, no idea which way to turn, and Cydney Parrish knew it. She might be a nut, but she was a perceptive nut.

Time to write a new Life Plan. He should have when *Dead Soup* hit it big. That's when his life went off track, when he'd let himself get sucked into the euphoria of fame and money. He'd written himself into bigger dead ends and written his way out, but this was his life, not Max Stone's, and there was no delete key if he screwed up. This would take some thought, Gus decided, and turned toward the car.

He headed south with his half lenses perched on the tip of his swollen nose and the scrap of paper where he'd jotted Cydney Parrish's address clutched in his right hand on the wheel. He drove through a quaint little shopping area with striped awnings over the storefronts, spied a florist and went in. He bought Bebe a bunch of daisies and a bouquet of chrysanthemums for Cydney.

By sheer dumb luck he found her street. By the birdbath in the front yard he found her brown brick and stucco house. The lawn was zoysia grass just beginning to turn winter beige in spots. A clutch of sparrows hopped on the lip of the birdbath—damned dangerous things, birdbaths—and a squirrel ran up one of the two shaggy pin oaks still clinging to their sharp-pointed gold leaves.

Gus followed the driveway past the house into a small hurricane of leaves. Not dull as they'd looked last night in the dark, but vivid, neon red maple leaves, swirling around a blue Jeep Cherokee parked in front of the open garage doors. The truck Cydney Parrish said she drove, Gus guessed, and glanced toward the backyard.

Cydney stood in the eye of the storm with a leaf blower in her hands. Gus could see enough of her through the funnel cloud of bright leaves to see that she had on jeans and a green sweatshirt, a pair of tan work gloves and clear plastic safety goggles.

She didn't see him or hear the Jag over the dull roar of the leaf blower. Gus parked next to her truck and sat watching her. With leaves dancing and swirling around her, she looked like a high-tech wood nymph. He smiled, changed his glasses for his Ray-Bans and picked up the bouquets he'd bought. He reached for the door handle, glanced in the rearview mirror and saw a Jag, a vivid, cranberry-red XJ8 coupe pull up the drive and stop a few feet behind his.

Aldo got out from behind the wheel. Gus raised a hand to him in the rearview mirror, but his nephew didn't wave back. He came around the nose of the car and leaned against the hood, crossed his arms and thrust out his chin in a scowl so belligerent it made Gus' head thud. He sighed and opened his door.

"This is *my* car," Aldo said when Gus got out of his, between his teeth, his voice tight, before Gus could open his mouth. "I paid cash for it. Paid the taxes, a year's worth of insurance and bought the license. It's mine free and clear, unless you plan to stop payment on the checks."

He uncrossed his arms, spread his palms on the hood and scooted an inch or two to the left so Gus could see the license plate. A vanity plate that said ILOVEBB.

"Hello to you, too. And I feel fine, thanks for asking." Gus walked around his Jag, laid the bouquets on the trunk lid and leaned against it facing Aldo. "What makes you think I'll stop payment on the checks?"

"Beats me, Uncle Gus. Maybe you storming in here last night and shoving my dad's will in Miss Parrish's face." Aldo jammed his arms together again and glared. "I'm a grown man and you made me look like a kid who can't wipe his nose without your permission."

Oops. Gus hadn't thought about Aldo when he'd jumped in his car and set a new land speed record between Crooked Possum and Kansas City. He'd only thought of Fletcher Parrish and his own ego.

"I'm sorry, Aldo. I went off half-cocked. I was trying to apologize for it when Bebe punched me and knocked me cold."

"You asked for it."

"I was speaking figuratively."

"I don't care if you were speaking Greek." Aldo raised his voice above the roar of the leaf blower. Leaves skipped over the chain-link fence and fluttered onto the driveway between them. "You scared Bebe half to death. She thought she'd killed you."

"Well. How rude of me to pass out." Gus picked up the daisies in their green tissue paper and thrust them at Aldo. "Give her these."

A tiny smile cracked the grim line of his nephew's mouth. "You brought some for Miss Parrish, too?"

"Yes." Gus laid the flowers back on the trunk. "And you can keep the car."

"You aren't gonna make me take it back?"

"No. Sunday was your twenty-first birthday. Seems like a great present to me. Happy birthday."

Aldo tilted his head to one side. Just enough to catch one of the long beams of late afternoon sun slanting through the maple tree. The light glowed on his mane of palomino hair and made Gus' chest ache. He looked so much like Artie it hurt, and Beth had worn her long, pale hair the same way, in a drawn-back ponytail with a wave of bangs.

"You know how much I paid for this car," Aldo said.

"Not to the penny, but I can guess."

"And you don't care?"

"I don't give a damn about the money, Aldo. I know that's how it looked last night, but I told you—I misunderstood."

"You thought Bebe was after my money?"

"The possibility occurred to me," Gus hedged. He hadn't thought that at all, but it was safer ground than what he did think.

"But you don't think so now?"

"No. I know better now." Cydney Parrish's ostrich-size nest egg had convinced him.

"So what do you think of Bebe?"

"She throws a wicked left."

"C'mon, Uncle Gus." Another inch or so of smile cracked the scowl on Aldo's face. "I mean really."

His nephew didn't want to know and Gus didn't want to tell him what he *really* thought. He thought Bebe Parrish was a few fries short of a Happy Meal, her aunt was a kook who talked to pictures of him cut out of magazines and her grandfather was a first-class SOB.

"She's very pretty," Gus said. "And she seems very sweet."

"So it's okay with you for us to get married?"

"I didn't say that." Aldo pushed off the Jag, his fists clenched, and Gus flung up a hand. "It might be okay if you can convince me that you and Bebe realize the responsibilities of marriage and that you're genuinely committed to each other."

"The State of Missouri says we're old enough to get married. We don't need your permission."

"No, you don't, but I hope you want my blessing."

"Sure I do. Why do you think I called you?"

"Why *did* you call? If you wanted me to think there was something not quite kosher about all this, that was the perfect way to do it."

"I didn't think of that," Aldo admitted.

"I didn't think much last night, either, and I'm sorry." Gus offered his hand to Aldo. "Want to start over?"

"Sure." Aldo threw his arms around Gus. "I'm sorry, too. I love you, Uncle Gus."

"Love you, too, Aldo," Gus said thickly, and hugged him tight.

The leaf blower switched off and Gus glanced toward the yard. Cydney Parrish stood near the fence smiling, her goggles on her head, leaves stuck in her hair and her eyelashes sparkling.

"I've reconsidered your invitation, Miss Parrish. What's for dinner?"

chapter
eight

"Chicken and noodles, thanks to my mother." Cydney smiled to hide her panic. If he'd said yes this morning, she could've had her nails done and bought a new outfit. Maybe scheduled a quickie liposuction. "Mother and Bebe should be here soon," she added, gathering up the cord of the leaf blower. "Why don't you take your uncle inside, Aldo, while I put this away?"

"You go ahead, Aldo," Angus Munroe said. "I'll help Miss Parrish."

He pushed off the Jag and picked up a green tissue-wrapped cone of flowers, one of two lying on the trunk lid. Chrysanthemums, Cydney guessed, by their spicy scent and purple-tipped lavender blooms.

Her best falling asleep fantasy of Angus Munroe involved an armful of roses. Peach roses, her favorite. He brought them to her first book signing, went down on one knee beside the table where her fans were lined up for her autograph, smiled and laid the roses in her lap.

"Miss Parrish," he said to her, starry-eyed and worshiping at her feet. "Cydney. I'm in awe of your talent."

Oh gag me, her little voice said. *Not that one again.*

"Stop right there." Cydney flung up her gloved right hand as Angus Munroe reached the fence. "I haven't found the wicket yet."

"I'll risk it." He unlatched the gate and stepped into the yard, the sunlight slanting through the branches of the maple tree winking on the lenses of his sunglasses. "I'm sorry about last night, Miss Parrish, and about the flowers in my room this morning. They were delivered to the wrong person. I hope you'll accept these with my apologies."

Holding the mums out to her, he waded toward her through the shin-deep leaves she'd blown away from the fence so they'd be easier to rake. He didn't see the wicket and neither did Cydney, though she supposed she should have. It was a natural, after all.

She did see the catch in his step, the startled O his lips formed when he put his foot through it. And a flash of the headline in tomorrow's *Kansas City Star*—AUTHOR SUES HOME OWNER FOR NEGLIGENCE—as he tripped and fell face first in the leaves with a crunching plop.

"Mr. Munroe!" Cydney dropped the leaf blower and raced toward him, skidding onto her knees beside him. "Are you all right?"

He didn't move, just lay sprawled on his face, the shoulders of his navy suede jacket and the backs of his blue-jeaned legs scattered with leaves. Cydney's hands fluttered around him. Did she dare touch him? Could a person suffocate in leaves?

"Uncle Gus!" She glanced up as Aldo came pelting toward them. "Uncle Gus! Are you all right?"

Cydney laid a hand on Angus Munroe's shoulder and felt him groan. So did she, certain that this time he'd call his attorney.

"Uncle Gus?" Aldo leaned over him. "You okay?"

Angus Munroe pushed himself up on one arm. The bill of his ball cap was crushed, his sunglasses bent and hanging off his face by one twisted earpiece. He plucked a hand-size red maple leaf out of his right ear and squinted a bruised eye at Cydney.

"I think I found your wicket, Miss Parrish."

A joke? Was that a joke? Cydney wasn't sure, but Aldo grinned as he caught his uncle by the arms and helped him up. Angus Munroe took a step as he stood and stumbled, favoring his right foot. Oh no, Cydney thought. *All aboard for the emergency room,* her little voice said.

Cydney dropped her gaze to the chrysanthemums. He'd

fallen on them and crushed them as flat as her last hope that he'd like her. That's all she'd wanted. Angus Munroe to like her, and to make a good impression for Bebe's sake. She picked up the bouquet and touched the squashed blooms. Was that so much to ask?

"I'm sorry about the flowers, Miss Parrish."

So was she. They weren't peach roses, but Angus Munroe had bought them for her. It wasn't her fantasy but it was close enough.

"That's all right, Mr. Munroe. It's the thought that counts."

Cydney handed the flattened mums to Aldo and crawled toward the fence. She found the wicket, stuck tight in the ground like it was embedded in concrete, pulled and tugged but couldn't budge it. She rose on her knees, grasped it in both hands and gave a mighty heave. It came free and tumbled her over on her fanny at Angus Munroe's feet.

He stood brushing leaves off his jacket and looking down at her, his sunglasses in his pocket, his crumpled hat pushed back on his head. Both his eyes were turning black, his nose so swollen it hurt just to look at it. Cydney realized she was staring at him and that he was staring back at her. Like she was depriving a village somewhere of an idiot.

"Got it," she said, raising the wicket in her gloved left hand.

"Good," he said. "For God's sake, don't drop it."

He offered her a hand. Cydney took it, noting the wince he made as she pulled herself to her feet.

"I think you've hurt yourself again, Mr. Munroe."

"Again, Miss Parrish? I didn't hurt myself the first time."

"Oh no. No, of course not. Bebe hit you, then Aldo and I dropped you and—" *You're blithering,* her little voice interrupted. *Like that idiot with no village.* "Never mind. I'm sure you remember what happened."

"Actually I don't. Just bits and pieces."

"Can I get you anything? An ice bag?"

"Relax, Miss Parrish. You warned me about the wicket. I'm not going to sue you."

"Thank God," she blurted, and Angus Munroe scowled. She snatched up the leaf blower and backed away. "Excuse me. I'll just put this away. And hide the croquet set where I'll never find it again."

Cydney hurried across the yard, gritting her teeth and crunching leaves beneath her feet. Damn Angus Munroe. She'd never again be able to enjoy watching leaves blow around her backyard. Or let them pile up until November, when she spent a whole Saturday raking and bagging. She loved those Saturdays. The spring of the rake tines in the grass, the ripe smell of leaves half decayed into compost. Her flushed cheeks and sore muscles, the hot chocolate and sleeping like a hibernating bear afterward.

The inside of the garage felt cool after the hot sun and the heat of Angus Munroe's scowl. Cydney tossed her goggles, her gloves and the wicket on the bench where she kept her gardening tools. She hung the leaf blower between two nails driven into the back wall and watched the cord swing from the handle. Make a nifty noose. Or maybe she could bend the wicket into a garrote. She couldn't decide which one Angus Munroe deserved more for barging into her life—hanging or strangling.

She'd liked him better when he was just a picture cut out of a magazine, a goal she could strive for and a face she could dream about. In person he was arrogant and hidebound and she didn't like him. Good thing, since she was sure he didn't like her, either.

Cydney hadn't felt this hurt and disappointed since the photographer from *People* asked her to stay behind him so she wouldn't accidentally end up in one of the pictures. Tears pricked her eyes but she blinked them away. She heard a slam in the driveway, drew a breath and walked back to the open overhead door.

Her mother's silver Lincoln Town Car sat behind her truck. Georgette and Bebe were already in the backyard with Aldo and his uncle, a nest of shopping bags at their feet. Bebe held the other bouquet Cydney had last seen on the trunk of his car. Daisies, she could see, as her niece peeled back one corner of the paper.

Georgette smiled and held out her hand to Angus Munroe. He said something that made her laugh but Cydney was too far away to hear. Bebe looked up at him from the daisies cupped in her hands, a dazzling you-like-me, you-*really*-like-me smile on her face.

Few men could withstand Bebe's innocently devastating smile, but Angus Munroe just stood looking at her. Like he was trying to decide what to make of her, Cydney thought. *Or maybe,* her little voice suggested, *what to do about her.*

"Uh-oh," Cydney muttered, frowning as she watched Aldo pick up Bebe's packages and lead her toward the house.

She waded gracefully along beside him despite the leaves and the air boot on her right ankle. Angus Munroe offered Georgette his arm, picked up her packages and escorted her toward the patio, limping just a little on his right foot. Aldo opened the French doors and helped Bebe up the step into the dining room. Angus Munroe did the same for Georgette and shut the door behind them.

Cydney stood in the open garage door, her hands clenched into fists. Why hadn't he stayed in Crooked Possum? He could've remained her secret fantasy then, and no harm done. She wished she could just stay out here in the garage, but she couldn't. For Bebe's sake she had to play gracious hostess and serve him dinner. Good thing her mother made the chicken and noodles before she took Bebe shopping. The way Cydney's day was going, she'd probably poison him.

Maybe you'll get lucky, her little voice said. *Maybe he'll choke on a chicken bone.*

If he did, she could save him—she knew the Heimlich maneuver. He might not like her, but he'd owe her one. The stuff of great blackmail if he continued to be difficult about the wedding.

Why was he being difficult? This morning he'd said he couldn't care less about Aldo's money. So if the fifteen million dollars wasn't the problem, what was? Why hadn't she thought to ask him? And why was she just standing here? She needed to change, set the table and fawn and fuss over Angus Munroe before he rethought the idea of suing her. Cydney shut and locked the overhead door and headed for the house.

Angus Munroe was already tucked up on the couch, his right foot on a cushion on her coffee table and an ice bag on his ankle. Her mother stood beside him holding another ice bag and a glass of water. Cydney didn't see Bebe and Aldo and didn't stop to look for them. She hurried to her bedroom, shut the door and stripped off her clothes, hopped into the shower in her bathroom and thought about drowning herself.

Too bad she hadn't thought of it *before* Angus Munroe found her talking to pictures of him. It might not have kept Bebe from hitting him and cracking his nose, or Aldo from dropping him, but at least she wouldn't have been around to see it. He could've fractured his skull on the birdbath or broken his neck when he'd tripped over the wicket. Boy, when life turned ugly, it took no prisoners.

Cydney dressed in black slacks and flats and a green sweater set—a scoop-neck shell and a cardigan with a single button on a loop—added the jade lariat necklace and earrings her father sent her from Hong Kong on his last book tour and declared herself as ready as she'd ever be.

Her mother was in the kitchen, whisking Bisquick and milk together for dumplings. She crooked her finger at Cydney.

"Start the coffee," she whispered, "then finish setting the table."

"Okay," Cydney whispered back. "Why are we whispering?"

"Angus Munroe is asleep. He took a pain pill." She jerked her head toward the living room. "Use my mother's china."

"Don't you think that's overkill?"

"After Bebe punching him in the nose, nothing is overkill. How could you let such a thing happen?"

"How could I *let* it? How could I have stopped it?"

"You're an adult, Cydney. Bebe is a child."

"If she's a child, then she has no business getting married,"

Cydney blurted, and blinked. Eek. She sounded like Angus Munroe.

Georgette said, "You sound like your father."

I should've stayed in the garage, Cydney thought. Why didn't I stay in the garage?

"All right, Mother." She sighed. "I'll use Grandmother's china."

Cydney filled the Krups machine and turned it on, then crept into the dining room, where she stored the set of eighty-year-old Spode, ivory with gold-banded edges, in the hutch. By rights the service for twelve belonged to Gwen, but Gwen had no interest in china unless *Time* or *Newsweek* wanted to send her there to photograph the Great Wall.

Georgette had already spread a white damask cloth on the table, tucked the napkins artfully into rings and set the daisies Angus Munroe brought Bebe to float in a crystal bowl between tall white tapers.

Cydney eased open the hutch doors so they wouldn't squeak. She laid places at each end of the table, two on one side for Bebe and Aldo, one across from them for Angus Munroe, and crept to the doorway between the dining room and living room to peek at him.

Poor man. Her left ankle, the one she'd wrenched when she slipped on the grape in the produce aisle, twinged in sympathy. He'd come to Kansas City to talk to his nephew, and now look at him. Packed in ice—one bag on his ankle, the other on his nose—dead leaves and dry grass stuck to his clothes, sprawled in a heap on her mauve sofa.

Weary and beat-up, but handsome as a sin heap, even with two black eyes, a shadow of beard on his jaw and a lock of dark hair falling over the ice bag pressed to his nose. Cydney had never seen a picture of him where his hair wasn't falling over his face. He must have a cowlick, she thought, right there in front.

He'd taken off his size 10 suede hiking boots, the ones she'd brushed mud off last night. Cydney could see bits of crushed leaf stuck to the toes of his socks. White, over the calf tube socks with ribbed tops and gray toes. She'd washed

them last night along with his sweater, size large, his jeans—
34 waist, 36 inseam—and his boxer shorts. Paisley silk that
slipped through her fingers like—well, like silk—when she'd
taken them out of the dryer.

If she'd had a night and a day like Angus Munroe, she'd be
cranky and out of sorts, too. I've been too hard on him,
Cydney thought. I should cut him some slack. For Bebe's sake.
Her decision had nothing at all to do with the picture forming
in her head, of Angus Munroe wearing those paisley boxers
and nothing else. Absolutely nothing.

Whoa, mama, her little voice said, just as Bebe and Aldo
came into the living room and bounced down on either side
of him, their weight dipping the couch cushions and knocking the ice bag off his nose. He caught it against his chest and
looked up, bleary-eyed, at Cydney standing in the dining room
doorway.

He smiled at her, a soft-edged, half-asleep smile that made
her stomach flutter. He has no idea what he's doing, Cydney
told herself, no clue, thank God, that you're thinking about
his underwear. He's half-looped, that's all, from the pain pill
he took.

"Check it out, Uncle Gus." Aldo leaned over him, un-
rolling a blueprint in his lap. "The house I'm gonna build for
me and Bebe."

"But we can't decide where to go on our honeymoon."
Bebe opened two travel brochures and spread them on top of
the blueprint. "What do you think, Mr. Munroe? Cancún or
Cleveland?"

"Cleveland?" He gave a raspy, not quite awake laugh that
made Bebe stick her lip out. "What the hell's in Cleveland?"

"The Rock and Roll Hall of Fame, Uncle Gus. Jeez." Aldo
laughed. "You gotta get out of Crooked Possum more
often."

"Dinner, everyone!" Georgette came out of the kitchen
ringing the little crystal bell she'd given Cydney with the
silver coffee carafe. No matter what cabinet or drawer Cydney
hid it in, her mother always found it.

Georgette lit the candles and everyone sat down, Cydney

at the end of the table closest to the French doors. Angus Munroe sat on her right, across from Aldo and Bebe, her mother at the opposite end. Cydney said grace and Georgette started the salad around.

Bebe chattered mindlessly, as Bebe always did, mostly to Aldo about shopping and school and his new Jag and shopping. Cydney kept waiting for one of them to mention the wedding, but they were off in their own little world. Angus Munroe didn't say a word, just ate steadily—two helpings of chicken and noodles—and watched them.

The subject didn't come up until dessert. A three-layer carrot cake Georgette found time to bake between laps in the pool, her hour on the Stairmaster and taking Bebe shopping. Sprinkled with pecans and coconut, dotted with orange icing carrots with green icing tops and served on a footed crystal cake plate and a white paper doily. Some days Cydney really hated her mother.

Angus Munroe ate two slices. Aldo finished a third piece, drained his glass of milk and grinned at his uncle across the table.

"Eat your heart out, Uncle Gus. Mrs. Parrish taught Bebe how to cook. I'm gonna eat like a king."

"Call me Georgette, Aldo." Her mother rose and laid a hand on his shoulder while she filled his glass from a crystal pitcher. Milk cartons were not allowed at the table in Georgette's presence. "Or Gramma George if you prefer."

"Okay, Gramma George." Aldo beamed at her, then at Cydney. "Can I call you Uncle Cyd, Miss Parrish?"

"If you'd like, Aldo."

Angus Munroe scowled. Either the pain pill's wearing off, Cydney thought, or he only smiles twice a year—when the royalty checks arrive.

"You certainly will eat like a king." He put his fork down and lifted his coffee cup from its saucer. "A delicious meal, Mrs. Parrish. Thank you. And wonderful coffee."

"Uncle Cyd made the coffee," Bebe chimed in. "She only drinks tea, but my Grampa Fletch says she makes the best coffee in the world."

"Does he?" Angus Munroe glanced at Cydney, her pulse jumping at the quick smile he gave her. "Well, I agree with him." He saluted her with his cup. "Delicious, Miss Parrish."

"Thank you, Mr. Munroe. Would you like a refill?"

"Yes, thank you." He put his cup down. "And thank you for inviting me."

"You're welcome, Mr. Munroe." Cydney filled his cup and put the server down, seated herself and smoothed her napkin in her lap, glanced up and saw her mother eyeing her with an arched, what-gives eyebrow.

"My, my, you two are awfully formal," she said, aiming her megawatt TV smile on Angus Munroe. "Since we're going to be family, please call me Georgette. Do you prefer Angus or Gus?"

The question caught him with his coffee raised partway to his mouth. His arm froze for just a second, then he put the cup down without drinking and looked at her mother.

"Angus will be fine. I don't hear it often and it's a fine old name."

"What do *I* call you?" Bebe asked him.

"I don't know, Bebe." He shrugged like he could care less and wiped his mouth with his napkin. "What would you like to call me?"

"Rude," she said flatly. "Uncle Cyd invited you to dinner and Gramma George baked you a cake, but you won't talk to them or to me unless one of us asks you a question. Don't you like us?"

Angus Munroe sat back in his chair, startled. Her mother looked like a deer caught in headlights. Cydney held her breath.

"Well, Bebe," he said slowly. And carefully, Cydney thought, feeling his way. "I've just met you and your family. I'm not terribly at ease with people I don't know well."

"I keep telling you, Uncle Gus." Aldo held his plate up to Georgette, who was cutting him a fourth slice of carrot cake. "You gotta get out of Crooked Possum more often."

"Yes, Aldo, you keep telling me that." He glanced at his

nephew, a flicker of irritation in his gray eyes. "But I like my life the way it is."

"All work and no play makes Angus a dull boy," Aldo said in a singsong voice, waving his fork back and forth. "When was the last time you met a hot chick in Crooked Possum, Uncle Gus?"

"Put a sock in it, Aldo." He gave his nephew a smile that said, "Or I will," and picked up his cup. "I'm not interested in hot chicks."

"Then I have a great idea!" Bebe cried enthusiastically. "You should ask my Aunt Cydney for a date!"

Angus Munroe choked on his coffee, grabbed his napkin and coughed. His water glass was empty and so was the pitcher. *Let him strangle,* her little voice said, but Cydney took the pitcher to the kitchen, her cheeks burning, filled it and brought it back to the table. *Atta girl!* her little voice cheered. *Throw it in his face!* But Cydney filled his glass and sat down.

Angus Munroe snatched up the water and drank, coughed again and wiped his mouth. "Sorry," he croaked. "Swallowed wrong."

Cydney just smiled. She'd keep smiling, even if it killed her. Or broke her heart, whichever came first.

"Enough about me, Aldo." Angus Munroe cleared his throat. "Let's talk about your wedding. When and where do you plan to have it?"

"A week from Saturday." Aldo caught Bebe's hand and laced their fingers together. A sign of solidarity in the face of the enemy, Cydney guessed. "The where, we haven't decided yet."

"We'd love to find a romantic, out-of-the-way place," Bebe said, a soft, dreamy glow in her eyes that disappeared when she sighed. "But that's out of the question because of my mother."

"Why? This is your wedding, not hers."

"But I want my mother at the ceremony, Mr. Munroe. She's a photojournalist and very much in demand. I'm afraid if I don't take her straight to the church when she gets off the plane from Russia some magazine editor will call and she'll be gone again before the organist can sit down to play 'The Wedding March.' "

"What if we get married in some really far-off place?" Aldo suggested around a mouthful of cake. "Like a sheep ranch in the middle of Australia? Bet they don't have many airports or flights to New York."

"Aldo," Bebe said patiently. "Sheep are not romantic."

"Yeah, but we could go four-wheeling in the Outback. And rock climbing and crocodile hunting."

Angus Munroe sat back in his chair, his right hand cupped over his mouth. Through his fingers, Cydney could just see the grin lifting one side of his mouth. Bebe sat back in her chair and stuck out her lip.

"Right. Not romantic." Aldo pointed his fork at Bebe. "But your mother would definitely be grounded once we got her there. And I bet they don't have many phones, either."

"I've been thinking about the telephone problem, Cydney," Georgette said. "I'm putting you in charge of taking Gwen's cell phone away from her."

"Oh no, Mother. I got the short straw last time Gwen was home."

You always get the short straw, her little voice pointed out, but Cydney ignored it. From the corner of her eye, she saw Angus Munroe's grin widen behind his cupped hand.

"But I'm sure we won't have that problem this time," she added hurriedly. "After all, this is Bebe's wedding."

"What about your Grampa Fletch, Bebe?" Angus Munroe asked.

"Oh, he's a writer, too," she said brightly. "But I don't know if he has a cell phone. Does he, Uncle Cyd?"

Angus Munroe shifted in his chair, made a fist of his hand and coughed. To keep from laughing out loud, Cydney was sure. He'd hurt her feelings when he'd choked at the thought of going out with her, but she would *not* tolerate him laughing at Bebe. One more snigger and she'd punch him in the nose herself.

"Yes, Bebe," she said. "Grampa Fletch has a cell phone."

"I know he's a writer, Bebe. I've read his books," Angus Munroe said. "I meant, is he coming to the wedding?"

"Hell no," she chirped cheerfully. "Only Gramps said, 'Hell no, Bebe-cakes.' That's what he calls me, Bebe-cakes. 'I've been to enough weddings of my own,' he said, but he invited me and Aldo to Cannes for Christmas."

"His treat," Aldo put in. "It's our wedding present from Mr. Parrish. Two plane tickets to Cannes."

"That's a very generous gift, Aldo." Angus Munroe folded his arms across his stomach, reminding Cydney of last night when Bebe knocked him out. His sweater had ridden up when he fell, just enough to give Cydney a mouthwatering glimpse of his washboard abdomen. "Tell you what. I'll pay for your plane tickets to Cleveland."

What a guy, her little voice said. *Rock hard, ripped—and cheap.*

"Oh, Mr. Munroe!" Bebe squealed, her eyes shining with happiness. "Thank you so much!"

"Uncle Gus, Bebe." He smiled at her. "Call me Uncle Gus."

chapter
nine

Desperation, not inspiration, was the true mother of invention. Any writer who'd ever cranked out the last hundred pages of a four-hundred-page manuscript in twenty-four hours to meet a deadline knew it. And Gus was desperate.

Aldo had defected. Gus had suspected it when he'd wakened in the hospital and found Cydney Parrish, not Aldo, at his bedside. He'd sold out for chicken and noodles, carrot cake and a hot chick. Gus could hire a chef, but he couldn't compete with Bebe and he knew it.

He also knew a brick wall when he saw one, and one sat looking at him across the table, Aldo and Bebe with their hands clasped together. The twelve-thousand-dollar diamond Gus had had a stroke over blazed on Bebe's ring finger. He could yank Aldo's money but that wouldn't stop the wedding. It would only make Aldo hate him, and he didn't want that. He wanted them to wait—until spring, maybe—to make sure they knew what they were doing.

Just a few months to be certain of their feelings, a few months to give Gus time to adjust to the fact that Aldo didn't need him anymore, to find a new focal point for his life. He didn't think that was too much to ask, but he was too proud to admit that he felt so vulnerable.

He'd come up with a plan instead. A plan to make Aldo stop and think beyond Bebe's delectable figure, a chance to give himself time to formulate a new Life Plan. He thought he could pull it off, but not in Kansas City. He was outnumbered here and on Parrish turf, but now that he knew Fletcher Parrish wasn't coming to the wedding, he could seize home-field advantage.

"I see your problem." Gus folded his arms on the edge of the table and spoke directly to Aldo and Bebe. "I don't understand it. I don't understand any parent who puts career ahead of children. But hey." He shrugged. "I'm the guy who needs to get out of Crooked Possum."

"That's not all you need," Cydney muttered into her teacup. Gus glanced at her. She smiled serenely. The lariat necklace she wore, a string of tiny jade beads, gleamed in the glow of the half-burned candles. All through dinner he'd fantasized about catching the Y-end in his teeth while he kissed the peach-toned hollow of her throat.

"I think I have a solution to your quandary about where to have the wedding." Gus swung his gaze back to Aldo and Bebe, swearing he'd keep it there. "Tall Pines."

His nephew's eyes sprang wide and his jaw dropped. Cydney Parrish's teacup clattered onto its saucer.

"Uncle Gus?" Aldo made the peace sign with his right hand. "How many fingers am I holding up?"

"Three," Gus said, just to be perverse. "Two fingers, Aldo, and no, I didn't hit my head that hard."

"What's Tall Pines?" Bebe asked.

"My home, Bebe. Mine and Aldo's," he said, just in case Aldo had forgotten. "Tall Pines was once a bed-and-breakfast. There are fifteen bedrooms in the house." Bebe's eyes widened. Her elbow slid onto the table to support her chin as she leaned closer to listen. "There's a great room we never use that will hold at least one hundred people. Huge stone fireplace, a wall of windows overlooking the lake."

Gus paused to let Bebe catch up. When her lips stopped moving and her eyes lit up, he continued.

"Pine floors and paneling throughout. The closest airport is in Springfield, one hundred and twenty-five miles from Tall Pines. And the best part is that Crooked Possum isn't on any road map." Gus leaned over the table toward Bebe. "Aldo gets lost every time he comes home. I guarantee your mother won't find her way out once you get her there."

"It's *perfect*!" Bebe crowed, leaping out of her chair and around the table. "Oh *thank you*, Uncle Gus! Thank you, thank you!"

Gus barely had time to get to his feet before Bebe flung herself at him. He caught her around the waist with his left arm and the back of his chair in his right hand to keep her momentum from knocking them over. He had to swing her halfway around to do it, looked over the top of her red head and saw Cydney Parrish gazing at him. Gus wasn't sure if the tilt of her chin meant she didn't believe him or she didn't trust him.

"You don't approve, Cydney?"

"Offering Tall Pines is a lovely gesture." She let go of her cup and tucked her hands in her lap. "Bebe clearly loves the idea. The decision is hers and Aldo's, of course, but I think Crooked Possum is too small and too far off the beaten track. We need a florist and a caterer, and it would be nice if the wedding guests had a prayer of finding the place."

"I only care about Mother, Uncle Cyd." Bebe turned and faced her aunt. "If she'll be stuck in Crooked Possum I'll be happy."

"I'm sure you can find everything you need in Branson," Gus said. "It's quite a booming little metropolis since country music came to town, and it's only a fifty-mile drive." Each way, but Gus decided not to mention that. "An easy trip."

If you're a mountain goat, his inner voice said. *Have you no shame, Munroe?* Absolutely none, Gus realized. And no scruples, either. He'd sell his soul to the devil if he hadn't already sold it to his publisher.

"And Branson is, what?" Cydney asked. "Two hundred miles from Kansas City? A wedding can't be planned long distance, Mr. Munroe, and we only have eleven days."

"Gus. So come to Tall Pines as soon as you need to."

Cydney arched an eyebrow. "Would tomorrow be convenient?"

"Tomorrow's fine. I'll have your rooms ready."

"Mr. Munroe." She rose from her chair, shaking her head as she started gathering dishes. "You're not being practical. Aldo and Bebe have classes here in Kansas City."

"School's not a problem, Uncle Cyd," Bebe said. "Aldo and I have mostly lectures this semester. We've talked to our professors and we've decided to wait till summer to take our honeymoon."

"Oh," Cydney said. Dismayed for all of five seconds, then she said "Oh," again, brightly, and gave Gus a smug look. "That's very *mature* of you and Aldo, but I see more problems than pluses with having your wedding in the middle of the Ozark wilderness."

"Branson is hardly wilderness, Cydney," Georgette said. "You were there last summer and you raved about the shops and boutiques."

"I was a tourist, Mother. I bought crafts and gifts. I wasn't buying a wedding gown."

"I *have* my dress, Aunt Cydney. Gramma bought it for me today. And my shoes and my veil."

"That's three things, Bebe. Three." Cydney held up as many fingers. "We have decorations and candles to buy—a million things. We know exactly where to find everything we need in Kansas City and we don't have to drive fifty miles to order the wedding cake."

"Tall Pines is *perfect*," Bebe said stubbornly, squaring off on her aunt over the corner of the table. "And it's *my* wedding."

"And Aldo's," Gus threw in, but no one paid any attention to him.

Not even Aldo, who was plowing through his carrot cake, oblivious to the snit Bebe was working herself into. She stood glaring at her aunt, who glared right back at her. Amazing, Gus thought. My plan is working already. He'd meant to cause dissention between Aldo and Bebe. Nothing major, just mix things up enough to pull their heads out of the clouds. Create a snag or two to make them realize they were planning a life together, not just a big party with cake and punch and nuts—provided by the Parrish family—for all their friends, but this squabble between Bebe and Cydney might work just as well. Get the whole family into it.

"Yes, Bebe, it's your wedding. And I admit Tall Pines sounds wonderfully romantic." Cydney finished stacking plates. "But I have a business to run and clients who depend on me."

"I depend on you, too!" Bebe's lip protruded and started to tremble. "I can't get married without you, Uncle Cyd!"

"If you get married in Kansas City you won't have to."

"That's blackmail, Cydney," Georgette said severely.

"It's the truth. I have to work to support myself and Bebe."

"You're forgetting something." Georgette rose and started gathering dishes at her end of the table. "In twelve days Bebe will be married and it will be Aldo's responsibility to take care of her."

"I know that." So Cydney claimed, but the quick, caught-short blink she gave her mother suggested that maybe she'd forgotten. Or had yet to accept it. "But if I don't take care of my clients, someone else will."

"So let someone else. You don't need to work sixty hours a week. You need time to finish that book you've been writing for ten years."

"Five years, Mother. It's only *five* years."

"Your father has written four books in that time," Georgette said. Slackard, Gus thought. He'd written six and the screenplay for *Dead Calm*, his fifth best-seller. "How many chapters have you written?"

"This isn't about me, Mother." Cydney ducked Gus a flustered, discomfited look. This was more than she wanted him to know about her and she didn't like it. "It's about Bebe and Aldo's wedding."

"*I* didn't bring you and your clients into this conversation, Cydney. *You* did."

"Yes, to make a point. Don't take this the wrong way, Bebe." She glanced at her niece, then faced her mother. "It's not fair to expect me to put my life on hold because Bebe wants to get married the second Gwen steps off the plane from Moscow."

"Of course it's not fair, but since you've put your life on hold for Bebe for the last five years, what's another twelve days?"

"Twelve days isn't the issue, it's the principle," Cydney retorted, her jaw set and fire in her eyes. The same blaze Gus

had seen there last night when she'd told him to shove the codicil to Artie's will where the sun don't shine. "And I still think Crooked Possum is too small, too far away and too hard to find."

"It doesn't matter what you think." Georgette stopped gathering dishes and looked down the length of the table at her daughter. "Let Bebe have her wedding at Tall Pines or on the moon or wherever she wants and let's all work together to make it a beautiful, memorable day."

"And don't worry, Uncle Cyd." Aldo finished the last of his cake and his milk and picked up his napkin. "Tall Pines is big enough that you won't have to see my Uncle Gus unless you want to."

In mid-wipe of his mouth, Aldo froze, an oh-m'God-what-did-I-say glaze in his eyes. Something he shouldn't have, Gus surmised, by the brilliant flush that shot all the way to Cydney Parrish's hairline. Well, wasn't this a kick in the pants? *He* was the reason she didn't want to come to Tall Pines.

"Aldo's absolutely right," Gus agreed. "I'm in my office most of the time. You'll have the run of the place. Carte blanche to do whatever you need for the wedding. I won't get in your way."

"All right. I know when I'm beat." Cydney sighed exasperatedly. "But don't blame me if the caterer can't find Crooked Possum."

"Then it's settled," Georgette said. "Bebe. You and Aldo will be married at Tall Pines."

"Oh thank you, Gramma! Thank you, Uncle Cyd!" Bebe flung herself at her aunt, catching her around the neck in a fierce hug that jerked her chin up and locked her eyes on Gus.

He smiled at her. His headache was pounding—and his temper right along with it—but he was determined to keep smiling even if he popped a blood vessel. Cydney Parrish flushed again, ducked his gaze and slipped out of her niece's headlock.

"Oh Aldo!" Bebe clapped her hands together. "I'm so happy!"

"Me, too, Beebs." He grinned and rose to catch her as she

danced around the table and into his arms, with remarkable grace in spite of the air boot on her ankle.

Gus watched Cydney Parrish stack dishes on a tray she'd taken off the sideboard. When she went to pick it up, he beat her to the handles.

"Let me help you," he said.

"No thank you," she said coldly. "You've done quite enough."

Then she yanked the tray from him and stalked into the kitchen.

"Don't mind Cydney," Georgette said, in a low voice at Gus' elbow as she came around the table, folding napkins as she gathered them. "It's tough to be the only girl in the family who isn't getting married."

"I'll take your word for it," Gus said, and she laughed.

"I've been saying no to Herb Baker for years," Georgette went on, "but I said yes Sunday, so here we are all of a sudden with three brides in the family. Bebe and I, and Gwen is supposed to marry some prince she picked up in Russia. I'd feel left out, too, if I were Cydney." She folded the last of the napkins—since they were soiled, Gus had no idea why—and smiled. "It was very nice of you to bring Bebe flowers. And very forgiving after what happened last night."

Gus glanced through the spindles on the half wall that separated the dining room from the kitchen. Cydney Parrish stood with her back to him rinsing dishes, in a cloud of steam that fogged the window and a halo of light cast by the round neon fixture she'd switched on. He hadn't seen the chrysanthemums he'd bought her since he'd fallen on them and she'd peeled them off the ground. She'd probably thrown them away.

"I don't hold grudges. I wanted Bebe to know that," he said to Georgette. "So I can expect you all tomorrow?"

"I think Thursday will be time enough. Give us a day to pack and get organized. I'd like to bring my fiancé, Herb, with us, if you don't mind. I'm sure we'll need an extra pair of hands."

"He's welcome. If you have a fax machine I'll send you a map to Crooked Possum and Tall Pines."

"Lovely." She touched his arm and smiled. "I'll give you my card."

Gus ducked into the living room to collect his jacket from the couch. When he came back, Aldo and Bebe were cemented in a lip-lock worthy of Super Glue. He cleared his throat and they broke apart.

"Don't worry, Uncle Gus." Aldo grinned and caught Bebe's hand as he turned around. "I won't get lost coming home this time."

For the last time, Gus thought, hiding the pang he felt behind a smile. "Just in case, oh mighty Pathfinder, I'm faxing Georgette a map."

"Here's the number," she said, handing Gus a gray linen card.

"I'll send the map tomorrow." Gus slipped the card into his wallet and the wallet into his jacket pocket. "And I'll see you all on Thursday."

"We'll walk you out, Uncle Gus." Aldo fished his keys from his pocket and slung his arm around Bebe. "We're gonna cruise in the Jag."

"I should be off as well." Georgette hooked her purse over her shoulder and glanced into the kitchen. "Need some help, Cydney?"

"Not now, Mother. I'm nearly finished." She shut off the water, crossed the kitchen and opened the top freezer compartment of the refrigerator. She took out a filled ice bag, an old-fashioned blue rubber one with a screw-on cap, brought it to Gus and handed it to him.

"For your nose," she said to him, then to Bebe, "Eleven-thirty, please. I'll be waiting up."

"Yes, Uncle Cyd," she replied in a weary singsong. "Eleven-thirty."

"Thank you for this." Gus gave Cydney a nod and the ice bag a toss on his palm. "And your hospitality."

"You're welcome. Good night, Mr. Munroe," she said curtly, then walked back to the sink and turned on the water.

chapter
ten

It took Gus twenty minutes after he left Cydney Parrish's house to find a Quik Trip that sold gas and road maps. He bought a Kansas City street guide and leaned against the right front fender tracing his way to the interstate while the Jag guzzled a tankful of super unleaded premium under a neon-lit aluminum canopy.

His ankles were crossed, his half lenses sitting almost straight on his not-so-swollen nose. A fuzzy moth swooping around the lights took a kamikaze dive into the map. Gus brushed it off, remembered the moth he'd wanted to pluck out of Cydney's hair last night and scowled.

Who did she think she was? Asking him if he knew what he was doing, muttering into her teacup at dinner, "That's not all you need."

She hadn't a clue what he needed. Neither did Gus now that Aldo was getting married, other than a giant-size thumb to plug the hole in his life. He'd known Aldo would leave home someday; he just hadn't expected it this soon. Maybe he should have, but he hadn't. He felt lost and abandoned and had no one to blame for it but himself.

When the pump shut off, he went inside to pay for the gas and the map. A plastic vase full of peach-colored roses— $1.99 each—sat by the cash register. Gus glared at them. He should be glad in all the talk of brides and weddings that Cydney Parrish had thrown the mums away without telling her mother he'd brought her flowers, too, but he wasn't. He was annoyed as hell.

He bought a dozen roses, had the clerk wrap the dripping

stems in waxed paper sheets from the donut case, stalked out to the car and drove back to Cydney's house.

The only vehicle in the driveway was her blue Jeep Cherokee, the back window fogged with dew. Good. It was just the two of them. Gus got out of the Jag with the roses, shut the door and looked at the house.

In the spill of light through the uncurtained French doors, he could see Cydney clearing the table. Gus let himself through the gate, crossed the yard and reached the patio just as she disappeared into the kitchen with the water goblets.

He waited by the picnic table until she came back, then stepped forward, tucking the roses behind him. He watched her fold the corners of the tablecloth toward the center of the table where Georgette had left her neat stack of napkins. She picked up the top one and wiped her nose, then her lashes, her head turned just enough that Gus could see the shimmer in her eyes. He didn't realize it was unshed tears until he'd raised his foot on the step, knocked, and she glanced up and saw him.

He'd come back to tell her she didn't know diddly-squat about him, not to trap her in another awkward moment and embarrass her. Part of him wanted to turn away and leave, the rest of him wanted to put his arms around her and comfort her. He smiled at her through the glass. She wiped her nose again, came to the door and opened it.

"Yes, Mr. Munroe?" Her voice sounded thick, like she had a cold. "Did you forget something?"

"Yes." Gus held the roses out to her. "My manners."

"*Ohhh,*" she said, on a sharp catch of breath.

No thank you, just that single, sucked-in syllable. She took the roses from him, gingerly, like he'd handed her a bouquet of poison ivy.

"If you don't like them," Gus said, "I guess I could fall on them."

She laughed, a bubbly warble that brought a fresh sheen of tears to her lashes. "Please don't. Peach roses are my favorite."

"Is that why you're crying?"

"No." She drew a shuddery breath that made the looped end of the jade necklace Gus still wanted to catch in his teeth quiver in the hollow of her throat. "I'm crying because I miss Bebe already."

"Cheer up. She'll be home at eleven-thirty."

"That's not what I mean." She looked at the roses and traced a shiny green leaf with one fingertip. "She's getting married a week from Saturday and leaving forever. I'm sure that sounds silly to you. I'm not her mother and I'm crying because she's leaving home."

"It doesn't sound silly at all. I feel the same way about Aldo."

She blinked up at him from the roses. "You do?"

"I've been his guardian since he was four years old."

"Oh my." She blinked again. "You were very young."

"Too young, really, but I had my aunt Phoebe. I couldn't have raised Aldo without her. She died five years ago and I still miss her."

"I'm so sorry," Cydney murmured, her eyebrows drawing together. Gus thought her sympathy was genuine. Everything about Cydney Parrish was genuine. Genuinely nice, genuinely sincere. And genuinely sexy, God help him, in her clingy little sweater set and neat black slacks. She traced the rose leaf again, then looked at him. "I have some coffee left. Would you like a cup?"

"Love one," he said, and followed her inside.

He stopped just inside the kitchen and watched her unwrap the roses, put them in a vase and fill it with water. There was a dishwasher built in under the microwave, but one side of the double, white porcelain sink was full of suds, the plates from dinner drying in a rack. Family heirloom, he guessed. Aunt Phoebe had hand-washed her china, a Blue Willow pattern she'd inherited from her mother. Gus hadn't eaten a meal served on china with flowers and candles since Aunt Phoebe died.

Five years. That's how long it had been since he'd stood in a kitchen smelling leftover chicken and warm coffee. Five years since he'd felt so at home in any place other than Tall Pines. No wonder Aldo defected. Good eats and hot chicks. Definitely plural, no matter what Bebe said.

"Please." Cydney waved him toward a white, tile-topped

table with an oak Lazy Susan in the middle. "Would you like a piece of cake?"

"No thanks." Gus took off his jacket, hung it on the back of the chair at the end of the table and sat down. "Any cookies left?"

"Macaroons?" She glanced at him over her shoulder, a thick white mug in each hand. "I think so."

There were eight left in a ceramic teddy bear cookie jar. She put them on a plate and brought them to him with his coffee. Gus thanked her and ate one while she made herself a cup of tea. She brought it to the table with the roses, put the vase down next to the Lazy Susan and took the chair on his left.

"The roses are lovely. Thank you, Mr. Munroe."

"Gus," he said, sipping his coffee.

"I'm sorry I made such a fuss about Tall Pines."

"Your concerns are valid, but I'm sure you won't have any trouble finding everything you need for the wedding in Branson."

He wasn't sure of any such thing, but he smiled and bit into another cookie. He hoped the Parrish women would have a hell of a time finding candles and flowers and a decent caterer. All the better to foul things up, make everybody take a deep breath and a good long look at what they were doing.

What are you doing, Munroe? his inner voice asked. *Lusting after Cydney Parrish while you lie to her through your teeth? Nice. Very nice. I'm ashamed to be your conscience.*

"Yeah? Well, get over it," Gus mumbled around a mouthful of macaroon.

Cydney's spine stiffened. "Get over what?"

Gus held up his index finger, thinking fast while he chewed, and took a swallow of coffee. "Your reluctance to come to Tall Pines."

"I suppose I should explain that." She put her spoon down and looked him square in the eye. "I said some things I shouldn't have to Aldo, last night while Bebe was in X ray. I was angry and upset. I told him you were rude and arrogant and I hoped I'd never see you again."

"Rude and arrogant," Gus repeated, heartened by the glint

he saw in her eyes. This was more like it. This was the little spitfire who'd told him to shove Artie's will, not the put-upon little doormat who'd caved in to Georgette. "You don't think I was pompous and pushy?"

"Well," she said, smiling. "I suppose you were a *little* pushy."

"I was a lot pushy. If I'd been you, I would've thrown me out."

"You asked for a punch in the nose."

"I asked for a good, swift kick. You suggested the punch."

"I never dreamed Bebe would hit you."

"Neither did I."

"I'm glad you came back, Mr. Munroe." She went to the wall phone by the microwave, came back with a pad of paper and a ballpoint pen and sat down. "There are some things we need to talk about."

"Gus," he said. "Like what?"

"Will the great room really hold a hundred people?"

"I'd say so, easy."

"Do you know the dimensions?"

"Really long by really wide."

"Is it longer than it is wide?" She laid her hands on the table in the shape of a rectangle, then a square. "Or wider than it is long?"

"Longer than it is wide." It was an excuse to touch her, so Gus did, took her small wrists in his hands and drew hers farther apart. He felt her tremble, or thought he did, but she slipped her hands free too quickly to tell and bent her head over her notepad.

"Like this?" she asked, sketching a long, wide room.

"That's it. There's a dais at this end that runs the width of the windows. Three steps up to it," Gus said, pointing with his finger. "The fireplace is on this wall."

"Where's the door? Here?" She drew a doorway at the opposite end of the room, tucked a curl of silver-blond hair behind her ear and turned the pad toward him.

Gus reached for his glasses, realized he'd left them in the car and leaned close enough to notice the jade drop earring pierced through her lobe. Oh God. More beads and delectable, peach-kissed skin to nibble.

"Perfect," he said.

"We'll put the minister on the dais, and if they're wide enough to stand on, Bebe and Aldo on the steps. You said the floor is hardwood, so we'll need a runner for Bebe when she comes down the aisle." She wrote "runner" in the corner of the page, then drew one down the center of the room with little rows of X's on each side. "And chairs." She wrote that in the corner and looked up at Gus. "What direction do the windows face?"

"Southeast overlooking the lake."

"Draperies?"

"Nope."

"Morning sun." She jotted "3"—slash—"4 P.M." and a question mark in the top corner. "We'll want an afternoon ceremony."

"We will? Why?"

"Because the room will be flooded with sunlight in the morning."

"Maybe Aldo and Bebe want to get married in sunglasses."

She frowned at him. "Maybe they don't."

"Why don't you ask them?"

"Of course I'll ask them. I'm merely making notes for Bebe and a list of things we need."

"Looks to me like you're planning the wedding."

"Someone has to get started on the preparations."

"How 'bout the bride and groom?"

"They're not here at the moment."

"That's my point. Aldo and Bebe want to get married a week from Saturday, but you're the one sitting here making notes and sketches while they're out cruising in the Jag."

"Cruising is what kids do for fun these days, Mr. Munroe."

"*Kids,* Miss Parrish. Responsible young adults park their butts at the kitchen table and plan their own wedding."

"Oh, I see." She slapped her pen down, grabbed the cookie plate and marched it to the counter next to the refrigerator.

"We're back to Bebe and Aldo aren't mature enough to get married."

"They aren't mature enough." Gus followed her to the counter and spread his left hand on the butcher-block top beside her. "The fact that you're here and they're not proves it. And if you think they're out cruising, then you've forgotten what's it like to be young and in lust."

"Bebe and Aldo are *in love*," she said hotly, glaring at him as she upended the plate over the teddy bear.

"Aldo and Bebe are *in lust*." Gus snatched a macaroon before they all spilled into the jar. "They can't keep their hands off each other."

She clapped the head on the teddy bear and turned to face him. "That's part of being in love, Mr. Munroe."

"Part of being in love, yes. But lust all by itself is a poor foundation for marriage."

"I agree. But I'm not sure you know the difference."

"Between love and lust? Sure I do."

"I wouldn't take it to court if I were you."

"I don't have to take it to court. I can prove it right here."

"Can you?" She raised an eyebrow and her chin an *oh-really* notch. "I'd like to see that."

"Then keep your eyes open," he said, and kissed her.

Hard and swift, like he'd been aching to all night, expecting her to push him away and ready to release her the second she did, but her lips parted—stunning him and thrilling him—drawing him deep into the Earl Grey–flavored sweetness of her mouth. Gus groaned and lifted her, pressed himself between her legs and swung her onto the counter.

Her mouth softened, her knees hooked his waist and pulled him into the V of her thighs. He bent his head to her throat, caught her jade necklace in his teeth and nibbled, felt her quiver, sucked the beat leaping in the hollow of her throat. He felt the catch in her breath, the moan that shivered through her.

She pressed hot, tiny kisses to his forehead, slid her tongue into his ear and lit him up like a just-struck match. Gus pulled her off the counter, light and yielding in his cupped hands, her eyes half-shut and dazed. He turned toward the hallway he'd seen her disappear into last night and whispered raggedly in her ear, "Where's your bedroom?"

Her eyes flew open, her arms shot out and her fingers caught the door frame. "*What?*"

"Your bedroom, sweetheart. Where is it?"

"I'm not your sweetheart, Mr. Munroe, which proves you don't know the difference between love and lust. Now please put me down."

"I think I proved it perfectly." Gus eased her to the floor, scrambling for a way to save face, to soothe the hurt and reproach simmering in her almond eyes. "You and I are sexually mature adults. We can enjoy lust and not confuse it with love. When I was Aldo's age I fell in love with every girl who tripped my hormones. And that was every girl I laid eyes on in the course of a day."

"Oh. Well." She lowered her eyes and smoothed her sweater, her cheeks flushed, a pulse beat still jumping in her throat. "Then I guess you proved your point, Mr. Munroe."

"Gus," he said, and sighed with relief. Saved again by desperation.

The phone rang. Gus stepped out of the way and Cydney ducked past him to answer it. "Hello?" she said, tucking the receiver beneath her chin. "Dad. What are you doing up?" She glanced at the clock on the microwave. "It's almost three in the morning in Cannes." Then she winced and held the receiver at arm's length. "Don't yell at me! I can't hear you when you yell!"

Gus bristled at the bellow he could hear clear across the kitchen. He wanted to grab the receiver from Cydney and slam it in Fletcher Parrish's ear, but stepped into the living room to give her some privacy.

"That's the most selfish thing I've ever heard, Dad. This is Bebe's life and Bebe's choice." Gus backed up a step, drawn by Cydney's furious hiss as she tried to keep her voice down. "No one has betrayed you, least of all Bebe. She fell in love with a sweet, funny, wonderful boy."

He heard Cydney's voice break, decided to hell with privacy, and wheeled back into the kitchen. She looked up at him, an angry glitter in her eyes, and nodded at him to stay.

"I won't discuss this." She listened a moment, her jaw clenched. "First, I don't want to. Second, the no-talent pretty boy is standing in my kitchen." She broke the connection with two fingers, banged the receiver down on the counter next to the microwave and turned to face him. "My father called you that. I apologize for repeating it."

"I've been called worse by book critics." Gus crossed his arms and his ankles and leaned against the counter. Any closer and he doubted he could keep his hands off her. "At least your father said I was pretty."

She laughed, but it was shaky. So was she, the pulse in her throat still jumping. Lust and temper pumped a lot of adrenaline.

"You'd feel better if you hit something. But please," Gus covered his nose with his hand, "not me."

This time her laugh wasn't quite as shaky. "Do you know my father, Mr. Munroe?"

"Gus," he said, and shook his head. The go-away-kid-you-bother-me brush-off Parrish had given him at the mystery conference hardly counted. "I take it he's not too thrilled with Bebe marrying Aldo."

"He's furious because she's marrying the nephew of the no-talent pretty boy who knocked him out of first place on *The New York Times* List, and he just found out about it."

"That was years ago. Ancient history." Gus had a framed copy of the list hung in a place of honor in his office to prove it. "Who told him?"

"My *sis-ter*," she said, making two distinctly annoyed syllables of the word. "Apparently Gwen talked to Bebe today and asked about Aldo's family. When Bebe told her Aldo is your nephew, she just *had* to call Dad. She couldn't let *me* tell him." She blurted the last, did an uh-oh blink and shot Gus a guilty look he didn't understand. "What I mean is, I can usually break things to Dad without him blowing a gasket."

It didn't surprise Gus that Gwen Parrish had ratted on him. Like father, like daughter, he thought, recalling the *People* magazine article about Fletcher and Gwen Parrish, the one that hadn't mentioned Cydney. Hmmm. Sibling rivalry. How could he make use of it?

That's the last straw, Munroe, his inner voice said. *I quit.*

"No one will miss you," Gus replied. Out loud, but fortunately just as Cydney hung the receiver back on the base. He didn't think she heard him over the plastic clunk until she glanced at him over her shoulder. "I'm sorry. What did you say? Miss who?"

"Your father," he ad-libbed. "I said it sounds like no one will miss him at the wedding."

"Gwen will. She and Dad are like this." Cydney crossed her first two fingers and smiled ruefully. "So will my mother, in spite of her so-called engagement to Herb Baker. A very nice man, but I'll be surprised if you receive an invitation to their Christmas Eve wedding."

She moved back to the table and sat down. Gus joined her.

"Oh—invitations." She smacked her hand against her forehead, tore her sketch off the pad and passed it to him with the pen. "Can you give me a list of how many guests you'd like to invite? If you'll fax the addresses to my mother, I promise I'll mail the invitations."

Gus stared at the pad and pen, his throat suddenly tight. Arthur and Bethany Munroe, he wished he could write. With all his heart he wished it. Miss Phoebe Munroe. Mr. and Mrs. Arthur Munroe, Sr. College buddies he'd lost track of, friends from Joplin he'd let slip away when he'd retreated to Crooked Possum.

"Can't think of a soul." He pushed the pad back to Cydney. "I'm sure Aldo has friends from school he'd like to invite."

She looked at him for a moment, then said: "You *don't* like us."

"I don't like you? Where did that come from?"

"Right here, *Angus*." She shoved the blank pad at him, so hard it spun in a circle on its cardboard back. "My father has so many friends he needs four address books to keep track of them."

"Fletcher Parrish is the party animal of the literary world,"

Gus replied testily. "I'm the guy who needs to get out of Crooked Possum."

"I thought you said you don't know my father."

"I know *of* him. Publishing is a very small and incestuous world. I have it on good authority that anyone with a liquor license knows your father on a first-name basis."

"That's a persona my father chooses to project," she replied coolly. "He thinks it increases his sales. I'm sure you and your publisher believe your hermit-on-the-mountain act does the same thing."

"It's not an act." It was the truth, and Gus felt like a dweeb, a total social misfit admitting it. "I've lost track of everyone I knew in Joplin. My parents are dead. Aldo's parents are dead. Aunt Phoebe is dead. I simply don't have anyone to invite."

"All right, Angus." She took the pad back and laid the pen on top of it. "I don't believe you, but if that's the story you intend to stick to, then we'll simply seat some of Bebe's guests on Aldo's side of the aisle and fill up the empty chairs."

"Why would I make up such an unflattering story?"

"It's what you do for a living, make up stories. And I think you'd do anything to cause trouble."

"Then why did I offer Tall Pines for the ceremony?"

"I don't know," she said, narrowing her eyes at him. "I haven't figured that out yet. But I will—and I'll be watching you."

"Well, you just watch away, *Cydney*." Gus got to his feet, yanked his jacket off the chair and pulled it on. He'd said it himself—she was a perceptive little nut. "You'll see me doing everything I can to make you welcome in my home and Aldo's wedding day the happiest of his life."

She snorted ruefully through her pert little nose. "I'll believe that when I see it."

"Then keep your eyes open," he shot back, and she flushed all the way to the roots of her silver-blond hair. "I'll see you on Thursday."

chapter
eleven

If Tall Pines had failed to make it as a bed-and-breakfast Cydney knew why. No one could find the damn place. Even with a map.

She thought the one Angus Munroe faxed Georgette was bogus, saw sabotage in directions he'd written in the margins, notes like, "Turn left off Double Y onto gravel road at Gib Elbert Senior's mailbox—not Junior's—then left at big oak tree with split trunk at third curve." Until she reached the third curve on the gravel road and realized there were no signs and no street names. Only landmarks like the big oak tree with the split trunk and Gib Elbert Senior's—not Junior's—mailbox.

Half an hour later, when a gray barn with a red roof failed to materialize on the south side of another gravel road where the map said it should, Cydney wasn't sure if she'd turned left at an oak or an elm. She was lost, hopelessly, and she knew it. Just like last summer when she'd tried to find Crooked Possum. She nosed the Jeep as close to the edge of the wretched road as she dared—there was no shoulder—and sat with her hands clenched on the wheel.

"Does any of this look familiar to you, Aldo?"

Cydney glanced in the rearview mirror but didn't see his blond head—or Bebe's red one—in the backseat, just Herb Baker's white Cadillac easing to a stop behind the truck.

"*Aldo!*" she shouted, and up he popped with Bebe, her lips red and bee-stung beside him.

"Yeah, Uncle Cyd?"

His face was flushed, and Cydney wanted to slap him. She'd offered to let Aldo take the wheel in Branson, but he'd declined. All the better to stay in the backseat and play feel each other up with Bebe.

"I said," Cydney repeated testily, "does any of this look familiar?"

"Uh," he looked out the windshield and the side windows. "Nope."

I think this is how the Donner Party started, her little voice said.

"Oh shut up," Cydney snapped, and Aldo blinked at her. "But I didn't say anything."

"Well, *don't*." In her mirror she saw Herb stretch out of the Cadillac and popped her door open. "And stay *vertical*," she warned, as she slid out of the air-conditioned truck into the warm afternoon.

The cloud of gravel smoke settling over the Jeep made her sneeze. She waved it away and walked toward the back bumper to meet Herb. Grasshoppers sawed in waist-high weeds and frogs croaked somewhere past the autumn gold trees bending over a wire fence. Bullfrogs, huge and deep-throated, the size of the Cherokee's tires by the sound of them.

Beyond that everything was still and stifling. This land-scape of haze-shrouded hills and rocky fields was as alien to Cydney as Mars. It made every nerve in her body jump. She'd spent last evening answering the door to trick-or-treaters, then stayed up till 4 A.M. finishing two jobs for clients who simply couldn't wait until she got back to town. She was so tired she had to force herself to smile at Herb, who leaned against the Cadillac waiting for her.

A nice man, she'd said to Angus Munroe, and he was, flipping up the clip-on sunglasses attached to his round, wire-framed bifocals as she came up beside him. His curly, gray-threaded dark hair and clipped mustache glistened in the sun. He had to be as hot and miserable as Cydney, but his smile was kind and patient. Maybe Georgette knew what she was doing after all. Her father would've been in a towering, screaming rage by now.

"Well, kiddo," Herb said, an oh-well cheerfulness in his

voice. "At this point I think we need a Global Positioning Satellite."

"Oh Herb, I'm sorry." Cydney parked her sunglasses on the top of her head and sagged against the Cadillac's dusty chrome grill beside him. "I think I turned at Gib Elbert Junior's mailbox."

"Well, then." Herb held his map up next to hers. "Let's go back to Double Y and find Gib Elbert Senior's mailbox. What do you say?"

Let's forget this whole damn thing and go home, Cydney wanted to say. "Sounds like a plan," she said wearily, and plucked a blue highlighter out of her pocket to mark the route Herb traced with his finger.

This was not the triumphant entrance to Tall Pines she'd envisioned. Sometime between 4 A.M. when she'd finally gotten to bed and six when she'd wakened with a jolt, too tired and too wired to sleep, she'd dreamed they arrived hours early at Tall Pines, stunning Angus Munroe with her uncanny sense of direction. She'd seen herself blithely tossing the map in his face as she sailed past him with her suitcase.

She'd dreamed about other things, too. The feel of his arms around her, the taste of his mouth, the rasp in his voice when he'd whispered, "Where's your bedroom?" All of it to make a point and prove his argument. What an *idiot* she was to think he'd actually wanted her.

Cydney heard a car door open and glanced over her shoulder at her mother, smiling serenely behind her Ann Taylor sunglasses as she came around the Cadillac, every champagne-blond hair on her head in place, her skin smooth and taut. She and Bebe had spent all of yesterday at Georgette's favorite day spa while Cydney ran herself ragged getting ready for the trip to Crooked Possum.

"How goes it, trailblazers?" Georgette asked, then glanced at the back window of the Jeep. She frowned and inched her sunglasses down her nose. "Where are Bebe and Aldo?"

"Hey!" Cydney shot off the Caddy and smacked her doubled fist against the tinted glass. "I told you to keep it *vertical*!"

She punched the window again and Bebe and Aldo sprang upright and apart on the seat.

Cydney turned around. Georgette slid her glasses another inch down her nose. "What was that about?"

"I've listened to those two pant and moan and paw each other all the way from Kansas City and I'm sick of it."

"Oh." Georgette leaned against Herb's shoulder. "Are we in Arkansas? I could swear I saw a sign that said Arkansas."

Sign? Cydney wanted to shriek, I'd kill to see a sign! She pinched the bridge of her nose and shut her eyes. She wanted to go home, clicked her heels three times but nothing happened. White leather Keds just didn't have the same magic as ruby slippers.

"How 'bout I take the lead for a while, kiddo?" Herb asked.

"Oh please, Herb. Thanks." Cydney opened her eyes and saw her mother gazing at her over her sunglasses with her right eyebrow raised.

"All righty, then. Onward and backward," he said jovially, escorting Georgette around the Cadillac and opening her door.

Cydney walked to the truck, got in behind the wheel and fastened her seat belt. She caught Bebe's eye in the mirror as she looked up. Her niece sat with her arms jammed together and her bottom lip stuck out.

"Buckle up, both of you." Cydney swiveled the mirror to include Aldo in the order. "That should keep your hands to yourselves."

"*Really,* Uncle Cyd," Bebe huffed indignantly. "Aldo and I are *engaged* to be *married.*"

Cydney flung herself halfway over the bucket seat, so furious she didn't care that she almost strangled herself in the seat belt. Bebe's eyes widened and she shrank into the corner of the backseat.

"If you don't suck in that lip and buckle that belt, young lady, the only thing you and Aldo are going to be *engaged* in is hitchhiking to Crooked Possum. You got me?"

"Y-y-yes, Uncle Cyd." Bebe fumbled herself into her belt. Aldo fastened his in a flash.

Cydney put the Jeep in gear and made a bumpy U-turn over the gravel humped in the middle of the road, stepped on the brake and waited for Herb to wheel the boat-size Caddy around. She heard sniffles, cranked her mirror and saw Bebe wiping her tear-filled eyes.

"Oh, turn it *off*," Cydney snapped disgustedly. "You've behaved like a couple of randy fifteen-year-olds at the drive-in all day long."

"Aldo and I are *in love*!" Bebe wailed tragically.

"You and Aldo are *in heat*!" she shot back, and blinked at herself in the rearview mirror. In lust, in heat—same thing. Damn Angus Munroe. And the peach roses he'd brought her, too.

A horn beeped and Cydney started, blinking at the Cadillac's red taillights. Herb waved at her in his mirror. She waved back and followed him down the rutted gravel road.

It took them an hour to find Double Y, where, sure enough, she'd turned at Gib Elbert Junior's mailbox. Damn it to hell. Cydney made a left behind the Cadillac at Gib Elbert Senior's mailbox, rubbed the headache pounding above her eyes and glanced at her watch. Two-thirty. Georgette had faxed Angus Munroe to expect them by one.

Cydney switched on the wipers and the washers to clear gravel dust from the windshield and turned behind Herb onto a narrow and pitted but mercifully paved road. The glass swept clean and at last she saw a sign, nailed to a weather-beaten post: CROOKED POSSUM, POPULATION 162, with an arrow pointing left. Herb made the turn and so did Cydney, slowing down behind the Cadillac at the 25 MPH CITY LIMIT sign.

"Don't blink or you'll miss it," Aldo joked.

Bebe sniffed. Cydney cranked the mirror toward her and saw Aldo's hand creeping toward hers across the backseat.

"Touch her," Cydney warned, "and you'll draw back a stump."

Aldo snatched his hand away, and Cydney looked at the

road in time to see a second sign, THANKS FOR VISITING CROOKED POSSUM. Y'ALL COME BACK, slide by on the right. Well, hell. She'd missed it.

"You've been a crab all day, Aunt Cydney," Bebe whined tearfully. "What's wrong with you?"

"I'm exhausted," she said, steering the Jeep through a right-hand curve behind the Cadillac at a Y-split in the road.

"You should've come to the spa yesterday with me and Gramma."

"Oh really?" Cydney challenged her in the rearview mirror. "If I'd gone to the spa who would've designed your wedding invitations and taken them to Kinkos to be printed? Who would've spent last evening addressing and mailing them because you and Gramma didn't want to chip your freshly manicured nails?"

"I don't know." Bebe's mouth trembled and her eyes filled. "You make it sound like it's all my fault."

"It *is* your fault, Bebe. This is *your* wedding, not mine."

"But Gramma said I should ignore you. She said you're in a bad mood 'cause everybody's getting married but you."

"*Did* she?" Cydney glared at Georgette's profile in the Cadillac's front seat. "Well, she's wrong. I do *not* feel left out."

Oh, who are you trying to kid? her little voice asked.

Okay. So she felt left out. She'd been left out of things before, like the *People* magazine article. That was tough, to feel so insignificant, but feeling undesirable, knowing Angus Munroe had kissed her just to prove his point . . . hearing him say he thought he'd proved it perfectly while she stood there in front of him, reeling and weak-kneed from the crush of his mouth against hers . . . That hurt.

A lot, but it wasn't the end of the world. Crooked Possum was the end of the world, and Tall Pines was the X marked on the map. Cydney plucked her copy off the dashboard, caught a look at her watch and realized she'd been blindly following Herb for a good ten minutes. Not bright if she wanted to find her way out of here again.

The road they were on dipped through a shady hollow at the foot of a wooded, round-topped hill. A mountain in Missouri, a big grassy hump with lots of trees on it in Colorado. The Ozarks were sloped and sleepy, friendly, nonthreatening mountains, unlike the sheer, steep Rockies that always overwhelmed Cydney.

"Whoa, Miss Parrish," Aldo piped up. "We just passed Tall Pines."

"We did?" Cydney stepped on the brake and looked in the mirror. All she saw was a solid wall of trees on both sides of the road, but she blew the horn at Herb and saw the Caddy's brake lights flash. "Where?"

"I'll hop out and show you," Aldo said, and sprang his door open.

"High time you did something," Cydney muttered, watching him lope up the long, curved hill they'd just come down.

Bebe turned to watch him through the rear window with a nose-in-the-air sniff at Cydney that was supposed to make her feel bad. It didn't. Bebe could pout and Aldo could call her Miss Parrish till the cows came home, and she wouldn't cave. She'd had enough of the two of them behaving like children. Spoiled, self-indulgent children who went cruising while she made lists and went to the spa while she designed invitations. Kids, not responsible young adults, who couldn't keep their hands off each other in the backseat. Just like Angus Munroe said. The smug, arrogant jerk. And to think she'd defended them.

No more, Cydney vowed, as she put the Jeep in reverse and backed up the hill. Halfway through the curve she saw Aldo standing in the middle of a wide blacktop drive edged by tall pine trees. The way their shaggy boughs overhung the edge of the road, it was no wonder she and Herb had missed it.

Cydney turned into the drive and stopped to pick up Aldo and wait for Herb. She could see the first curve in the drive, the edges marked by split-rail fences and pine trees. She looped her arms over the top of the steering wheel, leaned forward and peered up the hill. Uh, make that mountain, she amended, when she realized she couldn't see the top.

When the Cadillac turned in behind the Jeep, Cydney led

the way up the drive. It was twice as wide as the road and perfectly paved. Well, that was something. If the wedding guests made it this far, which she seriously doubted. A troop of Eagle Scouts led by a Sherpa guide couldn't find this place.

Instead of R.S.V.P. she should've written B.Y.O.C. at the bottom of the invitations—Bring Your Own Compass. She'd make signs, Cydney decided, and stake them along the road from here to Double Y, pithy little directives like, "Leave a Trail—You'll Need It" and "Ignore the Buzzards Circling Overhead."

Bebe would get her wish, all right. No way would Gwen find her way out of Tall Pines. Cydney only hoped she could find her way *in*.

Angus Munroe's driveway was 3.5 miles long—Cydney clocked it on the odometer—and wound up the side of the mountain in grades that took the steep out of the climb, the trees and the split-rail fence marching alongside. At the top they fell away where the road leveled and made a circle around a grassy area with five shaggy pines in the center.

Cydney bore to the right and saw the house once the Jeep cleared the trees—a massive, split-timbered manse with a shingled roof, two stories and two wings that flared away from a deep, covered porch that ran the length of the house.

"Oh Aldo," Bebe gushed. "It's *beautiful*!"

Cydney glanced in the mirror and saw them gazing adoringly at each other, their fingers welded together in the middle of the backseat. She opened her mouth, then shut it. Let Munroe pry them apart.

She drove past the wide, timbered porch steps and parked the Jeep with its tailgate pointed toward the house. Bebe and Aldo bailed out before she switched off the engine. Without a word, just slammed the doors, clasped hands and raced toward the house.

"Well, you're welcome," Cydney said.

The Cadillac stopped beside the Jeep and Herb got out. So did her mother, without waiting for Herb, leaving her door hanging open a scant inch from Cydney's. She rapped on the glass, but Georgette had already moved past the window.

Cydney turned the ignition key, pressed the button to lower the glass and called, "Mother! The door!" But Georgette was out of earshot, striding briskly toward the house with Herb.

It was déjà vu, just like Tuesday evening when her mother and Munroe and Bebe and Aldo trooped into her house and left her in the garage. No one had missed her. Why hadn't she stayed there? She could be there still, forgotten in her own garage in Kansas City rather than stuck in her truck on the side of a mountain in the Ozarks. When would she learn to seize these opportunities?

"Well, hell." Cydney lowered her window all the way, released her seat belt and crawled up on her knees to reach through the window and push the door shut.

A simple plan, but gravity was against her. The ground sloped away from the porch on this side of the drive, the Cadillac's nose pointed downhill and the damn passenger door weighed four times as much as the Jeep. Or felt like it. Twice Cydney shoved the door. Twice it failed to catch and swung open again.

Once more, she thought, she'd try once more. If she didn't get it this time, she'd give up and crawl over the gearshift. Cydney drew a breath, stretched out the window and reached for the door. Just as her hand closed on the top corner, she heard footsteps and saw a flicker of movement from the corner of her left eye—a tall man with broad shoulders and a lock of dark hair falling over his forehead.

"Need a hand?" Angus Munroe asked her.

chapter
twelve

Didn't it just figure that he'd catch her doing something stupid? Cydney leaned her hands on the rolled-down window, turned her head and saw Munroe leaning against the Jeep. He wore a gray Missouri Tigers T-shirt, denim shorts and brown loafers with no socks. His arms and ankles were crossed, his long tanned legs dusted with dark hair.

Cydney hung halfway out the window, her jeans heat-stuck to her fanny, the crisp white shirt she'd started the day in, a wilted mess. He looked cool and at ease and perfectly at home—which of course he was. She was hot, exhausted and out of her element. Out of breath, too. As much from the sight of his bare muscled arms and bare muscled legs as her fight with the door—which of course she'd lost.

"If you could just close the damn car door," she said to him.

"Whoa—profanity." Munroe grinned, straightened off the Jeep and effortlessly flipped the door shut with one hand. "Rough day?"

"Long and hot." She pulled her head in, rolled up the window and took her keys out of the ignition, clambered out of the Jeep and shut the door. "I got us lost. Twice, I think."

"You should've let Aldo drive."

"Aldo declined in favor of playing grope Bebe in the back-seat. You were right. Maybe they're in love—I don't know and right now I don't care—but my niece and your nephew are definitely, positively, without a doubt in major, roaring, unbridled lust."

So was Cydney, just looking at Angus Munroe. Good thing she was a sexually mature adult who could handle the sight of a gorgeous half-dressed man with grace and aplomb. *Who the heck are Grace and Aplomb?* her little voice asked, but Cydney ignored it.

She hadn't meant to blurt all that about Bebe and Aldo. She'd meant to stay mad at Munroe, stay away from him as much as she could and still keep an eye on him. Then he'd grinned at her and her pulse jumped and she'd realized she didn't want to be angry anymore. She wanted to hear him call her sweetheart again, even if he didn't mean it.

"Well." He leaned back against the Jeep and gave her a wry smile. His nose wasn't quite as swollen and the bruises around his eyes were beginning to fade. "That must've been hard to say."

"Actually, it wasn't," Cydney admitted. She'd just opened her mouth and it fell out. Kind of like her brain when she'd turned her head and saw him in those shorts.

"Oh, Cydney!" Georgette called from the top of the porch steps. "Bring my purse in when you bring the bags, would you?"

"*What?*" Cydney wheeled toward the porch, flinging up her right hand barely in time to catch the gold key ring her mother tossed her.

"The luggage. It's in the trunk." Georgette pointed at the Cadillac's boxcar-size back end. "Bebe and Aldo are exhausted and Herb has a bad back."

She waggled her fingers and went inside. Munroe scowled and pushed off the Jeep.

"Give me the keys. You are not hauling luggage." He held his hand out and she gave him her keys and Herb's. "Take her purse if you want, but I wouldn't. And tell Aldo to get his exhausted butt out here."

He moved behind the Caddy and opened the trunk. Cydney retrieved her mother's purse, climbed the steps and crossed the porch to the front doors. A big, handsome door with stained-glass panels. She opened one and stepped inside onto a raised foyer with a pegged-pine floor. There was an enclosed staircase on her left and a huge, open living room spread out before her, a glass wall at the far end with a triple set of solarium doors framed in the center.

Another staircase, a big, wide one on the wall she faced climbed to a gallery with an archway cut in the middle and the shadow of a hallway beyond. Bookcases covered the long wall beneath the gallery with two sets of pocket doors built into them. She'd drawn the doors on the left side of the stairs Tuesday night and knew they led to the great room. They stood partway open and Cydney could hear the echo of voices, her mother's and Bebe's.

"Hey, kiddo." Herb saluted her with a can of Budweiser from an oxblood leather bar stool. Aldo sat beside him, also with a Bud in hand, at a mahogany bar on the wall to Cydney's right. "This used to be the reception desk. Pretty neat, huh?"

"Very neat." Cydney came down the three steps from the foyer. "Aldo, your uncle wants you to help him with the luggage."

"Sure thing," he said, and hopped off his bar stool.

"I'll give you a hand," Herb said, and put down his beer.

"No, Herb. I'll help," Cydney said. "You rest your back."

"Nice of you, kiddo, but I'm sure your back's as tired as mine." He patted her arm as he went past her with Aldo. "I got Georgie's eight suitcases into the car. I'm sure I can get them out."

With a bad back? Eight suitcases? What had her mother packed? Why had she lied about Herb? And why did she let him call her Georgie?

"Darling, there you are. Come and *see* this room!" Cydney turned her head and saw her mother sailing toward her. "It's fabulous!"

So was the room Cydney stood in, big as a barn with a view of autumn-flamed woods through the glass wall and a stone fireplace with a hearth so huge the fire screen looked like a backstop. The pine floor gleamed where it wasn't covered with rugs and blue leather furniture.

"Don't stand there with your mouth open, Cydney." Georgette took her arm and turned her around. "Come and look."

"Here's your purse, Mother." She swung Georgette's Hermes bag off her shoulder and held it out to her.

"What? Oh—thank you." Georgette tossed the four thousand dollar leather bag on a chair. "You *must* see this room."

"In a minute. I have to bring in the luggage."

"Don't be idiotic." Georgette grabbed her hand and towed her across the living room. "Let the men get the bags."

"But you told *me* to get the bags, Mother. You also told me Herb has a bad back, but Herb says—"

"Oh, enough about the luggage. Look at *this*!"

Georgette reached the pocket doors, pushed them all the way open and flung Cydney ahead of her like she was a stone in a slingshot. She stumbled, straightened and stared around the great room.

"My God, Mother! It's *filthy*!"

"Of course it's filthy." Georgette swept past her into the room. The dust on the floor was so thick Cydney could see the tracks her mother and Bebe had already made. "A man lives here."

A rotten, devious man named Angus Munroe. As spotless and showplace perfect as the living room was, Cydney was sure he'd left the great room knee-deep in grime to dishearten and discourage them.

"Look past the dirt," Georgette said, proving that he'd have to try a lot harder to defeat her. "Look at the dimensions, the view—"

"What view?" Cydney batted a dust mote trailing all the way from the beamed ceiling out of her face. "The window's so dirty I can't see it!"

"Here it is, Uncle Cyd!" Bebe popped up on the dais steps, in front of a glass wall like the one in the living room, the solarium doors behind her zebra-striped with dirt.

"Think of the possibilities." Georgette moved ahead, sweeping her arms up and out. "An autumn garland on the mantel—" Cydney looked at the fireplace and its soot-blackened face. "Flowers in urns. Terra-cotta, I think. Baskets hung from the ceiling—"

"Not without a crane." Cydney frowned up at the cobweb-draped beams. "And a toxic-waste cleanup crew from the EPA."

"Must you be so negative?" Georgette spun around, her hands on her hips. "A little soap and water and elbow grease—"

"Oh no, Mother. No, no, *no*." Cydney backed away, shaking her head and her hands. "I am *not* cleaning this room."

"Of course you're not. Where do you get these ideas?"

"Tote that barge and bring in my purse," Cydney retorted. "Carry in the luggage and lift that bale."

"Bebe." Georgette turned her head halfway toward the dais. "Go on with your visualization. Close your eyes and *feel* the room the way you want it to look for your wedding. Can you do that, dear?"

"I'll try, Gramma." Bebe plunked down on the dais steps and screwed her eyes shut, so tightly that her entire face puckered.

"You come with me." Georgette crooked her finger and stalked to the far end of the room. Cydney sighed and followed. Her mother shut the pocket doors and took her by the arms. "Bebe nearly burst into tears when she saw this mess."

"So did I. How come you're so cheerful?"

"Paxil. And I'm not fooled by Angus Munroe and his mischief. Handsome as sin, but a real prick about this wedding."

"*Mother!*" Cydney gasped, torn between shock and laughter.

"For heaven's sake, Cydney, I've heard the word, and I was married to one for eighteen years. Divinely handsome, your father, but a real—"

"Right, Mother, I've got it," Cydney cut her off. "What are we going to do? And don't tell me sit on the steps and visualize."

"That was to distract Bebe. What we're going to do is hire professional cleaners. What we're *not* going to do is say one word about this to Angus Munroe. We're going to be gracious and serene and fawn all over him with gratitude."

Cydney looked up at the ceiling beams. "I vote for a rope."

"Lucky for us Bebe is marrying Aldo and not his uncle. It's bad enough he'll be an in-law. Impossible man." Georgette sighed, rubbed her temples and looked at Cydney. "Thank

God he isn't interested in you. Imagine the life you'd have with a man like that."

Cydney blinked, startled and suddenly awash in her most X-rated fantasies of Angus Munroe, real hot stuff dreams that went way beyond peach roses at her first book signing. Smoldering glances over candlelit dinners, trips to Hawaii to make love on moon-washed sands, a honeymoon in Paris on red silk sheets drenched with sex and champagne. Oh yes. Cydney could imagine it. So vividly all she could do was stare at her mother.

"It leaves me speechless, too." Georgette laid her hands on Cydney's shoulders. "Now. I'm going to finish this silly visualization thing I started with Bebe. You distract Munroe. He upsets her terribly."

"She doesn't look upset." Cydney leaned around her mother and peered at Bebe, sitting with her eyes shut, her elbows on her knees, her cheeks on her fists and her mouth slack. "She looks like she's asleep."

"She's traumatized. You know how insecure she is. She's positive Munroe hates her." Georgette took Cydney's elbow and propelled her toward the doors. "You keep him busy until I get her calmed down."

"Keep him busy doing what?"

"Make him show you the house. Ooh and ahh a lot. I don't know. Just go charm his socks off."

"Since he isn't wearing any, that shouldn't take long."

"Oh, for God's sake, Cydney, then tell him jokes. Seduce him. I don't care. Just keep him away from Bebe."

Georgette opened the pocket doors and pushed Cydney through them. She spun around, her mouth open to have the last word—at least once in her life—but the doors whacked shut in her face.

Cydney stared at them, closed her mouth and pressed her fingertips to the headache thudding above her eyes. She should've stayed in the garage. Why hadn't she stayed in the garage?

She heard muffled voices, creaky footsteps, and moved out from under the gallery. The fifteen bedrooms Munroe said

Tall Pines had must be up there, through the archway and down the hall. By the thumps and scrapes she heard, so were Munroe with Aldo and Herb and the luggage. Let her mother charm and distract him, Cydney decided. All she did was irritate and annoy him.

Cydney wandered toward the bar, saw a hallway beyond the second set of pocket doors and followed it into a dining room with wainscoted walls and tiny blue roses in stripes on creamy wallpaper. Another enclosed staircase rose up the back wall. The oval Chippendale table and cherry buffet reminded Cydney of her grandmother's furniture. The biggest breakfront she'd ever seen covered another wall, a lovely set of Blue Willow china behind its glass doors. Aunt Phoebe's, she thought, all of it.

The room proved how much Munroe missed her. It was a shrine—and it was immaculate. It smelled of potpourri and furniture polish. The finger Cydney wiped across the table came up clean. She felt tears in her eyes but blinked them away. She was tired, that's all, and madder than hell at Munroe for the cheap trick he'd pulled with the great room. She refused to be touched by how sweet and sentimental this room was.

She left it in a hurry, following another hall with a big, white-fixtured bathroom on one side and an even bigger butler's pantry with a double sink and built-in drawers and shelves behind glass doors on the other. The kitchen beyond had a bay window at the far end with a pine table and bench built into the curve of the window. There were more cabinets than Cydney had ever seen and a wood block center island with slatted wooden stools that cut the room in half lengthwise. The gas stove had twelve burners and four ovens, two on top, two on the bottom. There were two refrigerators—or maybe one was a freezer. Holdovers from Tall Pines' incarnation as a bed-and-breakfast, she guessed. The floor was brick red ceramic tile, the countertops gray-flecked granite.

"My mother will have an orgasm when she sees this," Cydney murmured, opening cabinets until she found a glass.

She took it to the sink, the size of a washtub and split into thirds, and ran herself a glass of cold water. While she drank it—wishing she had two Tylenol to go with it—she opened one of the stained-glass panels latched shut on the pass-through above the sink and saw the bar and the living room on the other side.

This will be perfect for serving hors d'oeuvres to the guests, Cydney thought, closing her eyes and taking a stab at visualizing the wedding. She could see her mother sliding trays of elegant munchies through the cutout, Herb arranging them on the bar, Munroe filching a couple with a drink in his hand. She could see Bebe in her wedding dress and Aldo in a tux, dancing and feeling each other up under the cover of Bebe's veil. She could even see Gwen, wearing a mother-of-the-bride corsage and enthralling the guests with her vivid presence, but she couldn't see herself anywhere—not even in the butler's pantry washing glasses like Cinderella in the scullery.

She couldn't see it, Cydney realized—any more than her mother could see Munroe being interested in her—because she didn't belong here. Forget Bebe's claim that she couldn't get married without her, the minute Gwen showed up Uncle Cyd would cease to exist. It had happened before; it happened every time Gwen put in an appearance. It would happen again, Cydney was sure, the second Gwen set foot in Tall Pines.

She'd be less than a guest at the wedding, she'd be a fifth wheel. The bride's old-maid aunt. If she had any guts, she'd save herself the hurt and humiliation of fading into the wood-work. She'd get her keys from Munroe, lug her suitcase out to the Jeep and take herself back to Kansas City. Before Bebe enshrined a dining room in her honor.

Cydney exhaled slowly, drew a deep breath and smelled Clorox, Pine-Sol and Soft Scrub. She opened her eyes and glared at her reflection in the stainless-steel sink. How did Munroe think he'd get away with this? The rest of the house so clean it squeaked but the great room a shambles? Did he think they wouldn't notice? Or did he think they wouldn't dare call him on it?

"Wrong on that one, pal." Cydney banged her rinsed glass down on the drain board, suddenly so angry she couldn't see straight.

She pushed through a louvered swinging door, moving quickly past the bar and aiming at the stairs until she saw the solarium doors standing open. She stopped and listened but the house was still. No bumps or thumps from upstairs, no muffled voices. Must be finished with the luggage, she thought, and made a beeline for the open doors.

'Scuse me, her little voice said. *I'd like to remind you that the last time you went off like this you wrote that letter to* People *magazine. Look where that got you.*

Good point, but you just couldn't ignore this strong a compulsion to kill somebody. Cydney stalked up three wide steps onto the dais in front of the solarium doors and stepped outside onto a deck. Empty except for a handful of Adirondack chairs and a breath-snatching view of the lake, a vast, curled finger of water rimmed in red and gold forests that filled the horizon.

It was spectacular. Tall Pines was spectacular.

Cydney had dreamed about coming here. She thought she'd been invited to a literary soiree or something. She couldn't remember why or what Tall Pines looked like in her dream. Not that it mattered. All that mattered was getting her keys back and her suitcase and going home.

She went to the rail and looked over. Nobody down there, either, just a flagstone terrace, a swimming pool drained and covered for the winter and a hot tub built inside a gazebo with steamed-up glass walls. Cydney could see herself in the tub, could almost feel the jets beating the sleep-deprived ache out of her muscles. When her brain tried to paint Munroe into the tub with her, she frowned and turned toward the doors.

Munroe stood there, leaning on the frame, looking her over, his gaze drifting from her head to her Keds and back again.

"Feel free to use the hot tub," he said. "You look like you need it."

"Gee, thanks for noticing," she shot back, her feelings stung.

"You look beat. That's all I meant." He straightened off the door frame and scowled at her. "I'm trying to make you feel welcome."

"Yes, you said that. You said you'd do everything you could

to make us feel welcome. Well, Mr. Munroe. I knew the second I saw the great room just exactly how welcome we are here."

"Gus. Good." Munroe smiled. "I hired a janitorial service from Springfield to clean the place up yesterday."

"Did you pay them extra to dump the dirt from the rest of the house in the great room?"

Munroe blinked at her and said, "Huh?"

"Bebe almost burst into tears when she saw it, but I'm sure that's what you intended. Happy now?"

"Confused," Munroe snapped. "What are you talking about?"

Cydney gave a rueful snort. "Like you don't know."

"I'll tell you what I know. You didn't want to come here in the first place." He leaned a hand on the door frame, an irritated, what-the-hell edge in his voice. "Second, you don't like me, and third, you're pissed about something but I'll be damned if I have any idea what."

If Angus Munroe wasn't one heck of an actor, then he really and truly had no idea what she was talking about. Uh-oh, Cydney thought, her stomach sinking. She'd done it again—leaped before she looked and jumped to the wrong conclusion. *I tried to warn you,* her little voice said.

"Did you inspect the house before the crew left?" She asked hopefully. If he said yes that would get her off the hook—sort of—but he said, "No," and scowled. "I just wrote the check. Why?"

"I think you should go look at the great room."

"I think we should *both* go look at the great room," Munroe said, and grabbed her hand.

Cydney let him tow her into the house, down the steps and across the living room. No point trying to duck this. She deserved it for shooting off her mouth. She'd take her lumps, retrieve her keys and her suitcase and slink back to Kansas City where she belonged.

The pocket doors her mother had slapped shut in her face stood ajar. When Munroe banged them all the way open with a crack like a pistol shot, Georgette and Herb turned away from the fireplace, a metal carpenter's tape stretched between them. Bebe was sitting on the dais, watching Aldo with a broom in his hands draw a giant heart pierced by an arrow in the dust on the floor, the initials *B.P. + A.M.* in the middle.

"My God," Munroe said, letting go of Cydney's hand. "It's *filthy*!"

"Oh Angus, it's just a little dust, a little dirt," Georgette replied in a swift singsong. "A little soap, a little water—"

"Don't you so much as touch a dust rag, Georgette. I paid a small fortune to have this place cleaned from top to bottom."

Munroe strode into the room and turned a circle looking up at the ceiling. He shook his head and glanced at Cydney with a rueful smile.

"You're right," he said. "I should've checked their work."

Wait a minute. She wasn't right. She was wrong. She'd accused him of creating this mess. Any second now he'd realize what she'd said and how she'd meant it. Then the dust balls would hit the fan.

Munroe walked up to Aldo and pursed his lips at the heart drawn in the dust. "Did you learn this in architectural drawing class?"

"Heck no, Uncle Gus." Aldo grinned. "It's just sort of impromptu."

"Take a picture of it. Then get a dustpan and sweep the floor so we don't track dirt all over the house." Munroe clapped a hand on his nephew's shoulder, then turned toward Herb. "Show Georgette and Cydney to their rooms, would you, Herb? I've got a phone call to make."

He glanced Cydney a nod—just a nod, no scowl—and strode out of the room. She was stunned, amazed that Munroe hadn't accused her of accusing him. She didn't realize until she heard a door close somewhere beyond the great room that he'd taken her car keys with him.

Her car keys and her chance to escape.

chapter
thirteen

For the second time in two days, Cydney considered drowning herself in the shower. Grace and Aplomb, whoever the heck they were, had totally abandoned her. If things didn't change—and *fast*—by the time she left Tall Pines she'd hold the world record for the number of times a so-called intelligent woman could put her foot in her mouth. And that was figuring she could get her keys back from Munroe and be out of here before dinner.

She felt funny using the shower, like she was imposing, since she knew she was leaving, but the hot spray beating on her shoulders felt *s-o-o-o* good. She'd need it for the long drive home, providing she could find her way out of here. Before she left, she'd suggest the signs she'd thought of and draft Aldo for the job. Munroe hadn't paid the cleaning crew to trash the great room, but that didn't mean he wouldn't put the signs up wrong and send the wedding guests to Arkansas.

It didn't mean he wouldn't try something else, either. The strong anti-wedding stand he'd taken with her in his hospital room Tuesday morning, followed by the one-eighty he'd made at dinner and his offer of Tall Pines for the ceremony just didn't add up. Cydney still didn't trust his motives, but it wasn't her wedding and it wasn't her problem. Her mother was wise to Munroe. Let her keep an eye on him. Cydney was going home to Kansas City where she belonged.

She'd come back on Saturday for the ceremony, slip in around noon and make herself useful washing glasses in the scullery. She could handle a few hours of being eclipsed by Gwen, but a week of knocking herself silly for Bebe, then

watching her niece forget she existed the second her mother
came through the door—not only no, but *hell* no.

Cydney shut off the water, opened the glass door and
reached for a towel. The Plexiglas shower surround was the
only modern convenience in an otherwise charmingly quaint
bathroom. A pedestal sink with a wood-framed mirror, a
washstand and open shelves and thick, loopy white rugs on the
tile floor. She dried off, wrapped up in the towel and padded
into the adjacent bedroom where her suitcase lay open on a
blanket box at the foot of the Victorian four-poster bed.

Because Georgette was an antiques freak, Cydney knew it
was old enough not to be a cedar chest. It was a lovely thing,
made of mahogany with a carved front and just enough dings
and dents to give it character.

All the furniture was antique, an oddly pleasing mix of
styles. A Duncan Phyfe desk, a Shaker dresser and a Chippendale chest, a Bombay chest that served as a nightstand. A
lovely wing chair with an ottoman sat in one corner with a
brass art nouveau floor lamp.

Munroe's Aunt Phoebe haunted Tall Pines as surely as if
she were a ghost. Cydney just couldn't see Munroe hanging
embroidered curtains, folding an afghan crocheted in ecru
yarn at the foot of the wedding ring quilt or tatting the lace
throw cushions.

What to wear, she wondered, staring into her suitcase. She
didn't want to look like she'd been planning to leave since
she'd come through the door. The cover story she'd con-
cocted was squirrels in the attic. Surely Munroe would buy
that, since he looked at her half the time like she had a bird's
nest for brains. She planned to say the neighbor she'd asked
to keep an eye on her house called on her cell phone to report
the squirrels. She'd lie and say she'd be back in a day or two.
When she got home she'd make up some other crisis to keep
her there.

She took a pair of navy crop pants and a blue shirt with
sleeves she could roll up out of her suitcase and put them on
with a pair of sandals. A little makeup—powder foundation,

blush, mascara and lip gloss. Picked out her damp curls and glanced at her watch. Ten past five. Her mother had set dinner for five-thirty so they could get to bed early. She had plenty of time to tell her squirrel story, come back for her suitcase, lug it out to the Jeep and be on the road before it was totally dark.

The room assigned to her was tucked into an alcove around a corner from the rest of the bedrooms. The stairs that led to the dining room were just outside the door. Cydney started toward them, heard a door open in the main hallway, then a thump and a loud "Shhh!" and poked her head around the corner, just as Angus Munroe stepped into the pine-paneled hall from the gallery at the other end. Bebe, with a black nylon tote bag over her shoulder, and Aldo, lugging a black duffel, froze in the middle of the long, carpeted corridor.

"What are you doing, Aldo?" Munroe asked.

He and Bebe blinked at each other, then Aldo put down the duffel and faced his uncle. "Moving my stuff into Bebe's room."

"Oh." Munroe nodded. "Why?"

"We aren't sneaking around. We're engaged to be married."

"Yes, I know. But until you *are* married, you don't sleep together in my house."

"My Uncle Cyd doesn't mind if we do it in her house," Bebe said.

"I most certainly *do* mind." Cydney stepped around the corner, stung that Bebe would say such a thing. "And I *never* gave you and Aldo permission to *do it* in my house."

"But you didn't say anything on Monday," Bebe argued.

"What could I say? I came home early and caught you in bed. You were there because you thought I wouldn't be. Your mother told you to celebrate your love. *I* told you to get dressed."

"Hey, Beebs," Aldo said sharply. "That's not what you told me."

"But—but," Bebe blubbered, her big brown eyes filling with tears. "I *love* you, Aldo! I just want to be with you!"

"You'll be with him for the rest of your life a week from Saturday," Cydney said. "In the meantime, this is Mr. Munroe's house, and you'll respect his rules and his wishes."

Bebe dropped the tote bag and whipped toward Cydney. "You're not my mother!"

She flung the words at her like a slap, then rushed past her into her room, half the length of the hall away from Aldo's, and slammed the door. Aldo muttered, " 'Scuse me," and went after her. When the door shut, Cydney looked at Angus Munroe. He scowled. Her face burned.

"I'm sorry," she said, just as he said, "I'm sorry." Not quite in sync, but close enough to make them both smile a little.

" 'We're engaged to be married,' " Cydney said, "was Bebe's justification for necking in the backseat."

"Aldo said they weren't sneaking," Munroe replied. "But it sure looked that way to me."

"Oh yes. They were definitely sneaking."

"I put them in separate rooms. I didn't think I had to spell it out."

"I can't believe Bebe said I didn't mind."

"It didn't sound to me like something you'd say."

Ahem, said Cydney's little voice. *The squirrels?*

"Oh right." She snapped her fingers. "The squirrels."

"Do you mean Chip and Dale or Aldo and Bebe?"

"I think Chip and Dale are chipmunks," Cydney said with a laugh. "I had a call from home, on my cell phone. My neighbor—"

She heard the door open behind her and turned around. Bebe and Aldo stepped into the hall. He picked up his luggage and put it back in his room, shut the door and walked back to Bebe.

"I apologize, Mr. Munroe," she mumbled to the carpet. "Aldo sleeping in my room was all my idea."

"I doubt it," Munroe replied dryly, and Aldo flushed. "But I accept your apology, Bebe."

"Thank you." She nodded and started toward the stairs with Aldo.

"Just a minute," Munroe said, and they turned back. "I think you owe your aunt an apology, too."

Bebe fixed a flat-eyed stare on Munroe. "Do I have to do everything you say while I'm in your house?"

"No, but it seems to me—"

"Then I'm not going to apologize," Bebe cut him off. "I'm an almost married *woman* and I'm tired of being treated like a *child*."

"Then stop behaving like one," Cydney shot back.

"You're *still* not my mother," Bebe hissed at her, then swept away with Aldo down the back stairs to the dining room.

"Sorry again," Munroe said quietly. "I meant well."

"It's not your fault. It's mine. Mine and my mother's." Cydney felt tears in her eyes, blinked them away and turned around.

Munroe leaned on one shoulder against the paneled wall. He'd changed into steel blue khakis and a windowpane checked shirt about the same color that made his gray eyes look navy, socks and a pair of black loafers with tassels. Darn it. She was hoping for one last glimpse of tanned, muscled skin dusted with dark hair.

"I think we went overboard," she said with a sigh, "trying to compensate for Gwen just dumping Bebe and going on with her life."

"When was that?" Munroe asked, his eyebrows drawing together.

"Bebe was three and a half," Cydney said, glancing away from him.

She shouldn't have blurted that about Gwen. She thought fast for something to soften what she'd said, something that didn't make her sister sound selfish and heartless.

"It really was the best thing for Bebe, but it's been hard on her. Hard on Gwen, too, believe it or not."

"I don't believe it," Munroe said, and Cydney swung him a sharp glance. He smiled. "I'll tell you what I do believe. I believe you're the nicest person I've ever met, Cydney Parrish."

"Gee, thanks. I've waited all my life to hear that from a man."

He laughed. Cydney didn't think he knew how, but the grin that came with the laugh flashed his white teeth and lit up his face, made his eyes shine and creased a dimple in his left cheek. It made her breath catch, too, and her stomach jump.

"Hal-loo-*ooo*!" Georgette yodeled up the stairs. "Din-*ner*!"

Then she rang the bell. *Cling-cling, cling-cling.* Cydney listened closely. It was definitely cling-cling, not ting-a-ling, ting-a-ling.

"That's not my bell," she said.

"It's Aunt Phoebe's." Munroe stepped forward and took her elbow. "She has a whole collection in the breakfront in the dining room."

"Oh God save us. My mother loves bells."

"So did Aunt Phoebe." Munroe steered her toward the back stairs. "She rang one to announce every meal. I hate the damn things."

"My mother gave me one made out of crystal, about this big." Cydney held two fingers a few inches apart. "No matter where I hide it she always finds it."

Munroe laughed again, a rich baritone rumble that spread a warm flush through Cydney. She'd made him laugh twice. It wasn't even close to any of her fantasies, but it was *real*. He was real. A living, breathing, warm male. She felt his hand on her elbow, smelled a whiff of his aftershave. He didn't want to drag her to bed and ravish her—damn it—but he thought she was the nicest person he'd ever met.

What about the squirrels? her little voice asked.

"Oh forget about the squirrels," Cydney said under her breath.

Chip and Dale—er, Bebe and Aldo—sat on one side of the dining room table. Aldo glanced up when Cydney came down the stairs with his uncle, then ducked his head over his plate. Bebe sat next to him, her nose in the air, her head turned pointedly away.

Herb sat at one end of the table, which left the chair between Georgette and Munroe at the other end for Cydney. He held it for her and she sat down, her mouth falling open at the food-heaped table. A platter of fried chicken, a bowl of potato salad the size of a vat, another of coleslaw, one of green beans cooked with bacon and onions, a plate of deviled eggs and sliced tomatoes and a basket full of steaming biscuits.

"Where did you get all this food, Mother?"

"I threw it together last night and packed it in the cooler," she replied. "The ingredients for the biscuits I found in the pantry."

"My pantry?" Munroe looked startled, sat down and spread his napkin. "You're kidding."

He said grace and Georgette started the food around. Bebe ate with her head turned away from the table, making a point of how upset she was. And waiting, Cydney guessed, for her grandmother to ask what was wrong so she could burst into tears and ruin everyone's dinner, but Georgette didn't ask.

The white sheers under the tied-back blue drapes on the window softened the sun setting behind tall red and gold trees and what looked like a bank of silver-edged storm clouds. Cydney thought she heard thunder, but maybe it was just Aldo's stomach. His fork was almost a blur moving between his plate and his mouth.

A pair of cranberry oil lamps flickered on the buffet. Electric wall sconces with tulip-shaped bulbs glowed on the walls. The white eyelet place mats Cydney recognized as her mother's, which accounted for two inches of space in one of the eight suitcases she'd brought with her.

For dessert, she served warmed-in-the-microwave apple pie with slices of sharp cheddar, something else "she'd whipped up and tossed in the cooler." Munroe ate two pieces, Aldo three. Cydney made herself a cup of tea, coffee for everyone else, carried it to the table and poured it.

"Thank you, darling." Georgette smiled at her, then at Munroe. "The cleaning crew can't make it until Tuesday, is that right, Angus?"

"That's what they said on the phone. I told them this was a rush job. The best they could do was promise to be finished by one."

"There isn't much we can do until Tuesday afternoon, then. Herb and I will finish the measurements this evening. Bebe decided on the decorations while she was visualizing. That gives us tomorrow, Saturday, Sunday and Monday to buy them, arrange for the chair rental, order the cake and the food and the flowers. Plenty of time."

"I wouldn't say plenty," Cydney said, sliding back into her chair.

"You would if you weren't so anal retentive. I have a detailed list of everything we need and a yen to see Eureka Springs."

"I am *not* anal retentive. And Eureka Springs is in Arkansas."

"I know where it is. I'm the one who saw the sign that said Arkansas, remember? Eureka Springs has some wonderful antique shops."

"We didn't come here to go antique hunting. We came to put on a wedding for a hundred guests and we have a little over a week to do it."

"Eureka Springs isn't that far," Munroe put in. "Only an hour and a half or so from here."

Cydney glanced him a butt-out look. He gave her a just-trying-to-help smile. When she turned back to her mother, Georgette was holding her hand out to Herb.

"How about it, handsome? Care to take me touring?"

Herb caught her fingers and squeezed. "Love to, Georgie-girl."

"*Mother,*" Cydney said sharply. "This is no time to go touring."

"It's the perfect time." Georgette turned and frowned at her. "If you intend to go postal over this wedding, Cydney, kindly wait until Monday and let me enjoy my weekend."

"I am *not* going postal!" she declared.

Her mother arched an eyebrow. "You'd be more convincing if you put down the knife."

Cydney blinked at the cheese knife clenched in her fingers. She flushed and hastily laid it aside.

"I simply think, Mother, that it would be prudent to shop

and make all the arrangements before you flit off to Eureka Springs."

"Do you? Then here's the list." Georgette pulled a folded sheet of paper out of her skirt pocket and slapped it into Cydney's hand. "Have yourself a happy little obsessive-compulsive weekend doing the shopping while I go to Eureka Springs."

"Since Gramma George and Herb are taking off," Aldo said quickly, before Cydney could reach for the cheese knife, "could I use your pickup tomorrow, Uncle Gus?"

"What for?" Munroe asked, lifting his coffee cup from its saucer.

"I'd like to take Bebe to Silver Dollar City. She's never been."

He pursed his lips, thought about it and nodded. "Okay."

"Thanks." Aldo wiped his mouth and stood up. "We're gonna see a show in Branson, too, so if it's late, we'll stay over and be back Saturday."

He moved behind Bebe's chair and held it while she rose, her lashes veiling her eyes, the sliver of a smug smile curving her mouth. Cydney stared at her, stunned. Munroe dropped his cup on its saucer with a *clunk*. He didn't say anything, just twisted in his chair and watched Bebe and Aldo waltz arm-in-arm out of the dining room. When they'd gone, he swung back to the table and looked at Cydney.

"I'll bet you they hatched the plan to borrow your truck while they were in Bebe's bedroom," she said. "But of course, they're not sneaking."

"Oh no, God forbid." Munroe wiped a hand over his mouth, leaned on his elbow on the table and scowled. "We've been had."

"Who's been had?" Georgette asked, glancing first at Cydney and then Munroe. "What did I miss?"

"The rehearsal for the performance you just saw," Munroe said.

While he explained to her and Herb what had happened in the upstairs hall, Cydney stared at her mother's list. She felt like such a fool. How had she missed the mile-wide, I'll-get-what-I-want-and-screw-you streak in Bebe? Was it genetic? God knew Cydney had seen Gwen pull enough stunts like this. Had she and Georgette created this—or just fostered it—by overindulging Bebe?

Her niece had what she wanted, Aldo in her bed—for tomorrow night, anyway—as if sex was all there was to being in love and wanting to spend your life with someone. Munroe had seen this from the jump. Why hadn't she? Was love really that blind?

"Hello?" Munroe waved a hand at her. "Earth to Cydney."

She started and blinked at him. "I'm sorry. What did you say?"

"I was explaining why I didn't insist Aldo and Bebe come home tomorrow. The roads around here are dicey, especially after dark and this close to deer season. A buck in rut will go right through a pickup to get at a doe. Much as it galls me to let them get away with this little trick, I'd rather they come back alive so I can kill them myself."

"Ah." Cydney smiled. "I like the way you think."

"Perhaps you're both making too much of this," Georgette suggested. "Youth and impetuousness go hand in hand."

"So does youth and immaturity," Cydney retorted.

"And youth and irresponsibility," Munroe added.

"Well, if you two don't sound like a couple of old poops." Georgette shook her head and held her hand out to Cydney. "Give me the list."

"Why?" she asked, clutching it possessively.

"It's mine and I want it back."

"What are you going to do with it?"

"Nothing until Saturday or Sunday and neither are you."

"Oh yes, I am." Cydney shoved the list in her shirt pocket and slapped her hand over it.

"I'm your mother, Cydney. It's my job to save you from these impulses."

"I'll save myself, Mother. You had your chance and you blew it." Cydney put down her napkin and stood up. "Go to Eureka Springs tomorrow and have a lovely time. You, too, Herb. I'm going shopping."

She turned on her heel and left the dining room, so rattled she didn't realize she'd walked right past the back stairs until Munroe caught up with her and curved his hand around her arm. A big, warm hand that felt oh so good cupping her elbow.

He winked at her and grinned. "Way to go, old poop."

"Thanks," Cydney said with a shaky laugh.

He led her toward the second set of pocket doors, the ones on this side of the gallery stairs, and pushed them open. "You okay?"

"I will be in a minute." She stepped past him and dropped into a brass-studded leather chair by the door. "That's the first time I've ever said no to my mother."

"Ever?" He raised an eyebrow. "In your whole life?"

"Ever in my whole life." Cydney drew a deep breath and pressed a hand to her head. "Whew. What a rush."

"Maybe you should put your head between your knees."

Cydney laughed. Munroe offered her a handshake.

"Congratulations, Uncle Cyd. Today you are a man."

"And all these years I thought I was a girl."

He laughed and they shook hands. Cydney heard another rumble and glanced at a glassed-in alcove at the far end of the room. It was the same size as the great room, but it ran at a right angle to it. She thought she saw a flicker of lightning through the glass, but it was hard to tell this far away from the window in the twilight-dim room.

"We need a drink to celebrate. I don't suppose you like beer?"

"Sure I do. What makes you think I don't?"

"Never mind." Munroe tugged her out of the chair. "Bottle okay, or do you want a glass?"

"A bottle is fine, thank you."

He led her to another bar like the one in the living room, only about half the size. He helped her up on a stool, walked behind the bar, bent down and came up with two longneck bottles of Budweiser. He popped the caps, passed her one and lifted the other.

"To liberation," he said.

"Liberation," Cydney said.

They clinked bottles and drank. Munroe flipped a panel of switches, came around the bar and swung himself up on the stool next to hers as lights winked on all over the room.

Soft, recessed spots behind the bar and around the edges of the room, tucked above book-crammed shelves built into the two longest walls. An antique pool table with webbed leather pockets sat in the center of the room, a poker table with chairs in a corner. Cydney saw a Ping-Pong table with one end pushed against a wall, and four lovely old library tables heaped with books. Three couches and a handful of built-for-reading chairs were spaced around the room just waiting to be plopped into with a book.

"This room is an interesting mix," she said.

"It's the R and R room. Research and recreation." Munroe took a pull on his beer. "I play Ping-Pong with the wall when I get stuck in a chapter."

Cydney had read that in a *Playboy* interview but didn't say so. She sipped her beer and looked up at three huge pinwheel chandeliers spaced among the beams along the length of the room. In the glass alcove at the farthest end of the room sat an ebony grand piano, the lid down and draped with a paisley shawl.

"Oh my God!" She smacked a hand—fortunately, not the one holding the beer bottle—against her forehead. "We didn't even *think* about music for the wedding!"

chapter
fourteen

A giant spear of lightning forked just outside the glass alcove. A huge crack of thunder shook Tall Pines and nearly jolted Cydney off her bar stool.

"That was a close one," she said as the lights flickered twice and went out, pitching the R & R room into total darkness.

"Stay put. This happens a lot." Cydney heard leather creak as Munroe slid off his stool. "I've got flashlights stashed all over."

Thunder boomed and a sheet of rain slashed the glass walls of the alcove. Lightning lit up the room like an X ray. She caught a glimpse of Munroe turning on a flashlight and passing it to her over the bar with the beam pointing away from her face.

"Can you see well enough to find your way to the dining room?"

"Yes." She blinked to focus her eyes and slid off the stool as he came around the bar with another flashlight. "Where are you going?"

"To shut down my computer and see if I remembered to buy gas for the generator. You'll find battery lamps in the pantry and a few more flashlights. I'll catch up with you in the kitchen."

Munroe hurried ahead of her through the pocket doors. In a flash of lightning beyond the living room glass wall, Cydney saw him take the steps up to the foyer in one bound and turn right up the staircase she'd seen in the foyer. So that's where his office is, she thought.

She understood Munroe's impulse to check his computer.

She'd shut down the MacIntosh in her office and the spare PC in her writing room, pulled the surge protectors from the outlets and tucked both computers under plastic covers before she'd left Kansas City.

Who says you're obsessive-compulsive? her little voice asked.

"Oh shut up," Cydney muttered, and made for the dining room.

The table was cleared and only one cranberry oil lamp burned on the buffet. The other sat on a kitchen counter, casting a pool of light over the sink where her mother and Herb stood rinsing dishes.

"Maybe Gus has a generator," Herb was saying as Cydney came into the room. "I sure would if I lived this deep in the boonies."

"He's gone to check it," she told Herb. "He says there are battery lamps and flashlights in the pantry."

"Loan me yours, kiddo, and I'll go look."

Cydney gave it to him and off Herb went, a man on a mission.

"Mother," she said. "Has Bebe said anything to you about music?"

"No, darling, she—oh my God!" Georgette shut off the water and spun away from the sink. "Music for the ceremony! How could I forget?"

"These things happen, Mother. Even with a detailed list."

"Never mind that damned list." Georgette rubbed her forehead, the only sign she ever gave that she was stressed. "How could I have forgotten music? If Angus had a piano, I could play."

"He does have a piano. A grand."

"Thank God." She pressed a hand to her throat. "Crisis canceled."

Too bad. It would've been fun—mean, but fun—to watch her mother sweat *j-u-u-u-s-t* a little.

"Let's find Bebe," Cydney suggested. "And ask her what music she wants for the wedding."

"Let's not. We'll end up with Goo-Goo Eyes and Nine Inch Snails."

"Goo-Goo *Dolls*, Mother, and Nine Inch *Nails*."

"Garbage, by any name. I'm playing it, so *I'll* pick the music."

"But this is Bebe's wedding, Mother."

"And Aldo's." Munroe pushed through the swinging door from the bar, his flashlight beam catching Cydney in the face. She swung her head away and blinked to clear the dazzle from her eyes. "I did forget to buy gas for the generator. I've got about a thimbleful in the garage."

"Good heavens, Angus," her mother said. "You're soaked."

"Well, Georgette, the garage is outside. And as folks around here say, it's rainin' pitchforks and little dogs."

"Here's a dish towel. At least dry your hair."

When Cydney could see again, she turned her head and saw Munroe rubbing a red-and-white-checked dish towel over his head. He leaned against the butcher-block island, his ankles crossed, his muscled arms rain-speckled and gleaming in the glow of the oil lamp. His khakis and his shirt were so wet they looked pasted to his long legs and broad chest, leaving nothing at all about his physique to Cydney's imagination.

"Oh Angus," her mother tsked. "You're dripping."

So was Cydney, into a little puddle of hormones on the floor.

Munroe dried his face and arms, ran a hand through his wet-spiked hair and draped the towel around his neck. Lucky towel.

"Cydney tells me," Georgette said, "that you have a grand piano."

"It's my Aunt Phoebe's." Munroe kicked off his loafers and peeled off his socks. His feet were long and strong and as gorgeous as the rest of him. Straight toes, high arches and narrow heels. "Is this about music for the wedding?"

"Yes," her mother said. "In all the hubbub of packing and getting here, we forgot about music. I play piano. Not well enough for Carnegie Hall, but I can play 'The Wedding March' with sheet music."

"There's music in the bench. You might want to look. We'll have to move the piano into the great room, then it'll have to be tuned. I don't know if Aldo and Herb and I can move it, but we can try. I'll call Aunt Phoebe's piano tuner in the morning and see when he can get out here."

Lightning illuminated the bay window, giving Cydney a glimpse of wind-bent trees and the anything-to-help smile on Munroe's face. Monday night he'd threatened to invoke the codicil to his brother's will to keep Aldo from marrying Bebe, now he was volunteering to move a grand piano. What was wrong with this picture?

Thunder crashed, needles of rain pelted the glass and Herb came back from the pantry with an armful of flashlights and four battery lamps. He switched one on and sent a laser-bright shaft of light shooting across the kitchen.

"These babies sure kick out the light, Gus," Herb said as he adjusted the beam. "We can signal the rescue plane, no problem."

Cydney smiled at his good-natured humor. Her father would've blown his stack at the first flicker of the lights and chewed Munroe to pieces for failing to keep gas for the generator on hand.

"I don't think we need to send up flares just yet, Herb." Munroe picked up a lamp and turned it on. "I'm going to change."

"Would you like a cup of cocoa, Angus?" her mother asked.

"Love one, thanks. I'll be right back."

He moved toward the swinging door with his loafers and the lamp, the beam pointing ahead of him. Be glad to help you peel off those khakis, Cydney thought, then jumped, startled, when he glanced at her over his shoulder and crooked a finger. Her mother and Herb didn't see; they were looking in the cabinets for a saucepan and mugs. She nodded and followed him through the door, into the pool of light cast by the lamp.

"I haven't seen Aldo and Bebe since the lights went out, have you?"

"No." Cydney shook her head. "Three guesses where they are."

"In the sack, probably. What d'you think I should do?"

"Yell 'Fire!'?"

He laughed and gave her a gentle squeeze on the shoulder that made her breath catch. "I like you, Cydney Parrish."

"I like you, too, Angus Munroe."

"Gus," he said, and smiled.

"Gus." She smiled back at him. He nodded and pointed his finger at her. "Wait till I change and we'll yell 'Fire!' together."

He turned toward the stairs and Cydney toward the kitchen, an old Barbra Streisand song, "He Touched Me," playing in her head. It snapped off with a jolt when she pushed through the door and saw Bebe and Aldo standing at the gas range stirring a Dutch oven full of cocoa with wooden spoons. Well, darn. She was looking forward to yelling, "Fire!"

Gus came back a few minutes later in jeans, a pair of his white over-the-calf tube socks with gray toes and a white T-shirt with a chest pocket. He swung onto the slatted stool next to Cydney's at the island and reached for a big red mug of cocoa floating with marshmallows.

"Don't tell me you found marshmallows in my pantry, Georgette."

"No," she admitted. "I brought them with me."

One bag of marshmallows, maybe two more inches of space in one suitcase, Cydney thought. What on earth had her mother packed?

The storm continued to crash and boom and flash like a strobe light. Gus turned on a portable radio and found an AM station crackling with static that said the National Weather Service had issued a severe thunderstorm watch for all of Taney County, which included Branson and Crooked Possum, until midnight.

"We won't get the lights back tonight," he said, leaning his watch close to a battery lamp. "It's eight-forty-five."

"You go on to bed, Georgie-girl," Herb said. "I'll finish the dishes."

Cydney couldn't recall her father ever offering to help with the dishes, let alone volunteering to do them. She remembered Fletch wolfing meals and racing back to his office, so absorbed in himself that he barely heard what was said to him, or snapped answers that made it clear he couldn't be bothered with a wife and kids.

It hadn't been that way at all, really. In those days he'd worked two jobs—columnist for the *Kansas City Star* by day, novelist by night and on weekends—but that's how it had felt to Cydney. Especially when his fourth book hit it big and he'd walked out on them.

She stole a glance at Bebe, feeding cocoa to Aldo on a spoon. How much had she been aware of when Gwen brought her home to Gramma's house and left her there after she won her first Pulitzer? Abandoned, not good enough to be included in her mother's newfound success?

"I will not leave you with all these dishes, Herbert," Georgette said firmly. "We'll finish them together."

"Let Aldo and me do the dishes, Gramma." Bebe dropped her spoon and spun her stool toward Georgette. "We're not tired."

"Yeah." Aldo hopped off his stool and started collecting empty mugs. "You cooked, Gramma George. We'll clean up the kitchen."

"Thank you, Bebe dear. You, too, Aldo." Georgette took Herb's arm and waggled her fingers. "Good night, Cydney. Good night, Angus."

They each took a flashlight and pushed through the swinging door.

"Need a hand?" Gus asked his nephew.

"No thanks, Uncle Gus. We can manage."

Gus glanced at Cydney. She gave him an oh-well shrug.

"Okay, then." He slid off his stool and helped Cydney down from hers. "Good night."

"Good night, Bebe," Cydney said as Gus pushed open the swinging door for her. "Good night, Aldo."

"Uncle Cyd?" Bebe called, and Cydney glanced at her over her shoulder. "I'm sorry I was such a brat today. I didn't mean to hurt your feelings. I love you." She picked at the dishrag in her hands. "That's all."

That was enough. "I love you, too, Bebe. Good night."

Cydney smiled and pushed through the door. Gus followed her and switched on a flashlight.

"Would you like some company on your shopping trip tomorrow?"

Cydney blinked up at his face, half in shadow and half in the light cast by the flashlight. "You?"

"Yeah, me."

"Well—don't you have a book to write?"

"I always have a book to write, but I can take a day off."

"Then—um—yes." Cydney's heart fluttered. "That'd be great."

"Good." He took her arm and led her across the living room to the gallery stairs. "Keep the flashlight. My bedroom is up those stairs," he said, nodding at the foyer. "Next to my office."

"Thanks. I can make it to my room from here."

"I'm sure you can, but I'll wait anyway." He gave her a lift onto the first step. "Up you go."

Cydney climbed to the gallery and turned around. "See? Made it."

"I knew you could. Good night, Cydney."

"Good night, Gus."

A sheet of lightning gave her light enough to watch him cross the living room and disappear up the foyer stairs. When she heard a door shut, she wheeled down the hall as fast as she dared in the dark, pushed open her door, flung it shut behind her and belly-flopped on the bed, her heart pounding in her chest.

He touched me, Barbra Streisand sang in her head. *He put his hand near mine and then he touched me. I felt a . . . a . . .* what? Cydney couldn't remember what Barbra felt. A sparkle? A glow? She felt shaky and on fire, rolled on her back and cupped her flushed face.

Who would've believed that behind Angus Munroe's scowl lurked a touchy-feely guy who liked to be called Gus, with a grin that turned her bones to goo? Cydney had no idea if cold showers worked, but she scrambled off the bed and made for the bathroom to find out. She did not want to end up a headline on the front page of *The National Enquirer*. She could see it now—GORGEOUS GUS MUNROE'S BIGGEST FAN SPONTANEOUSLY COMBUSTS IN HIS LIVING ROOM.

She lit three of the aromatherapy candles she always traveled with on the toilet tank and cranked on the shower, lukewarm rather than ice cold, stripped and got in. She stuck her head under the spray and then remembered the power failure, which meant no hair dryer. She'd look like Little Orphan Annie in the morning.

She couldn't imagine that Gus really wanted to go shopping with her. She thought he was being polite, since she'd gotten lost twice getting here. If he were up to something nefarious, he'd let her go alone, figuring she'd get lost again and the buzzards would have her bones picked clean by the time they found her with the wedding decorations.

He was behaving like a polite and considerate host, doing everything he could to make them feel welcome, and yet something about it didn't feel right. Cydney hated it when she did this, let a little thing like Gus' damn-the-hernia-be-glad-to-move-the-piano smile fester in the back of her mind. Why couldn't she just accept him at face value?

She didn't hear the bathroom door open, but she felt a draft of cool air and saw a shadow on the other side of the pebbled glass door. Her heart kicked and she fumbled with the taps to shut off the water.

"Who's there?" she called.

"It's me, Uncle Cyd," Bebe said. Cydney heard the toilet lid shut and saw Bebe's shadow shift as she sat down.

Cydney opened the shower door and reached for a towel. The candles flickering on the tank behind Bebe lit her mane of copper-red hair like a Renaissance painting. She wrapped the towel around her body and tucked the end between her breasts. "Yes, Bebe?"

"Why were you spying on me and Aldo in the hall?"

"I wasn't spying on you. I was on my way downstairs when I heard a thump and looked around the corner and caught you telling a bald-faced lie to Mr. Munroe."

"Aldo and I are engaged, Uncle Cyd. You keep forgetting that."

"How can I forget it? You keep reminding me of it every five minutes like it means something."

"It *does* mean something. It means we love each other, we're committed to each other and we have the right to make our own decisions."

"You and Aldo have intentions, Bebe. That's all it means to be engaged. You have an intention to marry and commit to each other. You do not have the right to behave like you're married or demand that people treat you like you're married until you *are* married."

"Marriage is just a ceremony and a stupid piece of paper!"

"Then why are you and Aldo bothering with it? Why did you drag your grandmother and me and Herb down here to the backwater of nowhere if marriage is just a stupid piece of paper?"

"Because I want my mother at my wedding!" Bebe cried, tears in her eyes and her voice as she jumped to her feet. "And you aren't her!"

"But I'm *here* and Gwen isn't. If she really wanted to be at your wedding, she would be. It wouldn't matter where you held it, and we wouldn't have to plot and scheme to keep her from leaving."

"The only person who's leaving is *you*!" Bebe shouted, pointing a finger at her. "I don't want you at my wedding!"

Cydney sucked a breath, so hurt she could hardly think. She'd read an article once about children leaving home who subconsciously picked fights with their parents to make the break less painful. For the child or the parent, she'd wondered, and now she knew.

"If that's the way you want it," she managed to say evenly. "It's your wedding, Bebe."

"Mine and Aldo's," she snapped, and spun out of the bathroom.

What's wrong with you? What happened to the sweet kid who apologized in the kitchen not fifteen minutes ago, Cydney wanted to shout, but her throat was clogged with tears. She trailed Bebe into the bedroom, watched her open the door and slam it behind her, hard enough to knock a painting of a sunny Ozark hillside on the wall askew.

Cydney sat down next to her suitcase on the blanket box at the foot of the bed, her insides shaking. She'd wanted to leave, but not like this. She got up and straightened the picture, walked to the window and lifted the embroidered curtain. Lightning still flickered, but the rain had stopped and she could see the moon behind a scud of racing clouds.

It would be practical and prudent to stay until morning and drive home in daylight, but she couldn't bear the thought of seeing Bebe or trying to explain this to her mother. And why should she? It was Bebe's decision to uninvite her—let Bebe explain it to Georgette.

She'd miss the shopping trip with Gus. Oh boy, would she miss it, but it was just as well. He liked her and that's all she'd wanted. She'd thought it was all she could hope for, but his easy, offhand touches stirred feelings in her she was sure he didn't share. If she stayed he'd break her heart. He wouldn't mean to, and he'd never know it, but he would.

Cydney glanced at her still-packed suitcase. All she had to do was shut it, throw on her clothes and she could leave. *You mean creep out the front door in the middle of the night, don't you?* her little voice asked.

"Call it what you want." Cydney swiped the flashlight off the bed and headed for the bathroom. "I'm going home."

She blew out the candles and left them on the back of the toilet. They were too hot to pack. Maybe her mother would think to collect them. She put on clean underwear, her crop pants and her blue shirt and left the shopping list on the Duncan Phyfe desk. She tossed her sandals in the suitcase, sat down to lace on her Keds and stubbed her toe on something on the floor next to the blanket box.

"Ow!" She rubbed her foot, reached for the flashlight and shined it on her laptop, the one with the blown graphics card she'd picked up from the repair shop on Wednesday and forgot to take out of the Jeep.

She tucked it in her suitcase and zipped it shut, tugged the pullman-on-wheels off the bed and raised the handle, slung her purse over her shoulder, gently opened the door and listened. All quiet.

Rather than risk the hallway and waking someone, Cydney took the carpeted back stairs, easing her suitcase down step by step. She couldn't remember where she'd left the map, but she had a plan. She'd get herself as far out of these hills as she could, then call the Highway Patrol on her cell phone and ask them to come find her.

She inched herself and her suitcase across the mostly bare living room floor so the wheels wouldn't squeak. She'd made it almost to the foyer when the moon broke through the clouds and silvery light poured through the glass wall, gleaming on the edges and curves of furniture and casting long pewter shadows on the pegged-pine floor. Cydney turned off the flashlight she didn't need anymore and put it on a table, lifted her suitcase up the steps and set it down by the door.

"Made it," she sighed, reaching for the handle.

She clicked the latch and *then* saw the alarm panel on the wall, one of the tiny red bulbs leaping from solid red to flashing red. Cydney jerked her hand away, expecting a siren to blare, but all she heard was a door banging open and footsteps thudding at a run down the stairs from Gus' bedroom.

A flashlight switched on, trapping her in the beam like a convict making a break for the wall. Cydney turned her head and saw Gus in the backwash, standing on the third step in red silk boxer shorts, the flashlight in his left hand and a baseball bat in his right.

"Going somewhere?" he asked.

"Yes. Home."

"Was it something I said?"

"No. Something Bebe said." Cydney tore her gaze away from his naked, dark-haired chest and looked at the floor. "Nice underwear."

"Oops. Sorry." He switched off the flashlight. "If I go put my pants on you won't leave, will you?"

She shook her head no and he turned up the stairs. Enough

light filtered into the foyer from the living room and through the stained-glass door panels that she saw a timbered bench on the wall behind her. She sat down and waited. Gus came back in his jeans and his white T-shirt, turned off the flashlight and sat down on the steps.

"You would've made a clean getaway if I hadn't installed a battery backup on the alarm."

"I wish I'd known that. I would've tried the window."

"What did Bebe say to you?"

"She accused me of spying on her and Aldo, which is ridiculous, but it started an argument and I think that's what she intended. She told me she didn't want me at her wedding and asked me to leave."

"Kids do that. It's unconscious, the experts say, but it helps them make the break when they leave home."

"I read that article, too."

"Doesn't help much, does it?"

"It doesn't help at all." Cydney's throat ached and her eyes filled. She raised a hand and wiped tears off her cheeks.

"C'mere, Uncle Cyd." Gus patted the stair beside him. When she hesitated he patted it again. "C'mon. I don't bite."

Cydney crossed the foyer and sat on the stairs, not beside him but on the step below his. He scooted down next to her, peeled off his T-shirt and handed it to her.

"Pretend it's a handkerchief," he said, and she burst into sobs, her face buried in his shirt, her elbows braced on her knees.

He drew her against his warm, sleek side, being kind and sympathetic, his arm around her shoulders, and that made her cry harder. She cried until she gave herself hiccups, and Gus went to the kitchen and brought her a glass of water. Cydney held her breath, drank every drop and wiped her last tear with the last dry inch of his shirt.

"Thanks." She sighed. "I feel better."

"Glad to hear it, 'cause you're gonna look like hell in the morning." Cydney laughed and he looked affronted. "I always do," he said, and she laughed harder, rocking back into the curve of his left arm as he looped it around her and smiled. "You don't really want to leave, do you?"

"No. But Bebe doesn't want me here and it's her wedding."

"It's Aldo's wedding, too, and this is *my* house. Bebe has no authority to kick anybody out of Tall Pines. If you're determined to go, I'll carry your suitcase out to your truck, but I'd like you to stay."

Cydney tipped her head back and looked at his face, the curve of his jaw etched in silver by the moon. "Really?"

"Really." He nodded. "Your mother scares the hell out of me."

She laughed and leaned her head against his shoulder. Just for a second, to see what it would feel like. It felt . . . wonderful. The warmth of his skin, the smooth tone of muscle beneath. He leaned his chin on her head and breathed into her damp hair, lacing a shiver down her back.

"Can I bring a guest to the wedding?"

Cydney's heart seized. You fool, she told herself, you idiot. Of course he already has somebody.

"Well, yes," she said, shooting straight up beside him and out from under his arm. "Certainly you can bring a guest."

"Then how'd you like to be my date for the wedding?"

Cydney turned sideways on the step to face him. He winked. Her throat swelled with tears and she bit her lip. Gus caught her hand and gave it a firm yet gentle squeeze.

"Bebe can't do a thing about it. This is my house and I'll invite who I please. The worst she can do is stick out her lip and risk falling over it on her way up the aisle. You can leave and come back for the ceremony, but I'd be damned if I'd let her run me off."

"You're right. I'll stay. And I'd love to be your date for the wedding." Cydney squeezed his hand and smiled at him. "Thank you, Gus. I think you're the nicest man I've ever met."

"Gee, thanks." He grinned at her. "I've waited all my life to hear that from a woman."

chapter
fifteen

Even critics who didn't especially like mysteries admired Angus Munroe's way with a plot, his "uncanny knack for moving characters through complex and emotionally charged scenarios."

That was fiction. This was real life. The Parrish clan had been here less than twenty-four hours and already the plot outline Gus had written, titled Grand Plan to Wreck the Wedding, was so far off track he wasn't sure he could get it back. Or that he wanted to.

This had seemed like such a great idea in Kansas City. He'd been sure Cydney Parrish would lose her appeal out of context, but he was wrong. She'd looked so damn cute yesterday, stuck in her Jeep in his driveway, a pissed-off little pixie with a smudge of gravel dust on her nose. He'd wanted to rub it off with a kiss. He hadn't, but he'd wanted to, and that was the Grand Plan's first wobble on the rails.

Gus stood at the big window in his office with Artie's ancient and dinged-up Louisville Slugger resting on his shoulder, the one he'd grabbed when Cydney tripped the alarm. He'd taught Aldo how to play baseball with this bat. It was way too short for both of them now, but it worked for hitting stones into the lake. Gus usually did his best thinking with Artie's bat in his hands, but not this morning. His brain felt as thick as the fog he could see curling off the lake.

If he'd been thinking yesterday he would've said yes when Cydney asked him if he'd paid to have the dirt from the rest of the house dumped in the great room. What a perfect opportunity to throw a monkey wrench in the wedding plans. A simple yes, and the Parrish clan would've gone straight back to Kansas City in a huff, but he'd just stood there, lost in a fantasy of Cydney naked and up to her nipples in bubbles in his hot tub. Gus turned the bat in his hands by its tape-wrapped grip and thought about whacking himself in the head with it.

How did she come up with stuff like paying to have dirt dumped in the great room? How come he couldn't?

'Cause men are from Mars, Munroe, his inner voice said. *And women are from Venus. Although Cydney Parrish could be from Pluto.*

"Yippee. You're back," Gus said to his AWOL muse. Or his conscience, or whatever the hell it was. "You can stay, but no bad-mouthing the woman I'm in lust with."

He wished it were only lust he felt for Cydney. He'd tried bed-hopping in college but it just wasn't in his nature. He had to like a woman before he could sleep with her and he liked Cydney. He liked her a lot. He liked her humor, her honesty and her sincerity. He liked the almond shape and color of her eyes and her pert little nose . . . the glimpse of cleavage she'd innocently given him when she'd leaned back into the curve of his arm on the stairs.

He didn't like petite women, but he thought Cydney was adorable. He didn't like blondes, either, but her silver-blond curls had felt like silk and smelled like lilacs when he'd laid his chin on her head. He wanted to do that again real soon. He wanted to do all kinds of things to her, starting with carrying her upstairs to his bed.

It wasn't in his nature to plot and scheme, either. In fiction, yes—in real life, no. But he'd come upstairs by flashlight after Cydney went to bed, patting himself on the back for being so damn smart. The electricity was still off, but he'd written the Grand Plan to Wreck the Wedding on his laptop Tuesday night when he got home from Kansas City. He'd forgotten to buy gas for the generator, but he always kept the batteries for the laptop charged. He nudged the PC's monitor aside to make room on his desk, fired up the laptop at 1:32 A.M.,

opened the file named GRAND PLAN and sat down to up-
date it.

What a stroke of genius to ask Cydney to be his date for
the wedding. Of course she said yes. He'd known she'd say
yes. He worked Bebe ordering Cydney to leave into the Plan
and added notes on how to make the best use of it. He'd
smiled and hummed while he typed, the last of the storm
rumbling away into the predawn darkness.

When he'd paused to think, leaning back in his chair with
his glasses and his fingers laced together on the top of his
head, his mind drifted to how soft and sweet Cydney felt
tucked in the curve of his arm. If the revised Plan held together, he could have the wedding in shambles by the end of
the weekend and Cydney in his bed. He remembered her hiccups and smiled, then her tears, and that's when it hit him—
the utter rottenness of what he was doing.

He'd damn near broken his neck jumping out of his chair
and backpedaling away from the laptop. He'd stared at the
screen, appalled at what he'd written. Who in hell did he
think he was, playing with people's emotions, jerking them
around by their heartstrings like marionettes?

He'd paced his office, telling himself the Grand Plan was
designed to serve the greater good, to save Aldo from making
the biggest mistake of his young life. It was his duty. Artie
had trusted him, counted on Gus to look out for Aldo. Made
sense till he ventured back to the laptop and had another
look at the Grand Plan. It didn't read like he was trying to
serve Aldo's best interests—it read like he was trying to serve
his own.

All right, he'd decided. He'd write another plan. A new
Life Plan for Angus Munroe. He sat down and opened a
new document, poised his fingers over the keys and hit a solid
brick wall of writer's block. He'd stared at the screen, unable
to type so much as a comma, the cursor blinking at him till the
headache he woke up with in the hospital Tuesday morning
came roaring back into his temples.

He'd shut down the laptop, took a shower and shaved, but
it hadn't helped. It was almost 8 A.M. now and he was tired

and hungry. His neck, his shoulders *and* his head ached. He'd napped a little in his reading chair by the window, but he hadn't been to bed. He couldn't face sleeping with such a selfish sonofabitch.

He wanted to blame his behavior on the concussion, but he'd been in full possession of his stinking, miserable faculties when he'd written the Grand Plan. Which was not to say that he knew what he was doing, because he didn't. Cydney nailed that right on the head.

Since Aldo's call on Monday he'd done nothing but react. First to the news that he was getting married, second to the leveler that he was marrying Fletcher Parrish's granddaughter. Gus had gone ballistic, and then he'd gone on the defensive, circling the wagons, closing ranks to protect the thing that meant the most to him in the world, his family.

The problem was that Aldo wanted a family of his own. He was entitled. So was Gus, but he'd lost his. He could've married and started another one, but he didn't want another family, he wanted the one he'd lost. He didn't think of himself as a man who lived in the past, but that's what he'd been doing. He'd convinced himself that so long as he had Aldo he still had Artie and Beth and his parents and Aunt Phoebe, or little pieces of them, anyway.

Aldo smiled just like Artie and laughed just like Beth. He had his mother's hair and eyes, his father's nose and chin. Sometimes he was scatterbrained like Beth, but he had a mind for math like Artie, and Aunt Phoebe's gentle heart. Gus didn't see much of his parents in Aldo, but he told him stories about his grandparents and he kept pictures of them and Artie and Beth and Aunt Phoebe on the piano in the R&R room.

So you won't forget them, he'd told Aldo. Gus called the photo array the Family Gallery. Aldo called it the Family Shrine. He'd asked Gus after Aunt Phoebe died why the photographs on the piano were the only things in the house Gus ever dusted.

Didn't have to be Freud to figure that one out. All these years he'd been trying to keep his family alive. Gus thought he'd accepted their loss, but apparently he hadn't. He'd barely gotten over losing his parents in a car wreck when the plane crash took Artie and Beth. He'd cried buckets. He and Aunt Phoebe cried a river between them, but maybe it took more than tears.

Maybe it took dismantling the shrine, tucking the pictures away in albums on a closet shelf. He could do that when he moved the piano, but what would he put in their place? What would he put in Aldo's place? Just thinking about it made his palms sweat. He wiped them one at a time on the thighs of his jeans, wrapped his hands around Artie's Louisville Slugger and thought he should probably put it away, too. It was a baseball bat, not a holy relic. He should save it for Aldo's son.

Now that was a scary thought, perpetuating the gene pool that produced Bebe Parrish. The more Gus saw of her the more certain he was that Aldo was making a colossal mistake. But it was Aldo's to make and Aldo's to pay for. No matter how nuts it drove Gus to think about having to put up with Bebe until the divorce. Or God forbid, the rest of his life.

The proper way to handle this was to tell Aldo point-blank how he felt. It was dirty pool to hold Artie's will over his head and plot and scheme behind his back, which meant the Grand Plan had to go. So did his plan to woo Cydney. He couldn't say no cohabitation to Aldo and then sleep with the bride's aunt. Well, he could. It was his house and he and Cydney were adults, but it was the old do-what-I-say-not-what-I-do thing, which he'd always tried to avoid.

And besides the scorching kiss they'd shared in her kitchen, Gus had no real proof that Cydney wanted to be wooed. She thought he was the nicest man she'd ever met. A far cry from, "Oooh, you stud, take me to bed." She'd think Jack the Ripper was the nicest man she'd ever met if he asked her to be his date for the wedding.

She wouldn't think he was Mr. Nice Guy if she saw the Grand Plan. Or if she knew he'd asked her to be his date just so he could keep her close to his bed. Well, not *just*, but mostly. Two more excellent reasons to hit the delete key. Gus turned toward the laptop and stopped. He still had Artie's bat on his shoulder. He took it off, held it in his hands and rubbed his thumb across the fly-ball dents.

Put it away, Munroe, his little voice said, and Gus did, in the closet next to the credenza, planting a kiss on the barrel before he stood the bat in the back corner, shut the door and drew a breath of stale, stuffy air.

The power and the air-conditioning had been off for almost ten hours. Gus opened the small windows flanking the big one overlooking the lake, inhaled cool, rain-freshened air and turned toward his desk. He sat down, opened the laptop and turned it on, brought up the Grand Plan to Wreck the Wedding and took one last look at it. Damn shame to delete it, really. It was some of his best work.

"Hey, Uncle Gus!" He nearly jumped out of his chair at Aldo's voice and the bang of his fist on the office door. "You up yet?"

"I'm awake. C'mon in."

Aldo opened the door and stuck his head past it. "Gramma George is making French toast. How many slices?"

Good ol' Georgette. Still trying to bribe him with food into seeing the wedding the Parrish way. All the tempting meals in the world wouldn't change his opinion of Bebe and this marriage, but what was the harm in letting her try? It wasn't plotting and scheming. But it wasn't honest, either. He'd be better off with the Chee-tos and Gatorade he had stashed in the credenza for breakfast.

"Tell her thank you, Aldo, but I—"

"Hal-loo-*ooo!* Angus?" Georgette called up the stairs behind Aldo. "Powdered sugar or just butter and syrup? Blueberry or maple?"

Blueberry was Gus' favorite. He thought about Chee-tos and caved.

"I'll have the works, please, with blueberry syrup," he called back to Georgette. "Be right down."

"Cool," Aldo said, and shut the door.

Bravo, Munroe, his inner voice said. *That's living your convictions.*

"Oh shut up." Gus pushed out of his chair and made for the door.

He hadn't smelled French toast in Tall Pines since Aunt Phoebe died, but the aroma—butter-fried bread drenched in egg and milk with a splash of vanilla and a pinch of nutmeg—filled his nose halfway down the stairs and made his mouth water. He hadn't laid eyes on his aunt's orange press in five years, either, but he saw it when he pushed through the door behind the bar, sitting on the island between Aldo and Bebe, dripping orange pulp.

"Hey, Uncle Gus." Aldo grinned cheerfully and handed him a glass of fresh-squeezed juice.

"Ready in a jiff, Angus." Georgette, her cheeks pink from the steam cloud rolling off the gas range, waved a spatula at him. "Bebe, dear. Check the syrup and make sure it's warm enough."

"Yes, Gramma." She rolled her eyes and dragged herself toward the stove and a small saucepan simmering on a back burner.

"Bebe's not a morning person," Aldo whispered to him.

"She doesn't seem to be much of an afternoon or evening person, either," Gus whispered back, and drank his orange juice.

Aldo frowned at him.

"Just my opinion." Gus gave him the glass and made for the bay window to help Herb open the pine table so he could put in the leaf.

"Morning, Herb," he said, taking hold of one end of the table. "Let me give you a hand."

"Thanks, Gus. Morning to you, too." Herb pulled his end open and seated the leaf in the gap. "Okay. Give her a shove."

They pushed the table together and tucked it back into the bay of the fogged-up window behind the bench. Gus opened the small side windows and the back door to let the heat out and turned around. He saw Aunt Phoebe's old stovetop coffeepot steaming on a trivet on the counter beside a pot of tea, but no sign of Cydney.

"Where's Cydney?" he asked Herb.

"Don't know. Haven't seen her yet this morning."

"Oh, she left," Bebe said offhandedly from the island.

Georgette switched off the flame under the cast-iron skillet and wheeled away from the stove. "What do you mean, *she left*?"

"I mean she left." Bebe shrugged and licked orange juice off her fingers. "About eleven-thirty last night."

"No, I didn't." Cydney marched into the kitchen from the hallway in jeans, a white knit pullover—and fire in her eyes.

Bebe spun toward her. "You said you were leaving."

"No. You said I was leaving. I decided to stay. Morning, Mother. Morning, Herb." Cydney picked up a set of ribbed green place mats Gus had never seen before, plates from Aunt Phoebe's set of everyday white stoneware that were stacked on the end of the island and brought them to the table. "Good morning, Gus."

"Morning, Cydney." He smiled at her and she smiled back.

She looked like hell. Her eyes were puffy from crying and her silver curls were a mess of tight, frizzy links. Looked like she'd stuck her finger in a light socket. And still Gus wanted to hug her.

"If I were cups," she said to him, "where would I be?"

"I'll get them." Gus paused on his way to the dish cabinet, spread his hands on the island and leaned toward Bebe. "I asked Cydney to stay. I need a date for the wedding and she agreed to accompany me. She'll be sitting on Aldo's side of the room with me. Any objections?"

"N-n-no," Bebe stammered, red-faced.

"Good." Gus looked her straight in the eye. "Subject closed."

Bebe stuck her lip out. It was childish as hell, but Gus stuck his lip out right back at her. Her eyes flew wide open.

"Breakfast is served," Georgette announced, lifting a steaming platter heaped with French toast off the counter.

Gus carried mugs and the coffee to the table and went back for the teapot. Cydney was already seated on the bench with Herb, catty-corner from Bebe and Aldo. Gus took the chair at the other end next to Cydney and set the teapot in front of her.

"Thank you," she said, and picked up her napkin, green cloth to match the mats. She spread it in her lap and laid a folded sheet of paper on top. She kept glancing at it and touching it. Gus had no idea what it was or what Cydney intended to do with it, until she finished her French toast, laid the paper on the edge of the table and wiped her mouth. Then she shifted on the bench to look at her niece.

"I've thought about what you said to me last night, Bebe. If you and Aldo are old enough to make your own decisions and decide the course of your lives, I'm sure you'll want to be in charge of every aspect of your wedding," she said, handing Bebe the folded piece of paper.

Everyone stopped eating, even Aldo. He blinked up from his plate with a drip of syrup in one corner of his mouth. Bebe plucked the folded sheet of paper gingerly from Cydney's fingers.

"What's this?" she asked.

"The list Gramma George made of the decorations you visualized for the great room."

"What am I supposed to do with it?"

"Go shopping."

"*Me?*" Bebe squeaked.

"Take Aldo with you. It's his wedding, too."

"But Aldo and I are going to Silver Dollar City today."

Cydney poured a cup of tea, added cream and sugar and didn't answer. Georgette started to say something, then pressed her lips shut.

"Here, Gramma." Bebe thrust the list at her.

"Herb and I are going to Eureka Springs," she replied.

"But it's your list!"

"And it's your wedding," Georgette said firmly.

Oh God. Gus gulped a slug of coffee and a deep breath. He'd volunteered to go shopping with Cydney, not spend the day alone with her in a house with sixteen beds and eight big, long, wide sofas. His imagination and his libido soared. So did a certain area of his anatomy he called Clyde. Gus hunched forward on his elbows and cleared his throat.

"Uh, Herb," he said. "Think you can find Eureka Springs okay? Cydney and I had other plans today, but we'd be glad to tag along."

Cydney paused with her teacup halfway to her mouth and arched an eyebrow at him. "We would?"

"Nice of you, Gus." Herb caught Georgette's hand and winked at him. "But we have other plans, too."

"Just thought I'd offer." Gus smiled gamely, then said to Georgette, "Wonderful French toast. Why don't you dump Herb and marry me?"

"Sorry, Gus. I saw her first." Herb grinned. "Tell you what, though. I'm told Cydney's French toast is just as good as my Georgie-girl's. You could always marry her."

Cydney choked on her tea, nearly dropped the cup getting it back in the saucer and snatched her napkin over her mouth and her nose. She made a noise in her throat that sounded like she was strangling—which pretty much deflated Clyde's spirits—scrambled off the bench and dashed for the bathroom.

"Oh my," Herb said bewilderedly. "What did I say?"

So much for scorching kisses in the kitchen. Gus excused himself and took his bent ego for a walk.

The rain had sucked all the heat out of the air and turned his backyard into a bog. The beat-up old brown loafers he'd stepped into after his 3 A.M. shower, with jeans and his gray Mizzou T-shirt, squished through sodden leaves. He slogged up the hill to the lake through rain-dulled autumn trees. He dug a couple fistfuls of muddy rocks out of the beach and sat on the edge of the dock skipping them into the lake. He'd been at it a while when Aldo dropped down on the dock beside him.

"Uncle Gus," he said. "You don't like Bebe, do you?"

"I don't like her behavior. I'm not real thrilled with yours, right now, either."

"What did I do?"

"That con job with my truck at dinner last night. Real cute."

"What con job? I want to take Bebe to Silver Dollar City."

"Baloney. You want to take her to the nearest motel and jump her bones, but you couldn't say that in front of her grandmother, could you? You figured if you asked me in private about the truck I'd put two and two together and say no."

"I should've driven my own car," Aldo grumbled.

"Why didn't you?"

"On these roads? Ruin my brand new Jag with gravel dings?"

"The way *you* drive. If you'd take your foot off the gas—"

"Aw jeez, Uncle Gus. Can I do anything right?"

"I don't know." Gus skipped another stone. "Think you and Bebe can manage to feed and dress yourselves once you're married?"

"Oh, that's funny, Uncle Gus." Aldo glared at him. "About as funny as you sticking your lip out at Bebe."

"It was stupid and childish and I'd do it again in a minute to show Bebe how stupid and childish she looks when she does it."

"You hurt her feelings."

"Bebe hurt Cydney's feelings. She sat on the steps last night crying because Bebe doesn't want her at the wedding."

"What d'you care? You got the hots for her?" Aldo smacked the flat of his doubled fist against his forehead. "Sorry. I didn't mean that."

"When I walked into the great room yesterday you had a broom in your hand. A sensible response to that much dirt, but you were drawing hearts on the filthy goddamn floor. Cydney brought the mess to my attention, which I take responsibility for because I didn't check their work before I paid the crew. Why didn't you tell me? Why did I have to tell you to sweep the floor?"

"I was getting to that," Aldo said between his teeth.

"You and Bebe want to be adults when it's convenient,

Aldo, when it doesn't cut into your play time. When it's not convenient, you dump your responsibilities on other people."

"You're gonna pull my trust fund, aren't you?"

"I don't give a damn about the money. I care about you and your ability to take care of yourself and a wife."

"You don't think I can, do you?"

"Frankly? No."

"What'll it take to convince you?"

"If you and Bebe can pull off this wedding in a week—on your own, without any help from anyone else—then I'll believe you're mature enough to be on your own and take care of yourselves."

"That's all?" Aldo slid him a dubious look. "I don't have to write one of those dopey Life Plans you're so big on?"

"No. Just plan the wedding all on your own. You and Bebe. Nobody else."

"How hard can that be?" Aldo said with a rueful snort. "Buy stuff and put up some decorations."

"A snap." Gus turned sideways on the dock and held out his hand. "How 'bout it, pal? We got a deal here?"

"Yeah, Uncle Gus." Aldo gripped his hand and gave it a firm, determined shake. "We got a deal."

chapter
sixteen

Gus didn't follow Aldo back to Tall Pines. He didn't dare until he thought of a way to keep his hands off Cydney.

When his nephew disappeared into the trees, he looked at the lake and considered dunking himself. This time of year the water was about forty degrees. Surely to God that would cool him off.

If you're gonna do it, his inner voice said, *go find a big rock and give yourself a couple good whacks on the head first.*

"Go away!" Gus shouted. "And leave me alone!"

The ring of his voice on the still morning air exploded a handful of ducks from a nearby clump of reeds. They veered away across the lake squawking. Gus watched them, squinting into the sun burning through the fog to keep the sick thud in his temples from splitting his skull.

He grimaced and rubbed his temples. He needed a pain pill. Maybe if he chugged three of the horse tabs the old coot doctor in Kansas City gave him with a can of beer he'd pass out for a week.

That's what he needed, a coma to get him through this wedding. And a reality check.

Reality Number One: Cydney nearly swallowed his tongue when he'd kissed her in her kitchen Tuesday night, but she also baked macaroons in that kitchen and kept them in a teddy bear cookie jar. You don't drag a woman like that to bed for a day of hot, wild sex. You court her. You make love to her. And then you marry her.

Reality Number Two: He didn't want to get married—he wanted to get laid. Crude, but the truth. So far as he knew, there was only one streetwalker in Crooked Possum. Mamie Buckles, who went door-to-door selling prickly pear jelly. Eighty if she was a day.

Reality Number Three: Cydney lived a sensible, prudent and well-planned life, a life he could admire and want to be a part of—if he wanted to get married, which he didn't—if only it didn't include Fletcher Parrish. Made him sound like he was thirty-five going on six, but it was the truth, this was a Reality Check and so he had to admit it.

Which still left the question—what was he going to do?

He hadn't a clue, but he knew what he wasn't going to do—spend the day alone at Tall Pines with Cydney. He'd take her sightseeing, maybe to Branson for lunch. There were a million motels in Branson but he'd slap an ice pack in his pants and leave his credit cards at home.

Gus levered himself to his feet, the butt of his jeans sagging from sitting on the soaked dock, and headed for the house. He was halfway up the almost-an-acre back lawn when he saw the brighter-than-daylight glare of the outside security lights wink on and heard a faint *waugga-waugga* wail. It was the alarm. The power must've come back on with a surge that triggered the system, and Aldo, who'd never figured out how to operate it, must have tried to shut it off and tripped the siren. Gus kicked off his mud-caked loafers and ran for the deck before every sheriff's deputy in Taney County showed up in his driveway.

"It's the switch on the left, Aldo!" he shouted when he reached the deck and yanked open the solarium doors, but the alarm blared on. "Your other left, Aldo!"

His nephew didn't answer. Neither did Herb or Georgette or Cydney when Gus called out to them as he raced across the living room. He stubbed his right big toe going up the foyer steps, tripped but caught himself on his hands, hissing between his teeth, on the wall beneath the control panel. Every light flashed, all the switches were flipped the wrong way. Gus flipped them back but the alarm kept screaming. He cursed and wheeled up the steps to his office.

Cydney sat at his desk, barely a foot from the master

switch on the alarm panel built into the wall behind her, staring at his laptop. Oh shit. Oh hell. The Grand Plan to Wreck the Wedding was still on the screen. Damn Georgette's French toast.

Cydney looked dazed, her almond eyes huge, her face almost as white as her knit pullover. She looked up when Gus burst into the room, breathing hard, his big toe throbbing and his hair falling in his face. She stared at him for a second, then grabbed the red Ping-Pong paddle on his desk and threw it at him.

A better man would've stood his ground and taken the shot, but a better man wouldn't have written the Grand Plan. Gus ducked. The paddle cracked into the door frame behind him. He jumped for the left side of the desk to reach the alarm and Cydney. She shot around the right side to avoid him. Gus shut down the system and spun after her just as she flung herself through the doorway.

"Cydney!" he shouted. "Cydney, wait, please!"

She didn't. Gus charged after her, too fast to make the turn on the landing at the top of the stairs. He bounced off the wall and careened onto the steps, caught just a glimpse of Cydney at the bottom and heard her yank open the front door. He grabbed the banister and smiled and took his time following her. She stood in the empty driveway, her arms jammed together, an angry glare on her face, when he came out of the house wincing on his smarting toe.

"Where's my truck?" she gritted at him between her teeth.

"I put it away last night." Gus leaned on the roof post at the top of the porch steps and nodded at the barn-size, six-car garage built in the middle of a paved turnaround at the end of the driveway a hundred yards from the house. "When I came out to check the generator."

"How did you—?" She broke off when Gus plucked her car keys out of his pocket and let them swing between his fingers.

He'd meant to give them back to her last night, but he'd gotten distracted; first by the cocoa-mustache on her upper lip he'd wanted to lick off in the kitchen, second by the shimmer of her hair in the moonlight glowing through the stained-glass windows in the foyer.

Cydney narrowed her eyes and thrust her right hand at him, palm-up. "Give me my keys, please."

"No." Gus slipped them back in his pocket and folded his arms.

She shoved her hands on her hips and her weight—all one hundred and ten pounds of it, maybe—on one foot. "I said please."

"So did I, but you ignored me."

"I plan to keep ignoring you." She turned on one heel and stalked toward the garage.

"Will you wait a minute?" Gus hurried off the porch, mindful of his bare feet and the needles shed by the pines growing in the circle lawn. Those that weren't rain-soaked and stuck to the puddled blacktop could be razor sharp. "I can explain the Grand Plan to Wreck the Wedding."

"No you *can't*!" She whipped around to face him, her voice breaking, her eyelashes glistening. "Don't even *try*!"

"It seemed like a good idea when I wrote it Tuesday night. I'd just gotten home from Kansas City. I was tired, I had a headache—" Gus reached for her but she shrugged him off and wheeled toward the garage. "Where are you going? The garage is locked and I've got your keys."

"Keep them." She dropped to her heels, pried one of the muddy, white-painted rocks out of the border edging the drive and marched on. "I've got a spare key in a magnetic box under the left front fender."

"I had a concussion, for God's sake." Gus limped after her, the throb in his jammed toe shooting up his foot into his ankle, the one he'd sprained in Cydney's backyard. "I'd been punched in the nose, dropped on a birdbath, tripped over a damn croquet wicket and—*Ow!*"

Gus fell against the split-rail fence edging the lawn at the sudden stab in his right foot and saw a pine needle sunk halfway into the pad of his big toe. He plucked it out, looked up and saw Cydney glaring at him.

"That doesn't excuse what you wrote," she said, her voice shaking with anger. "Or what you intend to do with it."

"*Intended*, Cydney. As in, I no longer intend."

"Of course you don't *intend* now. I caught you," she snapped, and wheeled toward the garage.

"Give me five minutes." Gus pushed off the fence after her, his big toe on fire. "Just five minutes to explain this. If you don't like what I say, I'll give your keys back and unlock the garage."

"No thanks." She spun toward him, hefting the rock in her hand. "I'd rather brain *you* with this, but I'll settle for breaking a window."

She took off again, making a beeline toward the timbered side wall of the garage and the window there. It was still speckled with rain, about chest-high on him and almost over Cydney's head. She could smash the glass but she'd never reach the window without a ladder.

"I read the Grand Plan when I went upstairs last night and realized I was playing with people's lives. Real people's lives, not characters I'd made up. I was going to delete the damn thing but Aldo interrupted me. I love French toast. I haven't had it since Aunt Phoebe died. I—"

"You wrote down every word I said to you last night." Cydney spun around, the rock clenched in her left fist, her eyes glittering. "You made Bebe ordering me to leave part of your Grand Plan. You were going to keep us at each other's throats and use it to wreck the wedding. That's the lowest, the sleaziest—the most selfish thing I've ever seen in my life."

"No it isn't," Gus told her. "This is."

He grabbed her by the shoulders and kissed her, muffling her protest with his mouth. She squirmed and wrenched, brought her right arm and her fist up between them. Gus caught it and stroked her knuckles with his thumb. Her fingers quivered and opened. So did her lips and her left hand, loosening her grip on the rock. It smashed onto his bare foot like a two-ton anvil, exploding stars behind his closed eyelids.

"*Ow!*" Gus flung himself away from her, against the rough-timbered wall of the garage, his weight on his forearms and his left foot, his right one throbbing like hell.

"Now give me my keys."

Gus opened his eyes, saw Cydney's right palm shoved under his nose and the flash in her eyes. "You did that on purpose."

"It was your head or your foot. Now give me my keys."

"You know where they are. Help yourself."

She slipped her hand into his pocket and fished. This is it, Gus thought dismally, as close as I'll ever get to Cydney Parrish sticking her hand in my pants. He felt her fingers close on her keys and sighed.

"Well now," drawled a deep and lazy Ozark voice. "I do believe this is the most intrestin' stickup position I've seen in some time."

Cydney whipped her chin around and blinked. Gus watched her gaze climb and her lips part. He glanced over his shoulder and nodded at Elvin Cantwell, Crooked Possum's one and only cop.

"Morning, Sheriff Cantwell."

"Mornin', Gus." The Sheriff nodded. "Mornin', ma'am."

Cydney just stared at him, all six feet six inches of him, all 275 pounds of him in starched tan khakis. Elvin stood with one hip cocked like John Wayne, fingers spread on the polished gun belt buckled around his waist. He had small, dark brown eyes, a headful of glossy black hair under his tipped-back Mountie hat and a toothpick stuck in his mouth.

"I said mornin', ma'am," he repeated, touching the brim of his hat.

Cydney didn't say anything, just blinked at him.

"Okeydokey." Elvin nodded to her, then at Gus. "Who might your purty little assailant be, Gus?"

"Oh, I'm not assailing Mr. Munroe, Sheriff. I'm assaulting him." Cydney picked up the rock and showed it to him. "With this."

"What are you *doing*?" Gus hissed at her, but she ignored him.

"Mmm-hmm." Elvin nodded. "And why might that be, Miss—?"

"Cydney Parrish." She shifted the rock to her left hand, stepped forward and shook hands with Elvin, her tiny little palm disappearing into his giant paw. "Lovely to meet you, Sheriff."

"Pleasure for me, too, ma'am, but I need to tell you 'fore

you say any more that you got the right to keep silent, that anything you say—"

"Elvin, wait a minute." Gus hopped around on his left foot, eased his weight onto his right, sucked air between his teeth but managed to stand straight. Shaky but straight. "Miss Parrish was reaching into my pocket for her car keys. She was not assaulting me."

"Yes I was." Cydney stuck her left arm out, turned her hand over and opened her fingers. The rock fell like a bullet and thunked into Gus' right foot. He felt something crunch and howled, tried to grab his foot and keeled over on his side in the wet grass. "Just like that. That's exactly how I did it."

"Mighty nice recreation," Elvin said. He meant re-creation, but he pronounced it without the hyphen, took a step toward Gus and dropped to his heels beside him, his gun belt creaking. "You okay, Gus?"

"Just peachy, Elvin," he croaked.

"Hang in there, hoss." He clapped Gus on the shoulder, poked the brim of his hat back and squinted up at Cydney. "I thank you kindly for showin' me how, Miss Parrish. Now if you'd kindly tell me why."

"Certainly, Sheriff." Cydney hunkered down beside Elvin and wrapped her arms around her drawn-up knees. "I dropped the rock on Mr. Munroe's foot because he kissed me and I didn't want him to."

"Did'ja tell him you didn't want him to kiss you?"

"I didn't have a chance. He grabbed me and wouldn't let go."

Gus groaned. He knew what she was doing—getting even. He closed his eyes and told himself he deserved this.

"Well." Gus heard Elvin's gun belt creak again, opened his eyes and saw the Sheriff looming over him, his shoulders so wide they blocked the sun. "We got us a domestic disagreement here, Gus? If'n so, I got no choice but to call in the Crisis Management Team."

"No, Elvin. No, no, *no*." Gus shot up on his hands, shaking his head emphatically. "This is *not* a domestic dispute."

"Mmm-hmm." Elvin walked the toothpick to the other

side of his mouth and glanced at Cydney. "You 'gree with that, Miss Parrish?"

"I suppose it depends on how you define *domestic*."

"For God's sake, Cydney," Gus nearly shouted, the pain in his foot snapping his temper. "Knock it off and tell him we aren't shacked up."

She wrinkled her nose at Elvin and said, "Not in this lifetime."

"Well then, ma'am. What the heck'er you doin' here?"

"I came for the wedding, Sheriff. My niece is marrying Mr. Munroe's nephew a week from tomorrow."

"Well, ain't that nice. 'Gratulations, Gus." Elvin offered his hand.

Gus took it. "Thanks, Elvin. Help me up, would you?"

"Glad to. Just as soon as you give Miss Parrish her keys."

Gus fished his keys and Cydney's out of his pocket and tossed both rings to Elvin. "Would you mind unlocking the garage?"

"Don't bother, Sheriff. I can manage." Cydney gave him a bright smile and took the keys out of his hand. "Thanks for your help."

When she disappeared around the corner of the garage, Elvin squatted beside Gus, his fingers laced together between his knees.

"She's leavin' for good, ain't she?" he asked in a low voice.

"Unless you arrest her."

"Don't think I can do that. Might be able to arrest you, though." Elvin took the toothpick out of his mouth. "That be any help?"

"I'd rot in solitary before she'd bail me out."

"What the hell'd you do wrong 'sides kiss her?"

"Everything." Gus could see that now and sighed.

"Well." Elvin put the toothpick back in his mouth, flipped it end over end, stood up and adjusted his gun belt. "Think I got a idea."

"Does it include helping me up?" Gus asked sourly.

"Just lay there lookin' feeble, hoss, and lemme handle this."

chapter
seventeen

Intuition told Gus he'd be smart to let Cydney go and give her a chance to cool off. Experience told him he was out of his mind to let Elvin handle this.

"I appreciate your concern, Elvin. Really," Gus said, trying to lever himself off the ground. "But I'm sure you've got better things to do."

"Happens I don't at the moment," he replied, ambling toward the driveway. "Lucky for you, 'cause I got a flare for this sorta thing."

"I have only three words to say to you—*Crisis Management Team.*"

"One li'l boo-boo." Elvin planted himself in the middle of the driveway and hitched up his gun belt. "B'hold the power of the badge, hoss."

When Cydney's Jeep came around the garage, its blue doors tracked with last night's rain and road dust, Elvin squared his shoulders and flung up his hand. Gus wasn't sure Cydney would stop, but she did. Wisely. Hitting Elvin would be like hitting a bridge abutment. She didn't look happy when she got out of the Jeep and came around the bug-spattered front end. She looked like she knew what was coming.

"Yes, Sheriff?" she asked hesitantly.

"Can't say you wasn't justified droppin' that rock on ol' Gus' foot, but assault with a deadly weapon is still assault with a deadly weapon."

Cydney blinked at him, incredulous. *"A rock?"*

"You'd be amazed, ma'am, what can turn deadly in a pair

o' angry hands. I recommend you fetch ol' Gus up to the hospital in Branson. If'n he's inclined to press charges"—*No, Elvin, no!* Gus wanted to shout at him—"I do believe the court would look kindly upon you."

Cydney swung a laser beam, you-slug-you glare on Gus. He sprawled on his back and let his head thud on the spongy grass.

"The court being you," Cydney said. "Is that right, Sheriff?"

"Yes, ma'am. I would be the court."

"And *I* would be the plaintiff." Gus pushed up on his hands. "If I were going to press charges, which I'm not. And I don't need to be fetched anywhere by anyone. I can fetch myself."

Just as soon as he figured out how to get off the ground. Elvin swung around to face him and Cydney peeked past him, took a look at Gus' bashed up and already bruised foot and winced.

"Big talk," Elvin said, "from a feller flat on his keister."

"If you'd help me up, *Your Honor,* I wouldn't be flat on my keister."

Elvin stepped toward him. Cydney opened the Jeep's passenger door wide on its hinges and said, "Load him up, Sheriff."

"No thank you." Gus clasped Elvin's broad-as-an-oak forearm and pulled himself up. "I'm just fine."

Except he couldn't stand on his right foot. Left, no problem—right, no way. He tried twice and ended up clinging to Elvin.

"You're lookin' like a fool here, hoss," he muttered in Gus' ear. "Git in the damn car. It's a hunnard mile round-trip t'Branson. Plenty o' time to sweet talk 'er into stayin'."

"That's your idea? A captive audience?"

" 'Course it is, idjet."

"Load me up, Sheriff."

Cydney was already belted in behind the wheel, the engine running, her head turned to watch Gus hop toward the Jeep, leaning on Elvin, his jeans soaked and baggy-assed, his gray T-shirt streaked with grass stains. Oh what a manly picture he made, said the raised eyebrow and puckered corner of her mouth. Elvin boosted him up into the seat and touched his hat brim.

"Drive careful, Miss Parrish." He shut the door and stepped back.

Cydney trod on the gas. The Jeep shot past Crooked Possum's one and only police cruiser and tore around the circle drive in front of the house, its tires squealing. Gus grabbed the door handle and hung on.

"I did not tell Elvin I was going to press charges."

"Fasten your seat belt and don't talk to me. I agreed to drive you to the hospital in Branson. I did not agree to listen to your lame, self-serving excuses."

"Ah yes, the emergency room." Gus buckled his shoulder harness. "What fond memories it brings of the night we met."

"Ah yes," she mocked, rocketing the Jeep through the first grade in the three-mile plunge down the side of the mountain. "The night you showed your true colors."

"Since I met you my colors are black and blue. And red." Gus frowned at his throbbing right foot. "My big toe is bleeding."

"Here." She reached into the back for the pop-up box of Kleenex on the seat and threw it at him. Gus caught it and said, "Thank you, Nurse Ratched."

He plucked a handful of tissues, raised his foot and wadded them around his toe. The Jeep screeched through the first switchback in the drive, an easy right-hand loop onto the second grade at thirty miles per hour—a close brush with g-forces at close to fifty.

"If you're trying to kill me," Gus said, "you could just let me get out and lay down in front of your truck."

She glared at him but took her foot off the gas. "Don't tempt me."

"I've been trying, but clearly you're above temptation."

"You aren't above anything, are you? I knew you were up to no good. The second you said have the wedding at Tall Pines I *knew* it."

"I *was* up to no good, but I'm not now. If you'd just listen—"

"So you can lie to me some more?" She wheeled the Jeep through the second switchback, this one a left, cutting it so close to the edge of the drive that the pine boughs overhanging the split-rail fence scraped her window. "No thanks."

"I did not lie to you. I told you from the jump I thought Aldo marrying Bebe was a crappy idea. I still do."

"You're entitled to your opinion. You are *not* entitled to scheme and connive and do everything you can to sabotage Bebe and Aldo getting married because *you* think it's a crappy idea."

"You're right. I realized that last night when I read the Grand Plan. Know what else I realized? If Aldo's dumb enough to marry your niece he deserves whatever he gets."

She slammed on the brake, screeching the Jeep to a stop. Gus glanced in the rearview mirror, saw ten feet of skid marks smoking behind the Jeep, glanced at Cydney and saw murder in her eyes.

"You arrogant, insulting—"

"Don't forget selfish," Gus cut in. "And if you want to see selfish up close and personal—not to mention spoiled stinking rotten and a few fries short of a Happy Meal—take a good look at your niece."

"Have a peek at your nephew, Munroe. Good thing he's a millionaire 'cause Aldo doesn't have brains enough to get a job pushing the menu buttons on the cash register at McDonald's!"

"They make a great pair, don't they? So do you and I, in case you haven't noticed. We raised them."

That one took the fight out of her. She stared at him for a second, then swung her head away, her knuckles white on the wheel.

"Hard to think up a snappy comeback to the truth, isn't it? I had the same problem when I tried to rationalize the Grand Plan. I told myself I was scheming and plotting to save Aldo from a fate worse than death. But that was my judgment, and the truth is, I was playing God with people's lives. Yours included, and I'm sorry."

She gave him a dubious frown, a fleck of mud on her jaw, another on the sleeve of her white pullover.

"I don't believe you. I think you're just trying to con me so the minute my back is turned you can start scheming and plotting again."

"No more sabotage." Gus flicked an X across his heart and held up his hand. "Swear to God."

"I don't trust you," she said flatly.

"Give me a chance to prove I've reformed." Gus undid his seat belt and inched toward her. "I want us to be friends again."

"I'm not sure I want to be your friend."

"Then let's try something else." Gus leaned toward her. When she didn't draw away, he leaned even closer. "How about lovers?"

Her eyes widened and her breath caught. He tipped his chin to kiss her, so focused on her parted peach lips he didn't see her left hand until it smacked him in the jaw. His head bounced off her seat, the Jeep leaped forward and Gus fell back against the door, his cheek stinging.

"That's your solution to everything, isn't it?" She shot him a flushed and furious glare, her foot hard on the gas again. "Grab the little blonde with the big case of hero worship and plant one on her."

Gus pushed himself up in the seat and rubbed his jaw. "What?"

"I probably am—no, make that *was*—your biggest fan." She clamped her hands on the wheel and squealed the Jeep almost sideways through the last switchback and the final drop to the county road. "Why do you think I have pictures of you tacked all over my writing room?"

He'd thought she was a nut. He'd asked her what kind of nut—Glenn Close or his biggest fan. She hadn't answered him and he hadn't wondered once since what all those pictures of him stuck all over the wall above her rickety old desk signified. Please God, she didn't remember what he'd said. He'd give anything to forget.

"I'll tell you what you thought. You thought I was a nut." She slammed on the brake and skidded the Jeep to a stop at the bottom of the drive. "Which way?"

"Left," Gus said. "I'm sorry I called you a nut."

"I'm sure I looked like one sitting on the floor talking to your picture." She turned left and floored the accelerator. "I was practicing what I'd say to you. I was so excited that at last I was going to meet you and be able to tell you how much I love your books."

All Gus had wanted from her father at that long ago mystery conference was an autograph and a chance to tell Fletcher Parrish how much his books meant to him. He knew what that felt like, to be let down by someone you admire. Gus leaned his elbow on the armrest on the door and wiped his hand over his mouth. Why was there never an abyss handy when he needed one to open up and swallow him?

"Why are you telling me this?"

"Why do you think?" She shot him a sizzling look. "I want you to feel like the sleazy, self-absorbed prick I think you are."

"That's what I thought. Just checking."

"How dare you sit in my dining room and tell me you don't read manuscripts by beginning writers? How *dare* you!" She beat her fist against the wheel. "My father is Fletcher Parrish, you arrogant jerk. If I want a published author to read my book, all I have to do is call Dad!"

"So finish the book and let your old man read it," Gus shot back. "Don't jump on my case 'cause you don't have what it takes to be a writer."

She hit the brake and slid the Jeep to a sideways halt in the middle of the road. Gus flung up his hands and caught himself on the dash.

"I've got what it takes," she said between her teeth.

"No you don't. If you did your book would be finished."

She made a disgusted noise, wrenched the Jeep straight on the road and stepped on the gas. "Like you know anything about my life."

"I know you've been writing the same book for five years." Gus grabbed the shoulder harness and fastened it.

"I've written six and a screenplay. If you'd put the amount of time into your writing that you've put into being Bebe's personal body slave you'd have finished your book a long damn time ago."

"Just put your butt in the chair, right?" she jeered, rocketing the Jeep up the long, curved hill that swooped down from the top of the ridge to the entrance to Tall Pines.

"That's ninety percent of it." Gus leaned toward the instrument panel and saw the digital speedometer flicking past 50. "Put your butt in the chair and keep it there until the book's finished."

"Easy for you to say. You're a recluse. You don't have a life."

"Yes I do and I value it. If you don't take your foot off the gas we're gonna be airborne when we hit the top of this hill."

She glared at him and glanced at the speedometer, lifted her foot from the accelerator and eased on the brake. The Jeep didn't take off but it bounced going over the crest of the ridge. Cydney kept her foot on the brake until the speedometer fell from 50 to 40 to 35.

"I do *too* have what it takes," she repeated, a quaver in her voice.

"Prove it. Finish the book."

"I will, damn you. I'll prove to you I've got what it takes."

"Don't prove it to me. Prove it to yourself."

She opened her mouth, snapped it shut and glared at him.

"Are you through yelling and calling me names?" he asked.

"For the moment." She swung her gaze back to the windshield and slowed the Jeep at a three-way split in the road. "Now where?"

"Straight through, then bear left."

She didn't say anything else and neither did Gus. The dash clock said it was 10 A.M. The thud in his head and the throb in his foot said it ought to be midnight. He leaned back in the seat, shut his eyes and opened them only when Cydney asked him which way to turn.

His body was one giant ache by the time they reached Branson. His joints creaked louder than the hinges when Cydney stopped the Jeep at the emergency room entrance and Gus pushed his door open. He swung his left foot out onto the concrete walk, his right foot numb but starting to prickle, and looked at the glass doors of the hospital entrance.

"Ten feet," he said. "I used to play hopscotch. I can do this."

He drew a breath and hopped toward the door. When he started to wobble, Cydney slid under his right arm and wrapped her left around his waist. Gus curved his arm around her, bent his head over hers and inhaled a noseful of her lilac-scented hair.

"Stop that." She jerked her head away and nudged him with her shoulder. "C'mon, Hopalong, before you fall and hurt yourself again."

"I'm going to say this one last time." Gus clenched his jaw. "I have yet to inflict pain or injury on myself in your presence."

"Oh, really? Who stepped on the pine needle? Who put his big foot through the wicket after I told him it was there?"

"Who dropped a rock on my foot? Not once, but twice? Who dropped me on a goddamn concrete birdbath?"

"Aldo dropped you on the birdbath. I had your feet."

They argued all the way to the ER check-in, where Cydney dumped him in a wheelchair and stalked off. Straight back to Kansas City, Gus was certain, but she was in the waiting room when he came limping out of ER on a cane three hours later.

He was so glad to see her sitting in a Pepto-Bismol pink chair, her arms and her legs crossed, her left foot hooked around her right ankle. She glanced him a warning, I'm-still-pissed-at-you look until she saw the blue paper slippers on his feet. Then she smiled, got up and walked toward him. She'd finger-combed her kinked-up hair, washed the mud off her jaw and tried to scrub it off her sleeve. Gus could see paper towel lint caught in the white ribbed fabric.

"You waited for me," he said, smiling at her.

"Of course I waited. I don't want your pal the Sheriff to arrest me for abandoning you at the hospital."

"Elvin would never arrest you. He offered to arrest me, but I told him you'd let me rot in solitary before you bailed me out."

She didn't deny it, just ducked her head and tucked her hands in her back pockets. "So how are you?"

"I'll live." Gus leaned on the cane they'd given him in ER and wagged his right foot in its paper bootie. "Little toe's broken and taped. They dug the rest of the pine needle out of my big toe and put Neosporin and a bandage on it."

He left out the jam in his big toe and the joint the ER doctor had popped. If she hadn't heard him yowl he wasn't going to mention it.

"Wait here," Cydney said, fishing her keys out of her pocket. "I'll bring the Jeep up to the door."

She did and Gus managed to lever himself up into the seat with the cane. "Are you hungry?" he asked.

She gave him a thanks-for-asking smile. "Starving."

"Hang a right down here and we'll drive through McDonald's. I'd take you someplace nice, but no shoes, no service."

Cydney ordered a fish sandwich and a Sprite, Gus two Big Macs and a Coke. They shared a large order of fries and inhaled their sandwiches parked in the back of the lot with the engine off and a cool autumn breeze fluttering through the rolled-down windows.

It would be Thanksgiving before he knew it and Christmas in the blink of an eye. Every year at Advent, Aunt Phoebe had invited the whole of Crooked Possum to Tall Pines for smoked turkey, oyster stuffing and mincemeat pie. Mamie Buckles always brought a pint of Jim Beam to spike the eggnog.

Gus missed that blow-your-doors-off punch and Aunt Phoebe nagging him to put up lights and the tree and hang wreaths on the mantels. He even missed ducking the mistletoe and Elvin's sister Louella. So much that his throat closed and he couldn't finish his second Big Mac.

Since Aunt Phoebe died, he and Aldo had spent Thanksgiving and Christmas eating Boston Market turkey and watching football. This year Aldo and Bebe were flying to Cannes to spend Christmas with Fletcher Parrish—his treat—and Gus would be alone.

Cydney collected the sandwich wrappers, napkins and his blue paper booties and slid out of the Jeep. Gus watched her walk to a close-by trash can and wondered what she'd be doing on Christmas. Knowing Georgette, there'd be a big family dinner and—Wait a minute. What had Cydney told him? Herb was a nice guy, but she'd be surprised if Gus got an invitation to the wedding, surprised if Georgette married him on Christmas Eve. That was it. That lifted his spirits. He'd see Cydney at Herb and Georgette's wedding. Maybe she'd forgive him by then.

Why should she, Munroe? his inner voice asked. *You've never forgiven Fletcher Parrish for cutting you dead.*

Gus scowled. Cydney stuffed the trash in a can and started back to the Jeep. Parrish brushing him off was one thing, but calling him a "no-talent pretty boy" was fightin' words. Cydney ducked her head, caught the cuff of her sleeve in her fingers and plucked at her hair. Gus smiled. She'd done the same thing Monday night when he'd caught her talking to his picture. He made her nervous, but did he make her hot? In her kitchen Tuesday night, yeah, baby, but now? Gus doubted it, but he would do just about anything—including forgiving her father—if only she'd forgive him.

"Look, they're hiring." He nodded at a banner stretched across the window when Cydney got in behind the wheel. "I'll tell Aldo."

Gus smiled at her but she didn't smile back, just started the engine and drove to the exit. "Which way?"

"Depends on where you're going."

She blinked at him. "Back to Tall Pines."

"Left." When she made the turn, Gus asked, "And from there?"

"Up to my room to write a book." She glanced at him, chin

up and eyes glinting. "Unless you want me to leave because I broke your toe."

"Are you going to yell at me some more?"

"I don't know." She frowned, not at him but at the traffic snarled ahead of the Jeep. "I haven't decided."

"Take the next right," Gus said, and Cydney did when the Jeep crept up to the intersection. "Is this the way we came in?"

"Nope, it's the back way. Branson was just a berg in the sticks till Nashville moved north. Now the roads are two-lane parking lots."

It was also a shortcut to Tall Pines that took fifteen minutes off the almost hour trip. Gus sat sideways in his seat with his legs stretched toward the console, telling Cydney where to turn and which way. She didn't so much as nod. Clearly she had nothing to say to him and didn't want to be anywhere near him. Every time Gus nudged his left knee closer to the console Cydney edged closer to the door. She kept frowning, like she had a headache. Maybe she was trying to think of a worse name to call him than a sleazy, self-absorbed prick.

It was 2:37 P.M. when the Jeep swung off the two-lane county blacktop and up the drive to Tall Pines. Cydney looked weary, her eyes smudged with dark circles in the deep shade cast by the pines.

"I'd like you to come up to my office," Gus said, "and watch me delete the Grand Plan to Wreck the Wedding."

"What difference will that make? It'll still be in your head."

"Call it an act of contrition."

"I think the only reason you're sorry is because I caught you."

"I'm sorry I hurt you. I never meant that."

"But you meant to hurt Bebe and Aldo." She steered the Jeep through the first switchback and glared at him. "You meant to break them up and break their hearts."

"I meant to stop this mad rush to get married in a week."

"Then why don't you freeze Aldo's trust fund? That's what you intended to do Monday night when you barged into my house."

"I didn't intend anything. I simply lost my temper and jumped in the car and drove to Kansas City."

"With the codicil to your brother's will in your pocket." She shot him a gimme-a-break look. "Sounds like intent to me."

Gus sighed and rubbed a hand through his hair. "How can I explain this so you'll understand?"

"You can't, so stop trying. You haven't said or done one thing since I met you that wasn't aimed at trying to stop this wedding."

"I just want Aldo and Bebe to wait a few months, that's all."

"I'll bet you do." She shot him another glare midway up the second grade. "It'll give you more time to plot and scheme to break them up."

"I am not trying to break them up," Gus insisted. "If Aldo and Bebe still want to get married in six months I won't stand in their way."

She stepped on the brake, slamming the Jeep to a stop that snapped Gus' neck. He whipped his head toward her just as she flung herself at him over the console, fire in her eyes and a twitch in her clenched jaw.

"You aren't going to stand in their way now. If you do one more thing, one tiny little thing to screw up this wedding any worse than it already is, I'll—"

"You'll what? Drop another rock on my foot? Threaten me with a croquet wicket? Come after me with a birdbath?"

A horn blew behind them, startling Gus and Cydney around in their seats—so quickly they almost bumped heads—to look out the Jeep's back window at Herb's white Cadillac. Georgette and Herb waved.

"Oh hell. They were supposed to be gone all day." Cydney waved back, straightened behind the wheel and stepped on the gas. "What's happened now?"

"Flat tire," Herb explained when he parked the Cadillac beside the Jeep and he and Gus opened their doors at the same time. "Took the Auto Club three hours to find us, so we just had lunch in Branson."

"Too bad," Gus said, levering himself out of the Jeep with his cane.

"Not the end of the world," Herb replied cheerfully as he walked around the Cadillac to open the passenger door. "Just a flat tire."

"We'll try for Eureka Springs tomorrow." Georgette rose out of the car, took a look at Gus over the dusty white roof and raised her sunglasses. "Good heavens, Angus. What have you done to yourself?"

"Uh, well, Mother," Cydney began, coming around the back end of the Jeep. "It's a long story, but the upshot is—"

"I broke my toe running for the alarm," Gus cut in. "The power surged when it came on and set the damn thing off. Cydney was kind enough to drive me to Branson to have my foot x-rayed."

"Well, come inside." Georgette gestured for him to follow her and Herb up the porch steps. "I'll fix you an ice bag."

When they disappeared through the front doors, Gus turned toward Cydney. "What is it with you people and ice bags?"

"You didn't have to lie for me." She leaned against the Jeep's tailgate, glaring at him. "I'd rather tell the truth and let my mother kill me."

"I did trip up the foyer steps. I can't prove it but I did. For all you or I or the radiologist know, that's when I broke my toe. And for the last time, I don't lie. But if I did, I sure as hell wouldn't for someone who thinks I'm a sleazy, self-absorbed prick."

"Do you want me to watch you delete the Grand Plan to Wreck the Wedding or not?"

"You bet I do."

"Then let's go. I've got a book to write."

Gus didn't need the cane going up the stairs, he had the banister to hang on to, and he managed to hobble across his office to his big blue leather swivel chair. Cydney perched one hip on the corner of his desk and watched over his shoulder while he performed the keystrokes to send the Grand Plan to the recycle bin. He poised the track ball over Yes to confirm and glanced at her.

"Care to do the honors?"

She shook her head. "You wrote it, you delete it."

Gus did, then followed the file to the trash bin. "Last chance," he taunted. "Sure you don't want a copy to show Georgette?"

"Oh, you'd love that, wouldn't you? My mother would pack Bebe out of here so fast it would make her head swim." She crossed her arms and tilted her head at him. "I'm surprised you didn't think of it."

Gus wished to hell he had. This was twice—*twice*—she'd seen a perfectly brilliant solution to ridding Aldo of Bebe Parrish, one that had gone right over his head. Too bad he was a sleazy, self-absorbed prick of his word and he'd sworn off sabotage. He clicked the file and Delete, sighed as the Grand Plan vanished into cyberspace, then swiveled his chair around to look at Cydney.

"Your thought processes absolutely amaze me," he said. "How do you think of these things?"

"Easy." She smiled and tapped her temple. "I've got what it takes."

chapter eighteen

The sleazy, self-absorbed prick could always rewrite the Grand Plan, but since he hadn't thought of giving it to her mother and she had, Cydney doubted that he would. What a dipstick. Sitting up there in his Ivory Tower with a bomb in his hands and too stupid to light the fuse.

How did he ever plot his way through a book?

If they were speaking, she'd ask him. Cydney sat in front of her laptop at the Duncan Phyfe desk in her room, chin on her fist, frowning at the cursor blinking at the end of the one and only line she'd typed more than an hour ago—"CHAPTER ONE."

"Great start, Cydney," she muttered. "Chapter one of what?"

Her mystery-in-progress was five years old and in Kansas City. She couldn't remember where she was in the story—or her detective heroine's name—so she'd decided to start a new book. She was determined to think one up. And she would, by golly, just as soon as she got over being mad as hell at Dipstick and hurt by his betrayal.

"Knock off the pity party, Cydney." She sat up straight and placed her fingers on the keypad. "Butt in the chair, fingers on the keys and—"

"Hey, kiddo." Herb tapped on the door. "Georgie-girl sent me to tell you dinner's ready."

"Thanks, Herb." Dipstick was the last person on earth she wanted to see. Maybe he wouldn't show for dinner, but if she didn't, Georgette would be the next person at her door. "I'll be right down."

Cydney changed into khaki trousers and another ribbed pullover, this one forest-green, and picked her hair out as best she could. She could've washed and dried it twice in the time she'd spent staring at the cursor and feeling sorry for herself, but oh well. She slapped on powder foundation, a little blush and lip gloss. Just in case Dipstick did show.

Halfway down the back stairs, she smelled pot roast. The sconces on the dining room walls and the cranberry lamps on the buffet were lit. So were the candles on the table, gleaming on the Blue Willow china—only four places set—and a small vase full of red and gold zinnias.

"Darling." Georgette pushed through the swinging door from the kitchen with a smile and a bowl of mashed potatoes. Herb followed with the pot roast. "Bebe phoned. She and Aldo are staying the night in Branson, so it's just you and me and Herb and Angus."

Yippee skippy, said Cydney's little voice.

"How went the shopping, or did Bebe say?"

"She's sure we'll love everything she bought." Georgette put the bowl down and looked at Cydney across the table. "W-a-a-ay cool stuff."

"Uh-oh," Herb said for both of them.

"Evening, all," Dipstick said, limping into the room in his stockinged feet without his cane.

He'd been in the shower—his hair looked wet—and he wore faded jeans and a blue oxford-cloth shirt with the sleeves rolled up. Just glancing at him, Cydney felt a stab of hurt and an ache of longing so sharp it snatched her breath. She pulled her chair out and sat down, angry with herself and wishing she'd stayed in her room.

"You're limping along pretty good there, Gus," Herb said.

"The foot feels much better," he said, sitting down on Cydney's left.

Right on the edge of her peripheral vision, right where she could *just* see him all through dinner. The harder she tried to ignore him, the more aware of him she was—the aura of warmth emanating from his body, the gleam of the candles on his fresh-shaved jaw. He seemed perfectly relaxed and totally oblivious to her, while every word he spoke and every move he made rubbed her sore feelings raw.

When her mother got up to clear the table, Cydney pitched in, rinsing dishes and stacking them while Georgette cut a blueberry pie—something else she'd whipped up and tossed in the cooler—and topped the slices with whipped cream. Cydney made coffee and tea from the kettle simmering on a back burner and offered her mother clean forks. When Georgette reached for them, she snatched them away.

"Pot roast is your best take-no-prisoners meal, Mother. Who are you trying to con, wheedle or browbeat?"

"What's the Grand Plan you and Angus were shouting about in the driveway?"

"None of your business."

"Then I'll pry it out of Angus."

"With a crowbar, maybe. Blueberry pie, no way."

"Bet me." Georgette filched the forks from Cydney.

"What do I win if you can't get him to talk?"

"Like that'll ever happen." Her mother rolled her eyes, slid the plates onto a tray and headed for the dining room.

Cydney followed with the tea and the coffee. Georgette doled out pie and Cydney filled cups. When Dipstick finished, he shifted in his chair to look at her mother and crossed his right knee over his left.

"Delicious, Georgette. I couldn't have asked for a better last meal."

Her mother blinked at him. "Last meal?"

"I figure that's what it'll be after you hear what I have to say. I'm totally, utterly and completely opposed to this wedding taking place next Saturday. I invited you to Tall Pines intending to do everything I could to see to it that it doesn't happen."

Cydney stabbed herself in the lip, dropped her fork and swept her napkin over her mouth. Her eyes teared and she tasted blood. The glint in her mother's eyes said Dipstick would be tasting it, too, in a minute.

"Can I say, Angus," she said tightly, "that I'm not surprised."

"You can say whatever you like, Georgette. I intend to."

"You have more to say?"

"I have plenty to say." So did Cydney, just as soon as her lip stopped bleeding and the feeling came back. "I told Cydney when she came to see me at the hospital Tuesday morning that arranging the wedding around Gwen's return from Russia is backwards. You're all rushing around to pull this off in a week so she won't be inconvenienced."

"No, that's not why. We're rushing around to pull this wedding off in a week because that's what Bebe wants."

"If Bebe wanted to jump off a bridge, would you let her?"

"Oh come now, Angus. That's stretching the analogy."

"No, Georgette, I don't think it is. What Bebe wants, Bebe gets, because you and Cydney give it to her. I know why you do it, because I do the same thing with Aldo. I overindulge him because I love him and he's all the family I have left. But mostly I do it because he lost his father and mother. I try to make up for their loss, just like you and Cydney try to make up for Gwen dumping Bebe and going on with her life."

"Baldly put," Georgette said, her nostrils flaring. "But accurate."

"I tried to voice my objections at dinner Tuesday evening, but you were all so caught up in where to have the wedding, no one heard me. That's what gave me the idea for the Grand Plan."

"Doan dooh dare do dis," Cydney said, her napkin pinched around her bottom lip. "Owl quill dooh."

"What the—?" Dipstick shot her a scowl that morphed into a startled blink. "What did you do to yourself?"

"Tabbed byslef wid by pork."

He fished a half-melted ice cube out of his water glass, tied it in a corner of his napkin and tossed it to her. "There's an ice bag. Put in on your lip and stay out of this."

"Ooh dude lub dat, wooden dooh, dooh—"

"Put the ice on your mouth and be quiet, Cydney," her mother snapped. "We can't understand you."

No one had ever understood her. She'd thought last night that Dipstick did, that they had a rapport going, but he was only setting her up to use her. Cydney grabbed the makeshift ice bag and pressed it to her lip, furious that she couldn't do anything else.

"Tell me, Angus." Georgette laid her arms on the table and leaned toward him. "Would the Grand Plan that came to you Tuesday night be the Grand Plan you and Cydney were shouting about in the driveway?"

"Yes. The complete title was Grand Plan to Wreck the Wedding. I wrote it when I got home Tuesday night. Cydney discovered it on my laptop when she went up to my office to turn off the alarm. She was understandably upset. That's why she dropped the rock on my foot."

Herb guffawed and winked at Cydney. Her mother shot her a nice-job-but-I'm-going-to-kill-you-anyway look, then focused her attention on Dipstick and listened to him tell the rest of the story. Accurately and dispassionately, which surprised Cydney. No lame excuses, no self-serving crapola, just the facts, ma'am, unflattering as they were to what he'd done and what he'd intended.

"I appreciate your candor, Angus," Georgette said when he finished. "I assume you'd like us to leave in the morning."

"Not at all. I'd like you to stay and have the wedding here at Tall Pines next Saturday. I'm still opposed to this marriage. I don't think it has a snowball's chance in hell of lasting—and frankly, I hope to God it doesn't—but I have no intention of trying to stop it. I gave Cydney my word. I don't think she believed me, even though she watched me delete the Grand Plan this afternoon. She doesn't trust me."

Georgette sat back in her chair, clasped her hands in her lap and eyed Dipstick speculatively. "Why should I trust you, Angus?"

"My nephew is the most important thing in the world to me, Georgette. If Aldo finds out about the Grand Plan, he'll never forgive me. He'll never speak to me again. If I break my word, all you have to do is tell Aldo. You won't get that kind of insurance from Lloyd's of London."

Georgette tipped her head at him. "Could you reconstruct the Grand Plan from memory?"

"Most of it, yes."

"Then I'd like to have it in writing, please."

"I thought you might." Dipstick drew a folded sheet of paper out of his right back pocket. "Handwritten, signed and dated."

"Thank you." Georgette took it from him and rose to her feet. So did Dipstick and Herb to hold the back of her chair. "I'll tear this up when Aldo and Bebe are pronounced man and wife."

"Then you'll stay?" Dipstick asked.

"Yes, Angus. It's more than you did for Bebe and Aldo, but I'll give you a chance. Finish clearing up for me, would you, Cydney?"

Her mother slipped the Grand Plan into her pocket, took Herb's arm and walked out of the dining room.

"Well." Dipstick sat down. "That went better than I thought."

Cydney touched her lip. It was fat and numb from the ice, but it had stopped bleeding. She laid the napkin aside and looked at Dipstick.

"I wasn't going to tell my mother about the Grand Plan," she said, *mother* sounding only a little like *mubber*. "Why did you tell her?"

"It was the only way I could think of to convince you that I'm telling the truth." He tugged another folded sheet of paper out of his pocket and tossed it on the table in front of her. "I never throw anything away. I found some carbon paper and made a copy for you."

"I never want to see that again." Cydney pushed the paper back at him. "Once was enough."

"Just look at it, will you?" Dipstick pushed it back to her. "It took me an hour to write it longhand with no mistakes."

Cydney eyed the folded sheet of paper. It would make good kindling for the Angus Munroe barbecue she planned to have when she got home. Burn a few pictures, grill a couple hot dogs.

"If I read it will you go away and let me do the dishes?"

"If you read it, I'll help you do the dishes."

Cydney sighed and unfolded the paper. His handwriting wasn't bad for a man, a little cramped and slanted to the right. She read the whole carbon-copied page and frowned at him.

"You changed it."

"Not much. I just left out what you said to me last night." He smiled and leaned toward her over the corner of the table, his hair dry enough to fall over his forehead. "That was private. Just between us."

He drew the *s* out suggestively, his gray eyes soft in the candlelight. Cydney's heart kicked over.

"Us? What us? We are *not* an us."

"I think we could be." He feathered a circle on her wrist with his fingertip that made Cydney's stomach flutter. "If you'd give us a chance."

"Like you gave Bebe and Aldo?"

He slumped back in his chair and scowled. "Why do you bring those two into every conversation we have?"

"I don't *bring* them. They're the only topic of conversation we have in common."

"We could talk about writing," Dipstick suggested. " 'Course, you'd have to sit down and actually write something first."

"I've written plenty, bub. Two hundred pages of my mystery!"

"In five years. Wow. Burnin' up the keys."

"You're trying to make me angry, aren't you?"

"I'm trying to talk to you about something besides Aldo and Bebe."

"We don't have anything else *to* talk about."

"We could find something. Or we could go upstairs, lock my bedroom door and make love. I'd carry you, but with this bum foot I'm afraid I'd drop you."

In her hottest fantasies, Angus Munroe had carried her up stairs to make love to her. And always, in every single fantasy, he said, "I love you," before he swung her into his arms like Rhett sweeping Scarlett up the stairs at Tara.

"You're twenty-four hours too late," Cydney said, her throat aching. "Last night I would've carried you upstairs."

"I said I'm sorry. I erased the Grand Plan. I gave you the power to take Aldo away from me. What else do I have to do for you to forgive me?"

"I don't know," Cydney lied. "I'm not sure I can forgive you."

Not until she heard the "I love you" she'd spent ten years of her life dreaming she'd hear Angus Munroe whisper in her ear. Cydney felt dazed and faint. How had this happened? How could she have fallen in love with a man she'd never met?

"I'm not going to beg. I might cry but I won't beg." He gave her a rueful smile, got to his feet and stacked their pie plates and cups and saucers together. "C'mon, Uncle Cyd. Let's get these dishes done."

It didn't take long. There were only four place settings of Aunt Phoebe's china to wash and dry and put away in the breakfront. Gus blew out the candles. Cydney extinguished the cranberry lamps and turned away from the sideboard. Only the brass sconces glowed on the walls, soft as stars on a warm summer night. Gus stood behind the chair she'd sat in, his hands resting on the back.

"I can't interest you in hot, wild sex, but how 'bout a couple games of Ping-Pong?"

"No, thanks. I've got a book to write."

"Ah. Your mystery," he said, and nodded. Boy, you don't know the half of it, Cydney thought. "Feel free to use the R & R room. Lots of reference books in there."

"Thank you. I will. Good night."

At the top of the back stairs Cydney stopped, turned around and saw Gus standing at the bottom, his right foot raised on the first step, his left hand on the banister.

"I'm really not a recluse," he said. "It's nice to have people in the house again."

"Is this another apology? 'Cause if it is—"

"No more apologies. I just wanted you to know that. And I want you to know I was only trying to save my family."

"The end doesn't justify the means with me."

"Too bad." He smiled at her. "Good night, Cydney."

She wheeled around the corner into her room, shut the door and leaned her forehead against it, her heart thumping. Only trying to save his family. What family? He didn't have one. All he had was Aldo.

She turned away from the door, toed off her Keds and sat down at the laptop. She had to figure this out, had to know how this had happened—how she'd fallen in love with a fantasy. At least now she knew why Dipstick's betrayal hurt so deeply. In her dreams he wasn't sleazy and self-absorbed. In her dreams, he was perfect. In real life, he wasn't.

Neither was she. She was confused and heartsore and still feeling dazed. She sat straight in her chair and put her fingers on the keypad, moved the cursor down a double-spaced line from "CHAPTER ONE," indented for the paragraph, drew a deep breath and started to type.

> *The worst day of my life was the last Monday in October. It started when I woke up at 7:12 A.M. My clock radio should have wakened me at six, but the alarm was set on P.M. instead of A.M. I'd forgotten to check it at 2 A.M. Sunday when I turned the clocks back from daylight savings time.*

First-person point of view wasn't commercially popular, but she could change that later. She was following the Fletcher Parrish Credo of Writing—puke it up, then clean it up.

Cydney typed four pages and read what she'd written. She was standing in the middle of the dozen eggs she'd dropped when Bebe came pelting into the kitchen wrapped in the bedsheet, staring with dismay at the huge diamond flashing on her niece's finger. Her hands were sweating. She wiped them on her trousers and plunged on.

She barfed up the story—her father would be so proud— through Dipstick finding her in her writing room talking to his picture. Her heart was thudding in her throat and her fingers were so damp they kept slipping off the keys. Her wrists ached and her fanny was numb. Her back screeched like a rusty gate when she tried to stand up. She grabbed the back of the chair and managed not to fall on her face.

No wonder. Her travel alarm on the bedside chest said 2:20 A.M.

"War isn't hell," Cydney moaned, limping on dead, leaden feet into the bathroom. "Writing is hell."

She took a hot, half-hour-long shower, washed and dried her hair, brushed her teeth—being careful of her lip—and creamed her face. Every muscle in her body creaked when she put on her pj's, green-striped seersucker with long pants and long sleeves, but her brain was wide-awake, humming and hot-wired into her story. She'd write a bit more, she decided, but not in the straight-backed chair she was sure Torquemada had used for the Inquisition.

Cydney shut down the laptop and dug for the spare adapter she always kept in her suitcase. She left the desk lamp on and headed for the R&R room down the back stairs and through the dining room.

The moonlight pouring through the living room glass wall helped her find the handles on the pocket doors. She slid them open and inhaled the scent of books. Ahh. Dipstick had turned the lights on behind the bar, but Cydney felt more switches on the wall above the chair inside the doors. The first three worked the chandeliers, the fourth one the spot-lights. She flipped it and soft pools of light came on, gleaming on the book spines lining the shelves built into the paneled walls.

Cydney tried out the couches, like Goldilocks, too hard, too soft, settled on an overstuffed chair with a big ottoman for her feet and a floor outlet for the adapter. She hooked up the laptop, brought up the chapter she'd just finished and read the last paragraph.

I heard the floor creak as if someone were walking across it. Then I felt it and my heart seized. I shot up on my knees, whirled around and saw Angus Munroe—tall, dark and drop-dead handsome in indigo jeans, hiking boots and a navy suede bomber jacket—jam a pair of wire-framed half glasses over a nose shaped just like Aldo's. He grasped the back of my old desk chair and leaned over it to take a closer look at the photos on my corkboard. That's when I wished I were dead.

No punch, her father would say. No hook. Hmmm. She'd make a cup of tea and think about it.

While the water boiled, Cydney ate a chicken leg left over from last night. It was almost 3:30 in the morning and she was starving. While her tea steeped, she ate a piece of blueberry pie. Then she rinsed the plate, poured her tea and went back to the R&R room, sat on the ottoman with the laptop on her knees, deleted *That's when I wished I were dead* and typed what Dipstick had said to her.

"My God. They are pictures of me. They're all pictures of me." Angus Munroe, my idol, the man of my dreams, yanked off his glasses and whipped his head toward me. "What kind of a nut are you?"

A darn good hook, even if she did say so herself. Cydney smiled, satisfied, and rubbed her arms. She had gooseflesh beneath her pj sleeves and her bare feet felt like ice. She yawned—she shouldn't have eaten—chafed her arms and got up to look at the books.

Dipstick's amazing collection of mysteries didn't surprise her. He had all of Ian Fleming and Alistair MacLean—and every one of her father's twenty-six books, in hardcover. She'd brought her camera so she could photograph the wedding. She'd take a picture of the shelf devoted to Fletcher Parrish in the no-talent pretty boy's library and FedEx it to her father. It would cost her a fortune, but it would be worth every penny. Then she'd call him and give him the raspberry long distance.

She found the slew of research tomes Dipstick had mentioned and a ton of books on sports, mostly baseball, and three trophies used as bookends. Little golden gloves with grass-stained balls tucked in the metal pockets, dated 1979, 1980 and 1981, all inscribed to Gus Munroe, second baseman. State tournament wins from high school, but no college trophies. Cydney wondered about that, then remembered what Dipstick had told her. He'd had Aldo since he was nineteen. How sad that he'd had to give up baseball. Cydney wondered what else he'd had to give up and if he'd resented it.

She felt a draft and shivered, heard something rattle and glanced toward the end of the room where Aunt Phoebe's grand piano sat with the lid down in the alcove walled by windows, gleaming in the half dark like a whale breaking the surface in a moonlit ocean. There were no spotlights in the alcove, but there was a floor lamp Cydney switched on.

The piano lid was covered with a paisley shawl and dozens of framed photographs. Baby pictures of Aldo with his palomino hair. Childhood pictures of two skinny, bony-jointed boys with dark hair and eyes, bats and gloves and buzz cuts, fishing poles and Christmas presents, scraped chins and birthday cakes, gaps in their teeth, and later, braces. Gus and his brother Artie, Cydney guessed.

Angus Munroe, the man who scowled most of the time and rarely smiled, who'd taken her breath away when he'd leaned against her Jeep and grinned at her yesterday, mugged and laughed and made faces at the camera. He looped his stick-thin arms around his brother, stood behind him and stuck two fingers up behind his head.

He was a little more subdued, but not much, in snaps with a tall, dark-haired man who looked like he'd spit both boys. Dipstick's father, Cydney guessed. There were pictures of his mother, a classy-looking brunette. With her boys and strings of fish; in a halter-top and shorts, squirting them with a hose and laughing; in a formal pose, wearing a sweater with a fur collar and her sons stair-stepped in front of her in suits and ties.

On the rim above the closed keyboard there were four more frames. Cydney sat down on the bench, turned on the light clipped to the music stand and felt her heart start to crack.

On Tall Pines' front porch, Munroe and Aldo—with a mouthful of braces—stood with their arms around a small, plump woman with bright red hair, pearls at her ears and her throat and a smile that crinkled her whole face. Aunt Phoebe. In a second photo, she sat at this piano in rolled-up jeans and sneakers, banging on the keys while a seven- or eight-year-old Aldo danced, wearing a white glove, sunglasses and a red jacket with gold-spangled epaulets.

A third photo of a wedding and a sylph-thin bride with a garland of roses in Aldo's white-blond hair. Her groom, Artie grown up and a ringer for Gus, stood behind her with his arms around her waist, his cheek pressed to her temple. Someone had clipped the corner of a napkin and tucked it under the glass. In gold script it read—"Artie and Bethany Munroe, June 10, 1975." At the top in blue crayon, written in a child's block-printed hand, it read—"Mommy and Daddy Getting Married."

The fourth photo was a snapshot in a small gold frame. Artie and Bethany, smiling and holding their maybe three-year-old son between them. Aldo laughing, his fat little arm outstretched, his stubby fingers reaching for the camera. In red crayon—"I Love You Mommy. I Love You Daddy. Love Aldo."

Cydney's eyes swam with tears. This was Gus' family—these pictures. This was what he'd tried to save, the plump little toddler with his mother's white-blond hair and blue eyes.

Oh God. And she'd told him the end didn't justify the means.

Cydney bent her arms on the music stand, buried her head in the crook of her elbow and sobbed.

chapter
nineteen

That's where Gus found her, flung over the piano in her pajamas, sound asleep with her head pillowed on her folded arms.

It was 6:15. He'd wakened in his boxer shorts and goose bumps, shivered out of bed into his office and looked out the window at the frost silvering the back lawn. He'd pulled on sweatpants, socks and a T-shirt and went down to the basement to check the pilot light before he turned on the furnace. He'd seen the pocket doors ajar, stepped into the R&R room and found Cydney slumped over the piano.

How could she sleep like that? Gus turned off the spotlights and started across the room to turn off the floor lamp, favoring his taped-up foot just a bit. Her laptop was plugged into the floor outlet next to the brown corduroy chair. A cup of tea, cold and filmy, sat on the floor next to the ottoman where the laptop sat humming away on screen save.

It was tempting, but reading what Cydney had written would be like going through her purse. He *should* pick up the cup. The way his luck was running, he'd forget it was there, kick it over, slip on spilled tea, and break his neck. So Gus picked up the cup and leaned toward the table next to the chair to put it down. He nudged the ottoman with his knee as he did and the laptop blinked off screen save. Imagine that.

He smiled and dropped to his heels. It said "Chapter 4" in the upper left corner of the top task bar. That's all he had a chance to read—peering and squinting at the LCD screen because his glasses were upstairs on his desk—before the piano bench creaked and he shot to his feet.

Cydney sighed, drew a breath—and snored. Once, softly,

her lips parted and peach-kissed even in sleep, a little blue welt on her bottom lip where she'd "tabbed byself wid by pork." Gus switched off the floor lamp and eased onto the end of the bench. Cydney stirred and snored again.

According to Aunt Phoebe, who'd snored like a freight train, ladies do not snore—ladies breathe deeply. So did Gus, content to just sit here and watch Cydney sleep. But it was cold, the furnace had just kicked on—he could smell dust burning off the vents—and her bowed-back sprawl over the piano couldn't be good for her spine.

He slid off the bench, just in case she woke up swinging, leaned over her and laid a hand on her shoulder. "Cydney. Cydney, wake up."

Her eyes opened, her head lifted and she blinked at him.

"Gus," she said, her voice a foggy croak. "Oh Gus."

She grabbed a handful of his T-shirt, pulled his head down and kissed him, her mouth slack but mostly on the mark. Gus fixed that with a quick slant of his head and pulled her up on her knees on the piano bench. He wrapped her in his arms, felt hers lock around his neck and her breasts moosh against his chest. Her nipples were hard. God, what a great way to start the day.

She curled her fingers in his hair, broke the kiss and looked at him, a luminous, wide-eyed smile on her face.

"Are you dreaming," Gus asked her. "Or am I?"

"I'm apologizing." She nodded at the Family Gallery, a glitter of gold and silver frames in the chilly morning sun slanting across the piano. "I didn't understand about your family, but I do now."

"Feeling sorry for Gus the Little Orphan Boy?"

"Oh no. I only meant—"

"It's okay, really. If I'd known, I would've pulled that rabbit out of my hat a lot sooner, that's all."

She laughed and bumped her forehead against his chin. Gus pressed a kiss between her eyebrows. She sighed. He drew a breath of her lilac-scented hair. Over her head he could see Artie standing next to Beth in their wedding photo.

It was probably a trick of the light, but he could've sworn his brother winked at him.

"My room or yours?" Gus murmured in her ear.

"What time is it?"

"Pushing seven, probably."

"My mother's feet will hit the floor any second. Your room. Tonight." She scraped a fingertip that made him shiver across his whiskered chin. "Don't shave."

"I'll throw my razor away."

He kissed her gently, mindful of her lip, and rubbed his hands up and down her spine. She made an oooh-ahhh noise in her throat and laid her head on his shoulder.

"*Ohhh* that feels good."

"I'll give you a massage." He'd give her the moon, Gus thought, the sun, the moon and all the stars in heaven. "Full body. Twice."

She made another oooh-ahhh noise and a purr of pleasure when he kneaded the small of her back.

"If you keep that up I'll be asleep in a minute."

"Maybe you should go to bed for a while. Rest up for tonight."

"I think I will." She drew away from him, stifling a yawn and wincing. "My back is killing me. How do you sit at a computer all day long?"

"I take breaks." Gus cupped her elbows and helped her off the bench, glanced at her laptop and breathed a sigh of relief. It was back on its teddy bear screen save. "I exercise and I don't sleep on pianos."

"Ah." She braced her hands on the small of her back and stretched. "That's what I did wrong."

She looked so damn cute hobbling over to the brown corduroy ottoman in her wrinkled green pajamas, her muscles so stiff she snapped, crackled and popped like a Rice Krispy. Gus let her shut down the laptop and unplug the adapter, then took it from her, tucked it under one arm and looped the other one around her.

"C'mon, old poop. Let me help you to your walker."

"Oh God, I feel like I need one," she groaned, leaning into him.

"Take a hot shower to loosen up those muscles. Sleep on your back with a pillow doubled under your knees." Gus walked her out of the R&R room and through the dining room, to the stairs. "If you're still tight when you wake up, lay on the floor with your feet up on a chair for about ten minutes. It'll help. Trust me."

She slipped out from under his arm at the foot of the stairs and took the laptop from him. "Do you have to do stuff like that?"

"Now and then."

"Oh God." She dragged herself up the stairs by the banister. "Maybe I don't have what it takes."

"Yes you do," Gus told her.

She smiled at him over her shoulder, her head cocked to one side. "Do you really think so, or are you just saying that so I'll sleep with you?"

"Both." Gus grinned and she laughed.

He waited at the foot of the stairs until he heard her bedroom door close, then wheeled through the house and up the stairs, through his office and into his bedroom. His alarm clock said it was 7:10 A.M. Georgette served dinner around six, she and Herb turned in about 10:30. Who knew about Aldo and Bebe. With any luck, they wouldn't come back.

His office was ready-for-inspection clean and orderly. He couldn't write in chaos, but he had no trouble sleeping in it. Gus figured he had fifteen hours to dig out the mess Aunt Phoebe called the Black Hole because stuff went into it and never came out. Like his socks. He had a bad habit of buying more when his drawer ran empty. He dug probably three-dozen pairs gray with dust out from under the bed and dumped them with the sheets down the laundry chute. He didn't think he and Cydney would end up *under* the bed but just thinking about the possibility made his pulse jump.

Down, boy, his inner voice said. *What happened to the old do-as-I-say-not-as-I-do thing? As I recall, you trashed the idea of seducing Cydney Parrish when you shit-canned the Grand Plan.*

"That was then, this is now," Gus said out loud. "She wants me."

God knew why after all the shenanigans he'd pulled. Maybe she felt sorry for him. Poor old stick-in-the-mud recluse, but he didn't care. She wanted him, he wanted her and for the moment that was enough.

He kept Aunt Phoebe's Hoover in the kitchen broom closet. Herb was at the table drinking coffee, Georgette at the stove in slacks and a white cardigan scrambling eggs in a cast-iron skillet.

"Good morning, Angus," she said. "I was just about to send Herb to fetch you for breakfast."

"I figured your excellent pot roast was my last supper."

"The Parrish family doesn't hold grudges, Angus." Georgette gave the eggs a fluff with her spatula. "We don't get mad. We get even." She smiled, but there was a glint in her eyes. "Sit down now before the eggs get cold. I'll go wake Cydney."

"Since she just went to bed, I wouldn't bother."

"Just now?" Georgette raised an eyebrow. "What was she doing?"

"Fell asleep reading," Gus fibbed. He wasn't sure why. "I found her when I came downstairs to turn on the furnace, and sent her to bed."

Georgette frowned. Gus smiled at her, poured himself a cup of coffee and carried it to the table.

"Morning, Gus," Herb said. "How's the foot?"

"Much better. Don't think I'll need the cane today."

"Are you sure, Angus?" Georgette brought the eggs to the table with a plate of bacon and sausage and a bowl of fresh fruit sprigged with mint. "Herb and I can postpone our jaunt to Eureka Springs."

Gus had forgotten Eureka Springs. Oh, what a beautiful morning. He wouldn't have to wait till tonight—he could wake Cydney up with nuzzled, whiskered kisses just as soon as Georgette and Herb left.

"How kind," he said. How fast can you get out the door, he thought. "But I'll manage just fine."

Gus wolfed his eggs and took his plate to the sink, rinsed it and reached for the cast-iron skillet.

"Angus, I'll do that," Georgette said to him from the table.

"Let me." He smiled. "I'm sure you'd like to get an early start."

But first, Herb had to drink the last cup of coffee. "Waste not, want not," he said, settling down at the table to take his time. Georgette insisted on helping Gus load the dishwasher. Then she had to find her sunglasses and take pork chops out of the freezer to thaw for dinner. Herb was still nursing that last damn cup of coffee. Gus was about to yank his head back and pour it down his throat when he finished.

At last, finally, at 8:45 they headed out the front door, Georgette looping her purse over her shoulder, Herb twirling his key ring around his finger. Gus herded them across the porch, down the steps and across the drive to Herb's dusty and dew-covered white Cadillac.

"Oooh, it's chilly." Georgette rubbed her arms beneath her short sleeves and turned toward the house. "I should take my sweater."

"I'll get it." Gus raced inside into the kitchen, yanked her white cardigan off the back of the chair where she'd left it and ran it back to her, his right foot and ankle twinging, but just a little. Testosterone, he thought, was a wonderful thing. "Here you go."

"Thank you." Georgette draped the sweater over her shoulders and gave him a curious, head-tipped look. "You're sure you'll be all right?"

"I'll be fine," Gus said. Just as soon as you get the hell in the damn car and leave, he thought. "Enjoy your day."

He smiled and opened Georgette's door. She started to say something, then shrugged, slid into the Cadillac and reached for her seat belt.

"Happy trails, Herb," Gus said to him over the top of the car.

"Tally ho, Gus," he said cheerfully, and got in behind the wheel.

The engine started and the Cadillac purred away. Gus half expected the Caddy to come back around the circle because

Georgette had forgotten something else. When it disappeared down the drive, he wheeled across the porch, shut the door and bounded up the stairs into the bathroom next to his bedroom. He squirted his toothbrush with Crest, shoved it in his mouth and got a good look at himself in the mirror. His hair and his whiskers were gray with dust. He was surprised Georgette had let him sit down at the table.

"Shit," he muttered around his toothbrush.

He turned on the shower while he brushed his teeth, stripped and jumped in. He washed his hair and soaped himself, his mind and his body on fire picturing himself in the shower with Cydney, his hands cupping her breasts, her peach-kissed nipples peeking at him through soap bubbles. Gus groaned and rinsed and shut off the water, shivered into a towel and saw the adhesive tape from his little toe and the gauze wrapped around his big toe stuck to the drain on the tile floor of the shower.

Last night he'd showered in a plastic bag because he wasn't supposed to get his foot wet. Oh well. He peeled the bandages off the drain and threw them away.

He toweled off, chased the dryer through his hair, pulled on a pair of purple silk boxers and the knee-length velour robe Aldo had given him for Christmas. It was striped in mauve and peacock blue and Gus hated it, but it was warm, and he didn't want to be a block of ice sliding into bed with Cydney.

The telephone rarely rang at Tall Pines. Less than a dozen people knew his phone number, but naturally the damn thing rang as he hurried across the living room.

"Hang up." Gus scowled at the cordless phone on the table next to the blue leather sofa nearest the stairs. "Whoever you are, hang up."

The phone chirped again like a cricket.

It could be his agent. His editor. An aluminum siding salesman. Or it could be Aldo. Gus swore, snatched up the phone and said hello.

"Collect call from Gwen Parrish," the operator said through her nose. "Will you accept the charge?"

"No." Gus banged the phone down and wheeled toward

the steps. He was halfway up them when the phone rang
again. He wheeled back to the table, grabbed the phone and
barked, "I said no!"

"Who the hell *are* you?" Gwen Parrish demanded. Gus
recognized her aged-whiskey voice from *60 Minutes*.

A man with a roaring, raging hard-on for your sister who'd
like to reach through the phone and rip out your tonsils, Gus
wanted to say, but shot back, "Who the hell are *you*?"

"Gwen Parrish. Put my mother on."

"She isn't here."

"Bebe, then."

"She isn't here, either."

"Oh for God's sake. Then I suppose I'll have to talk to
Cydney."

"She's asleep."

"Well, wake her *up*."

"I plan to." Gus pulled the jack out of the wall and took
the gallery stairs two at a time.

Cydney didn't answer when he rapped on her door and
called her name. He knocked again, turned the knob and pushed
the door open, peeked around it and saw her sprawled on her
back in the four-poster bed, her right arm flung over her eyes.
A wedge of sunlight from the east-facing window, dappled
with the pattern of the eyelet curtains, sliced across the foot of
the bed and the hump of a pillow tucked under her legs beneath the double wedding ring quilt.

Gus shut the door, went down on his knees beside the bed
and slid his outstretched arms under the covers. The sheets
were cool, Cydney's body soft and warm with sleep. Gus
cupped her to him and nuzzled his way past the buttons on
her pajama top, brushed her smooth, taut stomach with his
mouth and felt her quiver, sigh and curl around him, her right
arm draped over his shoulders.

"Ummm," she mumbled, her voice bleary. "Did I sleep all
day?"

"Nope. It's still morning." Gus raised his head and saw her
peering at him, puffy-eyed, her nose half-buried in her pillow.
"Your mother and Herb just left for Eureka Springs."

"Ohhh," she breathed, blinking and lifting her head. "I forgot."

"I thought they'd never get the hell out of here, but they just left."

"So what are you doing on the floor?"

"Praying you haven't changed your mind."

She smiled sleepily and turned on her back, kicked the pillow out from under her knees and stretched like a cat. "Come find out."

Gus slid out of his robe and into Cydney's arms. She drew the quilt over him, enfolding him in the warm cocoon of her body. He shivered and she rubbed her hands on his back, rocking him on top of her, his weight on his knees and his elbows.

"Ooh, you're cold," she murmured.

"I took a shower, but I didn't shave."

"Good boy." She kissed his whiskered chin, the scrape of her teeth like the flare of a match on his senses.

Gus pushed against her, tipping her head back and arching her throat. He buried his mouth in the peach-kissed hollow, felt her pulse leap against his lips and a shiver run through her. Over the moan that quivered up her throat, he heard Bebe's voice in the hallway.

"Gramma? Gramma, where are you?"

Cydney froze. "Did you lock the door?" she whispered.

"Uh—" Gus tried to remember.

"*Shit.*" She heaved him off of her, bolted for the door and flipped the lock half a second before Bebe knocked.

"Uncle Cyd?" she called, rattling the knob. "Are you in there?"

"I'm getting dressed," Cydney replied. "What is it?"

"Come see the decorations Aldo and I bought. Where's Gramma?"

"On her way to Eureka Springs with Herb."

"Where's Mr. Munroe?"

"Um—" Cydney glanced at the bed. "I don't know. I just got up."

Me, too, Gus mouthed at her and she flushed.

"Well, hurry up and come see, okay? Aldo!" Bebe called,

her voice drifting away from the door. "Uncle Cyd hasn't seen him, either."

"Oh God." Cydney shut her eyes and leaned her forehead against the door. "I *hate* sneaking."

Gus swung himself into a sitting position on the side of the bed, revved up and ready, his fists clenched on the mattress to keep back a howl of frustration. "You didn't hate it a minute ago."

"A minute ago we were alone." She whipped her head toward him and frowned. "Being alone isn't sneaking."

"Okay. I can follow that." Gus nodded. "It makes sense— sort of."

"I don't know what I was thinking." She rubbed a hand through her hair and sighed. "If Bebe and Aldo can't sleep together, then neither can we."

"I didn't say Aldo and Bebe can't sleep together," Gus said. "I said they can't sleep together in my house. I didn't say you and I couldn't."

"That's splitting hairs." She jammed her hands on her hips. "And I don't believe in double standards."

"I don't, either." Gus smiled and wagged his eyebrows. "But I do believe lust will find a way."

She just looked at him for a second, then hurried toward the big, teal green suitcase lying open on the blanket box at the foot of the bed.

"Give me time to get downstairs and distract Bebe and Aldo," she said, tossing a red tweed sweater and a pair of black twill pants over her arm. "If you use the back stairs, you should be able to get up to your room without them seeing you."

"Cydney, we aren't sneaking. We're adults and this is my house."

"And it's your rule." She looked up at him, an itsy-bitsy-teeny-tiny pair of white bikinis and a lace bra in her hands that made his mouth water. "If Bebe and Aldo can't sleep together without marriage then neither can we. And no, I don't want to marry you. Make love with you, yes. Marry you, no way in hell."

She snatched up her white sneakers and darted into the bathroom. The door shut like a slap and Gus sprang after her. The lock clicked and he spread his hands on both sides of the door, so aroused and frustrated he wanted to bash his head against it.

"What does that mean—'no way in hell'?"

"Keep your voice down," she hissed through the door. "It means I don't want to marry you."

"Not that I've asked you, but why not?"

She opened the door, tugging the cowl neck of her sweater into place. "Do you want to marry me?"

"No offense, but no. I don't want to marry anyone."

"Then stop huffing and puffing."

"I'm not puffing," Gus shot back indignantly. "Huffing, maybe—"

She rolled her eyes and shut the door. He grabbed the knob just as the lock clicked and froze it in his hand.

"All right, Cydney." Gus sighed. "Just tell me what I said wrong."

"You didn't say anything wrong." She opened the door, fully dressed, finger-combing her silver-blond curls into place. "You and I are sexually mature adults. We can enjoy lust and not confuse it with love."

"That sounds familiar."

"It should." Cydney ducked under his arm and headed across the bedroom. "You said it to me in my kitchen Tuesday night."

Ouch. Did it sound that stupid when he'd said it? He turned around in the bathroom doorway just as Cydney unlocked and opened the bedroom door and looked back at him.

"And yes," she said, as if she'd read his mind. "It sounded every bit as dopey when you said it. Give me five minutes."

She slipped into the hallway and shut the door. Gus wiped a hand over his mouth, snatched his robe off the floor and shrugged it on, so strung up on testosterone that his hands shook.

You said it, Munroe, his inner voice reminded him. *You don't drag a woman who bakes macaroons and keeps them*

in a teddy bear cookie jar to bed for a day of hot, wild sex.
You court her, you make love to her and then you marry her.

"Oh shut up," Gus snarled, and stalked out of Cydney's bedroom.

He took the back stairs through the dining room and into the kitchen. The swinging door behind the bar was closed. He could hear Bebe's voice but couldn't make out what she was saying. He tucked the front of his robe together, knotted the belt and eased the door open.

Cydney sat on the blue leather sofa by the gallery stairs. Bebe stood in front of her amid a pile of shopping bags, winding orange and black crepe-paper streamers around her aunt's shoulders. Gus could see three-quarters of Bebe's happy smile and all of the shell-shocked expression on Cydney's face.

"Won't this be *fun*, Uncle Cyd? A Halloween wedding!" Bebe gave the crepe paper a last flip over her shoulders and snatched up a shopping bag. "Aldo and I found all this neat stuff on sale in a party store in Springfield and thought, how *cool*! We can bob for apples after we cut the cake! And the best part, the absolute *most* fun is this. Ta-da!"

Bebe pulled a rubber gorilla mask out of the bag, put it on and threw her arms out wide. *"A masquerade reception!"*

Cydney just stared at her. Yesterday Gus would've danced a jig of joy. Today he didn't know what to do but feel for Cydney.

"You're not saying anything, Uncle Cyd." Bebe's arms wilted at her sides. "You hate it, don't you?"

"Uh—no." Cydney blinked, coming out of her stupor. "I'm just—um—wondering if a gorilla mask will go with your dress."

"Everything goes with pearls, Uncle Cyd. Gramma says so, and I bought lots of different masks. One for each guest." Bebe pulled out another one, took off the gorilla and tugged on a horrid rubber face with horns and warts. "How 'bout this one?"

"Eeeuu." Cydney wrinkled her nose. "What is that?"

"An ogre. I thought it would be perfect for Aldo's Uncle Gus."

"Little twit," Gus muttered, and pushed through the door.

Cydney frowned at him. Probably because he was still in his bathrobe. Bebe turned around, saw him and ripped off the mask. The front doors banged open and Aldo came down the steps staggering under the weight of a huge orange pumpkin.

"Hey, Uncle Gus. Gimme a hand, would you?" He panted. "I've got a hundred and twenty-five of these things."

Gus wrestled the pumpkin away from Aldo and grunted. The damn thing weighed forty pounds if it weighed an ounce. "What in hell are you going to do with a hundred and twenty-five pumpkins?"

"Carve them into jack-o'-lanterns." Aldo grinned. "They're the focal point of Bebe's decorating scheme."

"Just picture it, Mr. Munroe!" Bebe gushed excitedly. "The jack-o'-lanterns lit with candles. Streamers draped from the ceiling beams with fake cobwebs and orange icicle lights. And look at these!" She pulled a string of lights out of a bag, little orange pumpkins interspersed with black and white skulls. "Won't the great room look *cool*?"

"Very cool," Gus agreed, hefting the pumpkin onto the bar. "But your guests might think they're at a Halloween party, not a wedding."

"That's the whole idea." Bebe gave him a you-moron-you look. "It'll be the most different wedding anyone has ever attended."

"Different is good, Bebe," Cydney said, getting to her feet. "But this is your big day. Are you sure you want to share the limelight with a hundred and twenty-five pumpkins?"

Bebe whirled to face her. "You hate it."

"Not at all. Sounds like great fun to me, but I'm not sure what Gramma George will think."

"I don't care what Gramma thinks." Bebe stuck her lip out. "This is *my* wedding. Mine and Aldo's, and yesterday morning Mr. Munroe told Aldo we had to plan it all by ourselves, so that's what we did."

Cydney blinked and swung an accusing glare on him. Oh shit. What he'd said to Aldo by the lake—that's what Bebe meant.

"Wait a minute, Bebe," he said quickly. "I think Aldo misunderstood. That's not what I said."

"Yeah, it is, Uncle Gus." Aldo slouched up beside him with his hands in his back pockets. "That's exactly what you said."

Cydney's eyes narrowed and her nostrils flared.

"You asked what it would take to prove to me that you and Bebe are old enough to get married," Gus countered swiftly. "I said that if you could pull the wedding off in a week without any help from anyone else I'd believe you're old enough to take care of yourselves. I did not say you had to do it all on your own."

"Yes, you did," Aldo insisted. "You said, 'We got a deal here, pal?' I said yes and we shook on it."

"I should have known." Cydney sucked a breath between her teeth. "The whole time you were making up to me you had this little contingency plan in place."

"This is not a plan, Cydney. This is a misunderstanding."

"Did you or did you not say to Aldo, 'We got a plan here, pal?' "

"I did, yes, but that's not what I—"

"I've heard enough," she cut him off, and spun toward the stairs.

"Cydney, wait!" Gus called, bounding up the steps behind her.

She beat him to the gallery by two strides and bolted down the hall. Gus had to run to catch her. When he reached for her arm she spun around and stepped on his unbandaged broken toe.

"Yow!" He grabbed his foot and fell against the wall.

"I warned you. I told you if you did one more thing to screw up this wedding—"

"I'm not an idiot, Cydney. I confessed the Grand Plan to your mother. You can't possibly believe I did this on purpose."

"I don't know what I believe." She ruffled a shaky hand through her hair, tears clinging to her eyelashes. "Just when I think I can trust you, I turn around and it looks like you're up to no good again."

"I admit I dared Aldo." Gus pushed off the wall, his toe throbbing. "But I did it after breakfast, before I swore off plotting and scheming."

"You told me you gave up the Grand Plan *before* break-fast. You said you meant to delete it then, but you dared Aldo *after* breakfast."

"Aldo and Bebe can't plan their way out of a paper bag. That's the point I was trying to make—which they proved by buying gorilla masks and a hundred and twenty-five pumpkins—and I was angry. Bebe was hateful to you when you came into the kitchen."

"I see." She jammed her arms together. "You were de-fending me."

"Yeah, that's it," Gus agreed swiftly. "I was defending you."

"So I'd sleep with you."

"Yes. I mean no. I mean—"

"Go away," she said disgustedly, and spun toward her room.

"C'mon, Cydney." Gus hobbled after her. "Gimme a chance."

"I gave you a chance yesterday." She turned around in her bedroom doorway. "And today you're lying to me again."

"I'm telling the truth and I'm trying to explain," Gus said, taking a step toward her. "If you'd just listen—"

She back-stepped into the room and slammed the door. He plowed into it, saw stars and staggered backwards, stumbled and fell flat on his ass in his own hallway, his hands cupped over his throbbing nose.

Cydney opened the door and looked at him. "Are you all right?"

Gus lowered his hands and gingerly worked his nose up and down and from side to side. "I think so."

"You're bleeding," she said, nonplussed. "Go get an ice bag."

Then she shut the door and locked it.

chapter
twenty

So far, Cydney thought dismally, her acquaintance with Angus Munroe read like an episode of *ER*. He'd suffered a concussion, a cracked nose, a sprained ankle and a broken toe all more or less at her hands, and still he wanted to sleep with her.

Well, he'd wanted to until she slammed the door in his face. He might not now, but she hadn't hung around to find out. She'd dashed a note, grabbed her purse and her keys and ran for the Jeep while he was in the kitchen with Aldo and Bebe, letting them pack his nose in ice.

It wasn't in Cydney's nature to run, but she didn't know what else to do but disappear before her mother came back and strung her up in the great room by the orange icicle lights for giving the shopping list to Bebe. The only good thing about that scenario was they wouldn't have to cut her down— they could just leave her swinging from the ceiling beams as part of the decorations.

She remembered most of Gus' directions and found her way to Branson with only a half-dozen or so wrong turns. She filled the Jeep with gas and ran it through an automatic car wash to scrub the bug splats off the headlights. Then she went shopping. In all the hubbub of designing and mailing the invitations, she'd forgotten to pack something to wear to the wedding.

She found a mall built around a brick courtyard and spent the morning looking for a dress that would go with the paper bag she planned to wear over her head if Georgette couldn't talk Bebe out of a Halloween wedding. She wasn't hungry, but bought a cheeseburger and hot chocolate for lunch and took them outside to the courtyard where red-gold Bradford pear trees grew inside protective wrought-iron collars.

It was chilly enough to raise gooseflesh, even with the black wool blazer she'd grabbed out of her suitcase and tugged over her sweater, but she plunked down anyway at a black mesh table. The cheeseburger tasted funny, but Cydney ate it. She'd blown her chance to make love with Gus, so who cared if she caught pneumonia or ptomaine?

The stiff breeze chasing dead leaves around her feet reminded her of the maple tree in her backyard and the wicket. That damned croquet wicket, the doomed beginning to this whole debacle.

She shouldn't have run out of Gus' house. She should've followed her instincts and never set foot in it. Why had she slammed the door in his face? Wasn't dropping a rock on his foot and smacking him upside the head when he'd tried to kiss her enough? How was she going to face him? What was she going to say to him when she got back to Tall Pines?

Maybe you won't have to say anything, her little voice suggested. *If your mother finds out he dared Aldo and Bebe to plan the wedding, she might string him up by the orange icicle lights.*

Cydney made a face and gave up on the cheeseburger. More than likely, Gus had given up on her. She'd gone way beyond overreacting to what he'd said to Aldo. She realized that now and she wasn't angry anymore—well, not much—but she was mightily confused.

Thursday night Gus thought she was the nicest person he'd ever met. Yesterday morning he'd suggested they be lovers. What step had she missed in that evolution? And why did it seem so suspicious?

Was it her insecurities that made her think he *must* be up to something because he couldn't *possibly* just want her? Boy, that didn't paint a happy picture of her inner landscape.

"It's too good to be true," Cydney said out loud. "That's what's wrong with it. That's what makes it suspect."

She simply wasn't used to too good to be true. She was

used to Wendell Pickering being the best offer she'd had since the last time Gwen held a press conference to tell the world she was getting married.

Cydney sighed and finished her hot chocolate, stuffed the half-eaten cheeseburger in her empty cup, threw it away and headed for the Jeep. The map she'd picked up at the gas station said there were two factory outlet malls five miles off Highway 76, the main drag parking lot through town. Five miles and twenty minutes in gridlock, but she got there, found a sale on sweaters and shoes and a lovely peach-colored satin suit with a tea-length skirt that would go nicely with her paper bag.

It was pushing four when Cydney left the mall. The sky had turned gray with low-slung clouds. The wind was so strong it blew her across the parking lot and so cold it made her nose run. She turned the Jeep's heater on, blew her nose and headed back to Highway 76.

As she inched along in traffic, past the motels, music halls and strip malls crowding both sides of the road, she bent her arm on the door, spread her fingers on her temple and yawned. She felt achy from being up half the night and a headache from lack of sleep pulsed behind her eyes. Snapshots of Gus flickered through her mind, the lush hair on his chest, the long, gorgeous length of him in those purple silk boxers.

In her dreams he was kind, thoughtful and considerate. In person he was rude, arrogant and selfish. That was the problem—her stupid fantasies. She'd expected perfection and Gus wasn't perfect. He was human. Of course he seemed rude and arrogant and selfish. Of course he kept disappointing her. He'd keep on disappointing her until she snapped out of her dream world and accepted him as is, like a used car with no warranty. If it has tires or testicles, Gwen had told her once, it's going to give you trouble.

Cydney was tired of dreams. She wanted reality, wanted to feel Gus in her arms again, the sheer male weight of him on top of her. It wasn't all of her dream. He didn't want to marry anyone, so there'd be no "I love you," and no Rhett Butler sweep up the stairs, but part of a dream was better than none, wasn't it?

You sure about that? her little voice asked.

"No," Cydney admitted mournfully. "I'm not sure about anything."

She thought she remembered where Gus told her to turn to take the shortcut, but an hour later she was lost. Well, wasn't this the perfect end to the perfect day? She'd found her way out of Tall Pines but couldn't find her way out of Branson. Cydney pulled into a scenic overlook cut into the side of a tree-covered, autumn-flamed mountain and spread the map over the steering wheel.

Tall Pines lay west of Branson. That much she knew. What she didn't know was how she'd ended up here, on the east side of town with the sun slicing through the overcast to set in a tangerine blaze across the windshield. The wind buffeted the Jeep on its springs and seeped past the doors, cold enough to make her shiver. Three times she'd tried to get out of town going west and ended up making a giant loop. She didn't see much point trying again and reached for her cell phone.

Cydney dialed her mother and got the out of area recording. Bebe's cell phone dumped her into voice mail. She left a message—noting the time, 5:20—and sat huddled in the Jeep, running the engine every few minutes to keep warm. At six o'clock it started to snow, a swirl of tiny flakes skittering across the windshield. At 6:10 Cydney's nose started to run again. She gave up and dialed the number at Tall Pines Gus had faxed to her mother and Georgette had insisted she program into her phone before they'd left Kansas City.

He answered on the second ring with a curt, "Hello?"

Cydney opened her mouth, ready to admit defeat and ask for directions. Then Gus snapped, "Hel-*lo*?" and the memory of him sitting on the side of her bed in his purple silk boxers, wagging his eyebrows and saying, "Lust will find a way," seared through her heart. She punched end and tossed the phone into the passenger seat.

"If lust can find a way," she said grimly, "so can I."

As she started the engine and reached for the gearshift, her cell phone rang. At last, she thought, Bebe, and snatched it up. "Hello?"

"Why did you call and hang up?" It was Gus. "Where are you?"

Damn Caller I.D. "I have absolutely no idea where I am. Someplace east of Branson, parked in a scenic overlook."

"Stay put. I'll come and find you."

"No, don't. Just tell me—"

The connection went dead. Cydney redialed but the line just rang and rang. Terrific. She sighed, turned on the heater and folded her arms to wait. The longer she waited the bigger the snowflakes got—dime-size, quarter-size—and the more she worried about Gus. The Jeep had four-wheel drive. His Jaguar looked like a skateboard.

By the time the British racing green coupe skidded sideways into the overlook, there were three inches of snow on the ground and the flakes were the size of saucers. The Jag's wheels spun as Gus pulled up beside the Jeep, lowered his window and turned on the dome light. Cydney lowered hers and winced at his puffy red nose.

"You okay?" He called over the howl in the wind.

"Yes. Just cold."

"The roads are absolute shit. Aldo and Bebe took off in my pickup before the snow started, to catch a movie. I'm going to leave the Jag in Branson and ride back to Tall Pines with you. That okay?"

"Absolutely."

"Follow me."

Cydney did, the Jeep's transmission in four-wheel drive and her heart in her mouth watching the Jag slide down the mountain ahead of her. It was pitch-black and snowing like crazy, the flakes the size of dinner plates and piling up fast. She kept the wipers on high and the defroster blasting to keep the windshield clear.

Highway 76 was deserted. So were all the parking lots they passed, except those surrounding motels. Red neon NO VACANCY signs flickered through the snow. When Gus turned into a Chinese All-U-Can-Eat buffet, the Jag spun in a circle.

He straightened it out, parked it, hopped out and waved and ducked into the restaurant.

He's going to yell at me, Cydney thought. All the way to Tall Pines, like I did to him yesterday. She deserved it, but she couldn't face it trapped in her truck with no place to slink off to and cry. If she let him drive, maybe the snow would distract him until they reached Tall Pines. She could hide in her bedroom and make him yell at her through the locked door. It was the chicken way out, but Cydney took it, shoved the gearshift into park and climbed over the console into the passenger seat.

When Gus came out of the restaurant carrying two white bags, she lowered her window and waved him toward the driver's side. He squinted at her through the wind-driven snow, slipped and slid around the Jeep, opened the door and hiked himself in behind the wheel.

"Whew, it's cold." He slammed the door, shivered and passed her the two white bags. "Hope you like beef and broccoli."

Cydney tasted snow on her tongue, hot steamed rice and wok-fried meat. Her mouth watered and her heart ached looking at Gus, his cold-flushed face and his broad, snow-peppered, navy suede-clad shoulders.

"I love beef and broccoli," Cydney said. And I love you, heaven help me, she thought, as she bent over to tuck the bags between her feet.

This close up, his nose looked more red than it was swollen—maybe from the cold—and there was a scrape across the bridge.

"I'm sorry I slammed the door on your nose. Does it hurt?"

"Only when I laugh." He reached between his knees to release the seat, pushed it back to make room for his legs and gave her a rueful smile. "I'm sorry I didn't lock your bedroom door."

The defroster was blowing full tilt, melting the snow on the thatch of hair that was always falling over his forehead. Cydney raised her hand to brush it away, half expecting him to cross his index fingers and shout, "Back!" But he bent his head so she could reach him.

"Me, too," she sighed wistfully, just as the dome light winked off.

The red and yellow restaurant marquee glowed through the windshield, its neon glare softened by the snow piling up on the glass. Gus caught her wrist, raised just his eyes and looked at her.

"Does that mean you won't slug me if I kiss you?"

"It means I might slug you if you don't."

He made a noise in his throat, clamped his mouth over hers and lifted her over the console into his lap. All in one swift, strong scoop, spreading her legs over his without breaking the kiss, his lips cold but his mouth hot.

Hot enough to send her Angus Munroe fantasies up in flames. It didn't get any realer than the hard curve of his jaw and the deep, dizzying throb she felt behind the zipper of his jeans. Cydney clutched his shoulders, broke the kiss and gasped a breath.

"I've been like this all day," Gus said, gripping her hips. "Hard as a rock and ready to explode."

Cydney touched his stop-your-heart handsome face, the one she'd dreamed about and pinned pictures of to her corkboard. He rubbed his jaw against her palm, letting her feel the scrape of his beard.

"The rear seat folds down. And there's a blanket in the back."

"Don't tempt me." Gus slid his hands inside her sweater and touched her breasts, his cold fingers scurrying a chill up her back. "I want you but not in the parking lot of a Chinese restaurant. I want you in my bed, naked and screaming."

"Ohhh," Cydney said weakly. She'd never screamed, not once, in any of her Angus Munroe fantasies. "How fast can we get to Tall Pines?"

"Hang on and we'll find out." He lifted her over the console, started to draw away, then locked his mouth over hers again and bent her back in the passenger seat. When he raised his head, his eyes were dark and smoky. "Your mother called just before you did. She and Herb are stuck in eight inches of snow in Eureka Springs. Aldo and Bebe are staying the night in Branson again."

"Then we'll be all alone at Tall Pines." Thank you, fairy godmother, Cydney thought. "And alone isn't sneaking."

"Mark our place. I'd better drive while I still want to."

He gave her a quick kiss and straightened behind the wheel. Cydney thought she should sit up, but her bones had turned to goo. The imprint of Gus' mouth tingled on her lips. She watched him hook his seat belt and switch on the wipers, put the Jeep in reverse, stretch his arm across the back of her seat and glance down at her.

"You okay?" he asked.

"Oh—fine. Just afraid to move for fear I'll slide off on the floor."

He pulled her up and nuzzled her ear, the gnaw of his whiskers shooting shivers everywhere. "Honey, you ain't seen nothin' yet."

Cydney wrinkled her nose at him and scraped a fingertip across his prickly chin. "Promises, promises."

"I'm the FedEx of love, baby." He caught her finger in his teeth and swirled his tongue around it. "I deliver."

She laughed, pulled his head down and gently kissed his nose.

"I will never slam another door in your face. I won't hit you, pick up so much as a pebble, threaten you with a bird-bath or come after you with a croquet wicket."

"Sounds like a deal. I'll cancel the fitting on my body cast."

Cydney laughed again. He grinned and kissed her. She caught his bottom lip and sucked. The groan he made vibrated through every cell in her body. When she closed her teeth and nibbled, he crushed her to him, digging the gearshift into her ribs and making her head spin. Her cell phone—the one she'd tossed into the seat and forgotten—chirped beneath her right hip, startling her so badly she jumped and bit him.

"Ow!" Gus howled, clapping a hand over his mouth.

"Oh *no*!" Cydney reached between the seats, grabbed a handful of Kleenex from the box in the back and thrust them at him. Her cell phone bleeped again but she ignored it. "Oh Gus! I'm *sorry*!"

"It's okay." He took the tissues from her and wadded them against his lip. "Answer your phone."

Cydney dug it out from under her, switched it on and said, "Hello?"

"At last," Gwen said furiously, the connection crackling with static. "I've been calling and calling. Where have you been?"

"Shopping." Cydney never turned on her cell phone in a mall. She was one of maybe six people on the planet who thought it was the pinnacle of rude to stroll through a department store with a cell phone clamped to her ear. "Where are you?"

"In Moscow, wrapping things up. I called that Scrawny Pines place to talk to Mother—"

"Tall Pines, Gwen." Cydney watched Gus peel the tissue off his lip. It was spotted with blood and she winced. "It's Tall Pines."

"Some jerk answered and said Mother and Bebe were out. He told me you were asleep and hung up on me. When I called back no one answered. I think the jerk disconnected the phone."

"I doubt that, Gwen." Gus righted the mirror, put the Jeep in gear and steered it out of the icy parking lot onto snow-packed Highway 76. Cydney tucked the phone against her shoulder while she clipped her seat belt. "We're having a blizzard here."

"Good. Maybe it'll snow for a week and this wedding will be postponed. *Newsweek* called. They want me in Africa to shoot—"

"I'll shoot *you*," Cydney threatened. "We're twisting ourselves into knots to arrange this wedding around your schedule."

"Oh relax." Gwen's laugh crackled with static. "It's a joke."

"Very funny. Was there something you wanted?"

"Yes. Do you have your tripod with you?"

"Of course I do."

"Good. I lost mine and I need one to take the wedding pictures."

"You're the mother of the bride, Gwen. You're supposed to be *in* the pictures, not taking them."

"So the shots I'm supposed to be in I'll let you take."

"Gee, thanks, but I'd planned to take all the pictures." Cydney figured it would give her something to do besides wash glasses.

"*Vogue* has asked for a couple of candid shots of Bebe's wedding. Photos taken by Gwen Parrish, not her nobody kid sister."

"I am *not* a nobody, Gwen."

"This is *Vogue*, Cydney."

"This is my life, Gwen. *My* chance at *Vogue.*"

Her chance to be somebody besides Fletch and Georgette Parrish's other daughter. And her chance, Cydney realized, to get even with Gwen for a lifetime of I'm-so-superior barbs. It was *perfect.*

"Oh, all right." Cydney gave an exaggerated, aggrieved sigh. "Since it's *Vogue* I guess you can take the wedding pictures.

"Oh—one more thing. I talked to Dad and he said to tell you—"

A huge burst of static popped and broke the connection. Cydney shut the phone off and gave it a jaunty flip over her shoulder into the backseat. She could see it now. A soft-focus shot of Bebe in her veil and gorilla mask. Orange icicle lights and cobwebs draped in the background. Jack-o'-lanterns artfully arranged on the train of her gown.

And the name Gwen Parrish in the photo credit line.

Snow swirled across Highway 76 in a white haze, the wind behind it so fierce it howled and bounced the traffic light suspended above the intersection just ahead like a yo-yo on the end of the string. Cydney had to lean forward and peer over the dash to see that the light was red, just as Gus eased on the brake and glanced at her.

"Why were you and your sister arguing about who's going to take the wedding pictures?"

"Oh we weren't arguing," Cydney explained cheerfully. "Gwen was just putting me in my place. *Vogue* wants to run a couple of Bebe's wedding pictures. Shots taken by Gwen Parrish, not her nobody kid sister."

"So stop acting like her nobody kid sister." The light changed and Gus gave the Jeep gas enough to churn its way through the intersection. "Stop competing. Throw your camera away and finish your book."

"Oh I plan to." Cydney rubbed her hands together. With glee and to warm them up. "Just as soon as this wedding is over with."

"Don't lose your momentum. You wrote four chapters last night. Not that I recommend marathon stretches but—"

"You snooped!" Cydney flung herself sideways in the seat, almost choking herself on the shoulder harness. "You read what I wrote!"

"I did not." Gus made a right off Highway 76. Onto a street, Cydney assumed, though the snow was so deep it obliterated the curbs. He steered the Jeep up a long, drifted hill and glanced at her. "I bumped the ottoman when I picked up your cup of tea and knocked your laptop off screen save."

Cydney tried to recall what she'd written. *Angus Munroe, my idol, the man of my dreams.* Had she written that or just meant to and forgot? She couldn't remember.

"If you didn't read them, how do you know I wrote four chapters?"

"We use the same software, Cydney. It said 'Chapter 4' in the top task bar."

"Oh. Well," she said. But what else did it say? Had she written anything incriminating? Anything like, "Angus Munroe, the man I've been in love with from afar for the last ten years"? "Even so. What I wrote was personal and private and you shouldn't have read it."

"That works both ways, you know." Gus eased the Jeep through a glassy curve, stripped of snow at the top of the hill by the wind. In the rearview mirror, Cydney saw Branson falling away behind them in a foggy, snow-shrouded blur. "You shouldn't have read the Grand Plan to Wreck the Wedding, either."

"Well, I certainly didn't intend to," she said with a sniff. "I bumped your laptop while I was trying to shut off the alarm and there it was."

"Yeah, there it was." Gus shot her a frown. "Personal, private stuff *I* wrote, but you read it anyway, didn't you?"

"Yes, I did." Cydney squirmed. She'd wondered when this would occur to him. "And you're right. I shouldn't have."

"Damn straight you shouldn't have, but I didn't get all huffy and indignant when you invaded my privacy."

"I did not invade your privacy. Not intentionally, anyway."

"I didn't invade yours, *period*. You're the snoop and the coward."

"Coward?" Cydney blinked at him. "How'd I get to be a coward?"

"You caved in to your big-shot big sister. You should've stuck to your guns about photographing the wedding."

"Gwen is an AK-47, Gus. I am a peashooter."

"Only when you're up against somebody named Parrish. Me," he said, flicking his fingers off his chest, "you rip into like an Uzi."

"Well, just you wait. Every little peashooter has her day."

"What are you gonna do? Trade up to a pop gun?" He cocked a snide eyebrow at her, then sighed and forked a hand through his hair. "Sorry. I shouldn't have said that."

"Oh no. Feel free." Cydney gave an airy wave. "I'm a pushover."

"You don't have to be a pushover."

"Maybe I want to be." She flung herself around to glare at him, this time tugging the harness away from her throat so she didn't garrote herself. "Maybe I enjoy letting my family trample me into the ground."

"Aw, jeez." Gus let his hand fall back on the wheel with a disgusted slap. "I'm sorry I said anything."

"You should be. You don't know the first thing about my family."

"I know they're all loony and we can't have a conversation about them without you turning it into an argument."

"You're about to become a part of this loony family, buster."

"Only till the divorce, honey."

"Oh you *wish*. I hope you're around to watch Bebe and Aldo celebrate their seventy-fifth wedding anniversary." Cydney gave him an evil smile. "At Tall Pines."

"Over my dead body," Gus growled, his eyes narrowing.

"Keep it up and I'll see what I can do about that."

"With what? Your little peashooter?"

"No! The biggest damn rock I can find in Taney County!"

"Whoa—profanity. I'm really scared now."

That's when it turned ugly. He shouted at her, and why not? She'd screeched at him. Cydney had never screeched at anybody in her life but she couldn't seem to stop screeching at Gus. Of course her family was loony. Wasn't everybody's? Sure they used her, but he didn't have to say so. He didn't have to make it crystal clear that she was a chump and he knew it. He didn't have to call her a coward.

So she called him a jerk. A rude, insensitive jerk. He called her mother Lucretia Borgia and her father a pompous ass. Cydney said Aldo was a few clowns shy of a circus and Gus said Bebe was living proof that evolution can work in reverse.

"As for your sister—" He sucked a breath to keep the veins in his neck from bulging. "She's got bigger balls than I do."

"I'll take your word for it," Cydney snapped furiously.

He scowled at her. "What's that supposed to mean?"

"It means I have absolutely no desire *what*soever to see your balls."

"I wish to hell you'd decided that before I got us into this mess."

"What mess?"

"Take a look, honey."

He flashed on the brights and Cydney's breath caught as the headlights shot ahead. Wide and dazzling bright on the wind-driven snow swirling across the road in hubcap deep drifts that buried fences and hedgerows. Only the trees overhanging the road marked the dark, narrow edge. Most of them still had their leaves and sagged dangerously low under the weight of the wet, heavy snow.

"Yikes," she breathed. "Can we make it to Tall Pines?"

Cydney thought the slow, grinding *c-r-r-a-a-a-c-k* she heard was Gus gnashing his teeth at her, until she glanced at him and saw him twisting in his seat to look out the back window. She turned around, too, just as an old, suckered elm keeled over into the road, uprooted by the weight of the snow on its fully leafed-out crown. It landed with a muffled *whump*, like a drawbridge falling over a moat, completely blocking the road behind the Jeep and showering the back end with snow.

"That's that," Gus said grimly. "There's no turning back now."

chapter
twenty-one

No turning back from what? This butt-deep-in-snow spot in the road or this stupid, ridiculous argument? Everything Gus said to her was true, but she'd be damned if she'd apologize. She had not started the argument. She'd stood up for herself and her loony family.

Hate to interrupt while you're on a roll, her little voice said. *But calling yourself a pushover and a peashooter ain't exactly standing tall.*

"Oh shut up, you big-mouth know-it-all," Cydney blurted, and winced as Gus swung around and glowered at her.

"Five minutes ago I was a rude, insensitive jerk." He draped his left arm over the steering wheel and flipped his fingers at her. "Now I'm a big-mouth know-it-all. Am I moving up on your shit list or down?"

"I wasn't talking to you." Why not? Cydney didn't care if it made her sound loony. "I was talking to this little voice I have that pipes up in my head every once in a while."

"Well, at least you weren't talking to pictures of me."

"It's a lot easier to talk to your picture than it is to talk to you."

"At least I *try* to talk to you." He straightened behind the wheel, took his foot off the brake and eased on the gas. The tires spun until the Jeep found its footing, then it crunched forward into the snow, blurring in the headlights, it was coming down so fast. "I've tried to talk to you about writing—since you claim to be a writer—but all you want to talk about is Aldo and Bebe and this damn wedding."

"I do *not*—" Cydney stopped and thought about it. Well,

nuts. Bebe and Aldo were her only topic of conversation. Talk about obsessive. *And b-o-o-o-r-r-i-n-g,* her little voice tossed in. "If I'm so one-dimensional, why do you want to sleep with me?"

"Quite frankly—" He sighed and gave her a thank-God-I-came-out-of-my-coma blink. "I don't know that I want to anymore."

"Good. I don't want to sleep with you, either," Cydney replied coolly, amazed that she could sound so calm while her heart shattered. "I think it's an extremely bad idea."

"Oh yeah?" He shot her an affronted, tight-lipped glare. "I thought it was a damned fine idea till you said you had no desire to see my balls."

"You're incredible! How can you sit up straight with an ego that big and that bent out of shape?"

"This ain't ego. I've got the best-looking pair you'll *never* see."

"Send me a picture. I'll pin it on my corkboard!"

Here we go again, sports fans, her little voice said. *Off to the races.*

Hotter, heavier and lots nastier than the first heat. Slinging names and insults while the wind howled, the snow swirled and somehow Gus managed to weave the Jeep around mountain-sized drifts, half trees, whole trees and huge broken chunks of trees fallen into the road.

In a dim back corner of her mind, one that wasn't hazed with anger and heartache, Cydney knew what she was doing— venting her crushed hero worship on Gus. *And who better?* her little voice asked. It felt so good to just scream and let it all out. She couldn't hurt him. He didn't love her. He just wanted to show off his balls and get laid.

Well, fine. They were sexually mature adults. Obviously not emotionally mature or they wouldn't be shrieking at each other like ten-year-olds on a playground, but it was just the two of them. No one would ever know. And no one would care if they ripped each other to bloody shreds.

What an empowering realization. Just this once, she could be as bitchy as Gwen, as selfish as her mother. As pouty and shrill as Bebe, and get away with it because she wouldn't hurt anybody who loved her.

What a rush that gave her, almost as good as the first hot quiver of an orgasm. Which was probably as close as she was going to get to one tonight, so Cydney went for it, gathered up all her hostility and pent-up frustration—most of it sexual—and threw it in Gus' face.

He took it like a man. Every lousy, stinking thing she said to him and accused him of he hurled right back at her. It was wonderful. Exhilarating! Her face flushed and her blood pumped. Cydney wanted to laugh, but she was afraid it would break the mood.

By the time they reached the top of the bluff that swooped down to the entrance to Tall Pines, the veins in Gus' temples were pulsing. The Jeep nosed over the crest and lurched toward the ditch, the road ahead a vicious, glistening mess in the sweep of the headlights. Cydney could hear ice hissing against the windshield.

"Oh goddamned wonderful," Gus cursed, steering furiously into the slide. "Now it's sleeting."

"Be careful." Cydney grabbed the dash, her fingers clammy. She hated ice. Four-wheel drive was useless on ice.

"Calm down. I'm not going to wreck your goddamn truck."

"My goddamn truck is insured. I don't want you to kill yourself or me before Saturday. I want to live to see the look on your face when the minister pronounces Aldo and Bebe man and wife. Oh *no*!" Cydney smacked her hand against her forehead. "We forgot the clergyman!"

"Here we are in the middle of a goddamn ice slide—" Gus gritted his teeth and wrenched the Jeep out of another slither "—and all you can think about is that goddamn wedding!"

"It's better than watching you drive! You steer *into* the slide."

"I *am* steering into the slide!"

"You're *not*, or we wouldn't be sliding!"

"The whole damn road is solid ice!"

"No it isn't. There's a snowy spot right over there."

"Oh for crissake! Do you wanna drive or just tell me how?"

"If you think you can pull over without putting us in a ditch—"

"I'd like to put you in a ditch," Gus muttered.

"I heard that!"

Somehow, with all four wheels locked and skidding on the ice, Gus skated the Jeep down the long, curved slope. At the entrance to Tall Pines he stepped on the gas and sent the Jeep plowing through the grill-deep drift that had blown over and buried the lip of his driveway, shooting plumes of snow out from under the front fenders.

Cydney sighed with relief and glanced at the dash clock—11:15. It said 8:30 the last time she'd looked at it in Branson. A trip that should have taken an hour had taken almost three. No wonder she felt like every bone in her body had been stretched and snapped back into place.

"Whew." Gus blew out a breath. "I don't want to do that again soon."

Cydney couldn't imagine how he'd done it period. She peered into the sleety darkness at the snow-crusted hardwoods and ice-tipped pines slumping over the split rails edging the drive. Ice pellets skittered across the windshield and she shivered. "Great job," she told him.

"Be quiet." Gus steered the Jeep up the first grade, the tires slipping on the glazed-over snow. "It's a long way up and we stand a better chance of getting to the top if I don't have to fight the urge to pull over and stuff a snowball in your mouth."

"That was a compliment. I *meant* it."

"Oh I *know* you meant it."

"No. I *really* meant it."

"So did I." He scowled at her and swung the Jeep around a blue spruce that had toppled into the drive smack in the middle of the first switchback. The wheels bumped over its buried-in-snow crown, spun a little but dug in and churned the Jeep up the second grade. "Be quiet."

"You can't order me to shut up in my own truck."

"Yes I can. I'm trying to drive over here."

"*Trying* is the operative word."

"I mean it, Cydney." He steered the Jeep through the second switchback, the wheels spinning and the back end fishtailing all the way through the glassed-over curve. "Put a sock in it."

"So you drive and I'll yell. Sounds fair to me."

"That's it!" Halfway up the third grade, the last and the steepest, he slammed on the brake and shoved the gearshift toward park.

"What are you doing?" Gus ignored her, pushed his door open and bailed out of the Jeep. Cydney sucked a mouthful of sleet and frigid air and ducked her chin in the cowl of her sweater. "Where are you going?"

He swung around, his dark hair already dusted with ice crystals, and squinted a glare at her through the driving sleet.

"To make a snowball!" he shouted, and slammed the door.

Cydney gaped at him through the window. She couldn't believe he was actually doing this. She watched him grab the side mirror and use it to pull himself toward the front end. He made it and picked his way around the hood toward a snowdrift on the edge of the drive.

A nice fluffy drift full of heavy, wet snow that would pack down great into a big fat snowball that would probably choke her. If she were dumb enough to just sit here and let him cram it down her throat—which she wasn't. She was dumb enough—and mad enough—to unclip her seat belt, shove her door open and follow Gus out into the blizzard.

The wind snatched her breath, the sleet stuck her eyelashes together. She wiped them with her sleeve and saw Gus, leaning one hand on the snowy hood, making his way toward her. Cydney edged forward, slipped and grabbed the side mirror, the ice-encased chrome burning her bare hand. She thought she heard metal groan, thought she felt the Jeep move. Her head spun and her stomach clutched, but the sensation passed and she told herself it was only the wind howling in her ears. She clutched the mirror and skated up the side of the Jeep on her slick, rubber-soled Keds. She met Gus at the right front fender, her teeth chattering and her nose already frozen.

"Get back in the truck!" he shouted. "You'll freeze!"

"We'll both freeze! I'll shut up, I promise!"

"Too late!" He bent down and scooped up a handful of snow.

Cydney yelped and dove out of the way. Gus came up with a glob of snow, slipped and nearly fell. They both grabbed the Jeep and pushed off its nose at the same time—Cydney to propel herself and Gus to stay on his feet. Which Cydney managed to do until she slid on the ice and fell headfirst into the snowdrift.

She landed hung over the fence, the air knocked out of her lungs and that weird metallic groan in her ears again. She twisted around and stared, openmouthed, at the Jeep sliding slowly backwards away from her, snow and ice crunching beneath its tires.

"*My truck!*" Cydney shrieked, stretching a hand toward it.

Gus grabbed her and yanked her out of the way. She stumbled against him, wrenched around and watched the Jeep slide down the grade, crash through the split-rail fence and slam into a gnarled oak that snapped in half and collapsed onto the roof, showering her with a spray of ice. Cydney spat snow out of her mouth, blinked it out of her eyes and stared at her Jeep, the right side of the roof cleaved and crushed beneath the tree. The windshield was shattered but the engine was still running. Exhaust snaked from the tailpipe.

"My truck," she whimpered, stiff-lipped with cold.

"Stay here." Gus stepped around her and slid down the hill, caught himself on the side mirror and opened the driver's door.

He leaned inside and turned off the engine, shut the door and started back to her with the bags of beef and broccoli. He slogged up the edge of the drive where the snow gave him traction, in the navy suede hiking boots she'd brushed mud off of the other night. He stopped in front of her and held out her keys. She closed them, still warm from hanging in the ignition, in her frostbitten fingers and looked up at Gus.

"How did that happen?"

"My fault." He winced at her, his eyebrows spiky with ice. "The gearshift wasn't quite in park."

Not quite in park. That meant reverse or neutral. Cydney sucked in a breath and hit him. Square in the rock hard, ripped gut she'd glimpsed when he'd keeled over in her dining room like the oak tree had just keeled over on her truck. She didn't hurt him—she was a peashooter, after all—but he made a surprised little "Oompf."

"*You wrecked my truck!*" she screamed over the wind.

"If you'd kept your mouth shut like I asked—"

"If you'd used the hand brake this wouldn't have happened!"

"If I'd locked your bedroom door *none* of this would've happened!"

"Exactly! It's all your fault!"

"I just said it was!"

"Well finally! We agree on something!"

The wind slapped her in the face as she spun away, and knocked her back into Gus. Cold as it was, she felt a seep of warmth from his body and wanted to stay there, pasted against him, while the blizzard howled around them.

"Take the bags," he said in her ear, "and hang on to me."

"I'd rather *crawl*!"

"Fine—then crawl!" He sidestepped her and strode past her, his cleated boots breaking the crust on the snow piled up along the drive.

She almost had to crawl to make headway against the sleet whipping her around like a wind sock. She could barely see, but she floundered behind Gus, following his tracks. The second time she fell flat on her butt with her legs splayed and a jolt of pain shooting up her tailbone, he wound his fist in the cowl of her sweater, hauled her up and dragged her— stumbling, falling and spluttering with fury—toward the house.

He dragged her all the way up the last wretchedly slick

grade in his 3.5-mile-long driveway. Dredging her up when she fell, tightening his grip like a vice when she slipped, ripping stitches out of her blazer until she could feel the back of it flapping in the wind. When they finally reached level ground, he towed her like a sled; Cydney clutching his arm, her breath coming in sobs, an icicle frozen to the tip of her nose.

Gus pulled her up the buried front steps and across the icy porch, kicked the front door open and pushed her inside. The frozen soles of her Keds melted on contact with the warm pegged-pine floor and stopped her like she'd hit a patch of Super Glue. She whipped around, her breasts heaving, as Gus followed her inside and gave the door a push.

It didn't quite latch and blew open. He turned around to give it a boot, swinging the wet, torn bags of Chinese food within Cydney's grasp. She grabbed them—and when Gus spun around—she threw them.

The cartons inside split and broke when the bags smacked him in the chest. His mouth fell open and he stared at the rice stuck in clumps to the front of his suede jacket, the congealed beef oozing down his jeans.

"That's what you get for wrecking my truck!" Cydney sobbed, so furious all she could do was cry. "And for dragging me up here like a—a bag of frozen hash browns!"

That's how she felt—shredded, diced and freezer-burned—shivering to death in the snow melting off her clothes, glaring at him from under the ice-caked curls hanging over her forehead like crystal dreadlocks. Until Gus swiped a hand down his jacket, flipped beef and broccoli off his fingertips and leveled a livid, hot-eyed scowl on her.

Gulp, said her little voice.

"What do I get for a cracked nose, sprained ankle and busted toe?"

"How about a fat lip to go with them?"

He had her by the lapels of her blazer and drawn up on her toes before she saw him move. Nose to nose in the dark, Cydney's breath caught by surprise in her throat, the snow glowing through the stained-glass panels bright enough to show her the muscle leaping in his jaw.

"I've never been so goddamn mad or so goddamn turned on in my life. The more you yell at me the more I want to rip your clothes off."

"Oh Gus." Cydney flung her arms around him and clung to him, frozen cheek to frozen cheek, stretching to reach him, tears squeezing past her icy lashes. "All those terrible things I said to you."

"Say 'em again." He swung her off her feet, one arm around her shoulders, the other beneath her knees, his mouth barely an inch from hers. "Only this time say 'em like you mean 'em."

"You rude, insensitive jerk. You sleazy, self-absorbed prick."

"Oh baby, that's the one." He closed his eyes and quivered, his nostrils flaring. "Remember that one."

He had her up the stairs, through his office and in his bedroom before she stopped laughing. Before she could draw a breath he had her on the bed, his cold hands under her sweater, his shivery mouth on hers.

"You're freezing," he said in her ear. "You need a hot bath."

"I need you." Cydney locked her arms around his neck, afraid to let him get up. She could say the wrong word and start another fight. He could trip in the dark and break something vital. Like her heart, which he probably would before this wedding was over with, but she wasn't going to think about that. "You warm me up. Right here. Right now, you big-mouth know-it-all."

"Ooh, smut talk." He grinned and ripped open the zipper on his jacket, yanked it off and threw it across the room. "Your turn."

Cydney tossed what was left of her blazer on top of his jacket. His sweater followed, then hers, his boots and her Keds, their socks and his jeans. Last, her black twill pants, so stiff with ice he had to peel her out of them like a banana, following the fabric as he freed her of it with his mouth, touching off little fires where he kissed and licked her.

The inside of her thigh, a long, slow glide along her shin that left her flushed and quivering. The bruised spot on the back of her knee she worried might blossom into a spider vein. Thank God it was dark, barely light enough to see the outline of the bed in the glare of the snow cover gleaming through the big window on the far wall.

Her black twill pants came off at last and hit the floor with a wet plop that made Cydney's stomach jump. So did the flicker in Gus' eyes as he crawled onto the bed with her—hunger, need and just plain want that made her knees go weak and open to let him slide between them. He stretched himself on top of her, raised her arms over her head, laced his fingers through hers and settled in the V of her thighs. The hot, hard pulse of him made her shiver and melt with a moan he caught in a kiss.

Her Angus Munroe fantasies tried to creep in when he rolled her over so he could pull the bedclothes out from under them. *Wait a minute, he's doing this wrong. He should peel you out of your panties first and worship you with his eyes. Can't this guy follow a script?* Cydney wrapped her arms around Gus and pulled him down into a searing open-mouthed kiss that sent her fantasies yelping out of her head.

She didn't want them anymore. She didn't need them. She had the real thing in her arms, the weight of him on top of her again when he rolled her back on the sheets and drew the covers over them. He drove his tongue into the hollow of her throat, arching her head back against a pillow that had magically appeared beneath her.

Heat flared where his mouth touched. Her throat, her shoulders, cupped in his hands while he nuzzled her breasts. His thumbs hooked her bra straps and tugged her nipples free to be kissed and licked while his hands slid lower and pulled her panties past her hips. His fingers feathered her hipbones, his mouth still pulling on her breasts, tugging and sucking while Cydney gloried in the scrape of his beard on her swollen nipples. She held him against her, clutching his hair as his mouth moved lower, flushing heat up from her belly where he nuzzled her curls.

When he rose over her, tracking wet kisses up her torso, she felt him reach for the waistband of his boxers. She helped him slide them off, her fingers brushing his erection and making him shiver as he kicked the boxers aside and covered her with his body, her mouth with his and pushed against her, testing, hard and throbbing.

She raised her knees, wet and ready, and let him slide inside her. A slow, easy slide with a shuddered, drawn-deep breath as he settled on top of her, his weight on his knees, his hands gently cupping her head on the pillow. His thumbs brushed her temples while he stroked inside her. Kissed her nose, her eyebrows, her chin, stroking faster when her hips moved and she sucked his tongue into her mouth.

He was big but he was gentle, mindful of her size and her comfort, stroking fast, then slow, filling her gradually, letting her relax and revel and feel and taste, giving her his tongue whenever she wanted it. Petting her, touching her, snuggling his cheek next to hers on the pillow to gnaw her earlobe, rub his whiskered chin along her collarbone and make her giggle, chuckling deep in his throat when she did.

"Like that?" he murmured, or "How's this?" Kissing her again when she sighed, *"Yesss,"* savoring her, warming her, cherishing her. He slowed his pace, then sped, stilled and rose on his hands and looked at her with deep, dark eyes, a pulse hammering hard in his throat, his hair all over his head in spikes she'd put there with her tugging and pulling.

"Ready, babe?"

"Past ready, you arrogant, *pushy*—"

"Oh honey, that's the word." He drove into her, lifting her knees and her hips higher, arching her head back, thrusting and building heat and heat and more heat till it exploded in the pit of her and she clutched his hips and—

Screamed. Actually *screamed* as the mind-bursting climax ripped through her. She felt it tear up her throat, in her breasts, even in her nipples. It was wondrous. So glorious she screamed again as Gus locked his mouth over hers and sucked the scream into his throat. His last thrust tore a cry out of him that made her teeth vibrate. She clung to him, let him collapse on top of her and press his forehead to the side of her neck. She rubbed his back, slick with sweat, and felt him shudder, his heart thudding against hers.

"Am I too heavy?" he rasped in her ear.

"No." Cydney wrapped her arms around his rib cage, hooked her legs around his knees and snuggled. She rubbed her cheek in his chest hair, touched his flat, hard nipple with her tongue and felt him shiver.

He raised his head and smiled, stroking her temples with his fingertips. "Then I'd like to stay here a while."

How 'bout forever, Cydney wanted to suggest, but spread her arms out instead and smiled. "Make yourself comfortable."

Gus drew the covers over them and snuggled down on top of her, tucked his arms under her and cradled her, rubbing his nose in her hair, settling her hips deeper into the mattress. He stayed inside her, full and pulsing, her arms around his neck, stroking his hair, feeling his breath slow till he snored, once, softly in her ear.

"He touched me," Cydney sang softly off-key. "He put his hand near mine and then he touched me. I felt a—a—uh . . ."

"A sudden tingle when he touched me," Gus filled in groggily. "A sparkle, a glow."

Cydney laughed at the tickle of his breath on her collarbone, delighted that he knew the words. "I thought you were asleep."

"Nope. Just resting up." He wiggled closer and kissed the side of her neck. "Do you like Streisand?"

"Oh yes. Do you?"

"No. I just remember song lyrics. Now George Benson. That man can play the *gee-tar*," he drawled, sounding like his friend Sheriff Cantwell. "Want to swing from the chandelier in the great room next time?"

"Too high up. I'll get a nosebleed."

"We've got the house to ourselves. We should enjoy it before your loony—" He pushed up on an elbow. "Whattya say we don't go there?"

"Let's don't. How about the bathtub?"

"Great idea." He kissed her and rolled to his feet. Cydney heard a lamp switch click and Gus swear. "Power's out," he said, then she heard a crunch and a yowl, looked over the side of the bed and saw him on the dark, shadowy floor, gritting his teeth and clutching his right foot.

"Oh no," she mewed sympathetically. "Not again."

"Whacked the table when I reached for the lamp." He flexed his toes and winced. "I have *got* to remember to buy gas for the generator."

"Well, darn. I was looking forward to a bath."

"There should be enough hot water in the tank. But no heat." He rolled up on his knees and kissed her. "I'll light a fire."

"You just did," Cydney purred, winding her arms around his neck.

"I meant in the fireplace." Gus chuckled and tucked the covers around her. "Keep warm. I'll be back."

Cydney peered at his backside as he walked away from her but couldn't see much, just the paler shape he made against the darkness. When he disappeared into the bathroom—she caught a glimpse of the commode—she took her bra off and pitched it toward the clothes pile, hunkered down under the covers and pinched herself.

"Ouch," she said, smiling at the ceiling she could barely see.

Yep. She was wide-awake. Gus hadn't left her for dead in a snowdrift. He really had dragged her up his driveway, carried her up to his bedroom and made love to her. Next time she got caught in a blizzard she could just lie down in the snow and die a happy woman.

Oh boy. She couldn't wait to write this scene in her book.

Her bones ached and she felt sore spots in her hips that would likely be bruises tomorrow, but on the whole she felt wonderful. Languid and loved, even though she wasn't. Cydney turned her head on Gus' pillow and gazed at the window, at the pewter gleam streaming through the glass that meant the snow had stopped and the moon had come out. Pewter gleam. Ooh, she liked that. She'd have to remember it. Maybe, she thought, just maybe I do have what it takes.

"You've got what it takes and then some, honey."

Cydney shot up in bed, hand pressed to her heart and blinked at the top of Gus' head over the footboard. The footboard she hadn't been able to see until now. Through its wooden slats, carved in what looked like Southwest Mission style, she saw the flicker of a flame.

"You startled me. Did I say something?"

"You said, 'Just maybe I do have what it takes.' "

"Oh great. Now I'm talking to my little voice *and* myself."

"Don't worry about it, babe." She heard wood snap and watched the flame jump. "I've got one of those big-mouth know-it-all voices, too."

"Really? Do you talk back to it?"

"When I can get a word in, which believe me, ain't easy."

At last, thank God, something they had in common. A weird something, but a common something nonetheless.

The flame brightened through the footboard slats and glowed on the face of a stone fireplace with bookshelves on both sides. It was too dim to see what the jumble of shapes were on the mantel. A couple of baseballs, it looked like, and a Ping-Pong paddle, but she could see the bright reds and golds in the patchwork quilt she tugged with her as she walked down the bed on her knees and sat back on her heels. It was warm at the foot and bright enough to see Gus sitting on the carpeted floor feeding wood to the fire through a partly open black mesh screen.

She didn't feel the least bit shy being in his bed or ogling his lusciously naked body. Maybe because he'd been so tender with her, which was the only thing her fantasies had gotten right. She'd been so wrong about so much else. He glanced at her, held up a cigar and wagged it.

"Do you mind? The only time I want a cigar is after sex."

"Not a bit. Go ahead."

He lit the cigar with a strip of kindling and poked it back in the fire. "In case you're wondering, this is one stale stogie."

Cydney laughed, folded her arms on the footboard and

leaned her chin on her wrists. "The only time Max Stone smokes is after sex, too."

"You have read my books."

"I told you I was your biggest fan."

"Hmmm." He puffed on the cigar and squinted at her through the smoke. "I'm not gonna read about this on one of those Angus Munroe fan sites on the Internet, am I?"

"Heck no. I'm saving this for my memoirs."

"Are you?" He stuck the cigar in his mouth, raised his knees and looped his arms around them. "What are you going to say about me?"

"Well, let's see." Cydney leaned her chin on her hand and tapped a finger on her cheek, making it look like she had to think about it, which she didn't, because she already knew.

She'd say how much she loved him, how much it meant to her that he'd loved her—once, anyway, at least physically—and what a comfort it was to her, now that she was Bebe Parrish Munroe's old-maid aunt with a dining room enshrined in her honor. But she couldn't tell Gus that, so she parked her chin on her hand and gave him a wicked smile.

"I'll say you have the best-looking balls I never saw."

"How can you say that? Didn't we just—"

"The power's off." Cydney waved her hand. "No lights."

"I can fix that." He sprang off the floor, squared himself in front of the brightly burning fire and spread his legs. "Ta-da!"

Cydney clapped a hand over the startled squeak that escaped her and laughed. So hard she shrieked and keeled over on her side, wound in the quilt and howling with laughter.

"Gotcha." Gus bounced down beside her, chuckling, and gave her a playful slap on the rump. "Now you can't say you didn't see my balls."

"Boy, that's the truth." She sighed and wiped her eyes on the quilt. "But I can honestly say our night together moved me to tears."

He rocked back on his elbows, laughing, took the cigar out of his mouth and stretched out on his side next to her, smiled and touched a fingertip to a curl tangled on her forehead. "Have I told you that I think you're absolutely adorable?"

Cydney could see by the soft curve of his mouth and the warmth in his eyes that he meant it. It wasn't "I love you, be mine forever," but it wasn't bad. She blinked tears out of her eyes and told herself not to be maudlin, to be happy and grateful and enjoy this. She snuggled up to him and put a kiss on his chest.

"After our bath," she said, looking up at him through her lashes, "do you think we could try that naked and screaming thing again?"

chapter
twenty-two

The last time he made Cydney scream—or had she made him scream?—Gus' watch said it was 4:22 A.M. It was a Rolex and it lived on the table beside his bed because he rarely remembered to wear it. The next time he looked at it, cracking a bleary eye and peering at the 24-karat gold hands, it said 9:14 A.M.

That was his first awareness; his second, that he was drooling. He crept a hand out from under the pillow and wiped the corner of his mouth. That's when he felt the chill in the sheets, realized he was alone and flung himself over on his back.

A laser beam of sun shot through the window and damn near pierced his skull. He clapped a hand over his eyes until the strobe light in his head faded, then spread his fingers and frowned.

He'd fallen asleep with Cydney cuddled on his chest, her hand wrapped in his on his shoulder, his thumb stroking her wrist. Now there wasn't a wrinkle in the sheets, not a crease in her pillowcase.

Why wasn't she here?

Gus kicked off the covers and rolled to his feet. Her clothes were gone from the pile on the floor. His were neatly hung to dry over the shower doors in the bathroom. The towels he'd used to rub her down after he'd licked her dry were draped over racks. The bubbles he'd used to sculpt her a pair of Dolly Parton breasts while she leaned back between his legs with her head on his chest, laughing, had been rinsed down the bathtub drain. She'd emptied the ashes out of the soap dish he'd used as an ashtray, washed it and left it on the sink and blown out the candles he'd lit on the edge of the tub. She'd even trimmed the wicks.

His bedroom and bathroom looked like he'd spent the night with Aunt Phoebe. Why had Cydney done this? Why had she erased every trace that she'd ever been in his bed?

Time to put his pants on, go find her and ask her.

Gus brushed his teeth and his hair first, wincing at his face in the mirror. He needed a shave—he looked like Sasquatch— but he zipped on a pair of jeans, pulled on a T-shirt and headed downstairs.

He found Cydney in the R&R room, in a beige cable-knit sweater and jeans, curled in the oversized brown corduroy chair. One of the afghans Aunt Phoebe had crocheted in bright stripes of leftover yarn covered her drawn-up knees. He could see her toes curled in beige socks through the fringed hem. A big red mug sat on the table, her laptop on the overstuffed arm of the chair. She sat staring at the screen with her elbow bent and her fist curled, her knuckles pressed against her lips. So intently, she didn't see him when he stopped between the pocket doors she'd left open.

The floor felt warm beneath his bare feet, warmer than it should, Gus thought, until the furnace kicked on and Cydney sighed, so heavily he heard her clear across the room. She didn't so much as glance at him until he sat down in front of her on the ottoman. Then her chin jerked up and she blinked, her almond-shaped almond-brown eyes full of tears.

"Oh—good morning." She brushed quickly at her wet lashes with her curled index fingers and threw off the afghan. "The lights came on about an hour ago. I made coffee. What would you like for breakfast?"

"An answer." Gus caught her feet as she swung them out of the chair. "Why did you clean up my bedroom?"

"It was a mess. Clothes all over and wet towels—"

"I was gonna bronze those towels. Why did you do your damnedest to make it look like you'd never been in my bed? Was I that lousy?"

"Oh no. You were incredible." She put her feet on the

floor, hunched forward and slid her hands into his. "I slept with you because I wanted to. I had a wonderful, memorable night and that's all I want."

"Then why are you crying?"

"I can't tell you because it will start another fight."

"The goddamn wedding again."

"Not exactly." She tugged her hands out of his and laid them on her knees. "I know how you feel about Bebe but I love her. She's been the hub of my life. I feel like a wheel that's had all its spokes ripped out. I've been sitting here thinking. And wondering—" She drew a breath and let it go in a teary sigh, her eyes filling again. "What will I do without her? How will I fill the giant hole Bebe is going to leave in my life?"

"Well, for starters, throw your camera away—"

"And finish my book. Why didn't I think of that?" She clapped both her hands on his shoulders, picked up her cup and sprang out of the chair. "Thanks, Mr. Wizard. Problem solved, life fixed."

"Listen, Miss Snippy." Gus wheeled off the ottoman behind her and followed her out of the R&R room. "You asked me."

"No. I did not." She lofted a finger at him over her shoulder as she crossed the living room. "You asked me why I was crying and I told you."

"Well what the hell did you want me to say?"

"I didn't *want* you to say anything." She pushed partway through the swinging door and spun around, sloshing tea out of the mug in her left hand. "But that never seems to stop you."

The damn door almost did, flying back on its hinges straight at his nose from the shove Cydney gave it. Gus side-stepped it, stiff-armed it out of his way on its next swing and followed her into the kitchen. She wheeled away from the stove, a spitfire glint in her eye and a frying pan cocked in her hand.

"Bacon or sausage?"

"Sausage."

"Pancakes or French toast?"

"French toast."

She banged the skillet on a burner and grabbed a mug off the counter, filled it from the Krups machine and plunked it down on the island. "Orange juice or half a grapefruit?"

"Orange juice." Better keep her away from knives, Gus thought, and swung himself onto a stool.

She poured him a glass from the carton in the fridge, slid it to him across the island and stalked back to the stove with a package of sausage. Gus watched her fork links into the pan and adjust the flame.

"Ever ask yourself how Bebe got to be the hub of your life?"

Cydney ignored him, but Gus figured she would. She went back to the fridge for eggs, milk, butter and French bread. He waited till she'd cut a plate full of thick slices and tossed the knife in the sink. When she'd cracked the last egg and had no more to throw at him, he went on.

"It creeps up on you. One minute you're you, with your own life and your own stuff, and the next minute there's this little boy looking up at you. He's scared and he's confused, 'cause he doesn't understand why you're standing in Mommy and Daddy's place. He doesn't know where they went and he doesn't care. He just wants them back and he wants you gone 'cause you aren't them and you're never gonna be, and somehow he knows that."

She kept her back to him, poured milk over the eggs in a blue earthenware bowl, tossed in vanilla and nutmeg and snatched a whisk out of a crock. This whole thing was a crock. He was saying things to Cydney he'd sworn he'd never tell another living soul, but he was tired of fighting with her, weary of hearing about poor little obnoxious Bebe. And he was sick to death of Cydney's condescension. She'd never said, "Look, bub. You're a man. You just don't get it," but it was in her body language and the tone of her voice. Well yeah, he was a man but he got it and it was high damn time she knew it.

"You try to explain so he'll understand, but he's too little. The words you use scare him and make him cry. So you hug him and let him cry. That's all you can do. You let him hit you and kick you and scream for Mommy and Daddy. You hold him so he won't hurt himself and you let him cry till he falls asleep with his little arms limp and his soft, hot cheek pressed against your neck."

She was listening. Her chin drifted toward her shoulder, and the whisk in her hand, furiously beating the eggs, started to slow.

"You put him in his toddler bed, on his stomach like Aunt Phoebe said," Gus went on, "and you stand there looking at him. You're scared to death 'cause you're just a kid yourself, but you're all he has and you've got to stick this out. He's so sad you can feel it seep into your hand when you lay it on his back. You feel helpless. You don't know what to do but stand there with your hand on him. He whimpers in his sleep and you feel something inside you just—break. It hurts but you know it's nothing compared to what's hurting him."

Cydney stood with her back mostly to him, the head she'd beaten into the eggs hissing and settling into the bowl. Grease popped in the skillet and she jumped, dropped the whisk and grabbed a fork.

"Every night he cries himself to sleep. And he whimpers." Gus watched Cydney lay the sausages out to drain on a paper towel. "You sleep in a chair by his bed so you can pat him back to sleep. He's exhausted and pale when he wakes up in the morning. He opens his eyes and he sees you and he gives you this oh-hell-it's-you look that makes it hurt when you breathe, but you ignore it and you start over. Every day you start over. Tears and tantrums, the angry, bruised little eyes. Every night he cries and every night it's the chair and the whimpering and the patting till you think it's never going to stop."

Cydney swung the sausage pan into the sink. Her hand quivered as she lifted the cast-iron skillet onto the burner. She coated it with butter, dredged a slice of bread and tossed it, sizzling, into the pan.

"And then one morning he wakes up, blinks at you like he always does, and you're bracing yourself for the oh-shit-you-again look, and he smiles. Then he stands up on his knees and raises his hands and you pick him up. He puts his arms around your neck and his head on your shoulder. You kiss his little head and he hugs you, and that's it. He's yours and you're his and you'd lay down your life to make sure nothing ever hurts him this bad ever again."

A slice of soaked French bread hung from the fork in Cydney's hand. Gus watched the crust tear away and the whole thing plop back into the bowl. Smoke rolled off the cast-iron skillet, but Cydney just stood there until Gus got up. Then she dropped the fork and switched off the burner, wheeled and threw her arms around his rib cage, her face buried in his T-shirt. Gus held her, pressed his cheek to her hair and felt a sob shudder through her.

"It was rough with Bebe," she sniffled, "but nothing like that."

"I've been thinking. Maybe I'm wrong about Aldo and Bebe. Maybe they're not a disaster, maybe they're perfect together. Two abandoned little angels who managed to find each other."

"Oh Gus!" Cydney wailed and sobbed against his chest.

He let her cry, rubbing his hands on her back, molding her breasts to his chest. When she sighed, her warm breath fanned the tear spot on his T-shirt and stuck it to his left nipple. Gus felt himself stir and kissed the top of her head.

"Boy do I feel shallow," she said, a watery quaver in her voice. "No wonder you wrote the Grand Plan to Wreck the Wedding."

"Well thanks, but it wasn't the answer. Or the right thing to do."

"But now I understand why you wrote it. Poor Aldo." She gave a quivery sigh. "Poor little guy."

"Don't feel too bad for him. He doesn't remember those first few weeks after Artie and Beth died, and he figured out pretty quick how to work me. 'Course, I let him."

"Oh Bebe, too. My mother had such a guilt complex. She was sure it was her fault, that she must've done something or said something that gave Gwen the idea it was perfectly fine to dump her child and go on with her life. My mother bent over backwards to make up for it and I jumped right in and helped her."

"Ah, overcompensation. I know it well."

"I love my life. I really do." Cydney backed out of his embrace, tugged the dish towel off the handle on the oven door and used it to wipe tears from her amazingly long, amazingly dark eyelashes. "But I feel abandoned, like Bebe dumped me—just like Gwen dumped her. And I feel so damn angry because I did this to myself."

"I did the same thing, babe. Picked up the shovel when Aldo was a little guy and dug this hole in my life with my own hands."

"That's *exactly* how I feel." She smiled at him, a dazzling, sparkly-eyed smile that made his pulse jump. "And you do, too?"

Gus curved his hands around her hips, eased her against his zipper and felt himself stiffen. "I told you we had a lot in common."

"You tried to tell me." She laid her hands on his chest, scraped a fingernail on a tearstain, which made him shiver. "Now if I could just figure out what to put in Bebe's place."

How about me? The words jumped from his crotch to his tongue. But the phone rang—thank God the phone rang. Cydney loved her life. He'd given her a wonderful, memorable night and that's all she wanted. How lucky could a guy get? So why was he scowling?

Gus grabbed the phone on the wall by the swinging door, leaned his shoulder on the jamb and said hello.

"Hey, Uncle Gus. How's it look out there in the boondocks?"

He thought about it. For the two seconds it took to swing around and watch Cydney scrape the cast-iron skillet with a spatula as she carried it toward the sink and the garbage disposal.

"Pretty dim, pal. No lights and no heat," he told Aldo. "Wherever you and Bebe are, you better stay there."

Cydney blinked at him, the slice of French toast oozing

off the spatula, and arched a what-are-you-doing eyebrow at him.

"The plows have been out here in Branson," Aldo said. "The roads are clear and the sun's melting the ice like crazy."

"Cloudy as hell here. Looks like it's gonna snow again. Any second." Cydney plunked the skillet on the counter and swung a glance at the window. At the sun blazing through it and the icicles dripping like waterfalls off the eaves, then frowned at him. "The driveway's blocked, two trees down. I've gotta call Elvin and see if he can come out with his truck and tow bar. You and Bebe better sit tight in Branson."

"Okay," Aldo said cheerfully. "I'll call you later."

"Call me in the morning." Gus hung up and faced Cydney.

"Why did you lie to Aldo?" She stood at the sink with her hands on her hips. "Why did you tell him to call you in the morning?"

"I plan to be very busy the rest of today and tonight."

"Oh really?" She folded her arms and smiled. "Doing what?"

"C'mere." Gus crooked a finger at her. "I'll show you."

She dipped her chin and came toward him, smiling slyly through her lashes and plucking at her hair. Gus drew a breath—and cursed as the damn phone rang again.

"Don't move." He pointed at Cydney. She stopped and he answered the phone with a curt, " 'Lo?"

"Good morning, Angus. It's Georgette. How's the weather?"

"Looks like it's going to snow again. We've got trees blocking the road. No lights and no heat. How's Arkansas?"

My mother? Cydney mouthed at him. Gus nodded. She smiled.

"Herb thought we could make it back," Georgette said. "But not if the roads are blocked. When do you think they'll be clear?"

"Haven't a clue. Maybe not till tomorrow."

"What an awful shame," Georgette said happily. "I'll just have to do some more shopping. I trust you and Cydney are coping?"

"We're managing. We've got a nice fire going."

Gus winked. Cydney gave her eyebrows a hubba-hubba wiggle.

"No matter how bored you get, Angus, don't play Scrabble with her. She'll beat the pants off you."

"Too late, Georgette. She already whupped me at strip Ping-Pong."

Georgette laughed. So did Cydney, clapping a hand on her mouth.

"We'll see you tomorrow, then."

"Drive safely." He hung up and swung around, grinning at Cydney.

She took her hand off her mouth and grinned back at him. "She told you not to play Scrabble with me, didn't she?"

"Yep." Gus took two giant steps toward her, swooped Cydney up in his arms and spun her in a circle. She looped her arm around his neck, laughing. "What are you doing?"

"Filling the hole in my life." Her laugh snapped off and she blinked at him, her eyes huge. "Just temporarily. We're both in the same leaky boat. Don't see why we can't help each other bail."

"Oh—temporarily. Whew." She blew out a sigh that ruffled one of the curls she'd tugged over her forehead. "You scared me."

"What did you think I meant? Forever?"

"You? Me?" She pressed a hand to her throat. "Forever?"

Why did she say it like that? Like *you, me* and *forever* didn't belong in the same sentence? And why the you-gotta-be-kidding edge in her voice? Gus felt a scowl coming on but shrugged it off.

"Well, forever or next Saturday," he said. "Whichever comes first."

"Oh—fine. Next Saturday will be here long before forever."

"And tomorrow will be here before we know it." Gus wheeled toward the swinging door. Cydney pushed it out of the way, he carried her through it and stopped. "Okay. There are eight couches and sixteen beds, counting mine. Where do you want to start?"

"Twenty-four horizontal surfaces?" She cocked her head dubiously. "In twenty-four hours?"

"You don't think I can do it?"

"I don't think *I* can do it."

"C'mon, old poop." He gave her an affectionate jostle against his chest. "Let's give it a shot."

"Does last night count?"

"Maybe. If we get crunched for time, we'll count those four."

"Let's start with your bed. And it was five."

"It was four." Gus bounded onto the dais and swung up the steps.

"It was five. Twice in your bed." She held up as many fingers. "Twice in front of the fire. And—?"

"That's it." Gus carried her through his office. "That's four."

She slapped him on the chest. "You forgot the bathtub."

"I didn't forget the bathtub. I may have that bronzed, too." He put her down beside the bed, his breath quickening, and ripped off his T-shirt. "But the tub doesn't count."

He reached for her sweater but she jammed her hands on her hips, holding the hem of it firmly in place. "Why doesn't the tub count?"

"It's not a horizontal surface. It's curved."

"The back and the sides are curved, Gus. The bottom is flat."

"You're wasting precious seconds. Do I have to get a level?"

"No." She slipped her arms around him, rubbed her nose in his chest hair and smiled up at him. "You have to get the can of whipped cream and the jar of maraschino cherries in the fridge."

"Miss Parrish." Every inch of Gus quivered. "I'm shocked."

"We've only got twenty-four hours, bub." She kissed his chest. "We'll have to snack as we go to keep up our strength."

"Get naked." He gave her a quick, hard kiss. "I'll be right back."

Gus flew downstairs, nearly sprang the swinging door off

its hinges as he burst past it and flung open the refrigerator. The whipped cream was in the door but he had to hunt for the cherries, found them at last behind the leftover pot roast. How did Cydney know they were there?

Who the hell cares, Munroe, his inner voice said. *Get upstairs.*

Cydney lay naked in his bed, the sheet just covering her breasts. She smiled when he came through the door and stretched her arms over her head. The sheet slipped and so did most of Gus' brain. Straight to his groin. He'd spent a lot of time with his mouth and his hands on her breasts, but he'd seen them only by firelight or candlelight. In the bright sun bouncing off the snow and slanting through the window they gleamed soft and silky, small but perfect, her nipples peaked and peach-kissed like her mouth.

"I'll take that." She held her hand out for the whipped cream.

Gus tossed her the can and shucked off his jeans, loosened the lid on the maraschino cherries and put the jar on the table. Cydney plumped the pillows against the headboard, sat back on her heels and bit the lid off the whipped cream.

"Have a seat," she said, shaking the can.

Gus swung into bed and sank back against the pillows, hard and eager, every pulse point in his body leaping. God she was lovely. A slim, svelte little nymph with a wicked gleam in her almond eyes. She started with his toes, squirting them with cold whipped cream and licking it off with her hot little mouth. A dollop on his knees, couple on his thighs. He held his breath when she glanced up at him through her lashes, raised the can—and spritzed his navel.

He groaned with disappointment and she grinned, bent her head and made a long, slow stroke with her tongue that left him gasping and clutching the sheets. He reached for her when she slid into his lap, but she wagged a finger.

"Not so fast," she said, pressing the nozzle of the can to his chest and capping his nipples with whipped cream. "Hand me the cherries."

Gus did, his hand trembling. She unscrewed the lid and

plucked out a cherry. By the stem, with her teeth, capped the jar and gave it back to him. He gave it a toss and she laughed in her throat, the cherry trembling between her lips, then bent her head and dragged it over his chest. Back and forth, making him shiver and his chest hair prickle, rose on her knees and teased it across his mouth, slid her arms around his neck and buried her nipples in the mounds of whipped cream she'd smeared on him.

Gus grabbed her hips and dove, sucked her breasts clean, ringed her nipples with his tongue and felt her shiver. He glanced up at her, at the cherry glistening between her lips, caught it in his teeth as he lifted Cydney over him and thrust inside her. Once, twice, crushed the cherry in his jaw, and came hard, deep inside her, bucking her on top of him, scooped one breast into his hand and one into his mouth, his mind and his body a searing, red-hot blaze.

She clutched his hair and tugged his head back, clamped her mouth over his and pumped. Trembling and whimpering in her throat till she arched and he felt the spasm that shook her and quivered a cry up her throat. He sucked it into his mouth with her tongue and held her in his hands, sleek and shivering while the climax rippled through her.

When she moaned and went limp, he rolled her on her side, crossways on the bed, and cuddled down beside her. Tucked her left arm beneath his neck, kissed the pulse throbbing in her throat and drew the covers over them.

"Oh my." She sighed, a shudder in her voice. "Oh Gus."

"I have a confession." He nuzzled her collarbone. She stiffened and he glanced up at her. "I hate maraschino cherries."

She laughed and curled her arms around his neck, kissed his nose and slid her foot between his legs. Gus pulled her against him, breast to breast, and let her stretch, pressed his hand to the small of her back and rubbed himself against her.

"Mmmm. Maybe you can do twenty-four in twenty-four hours."

"I'm willing to die trying."

She laughed, slid her hand between them and stroked him gently. Gus felt himself stirring again, cupped her breast and tweaked her nipple, felt it peak and a breathy sigh tremble up her throat. He tucked a pillow beneath their heads. She snuggled into it, kissed his chin and feathered him delicately with her fingertips. He stroked her breasts, softly from the underside up to her nipples till they were both pebbled and hard beneath his thumb. So was he, pulsing in the hand she'd closed around him, her eyes bright and glazed, her mouth soft and dewy.

"Ready when you are," she whispered against his lips, circling the head of him with her thumb.

He rolled her over, raised and spread her knees and slid inside her wet, hot body, stretched her arms over her head, locked their fingers and kissed her, gave her his tongue and let her play with it, nip it and suck it while he stroked her. Slow and sweet, taking his time, watching her eyes and her breath, waiting till her lashes fluttered and she dug her nails into his shoulders, then drove into her hard and fast. She beat him to climax by half a heartbeat, a cry flinging her head back, then she wound around him, arms and legs tight, and held him while his mind blurred.

"My God." Gus rolled off her and caught her hand, drew it to his mouth and held it there, his heartbeat pulsing in his lips. "I had no idea I could do two in a row like that."

She rolled toward him and sighed. "Me, either, old poop."

Gus chuckled and kissed her hand. She nuzzled his shoulder, ran a finger across his lips. Gus sucked it and she purred, "Mmmm."

"What time is it?" He pushed up on his elbows and his stomach growled. Cydney popped up beside him. "Time to feed you."

She scooted to the edge of the bed, picked up her sweater and tugged it over her head. She stood up, yelped and turned to face him, a bright red stain of cherry juice splashed across her chest.

"Oops," Gus said. "Guess I'm buying you a new sweater."

She leveled a finger at him. "You're buying me a new truck."

"I'm buying you a new sweater and a new truck."

"Darn skippy. Got a shirt I can borrow?"

"In the closet." Gus watched the sweet little curve of her backside walk away from him and smiled.

She peeled off her sweater, tugged a blue cotton shirt off a hanger and slipped it on. The tails hung to her knees, the sleeves way past her wrists. She whistled as she did up the buttons and rolled the cuffs. God, she looked adorable.

"Be right back." She blew him a kiss and padded away on her small bare feet. What was she, a two? Her shoe size a five, maybe?

He'd have to find out so he could buy her a sweater. And lingerie. Oooh, yeah. He'd never bought lingerie for a woman, but he couldn't wait to get Cydney into Intimate Apparel. And out of it as fast as he could. He'd take her shopping tomorrow, soon as Aldo came back with his truck, which reminded him—Cydney's Jeep, crunched under the oak tree in the driveway.

He sat up, lifted the receiver on the clock radio/telephone that picked up AM stations in Canada on the handset but garbled all his phone calls. Because it was Sunday, he dialed Elvin at home.

"Sheriff Cantwell," he said, over a crackle of static and the murmur of a French voice. Quebec coming through loud and clear.

"Hi, Elvin, Gus."

"Hey, hoss. You talk that purty little Miss Parrish into stayin'?"

"I did," Gus said, rubbing his grumbling stomach. And she was coming back. With food and her hot little body. "You still got the tow bar on your truck, Elvin?"

"Sure do. Somebody stuck in a ditch?"

"Under a tree. Nobody hurt, we just need to pull the tree off."

"I c'n swing by after lunch."

Gus squinted at the time on his Rolex, 12:32. "Lunch today?"

"Hafta be. Gotta run up to Jeff City tomorrow." He meant Jefferson City, the state capital. " 'Spect me in about a hour."

"Thanks, Elvin." Gus hung up on the sheriff and Quebec, snapped on a pair of midnight-blue silk boxers and headed for the kitchen.

Cydney stood at the island smearing bagels with cream cheese. In his shirt and a bright nimbus of sunlight that made her hair shimmer.

"Well, hi." She gave a puzzled little laugh as he pushed through the swinging door. "What are you doing?"

Yeah, Munroe, his inner voice asked. *What are you doing?*

"Having the time of my life." Gus slid his folded arms on the island, leaned across the counter and kissed her. "How 'bout you?"

She licked cream cheese off her finger and tilted her head at him. "Beats croquet."

Gus laughed. "Keep me humble." He plucked a red grape out of the bowl beside Cydney and tossed it in his mouth. "Where did all the food in my fridge come from?"

"My mother brought some of it. I suspect she bought the rest of it after the Auto Club fixed the flat on Herb's Cadillac. Why?"

"Just wondering about the maraschino cherries. Our timetable has gone to hell. Elvin'll be here shortly to pull the tree off your truck."

"That'll take—what? An hour?"

"Minimum. Maybe two." He pulled another grape and ate it.

"Last night's five plus two is seven. Two hours to pull the tree off my truck. Twenty-four hours minus seven leaves seventeen more times in eighteen hours." She bit into half a bagel, chewed and swallowed. "Pretty tight. Think you can do it?"

"Might could kill me, as Elvin would say, but what a way to go."

"I wonder if my mother bought oysters?"

They laughed, bumping noses over the island. Gus licked cream cheese from the corner of her mouth. Cydney stuffed the rest of the bagel in his mouth and slid him the red mug of steaming coffee next to the fruit bowl. When he finished she handed him a napkin.

"We should get dressed before Elvin shows up." Gus picked her up and sat her on the island. "But first, I want to dance."

"Listen, bub." She let him wrap her legs around his waist and lift her, holding her raised right hand in his left. "If this is the pace you intend to keep on half a bagel and two grapes, you will kill yourself."

"I don't mean that kind of dance." Gus swung her around and waltzed her across the kitchen.

Cydney laughed, clutched his bare shoulder and pushed the swinging door open. "Why are you carrying me everywhere we go?"

" 'Cause you're little and cute and I can." Gus stopped next to the living room fireplace, holding her at eye level with his stereo and CD collection on the shelves built into its stone face. "I don't have any Streisand. Pick something else."

"Oh no." She shook her head. "This is obviously your fantasy, to dance around the living room in your shorts, so you pick."

"I've only got two hands, Cydney, and this isn't a fantasy. I'm having fun and I'm happy." And he was, Gus realized. Happier than he'd been in—hell, he couldn't remember. "C'mon. Pick something."

She pursed her lips, ran a finger along a row of CDs, sighed and flipped on the radio. An FM station and the Four Seasons belting out the redigitized version of "Oh What a Night" blared out of the speakers.

"This is peppy." She smiled and snapped her fingers in time with the beat. "And apropos."

Gus laughed and put her down, snatched the remote and kicked up the volume. Frankie Vallee's falsetto soared across the living room, hummed in his bones and made his heart swell watching Cydney boogie away from him backwards, shoulders wiggling and fingers popping.

"C'mon!" she shouted over the Mach 2 music rattling the glass wall. "You're the one who wanted to dance!"

Gus held the remote to his chest, raised his left hand and did a bebop little cha-cha to catch up with her. She laughed, her eyes shining at him over her shoulder as she twirled away, her arms swaying over her head. He caught her wrists and lowered her arms, held them out straight and danced along on her left like they were line dancing.

Cydney hooked his right arm around her, bumped his hip and grinned and did a Rockettes leg-kick. He tripped, kicked the wrong foot and knocked her off rhythm. Off balance, too, but he caught her and held her, both of them kicking in opposite directions, hopping in a one-legged circle toward the foyer and laughing—

Until Cydney's eyes flashed up and she gasped, a stricken, openmouthed stare on her face. She jerked to a stop, tripping Gus and swinging him around toward the foyer, where Fletcher Parrish stood. One hand on his hip, holding his brown leather trench coat open against a pair of taupe Armani slacks and a striped Boudini sweater.

Oh shit, said Gus' inner voice.

A dazzle of sun-kissed snow poured through the wide-open front doors behind Parrish, lighting his lion's mane of white hair. Only his eyebrows—Cydney's eyebrows, Gus realized—were still dark as sin.

He felt her shiver in the cold draft of air snaking around their ankles, pulled her protectively against his chest and cupped her shoulders, pressed the remote and turned off the music.

"Um—hi, Dad," she said, plucking at her hair.

"Cydney." He nodded to her, tapping the wool tweed fedora in his hand against his knee, and lifted his piercing, amber-brown eyes to Gus. "And you—*Munroe.* What the hell are you doing with my daughter?"

chapter
twenty-three

"She's not your daughter anymore, *Parrish*," Gus shot back, giving Cydney's shoulders a trust-me-babe squeeze. "She's my fiancée."

"*What?*" Cydney and her father shouted at the same time.

He doubted Parrish heard her. He didn't even look at her. He was glaring at Gus, the defiler, and his face was turning purple.

"Fletch!" A petulant, heavily accented voice—female and French, Gus thought—called from outside. "Help me with this damn bag!"

"Stay—right—there!" Parrish punctuated each word he snarled at Gus with a poke of his hat and swung back out the door.

"Hey!" Gus went after him, heading straight for the frozen tundra outside the door in his underwear. "Who the hell d'you think you are?"

"Whoa, wait!" He felt Cydney's hand on his arm and let her pull him around. She looked like she'd been pole-axed. Her face was pale, her eyes huge. "What are you doing? I'm not your fiancée."

"I apologize for that. But he's your father and for five crazy seconds I thought I could save face for you." Gus scowled at the open door, so angry he could see red spots pulsing at the corners of his vision. "Now I just want to knock his teeth out."

"He's not worth it. He left my mother the second his accountant told him he was rich enough. He dumped us"—There was that word again, Gus noticed—"because we cramped his style. I don't care what my father thinks of me or how I live my life."

"Well hell. I thought I was helping."

"I know you did." Tears spiked her lashes, but she drew a breath and gave him a plucky smile. "And I appreciate the gesture."

Gus wasn't happy anymore. He was pissed. He wanted to punch Parrish for putting tears in Cydney's eyes. Last time he'd hit somebody he was twelve. He'd lost his temper and popped Artie, who'd proceeded to clean up the floor with him.

"I'll tell your father the truth if that's what you want."

"I think Gwen convinced him to come. When she called last night she said, 'I talked to Dad and he told me to tell you—' That's when the connection broke. I think this is what she meant to say."

"Want me to tell him to hit the road?"

"Oh *do* I, but it would only start a war."

"Tell me what you want and I'll do it."

"I want to keep the peace. So do you think we could pretend for a few days, then fake a big fight and break up?"

"In a few days, babe, my house will be full of your loony family. I don't think we'll have to fake a big fight."

It was the pattern, and just thinking about it made Gus steam.

"Thanks." Cydney hugged him, leaned her chin on his chest and wiggled her eyebrows. "Think how cool this will sound in my memoirs."

"You're adorable." He kissed her. "And you're freezing." He started toward the door to shut it. "Was your old man born in a barn?"

"No, *Munroe.*" Parrish stepped inside, stopped and glowered at him. "I was born in Chicago."

He held a makeup case the size of a small safe in his left hand. On his right arm leaned a gorgeous brunette, swathed in sable. She looked to be about twenty and nearly as tall as Elvin, which meant she soared like a sequoia over Parrish. She smiled at Gus' blue silk boxers, raised her green cat's eyes and licked her lip. Oh yeah. She was French.

"Shut the door." Gus turned away, swiped one of Aunt

Phoebe's afghans off the closest couch, draped it around Cydney and laid his hands on her shoulders. "Preferably on your way out."

"I was invited here, *Munroe*." Parrish dropped the makeup case and came down the foyer steps. "To give my granddaughter away."

"Not by me you weren't." Gus tried to lift his hands off Cydney's shoulders, but she grabbed them and held on. "Shut the door."

Parrish swept his arm toward the steps. "Your house, your door."

"You left it open."

"I'm not your servant."

"You're number three on the *Times* List. I'm number one."

"*You no-talent pretty boy!*" Parrish roared, and lunged at him.

Cydney threw herself straight at his oncoming left fist. Gus' heart clutched and he grabbed for her, knowing he wouldn't reach her before the punch, but she ducked it—he had a feeling she'd done this before—and pushed her hands against her father's chest.

"Stop it, Dad. No fights."

"I'm not going to fight him. I'm going to knock him out."

"Oh, Fletch." The brunette rolled her eyes, her lips pursed in a bored pout. "Always must you do this?"

"Be quiet, Domino. Get out of my way, Cydney."

"I'm not moving, Dad. But you are, to a motel, if you don't stop."

"You're taking his side."

"Of course I am. He's my fiancé."

"In a pig's eye," Parrish sneered.

The spots swimming at the corners of Gus' eyes popped and spread a red haze across his vision. He drew back his right fist and slugged Parrish. His idol, Cydney's father. A man almost twice his age and half his size. Aimed the punch over Cydney's right shoulder and drove it into his chin. Two knuckles crunched and pain seared up his hand.

Parrish's head snapped and he hit the floor on his Armani-clad ass, blood spurting from his split lip.

"What are you *doing*?" Cydney shrieked at Gus, glaring at him as she dropped to her heels, fished a monogrammed blue linen handkerchief out of her father's trench coat pocket and pressed it to his lip. "This is not keeping the peace!"

"Sure ain't, Miss Parrish," Elvin said soberly. "That's my job."

She shot to her feet and stared at the Sheriff, standing just inside the still-open door, his huge frame draped with enough luggage to bring down an elephant. All of it calfskin with gold edges, probably Gucci.

It was Sunday so Elvin wasn't in uniform. He had a John Deere cap pushed back on his glossy black hair, wore a gray ribbed thermal shirt and a quilted, wool plaid jacket. Heavy denim work jeans, starched and ironed. He looked like a big, slow-witted rube, which he wasn't.

"Put those bags down, Elvin." Gus shook his throbbing hand. "You're not a porter."

"Just bein' neighborly." He gave the door a boot to shut it.

"I thought he was the hired man," Parrish said to Cydney.

"No, Dad. This is the Sheriff of Crooked Possum."

"Sheriff? Great! Hey—Barney Fife!" Parrish waved his handkerchief. "Get over here and arrest this hack for assault."

"I'd rather be a hack," Gus said, "than a has-been."

"*Has-been!*" Parrish tried to stand up, but couldn't get any traction from his slick-soled Italian loafers on the bare pine floor. "I'll show you has-been!"

"That's enough." Elvin raised an arm that probably had a hundred pounds of luggage hanging on it and pointed at Parrish, then touched the brim of his cap to Domino. "Where would you like your bags, ma'am?"

"You." She waved a vague, inch-long pink fingernail. "Cindy."

"*Cyd-ney,*" she and Gus said together.

"My room. Where is it?"

"At the Y'all Come Inn," Gus snapped the name of Crooked

Possum's only motel. "You'll love it. Very private. Only two guest rooms."

Built upstairs over Roylee Boyce's garage.

"Gus," Cydney said. Please, her eyes begged. I want peace, not war. "The room next to mine will be fine for Dad and Domino."

"Oh no-no-no." Domino waved her pink nail again. "Fletch and I we do not share in the same room."

Well now. Gus grinned. This was getting fun again. He glanced at Parrish, elbows bent on his raised knees, his handkerchief over his eyes.

Cydney blinked, but said smoothly, "How Continental. You take the room next to mine, Domino, and we'll put Dad somewhere else."

"How 'bout the garage?" Gus muttered.

"This way, Sheriff." As gracefully as if she were wearing taffeta and diamonds instead of his blue shirt and nothing else, Cydney gestured toward the gallery and turned to lead the way, kicking the afghan aside and elbowing Gus. "Peace," she said under her breath. "I mean it."

"Why don't you two fellers shake hands?" Elvin stepped aside at the foot of the steps to let the ladies go first. "Be a nice touch."

Domino slinked past, all legs and fur, winked at Gus and followed Cydney upstairs. Parrish plucked the handkerchief off his face and shouted at his daughter, "Put some clothes on while you're up there!"

When Elvin lumbered out of sight down the hallway, Parrish laid his elbows on his knees and looked at Gus. His sweater was spotted with blood. His lip had stopped bleeding but it was starting to swell.

"Do you want to shake hands, Munroe?"

"I'd rather wrap my head in aluminum foil and stick it in the microwave."

"You aren't going to marry Cydney."

"Why do you say that?"

He raised a hand toward the stairs, shrugged and let it fall. "Why would you want to?"

"On second thought, I'd rather wrap your head in aluminum foil."

"Oh come on. She's my daughter but I'm a realist. She can't come close to Domino."

"Apparently you can't either."

"Our marriage is a business arrangement," Parrish said loftily, but there were ruddy splotches on his throat. "She's good for my image and Gwen has gotten Domino a lot of modeling jobs. She's photographed her three times for the cover of *Vogue*."

And she wouldn't give her own sister an inside photo credit.

"What's the real story, Fletch? Can't get it up anymore?"

That got him off the floor, but Gus figured it would. He came up swinging, so wildly all Gus had to do was stick his fist out and let Parrish plow into it. A fountain of blood gushed from his nose, his eyes rolled and he keeled over, sprawled on his back and out cold on the floor.

"Goll dang it, hoss. Cain't I trust you no more?"

Gus bent over, stuck his hand between his knees and sucked his teeth to keep from screaming at the agony in his knuckles. Elvin clumped down the steps in his off-duty lumberjack boots, crossed the living room and dropped to his haunches beside Parrish.

"He took another swing at me."

" 'Magine he did, with you prancin' around in your skivvies and lil' Miss Parrish wearin' nothin' but your shirt." Elvin peeled up one of Parrish's eyelids, then pivoted on his heel toward Gus. "Reckon he'll live. Wouldn't bet the rent money on you, though."

"Cydney and I are adults. We weren't expecting her father."

"Even so, hoss." Elvin rose to his feet, his voice grave. "I got no choice but to call the Crisis Management Team."

"I'd best put my pants on, then."

"I'd advise it."

Kids taunted each other. Kids picked fights. He wasn't a kid, he was a grown man. He'd goaded Parrish the second time. He'd knocked him out. Maybe broken his nose. He'd behaved like a bully. A thug.

That's what Gus kept telling himself, between sticking his hand in the bowl of ice he took upstairs and trying to clean himself up, but he just couldn't feel bad. He wanted to hit Parrish again when he thought of what he'd said about Cydney.

The one thing he did feel bad about was the word *fiancée*. He'd meant well but his stupid attempt at gallantry had put Cydney in a bind. He'd saved her an awkward moment with her father, but what about Georgette? And Herb and Aldo and Bebe and her bitch sister, Gwen? He didn't think Cydney had stopped to consider them when she'd suggested keeping up the pretense. If Parrish didn't believe it, why would they?

And that was another thing. Why was it such an outlandish idea?

Cydney was cuter than a bug's ear. Funny and sensual. Genuine, honest and sincere. He could do worse.

Maybe she could do better, his inner voice said. *Think about that.*

Gus did, scowling at himself in the mirror while he attempted to shave left-handed. His right hand was a mess. Swollen and throbbing, his knuckles stiff and already bruised. It took him five minutes to zip and snap himself into a pair of jeans. By then he'd been upstairs almost an hour. Forget buttons. He pulled on a gray sweater with a black band across the chest and stuck his feet into loafers.

He almost ran into Elvin in the foyer, as the Sheriff came through the front door. Before he shut it, Gus caught a look at the porch, almost clear of snow, dry down to the pavement drive and the pine tree that had come down in the circle lawn during the storm.

"Want to move the tree before the Team gets here?"

"They're here, takin' tea in the dinin' room with Miss Parrish an' her daddy." Elvin stamped snow on one of Aunt Phoebe's braided rugs. "And the tree's took care of. Didn't need the truck or the tow bar."

"You moved *a tree* off Cydney's Jeep bare-handed?"

"Wasn't much of a tree, hoss, and it was already broke."

"You any good at moving pianos, Elvin?"

He explained and Elvin agreed to move Aunt Phoebe's grand into the great room. "Providin', o'course, that I don't hafta arrest you."

"You'll never take me alive, copper."

"That's what they all say, hoss."

He didn't think he'd be arrested. It depended on what Parrish told the Crisis Management Team. Gus doubted he'd repeat the comment that provoked him. He might confess it to Bob Dole. To the CMT, never. Parrish lived in his pride and his image.

His face was puffy and his eyes bleary, but he looked pretty good for a guy who'd been punched twice and knocked out. The split in his lip resembled a zipper but his nose was the pièce de résistance, a black-and-blue bulb smack in the middle of his face. Gus knew exactly what it felt like and smiled.

Parrish sat at the head of the table in navy trousers and a multicolored sweater. He lounged on one elbow in the armchair, a cigarette in a gold holder in an ashtray near his teacup.

"Here he is, ladies," he said with a sweep of his arm as Gus came into the room with Elvin. "My assailant."

"I believe that would be your alleged assailant," chirped Cloris Figgle, wife of Clovis Figgle, the mayor of Crooked Possum.

She sat facing the door, a notepad and pen next to her Blue Willow teacup. Her little black church hat sat on her tiny gray head, its net veil plucked over her forehead. When Gus winked at her she blushed.

Eighty-something Mamie Buckles sat next to Cloris. In a white lace blouse and flowered stretch pants that sagged on her like Saran Wrap with a bad case of static cling when she got up to bring Gus a pint jar with a little chintz collar on it.

"Here you go, Gussie. A jar o' my prickly pear jelly."

"Thank you, Mamie." She had a face like a hedge apple and bright, snappy blue eyes. He kissed her cheek and she patted his chest. "If you end up in the big house—" she slid

Elvin a look that said he'd better not "—I'll fetch you your supper ever' night."

"Sheriff." Parrish stood up. "Are you going to allow this?"

"It ain't against the law to give a neighbor a jar o' jelly."

In the case of Mamie's prickly pear jelly it probably ought to be, but Gus didn't say so. Parrish shut his mouth, sat down and reached for his cigarette. He took a puff, winced and pressed a finger to his mouth.

Cloris leaned toward him, peering at him with a raised finger so tiny it looked like a bird bone. "Is that the alleged split in your lip?"

"The split in my lip is not alleged, madam," Parrish replied. "It's there for all the world to see. What is alleged is who put it there."

"Thank you." Cloris wiggled her little bird finger at him and picked up her pen. "I'll just write that down so I don't forget."

A trill of laughter came through the swinging door. It was Cydney's and it gave Gus a zip up his back to realize he recognized it. She pushed into the dining room, carrying a tray with plates on it, cloth napkins and a platter of munchies, her head turned over her shoulder.

She'd put clothes on. Khaki slacks, a shimmery sweater the color of lime sherbet and woven brown flats. When she turned her head and her gaze fell on Gus, her laugh died. Her smile stayed but her eyes hardened and her steps veered toward the sideboard.

Louella Cantwell, Elvin's sister and the captain of the Crooked Possum Crisis Management Team, followed Cydney through the door. She was a nurse practitioner, warmhearted, good-humored. And God love her, in a forest-green pantsuit with a tunic top and a gold headband holding her glossy black pageboy, she looked like Elvin in drag. She carried a teapot tucked in a cozy crocheted by Aunt Phoebe. In Louella's hands it looked like it belonged to a child's tea set.

"Hey there, Gus." She put the teapot on a trivet in the

center of the table and glanced at him over her shoulder. "How's your hand?"

"Fine, Louella. I'm icing it." Gus stuck his right hand behind him and hurried to the sideboard where Cydney stood arranging the goody plate on a lace doily. He slid up beside her and reached for a cracker. A Ritz topped with cream cheese and a smoked oyster. "God bless Georgette."

Cydney slapped his hand away. "You won't be needing those."

"I didn't intend to hit him, babe. It just happened."

"Twice? I came downstairs after you'd knocked him out and Elvin was helping him up."

"I was provoked."

"Dad says he was provoked, but he won't tell me what you said."

"Coward. What I said is—"

"I think we should start now." Louella tapped her spoon on her teacup. "Please sit down, everyone."

She sat at the end of the table opposite Parrish, Cloris and Mamie on one side, Gus and Elvin with Cydney between them on the other.

"We always begin with a prayer." Louella folded her hands. "Dear Father in heaven—"

"No offense, madam," Parrish interrupted. "But I'm an atheist."

"I'll say a special prayer for you, Mr. Parrish." Louella closed her eyes. "Dear Lord, we ask Your guidance and wisdom—"

"I thought this was an intervention, not a prayer meeting."

"Mr. Parrish." Louella opened her eyes. Cydney shut hers and leaned her fingertips against her forehead. "Heavenly intervention is always welcome in our work with troubled families."

"Ah. But what about intellectual intervention?" Parrish leaned on an elbow, the cigarette in his hand trailing blue smoke. "A concise and unbiased gathering of the facts. The cold, critical eye of logic and reason. The irrefutable reality—"

"That you're making a fool of yourself?" Gus suggested.

"The reality"—Parrish glared at him—"that my daughter is not this man's fiancée and he has no intention of marrying her."

"Listen, you pompous sonofa—"

"You're right, Dad. Clever you." Cydney pushed to her feet. "Gus and I aren't engaged. We're having an affair. He told you I was his fiancée so I wouldn't be embarrassed. It was a kind and lovely gesture. I'll always remember it. And I'll never forget what you said—'In a pig's eye.'"

Parrish took a last drag on his cigarette and rubbed it out in the ashtray. "The minute I heard it I knew it was horseshit."

"That's because you're always right, Dad. Even when you're wrong you're right, and anyone who doubts that just has to ask you."

Parrish sat up straight, an affronted frown on his face. Cydney swung away from him and nodded to Cloris, Mamie and Louella.

"That's my statement, ladies. It was lovely to meet you."

Elvin stood up on one side of her, Gus the other. He wanted to go with her, but he wouldn't ruin her exit for the world. Elvin held her chair as she turned away, head high and shoulders straight, crossed the dining room and climbed the back stairs.

"I don't know you from Adam, mister, but I've known plenty of your sort," Mamie said bluntly to Parrish. "You're a horse's petoot."

"Mamie!" Cloris gasped. "It's the Sabbath!"

"My compliments, madam. You're an astute judge of character."

The twinkle in Parrish's eyes said he thought Mamie was a character. An old, dried-up back-country kook.

"And you're a jackass," she told him, then turned toward Louella. "I vote we let Gussie clobber him again."

"Let's don't rush to judgment, Mamie. Let's ask a few questions." Louella patted her hand and looked at Gus. "Is that what happened?"

"Pretty much." He and Elvin sat down. "That's when I clocked him, when he said, 'In a pig's eye.' "

"You and Cydney aren't engaged to be married?"

"No, Louella. I ad-libbed that."

"And not very well." Parrish lit the fresh cigarette in his holder and blew smoke through his nose. "The look on your face gave it away. The abject terror at the mere thought of marrying Cydney. Can't say I blame you, but you need to work on your poker face, Munroe."

"I was thinking I need to work on my right jab."

"Gus," Louella said sternly. "Now, Mr. Parrish—"

"I'd like to say something, Louella." Cloris turned in her chair and looked Parrish in the eye. "I believe you think that you have to be nasty to show people how smart you are. I also believe you must be a very angry and unhappy man to insult your daughter in front of strangers. I feel sorry for you, and I will surely say a prayer for you, but it's my judgment that you're an awful man and I vote with Mamie to let Gus clobber you."

Parrish sat a notch straighter, a startled, my-God-the-woman-has-a-brain flicker in his eyes. He wasn't the first person to mistake the citizens of Crooked Possum for half-witted, inbred hillbillies. He wouldn't be the last to misread their slower speech and pace, their faith and respectful manners for backwards, raised-in-the-holler lack of worldliness.

"But Cloris," Louella said, "we haven't heard from Mr. Parrish."

"Yes we have," she replied tartly. "I've heard all I care to hear."

"Gracious, ladies. Are you sure this is how you want to vote?"

"Did I mumble?" Mamie snapped. "Wore m'teeth so I wouldn't."

"Cloris? Are you sure about this?"

"Absolutely," she said firmly.

"Very well. I have your recommendation." Louella looked down the table at Parrish. "I don't agree with Mamie and

Cloris, which I will note in my report, but I've been outvoted. I'm sorry."

"Let me carry out the sentence for you, madam." Parrish slapped his hand and laughed. "There. I've been chastised."

"You ain't gettin' this, are you?" Elvin put on his I'm-the-Sheriff face and let Parrish have a good look at it. "This here is the Crooked Possum Crisis Management Team, duly empowered and granted full authority by the City Council to resolve domestic disputes by whatever means they deem appropriate. They jus' gave their recommendation. Now it's my job t'see to it that it's enforced."

"You have got to be kidding!" Parrish exclaimed with a laugh.

Elvin glanced at his sister. "Are we kiddin', Louella?"

"No, we are not." She spread her hands and shrugged. "The best I can offer you is the choice of where you'd like Gus to hit you."

"What do you mean, 'where'?"

"Face, body, arm, leg. Wherever you think you can take a punch."

"This is *outrageous*!" Parrish roared to his feet. "A travesty!"

"It's the law in Crooked Possum, Missouri." Elvin pronounced it Mizzou-rah and stood up. "You c'n abide by it or I c'n take you to jail."

"This no-talent hack hits me twice and your solution to a clearly unprovoked double assault is to let him hit me again?"

"In our opinion it wasn't unprovoked," Cloris answered. "In our opinion it was justifiable."

"There is no such thing, madam, as justifiable assault!"

"There is if we say there is, jackass." Mamie gave Gus a go-for-it swing of her fist. "Have at 'im, Gussie. Belt 'im a good one."

"Love to, Mamie." Gus stretched his hand across the table so she could see it. "But I don't think I can right now."

"Dang." She frowned at his bruised knuckles and glanced at Louella. "Could we let Gussie hit the jackass *with* somethin'?"

"No," Louella said firmly, gave Gus a thank-you smile and turned to Elvin. "What do you suggest, Sheriff?"

"A suspended sentence till Gus' hand heals up. With the understandin'—" Elvin shot an I-mean-this-hoss look at Gus and frowned at Parrish "—that you two keep your hands offa each other till this weddin's over. B'lieve that's why you're here, ain't it, Parrish?"

"To give my granddaughter away, yes," he said stiffly. "The second she's married I'll be on my way back to Cannes. In the meantime, I give you my word, Sheriff, that I will avoid this hack like the plague."

"I'll give the has-been a wide berth," Gus told Elvin. To Parrish, he said, "Cydney wants you here, so you can stay. Go find yourself a room that isn't already occupied. And haul your own damn luggage."

"Ladies." Parrish nodded to them. "Sheriff," he said to Elvin.

He ignored Gus and strode out of the dining room.

"Make you a poultice for that hand, Gussie," Mamie offered. "Sure would like to see you coldcock that jackass 'fore he leaves."

Somebody ought to coldcock you, Munroe, his inner voice said. *What d'you mean you can't think of a soul to invite to the wedding?*

"Don't remind me," Gus snapped. "I mean, that reminds me. There wasn't time to mail invitations, but you're all invited to Aldo's wedding next Saturday. The whole town, spread the word. It's three o'clock. Maybe four. I'll check with Cydney and let Elvin know."

"Ooh, a wedding!" Cloris clapped her hands. "I just love weddings!"

"Thank you, Gus." Louella gave him a misty-eyed smile. "I don't think we've all been up to Tall Pines since Phoebe passed, Lord rest her."

Five years. My God. Gus felt small and mean-spirited. Like Parrish, like he'd had his head stuck in a hole—or up the butt of his own misery—until Mamie winked and said, "I'll bring a li'l somethin' for the punch."

"You do that, Mamie." He laughed. "Louella, Cloris, thank you."

"I don't think we accomplished much." Louella gave her teammates a hard look. "But you're welcome, Gus."

"I need a favor," he said to Elvin. "My car's in Branson. Could you run me in to pick it up?"

"Sure thing, hoss."

"Let me tell Cydney. Be right back."

Gus raced up the back stairs. Maybe she'd want to ride along, get away from her old man. He could buy her dinner, maybe some lingerie. He tapped on her door and called her name but she didn't answer. Domino did, from the room across the alcove at the end of the hall, sliding into the doorway in a short, silk robe that showed lots of leg below and lots of bosom up top.

"Cindy is not there," she said.

"*Cyd-ney*. Where'd she go?"

"For the little walk. I loan her my fur and she went."

So did Gus, with a curt "Thanks," dashing through the house and out onto the deck. He saw lots of tracks in the snow, mostly deer and coyote. He tried the porch next, went back inside for an old sheepskin jacket in the foyer closet, and jogged out to the garage, then partway down the drive, but there was no sign of Cydney. She could walk to the North Pole on dry pavement and be warm as toast in a sable coat, but she wouldn't get far overland without snowshoes. Under the trees along the drive, the ice-crusted snow was about eight inches deep. In the open, where the almost fifty-degree sun had melted huge chunks of it, the bare ground was a muddy slop hole.

He gave up finally, hiked back to the house and met Elvin by his truck, a big red Chevy 4x4. Louella's dark green Suburban sat next to it, and she and Cloris and Mamie were just coming down the porch steps.

"Find her?" Elvin asked.

Gus shook his head no. "Beats the hell outta me where she went."

"She'll be fine, Gus." Louella opened the Suburban's passenger door, lifted Mamie first and then Cloris off their feet and up into the high-rise truck. "Don't worry about her."

But he did, all the way to Branson and back. He worried that she was stuck in the woods, knee-deep in mud and being circled by a coyote. Or stuck in the house with Parrish, being circled by her father and his bitter tongue. He shouldn't have left her; the Jag could've waited.

It was almost six and almost dark when he got back to Tall Pines. He parked the Jag by the front porch and switched off the engine. He didn't see any lights on in the house, grabbed the bags of Chinese food he'd bought in Branson and dashed up the steps.

"Is that beef and broccoli?"

Gus swung around and saw a lump of fur in one of the Adirondack chairs. "Yeah, it is. I thought maybe this time we could eat it."

Cydney laughed, straightened her jean-clad legs toward the porch rail and leaned her heels on it. Her white Keds were caked with mud.

"What are you doing out here?"

"Watching the stars come out."

Gus put the bags by the door, crossed the porch and sat on the arm of her chair. She leaned her head against his side. He ducked his chin and looked under the porch eave at the tiny diamonds of light dotting the gray and purple sky. He smelled snow in Cydney's hair and a reek of perfume from Domino's sable coat.

"How far did you walk?" he asked.

"Not far." She raised her arms and let the fur sleeves slide past her wrists. "It dawned on me I could be mistaken for a bear and shot."

Gus chuckled. It wasn't cold, just chilly enough that he could see his breath. "Have you been outside the whole time I was gone?"

"In and out. Louella came back to check on me. Then Elvin showed up to say he'd dropped you in Branson and you'd be home directly." She tipped her head up and looked at him, her eyes glistening in the twilight. "Louella said you were worried about me."

"I was afraid you'd get lost."

"Oh." She sighed and turned her head away. "Louella and Elvin moved the piano, just lifted it right up onto the dais in the great room like it weighed nothing. A grand piano."

"Louella is Crooked Possum's only EMT. I saw her roll a pickup off a guy once. He was pinned underneath it." Gus slid his arm around her. She resisted for a second, then settled against him. "Still mad at me?"

"I wasn't mad at you. I was just mad period." She curled her fist on her chin and gazed over the porch rail at the fog beginning to rise off the cooling snow. "I tried to work on my book. I wrote two whole words."

"That's better than no words. Which two did you get?"

"*Chapter Five.*"

"Some days it's tough." Gus kissed the top of her head. "Did Louella tell you how it went with the Crisis Management Team?"

"No. What happened?"

Gus told her, doing his best to mimic Cloris and Mamie. Cydney smiled, then she grinned. At the end, she laughed, then stretched her arms out again and cocked her head at him.

"Domino gave me this coat. I'm not keeping it, but she gave it to me. It belongs to last year, she said. 'Fletch, he will buy for me the new one.'" She frowned and shook her head. "Be damned if I would."

"Cydney," Gus said in her ear. "I think your father's impotent."

"You're kidding!" She flung herself sideways in the chair and stared at him. "That's what you said to him, isn't it?"

"Uh, well—more or less, yeah." He tensed, waiting for the punch, but she blinked into space for a second, then focused on his face.

"That's why he has to buy Domino a new sable every year, isn't it? Cloris is one sharp little cookie."

"The real power behind the throne of our mayor, Clovis Figgle."

"No wonder Dad flew into such a rage when he barged in on us." She laughed, her eyes sparkling. "He was *jealous*!"

"That hadn't occurred to me. I thought he was just an SOB."

"Well, that, too." She leaned her chin on his knee and looked up at him through her lashes, her amazingly long, amazingly dark lashes. "Want to get naked and eat Chinese food in your bed?"

"Beats croquet." He shrugged, and she laughed, wrinkled her nose at him, slipped her hand in his and let him help her out of the chair. "By the way, I invited everybody in Crooked Possum to the wedding."

"Wonderful." She stretched up on her toes and kissed his chin. "I'll tell Bebe to make sure Louella catches the bouquet."

chapter
twenty-four

At 9:17 Tuesday morning, Cydney sat on the blue leather sofa in the living room, the one that faced the foyer and the front door. She'd spent half of Monday there, too, sipping cups of tea while she waited for her mother to return from Eureka Springs. Georgette called while Cydney was in the bathroom, naturally, and told Gus she and Herb were staying over one more night so she could bid on a pump organ at an auction.

"Did you tell her Dad is here?" Cydney had asked.

"Doesn't she know?"

"Did *we* know?"

"Good point. You *think* your sister knew he was coming. But if Georgette doesn't know he's here, then who the hell invited him?"

Gus had frowned at her, then said just as she did: "Bebe."

This morning Cydney was playing it smart. No tea, just her laptop on her knees. She'd debated calling her mother back yesterday to warn her Fletch was here, but Gus had carried her off to the hot tub. They'd emerged an X-rated hour later to find a message from Aldo on the voice mail. He and Bebe had run into some friends from UMKC in Branson and wouldn't be home until today. Cydney had thought then, at 3 P.M. Monday, about calling her mother, but Gus had lured her back to the tub, so she still wasn't sure Georgette knew Fletch was at Tall Pines.

She hadn't seen her father or Domino since Sunday. The second time she and Gus had emerged from the hot tub, they'd found an ashtray full of cigarette butts on the island, the fridge raided, and the kitchen in a shambles. "Looks like raccoons broke in," Gus had grumbled. More likely, Cydney thought, her father was keeping his promise to Sheriff Cantwell to steer clear of Gus.

Cydney was surprised Georgette hadn't already come through the door. She hadn't heard a peep from her father or Domino yet today, and she'd been here on the couch since 6:30. Gus had shot awake at 5:20, thrown off the covers and grinned at her.

"That's it." He'd yanked on his jeans sans his boxers. "That's what Max needs to do in chapter twelve."

She'd struggled groggily up on one elbow and said, "Huh?"

"I'll be in my office." He leaned one knee on the bed and smacked a kiss on her mouth. "See you later."

She'd dragged herself into the bathroom, expecting him to join her as soon as he heard the water crank on, but she showered and washed her hair, dried it, brushed her teeth and dressed in jeans and the pink sweater she'd brought with her, all alone. When she stuck her head into his office, she'd seen Gus at his desk. Glasses on, mouth slack and partway open, his attention totally consumed by the PC.

"What?" he said absently, without looking up.

"Um—coffee or anything?"

"No." The clip in his voice was distracted, preoccupied, not at all sharp, but it hurt.

When she gathered her things and left, Gus didn't so much as glance up from the cursor spewing out words at Warp 6. That hurt, too.

The impulse to pick up her laptop on her way downstairs was pure I'll-show-you get-evenness, so of course it back-fired. She'd been sitting here for the last two hours staring at the words *Chapter Five* on the screen. She hadn't shown Gus a damn thing. She'd shown herself that she was not dealing at all well with the end of their idyll. *There's a news flash,* her little voice said. *I'll alert the media.* Her mother would be back today and Cydney couldn't imagine trying to sneak into Gus' bed with Georgette Parrish, the woman who'd always known when she'd had her feet on the couch, sleeping three doors away.

At least she'd had an extra day and night with Gus, but she was sure gonna miss beef and broccoli. She'd never be able to look another plate of it in the face after Gus had eaten most of his off her stomach and from between her breasts on Sunday night. Her heart fluttered, but she pushed the image of his mouth nibbling rice and her nipples out of her head.

Maybe if she read what she'd already written it would jump-start her brain. Cydney minimized chapter five, brought up chapter four and read the last couple pages.

"Hello, Mr. Munroe." I put on my best smile and offered my hand to his book jacket photo. "It's a pleasure to meet you."

My voice sounded funny over the tinny ring in my ears from the whack I'd taken on the back of the head. It made the deep voice that answered me—from the depths of my imagination, I thought—sound like it was coming from the bottom of an empty fifty-five gallon drum.

"Nice to meet you, too, Miss—?"

"Parrish. Cydney Parrish. I'm Bebe's aunt."

"I thought she had an Uncle Sid."

"That's Bebe's nickname for me, Uncle Cyd." I laughed, pretending. "I've read all your books, Mr. Munroe."

"So I see." The deep voice didn't sound hollow anymore. It sounded like Angus Munroe was really in the room, standing behind me, eyeing his books lined up in the bookcase. "Are those pictures of me?"

"Pictures?" I laughed again. "What pictures, Mr. Munroe?"

"The ones in your lap." The voice sounded sharp and edgy and very close. "The ones on the wall over the desk."

I heard the floor creak as if someone were walking across it. Then I felt it and my heart seized. I shot up on my knees, whirled around and saw Angus Munroe—

"Tall, dark and drop-dead handsome," Gus read aloud over her shoulder. "Hey, I like this part."

Cydney slapped her laptop shut and glared at him. He leaned on the back of the couch, one arm propping his chin on his hand. A grin on his face, his glasses slipped down on the end of his nose.

"Snoop. You snuck up on me."

"Did not." He vaulted over the couch and bounced down beside her, in his jeans and a red sweatshirt, and looped her under his arm. "I came downstairs, said, 'morning,' you said nothing. I went into the kitchen and drank a cup of coffee. I stuck my head past the door, said 'Wanna go upstairs and get naked?' You didn't answer, so I tiptoed over and had myself a peek." He raised his head and looked at her through his half lenses. "A peek not a snoop."

Cydney laughed and leaned her head against his chest, her heart aching and melting at the same time. Gus jostled her against him, chuckled into her hair and said, "You're still stuck, aren't you?"

"Boy, am I. I just can't think what happens next."

"You know what happens next, you were there."

"Yes, but I just—can't think how to say it."

"Want some help?"

Cydney drew her head back and looked at him.

"Just offering." He flung his hands up. "You could take advantage of something besides my body, you know."

"I appreciate it, Gus. I really do, but I have to find out if I can do this on my own."

"You think I never get stuck? Think your father never gets stuck? Sure we do, and I'm telling you from experience that it's a one-way ticket to writer's block to sit here beating your head against the screen if you don't have to. It only makes it worse."

"This is killing you, isn't it? I'm writing about you and you can't stand it. You're dying to read it."

"By inches I'm dying. By centimeters. By millimeters—"

"Oh stop." Cydney laughed and opened the laptop. Gus could hate it. Pick it to death. Tell her she didn't have what it takes. *Get real,* her little voice said. *It's about him. He'll love it.* "Here's where I'm stuck, at the end of chapter four. I don't know where to go from here."

He pushed his glasses up his nose and leaned closer to the screen. "Scroll up a few pages." Cydney did until he said, "Stop," nudged her fingers off the page up and page down keys and took over.

Her heart banged while he read. When he reached the end of chapter four, laughed and kissed the top of her head, she let go of the breath she hadn't realized she'd drawn and held.

"Funny, babe. Almost as cute as you. Nice job."

"Thanks. Where would you go from here?"

"Right this second? Upstairs with me." Cydney poked him in the ribs and he grinned. "Are you gonna stick with first-person?"

"No. That's just so I can get the story down."

"Then I'd change point of view."

"Get into your head?"

"You've been in my pants. Why not my brain?"

"I thought that's where your brain is."

"Only when I'm around you. C'mon. I'll help you get started."

"Oh Gus. I don't know."

"Be brave." He gave her a buck-up knuckle on the shoulder. "Live dangerously. Bring up chapter five."

Cydney did, her fingers clammy. "If you pick on me, I'll cry."

"I'm not going to pick on you. Just type what I say. The last line of four is 'What kind of a nut are you?' So the first line of chapter five is, 'A very fetching nut, Gus could see, now that she stood on her knees facing him.' " He kissed her temple and Cydney smiled, feeling loved again, even though she wasn't. " 'Probably harmless, but still a nut.' "

"A nut with no idea how to explain what she's doing," she said, laughing up at the grin on his face. "A nut who wishes she were dead."

"That's good. Write it down." He gave her shoulders an

encouraging squeeze. "Now this. 'She had lovely, almond-brown eyes tipped up at the corners and oddly dark brows for someone with such silvery-blond hair. A gamine face, the face of a pixie.' "

"What's a gamine and how do you spell it?"

"G-a-m-i-n-e, Scrabble whiz, and it's an urchin."

"Oh how flattering."

"Well, that's what you looked like. All waifish and woebegone—"

"Ooh, I like that," Cydney said excitedly, and typed it.

"I wanted to say, 'Aww.' " He breathed it in her ear from deep in his throat, tickling her with his breath. "But then it dawned on me that maybe you weren't being charmingly coy, but coolly calculating."

"Oh right." She smirked. "Like I knew you were coming."

"That's pretty much what my big-mouth know-it-all voice said. Like you knew I was coming and planned it. Like all the women I think are after me because I'm a rich, famous writer lay awake nights dreaming up screwball scenarios to get my attention."

"Do women really do that kind of thing to you?"

"No." Gus snapped his fingers. "Damn it."

"Aldo said that's why you moved to Crooked Possum, so nobody could find you unless you wanted them to."

"I moved us to Crooked Possum so nobody could find Aldo unless I wanted them to. I bought this place for Aunt Phoebe. Her dream was to own a bed-and-breakfast, but her heart gave out before she could open Tall Pines." Gus tossed his glasses aside, rubbed his hand on her arm and gazed around the living room. "I ought to sell it, but I just can't."

He looked so wistful, so handsome, like such a little boy with his hair falling over his eyes. Cydney's throat ached looking at him. He'd kept Tall Pines for Aunt Phoebe, kept the dining room just the way she'd left it and built a shrine from Aldo's baby pictures on her grand piano.

"By the way," she said, blinking at the tears in her eyes. "Louella and I packed all your pictures in a box till after the wedding."

"I might just leave them there." He sighed. "I think it's time."

Oh Gus. Oh please, she prayed. Don't say another word. Don't even think about broken little angels who managed to find each other.

"So what do you think of chapter five?" He glanced her a smile, blinked and frowned. "Why are you crying? Did I pick on you?"

"Oh no. No, no, no." Cydney kissed his chin, hoping he couldn't feel the teary shiver in her mouth. "You were a big help. Thanks."

She swung her head away, hit Save and sucked a breath. This was so hard, but she'd vowed to enjoy it, to enjoy Gus as long as she had him. She slanted a hey-big-boy smile at him through her lashes, laid her hand on his thigh and let her fingers creep toward his fly.

"Are you still not wearing any underwear?"

"Unzip me and find out."

Cydney shut down the laptop and put it on the table, leaned into him and reached for the snap on his jeans. Gus bent his head, his eyes smoky, his lips parted. Cydney heard a doorknob turn, footsteps skid to a halt and looked over her shoulder.

At her mother, standing on the foyer in pink knit slacks and a creamy turtleneck, every strand of champagne hair in place, her makeup perfect and fire in her eyes. She threw her blue wool coat and her Hermes bag at a chair and thrust her hands on her hips.

"What the hell is going on here?"

"Beats me, Mother." Cydney stood up with Gus beside her, his hand on the small of her back, and squared off on Georgette. She was thirty-two, not seventeen, and she was sick of having her privacy trampled. "What do you think is going on?"

"I think you've all lost your minds, that's what I think. How could you let your father just waltz through the door?"

"How were we supposed to stop him, Mother?" Cydney

waved at the open door behind her. "He barged through it exactly as you just did."

"Did I barge? I'm sorry." Georgette pressed one hand to her breast. "I meant to storm through the door screaming and throwing things."

"Now, now, Georgie-girl." Herb stepped inside, shut the door and slipped an arm around her. "We're all intelligent, rational adults. For Bebe and Aldo's sake, we can make the best of this awkward situation."

"*You* are intelligent and rational, Herbert." Her mother turned toward him on one foot. "*I* am intelligent and rational. Fletcher Parrish is a moody, petulant, hypercritical egomaniac with a mean streak."

"My finest qualities, George. Those of which I am proudest."

What Cydney heard in her father's voice was a wry, almost self-deprecating twist, not his usual sneer. She looked up at him coming down the gallery stairs in mauve silk pajamas, a matching dressing gown and leather mules, a fond smile on his face as he gazed at her mother.

"I'm warning you, Fletch." She stepped down from the foyer, one perfectly manicured nail thrust at him like a dagger. "One tantrum, one snit, and you'll pay me alimony until the day you die."

"Is this your intended?" Her father smiled sweetly at Georgette and offered his hand to Herb. "Fletcher Parrish. You're a lucky man."

"Herb Baker." Herb shook his hand. "Your loss is my gain."

"Right you are. Let me buy you a cup of coffee." Fletch laid an arm on his shoulders and glanced at Cydney. "I trust you made some?"

Not for you, she wanted to say. *Well, then say it,* her little voice egged her on, so Cydney did. "I didn't make it for you," she said boldly. "But yes, I made coffee."

"Brews the best pot on the planet, our Cydney." Fletch ignored the zinger and swept Herb across the living room, pushed the swinging door open, held it and glanced back at Georgette. "Are you joining us?"

"You bet I am," she growled. "I'm not taking my eyes off you."

And she didn't until she reached the bar and the 125 pumpkins piled on it caught her eye. She turned toward Gus and said, "Pumpkins are fruit, Angus. These will store much better in a cool place," then she wheeled through the door behind Herb.

Fletch turned to follow her, paused and looked at Gus. "How's the hand, Munroe?"

"I may never play the violin again."

"Glad to hear it. My nose hurts like hell," he said, but he smiled and pushed through the door.

When it swung shut Gus laid his hands on her shoulders. "What do you think? The body snatchers came last night?"

"Dream on." Cydney turned to face him. "He's up to something."

"Who's gonna tell Georgette about the pumpkins?"

"Not me. I'd rather put on Domino's coat and go stand out in the woods. At least I'd stand a fighting chance of *not* being shot."

"Then let's go change." Gus cupped her elbow and turned her toward the gallery. "I'll take you shopping."

"I was kidding about my truck, Gus. It's insured," Cydney said. Which reminded her, she had to call her insurance agent.

"I'm not buying you a truck. I'm buying you a sweater." He gave her a wicked, hot-eyed smile. "And lingerie."

Cydney shouldn't have let him, but he had so much fun in the Victoria's Secret wannabe boutique they found in Branson. He growled in his throat and panted like a dog over her shoulder as she looked through the racks. Knowing he'd never see her wear any of this stuff made her heart hurt, but she played along and laughed when he looked up at the ceiling, whistling, and tried to follow her into the changing room.

She cried a little while she was back there, where he couldn't see or hear her, and dabbed her eyes with her bra. The tear-stains were dry by the time he took her to lunch at a lovely wood-beamed and wood-paneled restaurant perched half-way up a mountain.

The hostess seated them at a table by a big window, lit a candle in a glass globe and left. Cydney leaned her chin on her hand and gazed at the snow-studded hills gathering mist in the valleys and hollows between them. In her dreams she'd been to places like this with Gus for romantic dinners, basking in the heat of passion in his eyes, serenely ignoring the murmured conversation she overheard from the next table:

"That's Cydney Parrish, the famous author."

"*Ohhh*. Who's the guy with her?"

"Dunno. Looks kinda familiar. Maybe he used to be famous."

Cydney rolled her eyes at her reflection in the window. You dweeb.

"Something bothering you?" Gus asked.

She glanced at him, looking up at her from the menu over the wire rims of his glasses. "Nope," she said. "Not a thing."

He half cocked an eyebrow and went back to the menu.

"Well. There is one tiny little thing."

He sighed and shut the menu. "The wedding."

"The pumpkins. I keep wondering if Bebe and Aldo have made it back to Tall Pines yet and told my mother."

Gus cupped his ear to the window. "I can't hear her screaming."

Cydney laughed. He smiled. "We'll eat and head back."

It was almost two when Gus turned the Jag up the drive to Tall Pines. The blue spruce that had come down during the storm had been cleared away. Only a scatter of needles and small branches marked where it had fallen over the first switchback.

"Looks like Elvin's been here," he said.

When the Jag swooped around the circle lawn, past the broken pine in the middle that made the others look like a gap-toothed smile, Cydney saw Sheriff Cantwell's squad car parked by the porch steps. Next to a white Ford Bronco with red doors and a light rack on the roof.

"Louella's here, too." Gus frowned as he switched off the engine and popped his door. "That's her ambulance."

"Oh no." Cydney's heart sank as she shoved her door open. "I told you my father was up to something."

And he was, up to his elbows in rubber gloves and a bucket of Spic 'n Span, scouring the stones on the front of the fireplace in the great room. Herb stood on the raised hearth scrubbing above the mantel. Aldo stood on a ladder with a sponge mop wiping down the paneling. Elvin steadied another ladder in the middle of the room so Louella could reach the cobwebs in the rafters with a towel-covered broom.

The reek of ammonia almost knocked Cydney over when she and Gus raced through the pocket doors, hand in hand and out of breath. Georgette stood on a stepladder in front of the glass wall, a rag black with grime in one of her rubber-gloved hands and a scarf tied around her hair. Bebe knelt beneath her with a rag in one gloved hand, the other one bare and pinching her nose shut.

"What are you people doing?" Gus asked.

"The cleaning crew called and canceled, Angus, so here we are." Georgette laid her rag on the top of the ladder and climbed down. "Elvin and Louella stopped by and kindly offered to help."

"Hey, Gus. Hi, Cydney." Louella wore green hospital scrubs and waved her dusty broom from the top of her ladder. "Cloris and her sisters and Mamie and Sarah Boyce should be here directly."

"That's very kind of you all," Gus said. "But it's not necessary."

"It is if you want to have a wedding in here on Saturday," Louella replied firmly. "When was the last time you cleaned this place?"

"Get changed and get busy, Angus," Georgette said to Gus, peeling off her rubber gloves as she came toward them. "Cydney, that goes for you, too. I need your help in the kitchen. We'll have a crowd to feed."

I'll be waiting with my rubber hose, said the look her mother gave her as she swept past. "Right there, Mother," Cydney said to her. "Here comes the third degree," she said under her breath to Gus.

"Remember you're an Uzi, not a peashooter." Gus drew her into the living room and kissed her forehead. "I'll take your goody bag up to my room. You can decide later which luscious ensemble you'd like me to peel you out of tonight with my teeth."

"I've already decided," Cydney said, knowing she wouldn't make it to his room tonight or any other night. "The lavender lace."

"Excellent choice." He kissed her again between her brows. "Better go before your mother sends out a posse."

Cydney went, first to her bedroom for her jeans and a slightly ratty green sweatshirt she'd brought along just in case and headed for the kitchen. Via the gallery stairs, hoping she'd run into Gus for another quick kiss. She didn't, but she saw that the pumpkins were gone from the bar, pushed through the door into the kitchen and saw her mother at the sink washing mushrooms.

Rice cooked in a lidded saucepan on the stove and bacon sizzled in a skillet. On the cabinet, two pumpkin pies waited to go in the oven.

"Did those pies come from where I think they came from?"

"One down," Georgette said. "One hundred and twenty-four to go."

Damn. There went her perfect get-even-with-Gwen scheme. Cydney moved to the stove to turn the bacon and check the rice.

"How'd you talk Bebe out of a Halloween wedding?"

"She'd talked herself out of it while she and Aldo were snowed in in Branson. Now we have a Harvest Bounty theme." She glanced at Cydney over her shoulder. "I'm putting Angus in my will. Anyone who can punch Fletcher Parrish and live to tell about it deserves a reward."

Cydney's stomach clutched, but she had to know. "Did Dad tell you why Gus hit him?"

"No. He only said that Angus provoked him. What happened?"

"I don't know," Cydney said, hoping she was lying about the right thing. "I was upstairs with Domino. I came down just as Sheriff Cantwell was helping Dad off the floor. He said the same thing. Gus had provoked him. Gus said Dad provoked him."

"Must be some macho, silly man-thing, then." Georgette shut off the water to drain the mushrooms. "What's the French bimbo like?"

"She doesn't sleep with Dad." Cydney figured she might as well tell her mother 'cause she'd find out soon enough. She also told her about the sable coat and the size of Domino's makeup case.

Georgette loved it and forgot all about the punch, which suited Cydney. She couldn't figure out why Fletch had told her mother about the second punch but not the first one. It was totally out of character for him to pass up an opportunity to humiliate someone.

"How'd you get Dad to pitch in and help?"

"I didn't. Herb filled a bucket with Spic 'n Span, your father filled a bucket. Herb picked up a scrub brush, your father picked up a scrub brush." Georgette slid her a coy little smile on her way to the fridge. "I think it's very sweet."

Cydney thought it was a stick of dynamite with a burning fuse.

The ladies of Crooked Possum arrived with their own buckets, rubber gloves, brushes and rags. Cloris Figgle and her three sisters, Mamie Buckles and Sarah Boyce. They called cheerfully to Gus and Aldo, Sheriff Cantwell and Louella when they entered the great room, nodded "How do" to the Parrish family and set to work like a hive full of bees.

Louella took command and appointed Cydney gopher. She fetched buckets of hot water and clean rags, shook dust mops off the deck rail, fetched coffee and iced tea and snacks on break times. Midway across the living room there was a head-spinning collision of scents—a Spic 'n Span and Pine-Sol overlay on top of stuffed mushrooms and the chicken and wild rice soup simmering in the kitchen.

It made Cydney dizzy and light-headed. So did the glances Gus shot her when she passed, sometimes soft-eyed and smiling, the rest sexy and sizzling. "Lavender lace," he whispered in her ear when she brought him a fresh pail of hot water. His breath on her neck made her shiver and her grip slip on the bucket handle.

By six o'clock the great room was mostly clean. At 6:30 the menfolk arrived, Mayor Figgle with a floor buffer that belonged to the Elks Lodge. While Roylee Boyce set to tuning Aunt Phoebe's piano on the dais, Mayor Figgle started on the floor. Gus and Aldo, Sheriff Cantwell and the rest of the men finished washing the walls and knocking cobwebs down from the rafters.

The ladies bustled into the kitchen, washed up and tied Aunt Phoebe's aprons over their work clothes and helped Georgette lay out supper on the bar. Stuffed mushrooms and a relish tray, vegetables with spinach dip, the soup in a steaming crock and sourdough bread hot from the oven. Before Georgette could reach for a bell, Louella hollered for the menfolk to come and get it.

Everyone filled plates and bowls, coffee cups and iced tea glasses and settled around the living room in pairs. Her mother and Herb, Mayor Figgle and Cloris, her three sisters and their husbands, Aldo and Bebe, Roylee and Sarah Boyce, Sheriff Cantwell and Louella. Even Domino came downstairs and sat with her father nibbling veggies.

Everyone had somebody, spouse, sibling or friend. Everyone but Cydney, who turned away last from the bar and saw Gus sitting on the hearth with Mamie. He closed the black mesh screen on the fire he'd just built, the tiny flame flickering in his eyes as he laughed at whatever she'd just said. Everyone was filthy and everyone's hair—except Georgette's—was ratted with dust, but everyone smiled and talked and laughed.

Everyone but Cydney. She stood by the bar like the last kid

to be picked for dodgeball. She could wade in anywhere, be welcomed with a smile and given a seat, but she stood on the fringe watching Bebe feed mushrooms to Aldo and felt tears burn in the corners of her eyes.

Gwen wouldn't be here till Thursday, but already Uncle Cyd had begun to disappear. She was losing them both, Bebe and Gus.

It was time, Cydney decided, to go wash glasses in the scullery.

chapter
twenty-five

Cydney didn't think Gus would miss her, but he missed her almost instantly. He glanced toward the bar where he'd seen her just a second ago filling a plate, and saw that she was gone. What the hell?

He started to get up and go look for her, just as Mamie leaned forward, plunked her elbows on her knees and cut off his exit.

"Tell you somethin', jackass." She pointed a crooked finger at Parrish, who sat with Domino on the closest blue couch. "Didn't think you knew how to work, but you've a fair hand with a scrub brush."

"Thank you, madam." Parrish nodded. "High praise, indeed."

"What does this mean?" Domino asked. "This *jackass*?"

"It's a term of endearment." Georgette shot a dazzling smile at Parrish, "Isn't it, jackass?"

Everyone laughed, even Parrish. With a gleam in his eyes Gus supposed could be malice, but he thought was amusement. He'd realized earlier that Cydney had her father's eyes as well as his dark brows. Same almond-brown color and almond shape. It had given him a hell of a jolt, but he was determined not to hold it against her. He just wanted to hold her.

"Cup of coffee?" Gus asked Mamie.

"Why thank you, Gussie. I'd love one." She sat back, clearing his path to the bar and wherever Cydney had disappeared to from there.

The kitchen was the likeliest place. Gus was two steps shy of the swinging door when Elvin's hand fell on his shoulder.

"Have a word, hoss?"

"In a sec, Elvin. I promised Mamie coffee and I need a clean cup."

"Here's a couple hidin' out behind the soup." Elvin turned him toward the bar. "Right proud of the way you and Parrish is gettin' along."

"Thanks." Gus filled a white mug from Aunt Phoebe's everyday stoneware with coffee. "And thanks for your help with the great room and moving the tree out of the drive."

"That's why the Good Lord give us friends, hoss, to lend a hand where and when we can." Elvin filled a mug for himself and emptied half of it in one swallow. "Glad t'see you comin' out o' your depression."

He pronounced it *de*-pression. Gus blinked at him. "My what?"

"*De*-pressed," Elvin said solemnly. "That's what Louella says you been since Miss Phoebe passed, God rest her. Said she didn't think it was cynical, though, and likely you'd git over it in time."

"Clinical, Elvin. I think Louella meant clinical depression."

"That's it." He snapped his fingers. "Cain't keep them medical terms straight. Anyhow. Mighty glad t'see you bein' your old self, hoss."

"Good t'be m'old self, Elvin." Gus clapped him on the arm and headed across the living room with Mamie's coffee.

De-pressed. My God. Could he have been and not realized it? Sometimes he couldn't sleep. He tended to forget to eat when he was heavy into a book. He was not suicidal. But the kicker was Cydney. Until she'd come along with her silver curls and wood nymph body he and Clyde had only occasionally shaken hands in the shower.

"Here you are, Mamie." Gus bent down and handed her the mug.

"Thank you, Gussie." She patted his cheek and smacked him a kiss.

Gus winked at her and made a beeline for Louella. Fortunately, she was sitting on the dais steps or he would've had to fetch one of the ladders to peck a kiss on her cheek.

"I'm fine, Louella." He sat down beside her and puffed out a breath. "But next time you think I'm not, I want you to tell me."

"Elvin and his big mouth." Louella aimed a sour look at her brother, then smiled at Gus. "I was keeping an eye on you. I figured you'd snap out of it once you had a reason." She looked around the room and frowned. "Well, where did Cydney go?"

"I don't know. She was over by the bar just a minute ago."

And a minute ago he'd realized on his own what Louella had just said. Gus felt a zip up his back and swung around to face her.

"What a second. What are you saying?"

"I ain't sayin' nothin', hoss." She let her drawl creep out, winked at him and clapped a hand on his knee. "You figger it out."

Or would you just like me to tell you? his inner voice asked.

"I'd like you to shut up and leave me alone," Gus muttered, and started across the living room for the kitchen. Just as he reached for the swinging door, he felt a hand on his arm, turned and saw Aldo.

"Got a minute, Uncle Gus?" He looked nervous and worried.

Uh-oh. "Sure, pal." He followed Aldo up the steps into the foyer, out of the noise and chatter and laughter in the living room.

"There's a lot more to this getting married stuff than I thought." Aldo leaned on the wall at the foot of the staircase. "I gotta have a tux, Bebe said, or I'll look like a dork. I never even thought of it. I've never even worn one."

"You are the groom, pal. You should wear a tuxedo," Gus agreed.

"And I gotta have a best man. Bebe's Grampa is giving her away, but she says I need somebody to stand up with me. So I was wondering." Aldo looked at the floor, then back up at Gus. "I know you're not crazy about me and Bebe getting married, but would you be my best man?"

"Well—sure. But if you'd like to ask one of your buds from school—"

"No. It's gotta be you, Uncle Gus." Aldo looked at him with Beth's blue eyes and Artie's jaw set in a firm, my-mind's-made-up line. "You're the best man I know."

"Then I'd be honored. You're the best man I know, too."

Gus offered his hand but Aldo threw his arms around him. Gus felt the scrape of his nephew's beard against his cheek and for just a second, just a whisper of memory, the soft, hot brush of a toddler's tear-dampened cheek. He swept Aldo into a fierce hug and pressed his mouth to his hair.

"I love you, Uncle Gus."

"I love you, too. Tell you what." Gus cleared his throat and held his nephew at arm's length. "If you'll get a haircut I'll buy you a tuxedo."

"Beebs mentioned that, too. Like my hair is longer than hers."

"Then we'll get your hair cut tomorrow and buy you a tux."

Aldo grinned. "One for you, too, best man."

"One for me, too." Gus clapped him on the shoulder.

"Dessert, everyone!" Georgette called. "Pumpkin pie!"

Gus turned and saw her sailing across the living room with a tray full of plates. Cydney followed her with a bowl of whipped cream and a big spoon. Aldo scurried back to Bebe, Gus went back to the hearth and his place beside Mamie.

When Georgette came his way with the pie and Cydney with the whipped cream, Gus' heart kicked at the glow the fire kissed on her brow, the lights it lit in her hair. He let Mamie dip first into the whipped cream, the perfect line—"What? No maraschino cherries?"—poised on his lips, but Mamie scooped a second spoonful and plopped it on his pie.

"There y'go, Gussie," she said cheerfully.

And there went Cydney, his silver-haired pixie, sliding a smile at him over her shoulder as she turned away and held the bowl out to Roylee and Sarah Boyce. This was wrong, damn it. She shouldn't offer whipped cream to anybody but him, and the second he peeled her out of the luscious lavender lace bra and teeny tiny panties he'd tell her so.

But he never got the chance. Dessert ended and everybody pitched in to put the food away and do the dishes. Louella and Mamie, Sarah and Cloris and her sisters promised to come back tomorrow to finish the great room and help with the decorating.

Georgette thanked them all, sent everyone home with a pumpkin, shut the door, turned around and gave Cydney a high five.

"Fourteen down. One hundred and eleven to go," she said, then clapped her hands. "Bedtime, everyone. We've lots to do tomorrow."

Gus raced upstairs. He changed the sheets, put clean towels in the bathroom and lit the candles, stripped down to his boxers and emptied the giant-size bag of lingerie on the bed. He spent a heart-pounding forty-five minutes arranging and rearranging the two dozen delectable little ensembles on Aunt Phoebe's quilt. He paced for another fifteen, jumping at every creak the floor made. He lost count of how many times he flew to the stairs expecting it to be Cydney this time for sure.

At 11:45 he yanked on sweats and socks and a T-shirt and went to get her, hurried down the steps, swung around the corner into the living room and slid to a stop. Georgette and Fletch sat on the hearth in robes and pajamas, roasting giant marshmallows on long barbecue forks over the glowing remnants of the fire Gus had banked and left to die. Where the heck, Gus wondered, was Herb?

"Angus." Georgette smiled. "Would you like a marshmallow?"

"Sure." If he could get to the kitchen he had a straight shot up the back stairs to Cydney's room. "How 'bout a cup of cocoa to go with it?"

"Cydney's making some. She couldn't sleep, either."

"Really?" Gus' pulse leaped. "I'll give her a hand."

He wheeled toward the swinging door just as she backed through it, a tray with mugs and spoons and a steaming china pot in her hands.

"Oh—hi there, Uncle Gus."

She blinked at him. If she'd had a free hand, she would've plucked her hair; she always did when she was nervous. Why had he spent a bloody fortune on sexy lingerie? She looked alluring as hell in the oversized white terry cloth robe belted over her green-striped pajamas.

"Hi yourself, Uncle Cyd." He went to her and took the tray, let his fingertips graze her knuckles as he lifted it out of her grasp.

"I tried to get to you," she whispered. "But Mother and Dad—"

"I'll try later," Gus whispered.

"No. Early. In the kitchen so we can talk. Say about—"

"Cydney," Georgette cut her off. "The marshmallows are burning."

So was Gus, to touch Cydney, to feel himself inside her. He carried the tray to the hearth and thought about dumping it on Georgette's head.

"I'm beat." Cydney gave an exaggerated yawn when she finished her cocoa, curled her arms in a stretch behind her head and caught Gus' eye. "Think I'll turn in so I can get up *early*. The *earlier* the better. Six-thirty isn't too *early*. It's the *early* bird that catches the worm, after all."

"What the hell are you doing?" Georgette looked at her like she'd grown another head. "Speaking in some kind of code?"

"Sorry, Mother. I'm just s-o-o-o tired." Gus grinned at Cydney and winked, gave her an okay-I-got-it nod. "G'night, all."

Gus set two alarms so he wouldn't oversleep. Not that he slept. He turned and twisted and burned all night. At 5:45 he was in the shower, throbbing and groaning at the tortured stirring the warm water raised between his legs. He spread his hands on the tiled wall and wanted to bash his head against it.

He shaved and brushed his teeth, dried his hair and frowned at the cowlick in the front. He should probably get a haircut today, too. He hissed through his teeth as he zipped himself gingerly into a pair of jeans, put on a navy sweater with a thin red stripe in it, socks and his loafers and headed downstairs at 6:17.

He stopped just shy of the swinging door behind the bar to adjust himself and mutter at Clyde to knock it off. When he reached to push the door open, he heard Parrish's voice in the kitchen and stopped.

"You lied to me and your mother, Bebe. Your Aunt Cydney and Munroe are no more trying to wreck your wedding than I am."

"But they were, Gramps. I told you on the phone, they were awful to me and Aldo. Just ask Gramma."

"I asked your grandmother. She and I had a very enlightening conversation late last night in front of the fire."

So that's what they were doing, Gus thought. Discussing Bebe.

"Damn smart of you to make your hysterical calls to your mother and me while your grandmother was in Arkansas and I couldn't reach her by phone. If she'd told me two days ago what she told me last night I wouldn't have come."

"But Aunt Cydney and Mr. Munroe knocked it off the second you came. See, I knew they would. I knew the minute you got here—"

"I got my lights punched out and I deserved it. I came here loaded for bear. I believed you—in Munroe's case because I wanted to—but I should've known better about Cydney. I'm ashamed of myself and I'm ashamed of you."

"But I didn't do anything!" Bebe wailed, and burst into tears.

"The hell you didn't. You threw a tantrum because you couldn't get your way. You made up lies to get even because your aunt and Munroe thwarted you. Does Aldo know you pulled this shit?"

Bebe's tears snapped off. "Don't tell him, Gramps. Please."

"Give me one good reason why I shouldn't. I think he deserves to know what he's got in store for him the first time he crosses you."

"I love Aldo, Gramps. I'd never be mean to him. I just got so upset because I couldn't have things the way I wanted."

"Nobody gets everything they want just the way they want it. Why the hell d'you think you should? I've spent my entire life trying to achieve it, gone through six wives in the process and I still don't have everything I want just the way I want it. Know why? 'Cause it's a perfect state of being and we live in an imperfect world. I wish somebody had explained that to me when I was your age and I'd had the brains to listen. It would have saved me a lot of anger and frustration and a whole lot of money."

"Oh but Aldo has lots of money. You don't have to worry—"

"Knock off the dumb bunny routine. It's a nice little act, though. It's cut a lot of corners for you, gotten you out of lots of boring little things you don't want to be bothered with, but nobody who's as stupid as you pretend to be could outsmart me *and* your mother at the same time."

"You won't tell, will you? It's my ace in the hole."

"Depends on how you conduct yourself. Show me you can see past the end of your own nose and I might keep quiet."

"Promise me, Gramps?"

"Hell no I won't promise. You got around me once, Bebe. Don't try it twice. I'm older, craftier and meaner than cat shit if you cross me."

"Do I have to apologize to everybody on the planet?"

"For what? Only your grandmother and I know what you did. I *am* going to tell your mother, however, so I advise you not to make any more hysterical phone calls."

"Oh Gramps, please don't tell her. If she gets really mad she might not come and I want her here more than anything."

"You should've thought of that before you pulled this. I won't let Gwen walk in here with a chip on her shoulder like I did. If she decides not to come, tough cookies. It'll be on you and nobody else."

"Gimme a chance, Gramps. I'll be good. I'll change, I promise I'll—"

"Oh brother." Parrish laughed. "If I had a nickel for every time I told your grandmother I'd change, I wouldn't have to write like a rabbit in heat to pay her alimony. You remind me of me."

"That's why you love me. That's why I'm your little Bebe-cakes."

"No, Bebe. That's why you scare me. Munroe's nephew may not be the sharpest knife in the drawer but he's a nice kid and he's nuts about you. You say you love him. I hope you do, 'cause I'd hate to see you end up like me with a train wreck for a life."

"That's the meanest thing you've ever said to me."

"It's the most honest thing I've ever said to you. Don't mistake kindness for weakness, Bebe. Now go away so I can drink my coffee."

Gus ducked out of sight behind the bar as Bebe slammed through the swinging door. The hinges shrieked and the door whacked into the wall. He rose from a crouch as she stormed past him. He watched her cross the living room and stomp up the gallery stairs. A second later a door banged. Gus leaned his arms on the bar and grinned.

"Got yours, little girl." He turned toward the door, reached for it again and stopped again when he heard another voice in the kitchen. Cydney, this time. She must've come through the dining room.

"Morning, Dad."

"Thank God it's you," Parrish replied. "Make me a decent pot of coffee, would you?"

"Sure. Did Bebe make this one?"

"Hell no, I made it. I wouldn't let my darling granddaughter near anything I plan to eat or drink. Arsenic leaves no trace, you know."

"Dad," Cydney said soberly. "I didn't mean to, but I heard everything you said to Bebe." Gus heard the tap turn and water run. "Boy, do I feel like a chump. She had me fooled."

"Bebe had us all fooled. I didn't realize I'd been manipulated by a master till I got here. I'm damn lucky Munroe only punched me twice."

"That little *bitch*!" Cydney shrilled, and something slammed hard against the granite countertop. "Do you know what she *did*?"

Gus hiked himself up on the countertop behind the bar, leaned the heels of his hands on the edge and listened to Cydney tell Parrish about the codicil to Artie's will and Bebe punching him in the nose. He'd meant to leave, had turned away, in fact, but changed his mind when he'd heard Cydney screech, "That little *bitch*!"

"Bebe knew damn good and well what that codicil meant and she was furious because she wasn't going to get her way," he heard Cydney seethe through the pass-through. "But she trotted out her dimwit act and got away with slugging Gus and knocking him out. She put him in the hospital, Dad. With a concussion and cracked cartilage in his nose!"

Parrish laughed. Gus grinned. He should be madder than hell, but this was just too rich. If he wrote it in a book no one would believe it.

"Dad," Cydney snapped indignantly. "This is not funny."

"Yes it is, honey." Parrish chuckled. "Isn't it, Munroe?"

Gus had been happily swinging his feet but froze, caught.

"Oh, c'mon in here," Parrish called. "I know you're out there."

The has-been didn't sound angry. Cydney didn't look angry, either, just surprised to see him when he pushed through the swinging door. She stood against the counter with her arms folded, the granite top strewn with coffee grounds. That's what she'd slammed, the basket of the Krups machine.

"How'd you know I was out there?" Gus asked Parrish.

"The bird and the worm and six-thirty isn't too early gave it away." Cydney flushed and plucked at her hair. "I didn't intend to get in your way. I came down for coffee and Bebe followed me. I take it you heard my conversation with her, too?"

"Every word," Gus admitted. "She's a piece of work."

"How angry are you?" Cydney asked, biting her lip.

"Not at all." Gus grinned and ruffled a hand through his hair. "I should be but this is just too good." He met Parrish's gaze, saw the grin on his face and the laughter in his eyes. "Guess we're even, huh?"

"Thanks to my Machiavellian little granddaughter, yes, we're even." Parrish slid off his stool and offered his hand. "I apologize for the 'no-talent pretty boy.' "

"Sorry about the 'has-been.' " Gus stepped toward him and shook his hand. "I own all your books in hardcover."

"Same here." Fletch winked. "Gotta keep up with the competition."

"All righty, gents." Cydney clapped her hands, a bright but quivery smile on her face. "What'll it be for breakfast?"

"French toast," Gus and Parrish said together. "It's my favorite," Fletch said. "Mine, too," Gus replied, and swung himself onto a stool.

What a love fest, his inner voice said. *I'm gagging here, Munroe.*

"And the mistress of French toast is here to prepare it." Georgette breezed into the kitchen from the hallway, with Herb behind her. "Fry sausage, Cydney," she said, nudging her aside at the stove. "Kindly cut the grapefruit, Herbert. Angus, set the table. And Fletch, stay on that stool and out of my way."

"Well, I like that. Just when I was about to offer to take you back."

Georgette swung a look at him over her shoulder, Aunt Phoebe's king-size cast-iron skillet in her hand. "For my French toast, of course."

"Absolutely." Parrish slid her a wicked smile and twisted a cigarette into his gold holder. "What other reason could I possibly have?"

Georgette glared at him, but her eyes twinkled as she banged the skillet on the front burner. "You're a wretch, Fletch."

"You're a poet, George."

They laughed at each other across the kitchen, trading a look that didn't quite strike sparks but came close. Cydney and Herb popped out of the fridge side by side, Herb clutching four fat, red grapefruit; Cydney a package of sausage on top of the butter dish, a dozen eggs and a half gallon of milk, an uh-oh pucker between her brows. Gus folded his arms on the island and smiled. This was getting fun again.

Cydney scurried toward the stove, splitting a what's-going-on-here look between her parents. Herb plunked a cutting board on the far end of the island and a grapefruit on top of it. Fletch lit his cigarette, inhaled and blew smoke. Herb waved a hand in front of his face.

"Must you smoke in here?"

"Sorry." Fletch slid off his stool. "Call me when breakfast's ready."

He pushed through the swinging door, a thin, blue curl trailing behind him. Herb watched him go, picked up a cleaver and whacked the grapefruit in half, hard enough to squirt juice in Gus' eye.

"Oops. Sorry, Gus."

"It's okay, Herb." He rubbed his stinging right eye and took himself out of the line of fire to set the table.

When Fletch came back he had Aldo with him. "Look who I found," he said. "The handsome groom."

"And where's the beautiful bride?" Georgette asked, a razor-thin edge in her voice as she put a platter of French toast on the table.

"She's got a headache. Bride nerves, she said, whatever that is." Aldo shrugged and grinned. "I offered to take her breakfast, but she said she wasn't hungry and I could have hers."

Georgette slid a look at Fletch, and Cydney one at Gus that said, "What do we tell this poor dumb schmuck nephew of yours?" He gave her a nothing-yet shake of his head and sat down at the table.

"Aldo tells me the two of you are off to buy tuxedos today," Fletch said to him halfway through breakfast. "Mind if I tag along?"

"Not a bit." Gus sipped his coffee. "How 'bout it, Herb? You game?"

"No thanks, Gus." He lifted Georgette's hand from her lap and kissed her fingers. "I'll stay here and be muscle for the ladies."

Georgette smiled at Herb. Fletch frowned. Cydney bit worriedly at her bottom lip. Gus wiped his mouth with his napkin to hide the grin on his face. Aldo kept on eating, his share and Bebe's and then some.

He was still eating when Louella and Mamie and Sarah and Cloris and her sisters arrived and trooped into the kitchen for a cup of coffee. Everyone got a laugh out of him following his plate in Georgette's hand toward the sink, still wiping up the last bit of syrup on the last piece of French toast and forking it into his mouth.

It was possible that Aldo was fully aware of Bebe's modus operandi and saw nothing wrong with it, although Gus hoped not. He'd hate to have to kill his nephew four days before his wedding. If Aldo were truly clueless, and Gus bet he was, then the question was how much and who best to tell him. He hoped Parrish had a reason for tagging along on the tux trip, because he really didn't want to be the one. Aldo wouldn't believe him, anyway. Gus wasn't sure he'd believe anyone.

They left for Springfield, where Gus figured they'd find a better selection of tuxedos, right after breakfast in his red extended cab Ford 4×4. Jags were ho-hum, Fletch claimed, and it had been years since he'd ridden in a pickup. He spent the trip telling Gus how to drive and asking Aldo about his studies and his plans for the future.

They did the tuxedo thing first at a specialty store in the Battlefield Mall. Time he bought himself a new monkey suit, too, Fletch said. Aldo cracked up at the phrase, which he'd never heard. Parrish made a big deal out of Aldo, said how proud he was to have him as his grandson-in-law. It made Aldo flush, and it made his eyes shine. As soon as the salesman found out his customer was Fletcher Parrish, they were fitted at the speed of light and told their tuxedos would be ready at 3 P.M.

Next stop the barbershop. Gus choked up watching Aldo's mane come off, revealing the strong line of his jaw and the cords of muscle in his neck. It reminded him of the first time he'd taken his nephew for a haircut, especially when the barber finished and Aldo swept one long tendril off the floor.

"To save for Beebs," he said, and Gus had to wipe his eyes.

Aunt Phoebe had wiped her eyes, too, when she'd plucked a white-blond curl off the barber's chair to press into the baby book Beth had started for her son.

Fletch offered to buy lunch. "But no mall food," he insisted, and he insisted on driving in their search for a suitable restaurant. God, what a riot. Little bantam rooster man versus the big-ass truck. Gus practically had to lift him up behind the wheel. Aldo gave him a bright blue Kansas City Royals baseball cap. Fletch grinned, put it on backwards, and off they went, gears grinding, clutch squealing and dual exhausts belching.

He and Fletch ate 16-ounce T-bones for lunch, Aldo a 32-ouncer, in a swank red leather and dark paneled steak house. Gus had coffee after, Aldo a giant-size hot fudge sundae and Fletch a whiskey sour and a cigarette that made Gus yearn for a cigar.

"Bebe's a lucky girl." Fletch leaned his elbow on the table and pointed his cigarette at Aldo. "You're a fine young man."

"No, Mr. Parrish. I'm a lucky guy." Aldo caught a chocolate drip at the corner of his mouth with his spoon and grinned. "Beebs tells me that all the time. And she tells me not to forget it."

With her big brown bedroom eyes and her lush body. When he was Aldo's age, Gus would've believed anything that came out of a mouth like Bebe's.

"I'm sure you've noticed that now and then Bebe is a bit, hmmm ..." Fletch rubbed his chin. "Shall we say, high-strung?"

"You mean like she cries a lot and stuff?"

"That's what I mean." Fletch laid a hand on his shoulder. "Could I give you some advice, Aldo? A few tips on how to handle Bebe?"

"Sure." Aldo laid his spoon in his empty dish with a clink. "I get a headache sometimes, she cries so much."

"How 'bout some coffee, guys?" Gus wiped his mouth and stood up. "I'll send the waitress over on my way out."

"Where are you going, Uncle Gus?"

"Uh—to buy cigars, Aldo. Can't have a decent wedding without cigars. I'll be back in—?"

"An hour." Fletch glanced at him and laid his hand on Aldo's shoulder again. "Never think a woman's tears are just tears, Aldo. She may be sad and cry, or angry and cry, but she is never just sad or just angry. There's always a deeper emotion, something else going on beneath the surface of her tears. The trick is figuring out what. If she tells you she's just sad, or just angry, don't believe her."

Gus stood beside the table listening and thinking of Cydney. The tears in her eyes when he'd found her in the brown chair on Sunday, the ones she'd blinked back when he'd helped her with chapter five, the quivery, watery smile on her face this morning.

"Gus." Fletch shot him a get-outta-here look. "Forget something?"

"Uh—no. Back in an hour."

Gus went, wondering what all those damn tears meant. What was Cydney trying to tell him that he was too dumb to figure out?

chapter
twenty-six

Bride nerves, Cydney's left big toe. Bebe no more had a headache than she did. She was upstairs plotting while Cydney and her mother and Herb and the ladies of Crooked Possum slaved downstairs to get the great room ready for her wedding. It was 12:45. How much longer was Georgette going to let Bebe get away with this?

Why are you waiting for your mother to do something? her little voice asked. *Why don't you take charge, for a change?*

" 'Cause I'm not supposed to know about this," Cydney muttered.

"You aren't supposed to know about what?" her mother asked.

From the foot of the stepladder Cydney stood on, startling her so badly she had to grab the mantel to keep from falling. She glanced at Georgette over her shoulder and frowned.

"I wish you wouldn't sneak up on me, Mother."

"I didn't sneak up on you. You didn't hear me because you were talking to yourself. You do that a lot, you know. It's very disconcerting to other people, Cydney."

"All writers talk to themselves, Mother."

"I talk to my secretary. It's called dictation. What aren't you supposed to know about?"

Cydney looked at the far end of the great room, where Herb and the ladies were putting a spit and polish shine on the bar. She doubted they could hear her, but she kept her voice low anyway.

"I'm not supposed to know Bebe isn't a dumbbell. Or that she's a selfish, spoiled, lying, scheming—"

"Come down here." Georgette crooked a finger.

When Cydney reached the floor, Georgette caught her arm and towed her up on the dais, put a bottle of Windex and paper towels in her hand.

"Don't use the whole roll." Georgette ripped off a fistful of sheets. "I'll need at least half of it to shove down your father's throat."

"Dad was not indiscreet. I overheard a conversation he had with Bebe in the kitchen this morning."

"You mean you eavesdropped."

"Yes, Mother. Just like you do all the time."

"And here I thought all my training had failed. Squirt me."

Where? her little voice asked, but Cydney ignored it. She spritzed the glass wall with Windex and they both wiped ammonia streaks.

"So why were you up the ladder muttering about this?"

"I'm angry. Bebe used us, took advantage of us. I think she has Aldo totally hoodwinked. That's not right, Mother. It's not fair to Aldo."

"Of course it isn't. That's why your father tagged along to buy a tuxedo. If anyone can find a gentle way to break it to Aldo that Bebe is a shameless manipulator, it's Fletch." Georgette paused in mid-wipe and smiled at her. "Since it takes one to know one."

"I'd also like you to explain to me why we're down here working our butts off while Bebe is upstairs lolling on hers."

"I don't think she's lolling. If she's doing anything up there, she's making voodoo dolls."

Cydney held her hand out to her mother. "Bet me."

"All right." Georgette shook her hand. "Bet you what?"

"Bet me Herb's the next one to punch Dad in the nose."

Georgette's nostrils flared. "You said your father wasn't indiscreet."

"He didn't have to be indiscreet. I was in the kitchen this morning and so was Herb when Dad flirted with you and you flirted right back. Dad is a married man, Mother. And you are engaged to Herb."

"Stop right there before we end up on *Jerry Springer*." Georgette threw one hand up like a traffic cop. "Go get Bebe."

"Missed a spot." Cydney pointed at a streak on the glass, handed her mother the paper towels and sashayed out of the great room.

Being mature and in control was heady stuff. Now if she could stay in the zone until she talked to Gus. She had a sexually mature adult speech all prepared. If she could just deliver it without falling apart.

Cydney took the back stairs, planning to make a pit stop before she dragged Bebe down to the great room by her hair. Her Keds, mud-free at last from her walk on Sunday, didn't so much as squeak as she crossed the alcove at the end of the hall and opened her bedroom door.

Bebe spun away from the Duncan Phyfe desk, her eyes and her mouth wide-open. With guilt and surprise at being caught, Cydney thought and felt a sick clutch in her stomach. She'd left her laptop on the desk, plugged into the outlet and running on screen save.

"If you touched one file," she threatened, "one chapter of my book, I'll make you eat the hard drive."

"I didn't. Honest. I just brought you something."

Bebe sidled away from the desk, lifting her hand awkwardly at a single red-gold zinnia tucked in a small white vase next to the laptop. A square pink envelope sat propped up against it.

"I'm sorry, Aunt Cydney. Really, really sorry. That's all."

Cydney stepped into the room away from the door. "Get out."

A bright vermilion flush shot up Bebe's throat. Her eyes filled with tears but she went, head down, and pulled the door quietly shut.

Cydney raced to the laptop and checked her files. All there. All safe. Thank God. She dashed to her suitcase, rummaged for a box of disks, flew back to the desk, sat down and copied all five of her precious chapters. Twice. When she finished, she sagged back in the chair, her hands and her insides trembling, her face hot, her fingers icy.

She stared at the zinnia and the pink envelope. She shouldn't open it. She should just throw it away, but she picked it up and opened it, pulled out a white card and read:

I'm sorry. I love you. Please forgive me.—Bebe

Her father was fifty-nine with a life like a train wreck. She was thirty-two with a life she despised, one spider vein and two gaping holes in her heart. One named Gus, the other named Bebe.

Gus thought she was the nicest person he'd ever met— *Whoop-de-doo,* her little voice said—but he didn't want to marry anyone. He'd told her so through the bathroom door and she'd driven onto the tracks with the guard down and the lights flashing anyway.

Maybe this was another one of Bebe's spoiled, selfish tricks, but she was just a kid, an abandoned little angel, and Cydney loved her. She got up and opened her bedroom door. Bebe was there, pacing the alcove and twisting her fingers together. She spun toward Cydney on her air-booted foot, her heartbeat leaping in the base of her throat.

"I heard you and your grandfather in the kitchen this morning."

"I know. Gramps told me before he left with Aldo and Mr. Munroe. He said you called me a bitch. That hurt so bad I couldn't breathe."

"Now you know how I felt when you said you didn't want me at your wedding."

"But I do. I want Mother, too. I just want—everything." She made a gawky sweep with one arm, her eyes filling again, her nose red from crying. "I don't think Mother will come once Grampa calls her. If she doesn't he said it would be on me and he's right. He's right and there's nothing I can do but hate myself. Everybody else does, so why not?"

"I don't hate you, Bebe. I feel used and betrayed and I'm so angry I can't see straight. But I love you and so does Aldo."

"But Aldo thinks I'm stupid. It was one of the things that

drew us together." Bebe twisted her fingers again, a genuine rise of panic in her voice. "If he finds out I'm not, I'm afraid he won't love me anymore."

"That's ridiculous. You figured out the codicil to his father's will in about ten seconds—I realized that, looking back on it this morning—and Aldo didn't stop loving you. I'm not sure he realized you figured it out. That could be a problem." Cydney ruffled a hand through her hair. "I don't understand why you thought you had to pretend to be stupid."

"This is gonna get me in trouble." Bebe plunked down on the top step of the back stairs. Cydney crossed the alcove and sat down next to her. "Look at Mother. Articulate and successful and divorced three times. Look how intelligent Gramma is and how long it took her to find Herb, who isn't at all intimidated by her. And look at you, Aunt Cydney." Bebe did, almost wincing. "So smart, so together and alone. I don't want to be alone like you and my mother and Gramma. So I played dumb."

"And look where it got you," Cydney pointed out. As gently as she could, putting aside her own hurt at Bebe's bleak but true take on her life.

Her niece's mouth trembled and her eyes filled. She bent her elbows on her knees, covered her face with her hands and sobbed. Cydney put her arms around her, held her and let her cry until she pulled away and wiped her eyes on her sleeve.

"I know I have to tell Aldo I'm not as dumb as a box of rocks. But I'm so scared," she said, sniffing. "He may not be the sharpest knife in the drawer, like Grampa says, but he's good and kind and funny and sweet and I—I really love him, Aunt Cydney."

"You do have to tell Aldo, but I don't think you have to hit him with it right between the eyes. You could let him in on your little secret bit by bit. One week you could learn to balance the checkbook, the next how to program the VCR. Things like that. And share it with him, Bebe. Just don't lord it over him and make him feel inadequate."

"You think it'll work?"

"Yes, I do, but you have to realize that you aren't going to get everything you want every time you want it. Nobody does. If you're lucky, you'll get part of what you want, or maybe most of it, but rarely do you get everything. It's hard, I know." Oh boy did she know. Like two glorious days with the man you've been in love with from afar for ten years and then *hasta la vista*, baby. "But you have to learn to accept it."

"Well, that blows," Bebe grumbled, then shot Cydney a shaky, watery grin that made them both laugh. "I should go face Gramma."

"I would, and get it over with."

"Come with me?"

"Sure." Cydney rose and let Bebe and her air boot go down the stairs first. "Isn't it time for that thing to come off your foot?"

"Yeah, but I'm s'posed to let a medical professional take it off."

"Let's ask Sheriff Cantwell's sister. She's an EMT."

Louella was happy to trot out to her Ford Bronco ambulance for her medical kit and remove the air boot. While she examined Bebe's ankle, Cydney sat on the living room hearth next to her mother.

Louella made Bebe walk for her and pronounced her ankle healed. Bebe stood up, drew a deep breath and walked over to Georgette.

"I'm sorry, Gramma. I'm sorry I misled you and Aunt Cydney."

"You never misled *me*, Bebe. I knew all along that no grandchild of mine could be as dumb as you pretended." Georgette rose and pinched Bebe's cheeks together. "Now go put on your other shoe and get to work."

She kissed Bebe's puckered mouth and swept away. Bebe watched her go, then cocked an eyebrow at Cydney.

"She's lying through her teeth."

"Absolutely. She lives to be right and rub all our noses in it."

"Were you fooled, Uncle Cyd? I mean, really?"

"Mostly, yes," Cydney admitted. "I did wonder a time or two when we played Scrabble. Though truthfully, I thought you were cheating."

"Never again, Uncle Cyd. I promise." Bebe kissed her and went upstairs for her other Reebok.

A delivery truck from a rental company in Springfield arrived with a toot of its horn and backed up to the front porch.

"Would'a been here a hour ago," the driver explained, "but we couldn't find the dang place."

While Herb helped him and his assistant unload chairs, Cydney made a fresh pot of coffee. Both men drank a big mugful when they finished, thanked her and left. Cydney put together a coffee tray and carried it into the great room, where Bebe and Herb were unfolding chairs and placing them in neat rows. In the back of the room, the Crooked Possum ladies and Georgette were emptying bags and boxes of flowers and ribbons and baskets and greenery onto the bar.

"Where did all this stuff come from?" Cydney asked her mother as she handed her a mug of decaf with Sweet 'N Low.

"I went shopping in Eureka Springs. Thank you, dear." Georgette smiled over the rim of her cup. "You didn't think I'd given you the only copy of the list I wrote from the decorations Bebe visualized, did you?"

"Yes, I did," Cydney said sourly. "And I spent the whole day after the Halloween wedding debacle worried silly that you'd string me up by the orange icicle lights Bebe bought, for giving her the shopping list."

"Then let this be a lesson to you, darling." Georgette put her coffee down, patted her cheek and went back to work.

So did Cydney, on the ammonia streaks on the glass wall. This whole last week had been a lesson. Most of it glorious, some of it painful—with the biggest hurt of all, saying goodbye to Gus, still looking her in the face—but she wouldn't trade a second of it. Now she had something wildly romantic to write about in her memoirs.

And changes to make in her life. Big scary ones, but she wasn't a pauper. She had the God-Save-Me-and-Bebe Fund and she could rent the apartment over the garage for extra income. She'd decided to move her writing room into Bebe's bedroom. She'd have to keep her studio up for a while, until she either sold or phased out Sunflower Photo.

And don't forget, her little voice said. *You have to get a cat.*

"Oh shut up," Cydney muttered.

Louella came to help her, climbing up on a ladder to reach the streaks Cydney couldn't, even with a ladder. Her shoulders ached by the time they finished, but the glass wall sparkled. Not a single dust mote floated in the soft, golden autumn sun filtering through the trees outside the house. Cydney glanced at her watch—3:45.

"The ceremony is scheduled for four," she said to Louella. "The light is just perfect, don't you think?"

"I surely do." She smiled and nodded at the great room "This is all shaping up real pretty."

A country understatement if she'd ever heard one, Cydney decided, when she turned around on the dais and caught her breath.

The floor glowed and the paneling gleamed. The chairs sat in neat, straight rows, those on the bride's side of the room upholstered in rich, forest-green, those on the groom's side in a deep, pumpkin-orange. The runner down the middle picked up the same colors, forest-green in the center with vivid pumpkin edges. Silk autumn leaves clustered around the candles on the mantel, pumpkins sat on the hearth, with more candles and silk leaves and a straw cornucopia spilling gourds and flowers and teeny pumpkins.

Mamie and Sarah on one side of the room and Cloris and her sisters on the other pinned ribbons and little nosegays on the chairs. Fat candles on terra-cotta pillars looped with green and blue and peach and pale orange ribbons stood by the doors. And here came Herb with the pillars that would stand on the steps leading up to the dais.

"Oh Louella." Cydney sighed. "It's just beautiful."

"Sure is. Wouldn't mind getting hitched in here myself."

The peach suit she'd bought in Branson would look perfect, Cydney thought. Which reminded her, it was still in her truck. And her truck was in the garage, Gus had told her, where Sheriff Cantwell parked it after he'd pulled the tree off the roof and driven it up the hill.

"Thanks for your help, Louella." Cydney gave her a

grateful smile, tripped down the steps and called to her mother, "Be right back."

She met the insurance adjustor she'd called after breakfast in the driveway. He followed her toward the garage, apologizing for being late.

"Said I'd be here by two, but I got lost," he said. "Twice."

Signs. Cydney smacked her hand on her forehead. I have got to make those signs. She unlocked the garage with the key Gus had given her before he'd left this morning and she'd mentioned she was going to call her insurance company. The adjustor rolled the door up and she backed the Jeep outside. With the roof crushed, she barely fit behind the wheel. She couldn't imagine how Sheriff Cantwell had squeezed in to drive the truck up here.

"You can have your Jeep repaired here," the adjustor said, when he'd finished his estimate. "Or we can tow it back to Kansas City and you can rent a car to drive home. Your choice."

Cydney thanked God she paid through the nose for tow coverage.

"Then let's tow it, please." She signed the forms he gave her and shook his hand, walked him to his car and headed back to the garage.

It felt good to be outside. The sun was bright, the air cool and crisp. She could smell the pine trees and the little bits of snow left here and there. She could see the lake, a tiny blue flash through the trees. Tall Pines was such a lovely place, even if no one could find it. No wonder Gus couldn't bear to sell it.

Cydney wasn't sure she could bear to say good-bye to it, or to Gus. She climbed into the Jeep and just sat there with the driver's door open, her stomach a cold, icy ball, her heart hammering in her ears. She loved this place, all of Aunt Phoebe's little here and there touches. And she loved Gus so much tears welled in her eyes just thinking about him.

Oh no. She was falling apart. She could not go back in the house like this. She had to get a grip on herself and get back in the zone. *Visualize,* her little voice said. *See yourself calm and in control. It worked for Bebe and the wedding decorations.*

Couldn't hurt. Cydney turned sideways in the seat and tucked her feet under her Indian-style, laid her hands on her knees with her middle fingers touching her thumbs and drew a deep breath. Closed her eyes and pictured herself being cool and collected. Suave and sophisticated. Laughing and dancing at the wedding and—Oh hell! They'd forgotten music for the reception!

Hey! We're visualizing here! her little voice yelled. *Save the panic attack till we're finished!*

"Sorry," Cydney murmured, and drew another deep breath. Where was she? Oh yeah. Being charming at the wedding. Laughing and dancing. Though how she was supposed to dance with no music—

"What the heck are you doing, babe?"

It was Gus. Cydney jerked her eyes open and saw him standing beside the Jeep, grinning at her with his arms folded and a navy blue baseball cap turned backwards on his head. His red truck sat by the front steps behind Louella's ambulance and Sarah Boyce's old wood-paneled station wagon. Her father wore a royal blue hat backwards on his head and Aldo a bright red one. She could see them over Gus' shoulder, trotting up the steps with four huge pizza boxes in their arms.

She let her breath go in a sigh. "I'm visualizing."

"Me, too. Lavender lace." Gus took a step toward her, his voice husky. "Think we can swing it tonight?"

"Good Lord willin' and the crik don't rise." Gus laughed and she grinned. "Mamie said that at lunch. What's with the rally caps?"

"Your father's idea." Gus turned his hat around, took another step toward her and cupped his hands over her knees. "Why don't you get a headache during supper, tell everybody you're going to bed and sneak up to my room while they're still at the table?"

Cydney cocked her head at him. "You're kidding, right?"

"No, I'm not kidding." He unfolded her legs and hooked them around his rib cage. "I'm desperate."

"Well, you know what they say." Cydney laid her hands on his shoulders, fighting with her breaking heart to keep her voice light, and kissed his nose. "All good things must come to an end."

"What end?" Gus scowled at her. "We're just getting started."

"We agreed on forever or next Saturday, whichever comes first."

"This is only Wednesday."

"I was a wreck last night waiting for my mother to go to sleep. When I finally dared to creep downstairs, there she was with my father. Fletch is king of the night owls. He prowls from midnight till dawn. We don't have a prayer of making this work with the house full of people."

"Well, goddamn it, we can try."

"When, Gus? And where?"

"Right goddamn here and right goddamn now. I'll pull my truck in the garage, lock the door and—"

A sudden, deafening wind roared out of nowhere, cutting Gus off and drowning him out. The deep, throaty pulse in it jarred Cydney's bones. She glanced up just as Gus did and saw a helicopter skimming toward them over the treetops beyond the garage.

It shot over the Jeep in a huge whoosh of air that snatched her breath and Gus' hat off his head. Cydney flung her arms around him, held on and watched the helicopter turn a circle above the house and settle on skis in the middle of the circle lawn, the rotor whipping the pine trees into a frenzy.

"Oh no," Cydney breathed in Gus' ear. "It think it's Gwen."

"Oh, hell." He groaned, his head thumping against her collarbone.

The Plexiglas cockpit door popped open, and sure enough, out hopped Gwen, her caramel-blond hair barely stirring in the wake of the rotor. It wouldn't dare. A tall man with reddish-brown hair slid out onto the grass beside her and reached inside for two very large nylon bags. He passed one to Gwen and slung the other one over his shoulder.

"I think the Prince is with her," Cydney said in Gus' ear.

"Oh double hell." Gus groaned again.

He turned around between her knees as Gwen and her companion ducked the blades and started up the lawn toward the house. When they reached the drive, they turned and waved. The helicopter lifted off, whipping the pines again, and swooped away over the trees, toward Branson.

"Well, damn it," Gus said. "What's she doing here a day early?"

"I don't know. I just hope to heaven Dad talked to her."

"He made a couple calls on his cell phone today but Aldo and I didn't listen. We took ourselves elsewhere."

The front doors sprang open and a redheaded blur streaked across the porch. Bebe. Her joyful, *M-o-o-t-h-e-r!*" and her flung-open arms sprang tears in Cydney's eyes. Gwen dropped her bag and hugged her, rocking her from side to side. Cydney smiled and sniffled.

Gus spun on one foot and frowned at her. "You're crying."

"These are happy tears. Bebe hasn't seen her mother in two years."

"You must be the happiest woman on the damn planet. Every time I've looked at you the last four days, you're crying."

"Weddings are very emotional. Everybody cries."

"The wedding isn't till Saturday. This is Wednesday."

"So I can't cry till Saturday?"

"I'd just like you to be honest about why you're crying."

"Look at my mother." Cydney took Gus by the shoulders, turned him around and nodded at Georgette hurrying down the porch steps with a smile on her face and a hankie in her hand. "See? She's crying but she's smiling." She gave his shoulders a shake. "Happy tears, Gus. Happy tears."

"All right, all right." He sighed. "Goddamn happy tears."

Gwen lifted an arm from Bebe's shoulders and swept her mother into a three-way hug. Fletch hopped down the steps and shook hands with Gwen's friend. He nodded his head and bowed.

"Yep. That's the Prince." Cydney slid her arms around

Gus and pressed her cheek to his temple. His hair smelled like shampoo and cigar smoke. He sighed and leaned against her, laid a hand over her wrists clasped on his chest. "The joint's really gonna be jumping now."

The group hug ended. Gwen slid one arm around Bebe, the other around Georgette. They started toward the porch with Fletch and the Prince—Somebody Romanoff, Cydney thought—trailing behind.

"Aren't they forgetting something?" Gus said.

"What?" Cydney asked.

He braced his elbow on the seat between her knees and frowned at her over his shoulder. "You."

Cydney laughed. She could tell he'd gotten a haircut, but the ball cap and the helicopter had wrecked it. Instead of falling over his forehead, his hair stood straight up, as indignant as the edge in his voice.

"You did the same thing to me last Tuesday. Walked into my house and left me standing in the garage."

"I did?" He blinked at her. "When?"

"Never mind, Gus." She put a kiss on his nose. "It doesn't matter."

"Yes it matters." He spun all the way around. "You matter."

"I will as soon as my father wants a cup of coffee."

"Or your mother wants the bags brought in the house. I can't wait to find out what your sister expects you to do for her."

"Is this the big fight you said we wouldn't have to fake as soon as the rest of my loony family gets here?"

"It is if you turn back into a peashooter."

"What do you care if I'm a peashooter or an Uzi?"

I care plenty, Gus wanted to say. He'd realized it when she said all good things must come to an end. His gut clenched at the thought of never seeing her again, never holding her again. He wanted to tell her so, but not out here in the damn driveway, not after he'd tried to pick a fight with her because he thought she was about to dump him.

"I thought we were friends," he said.

"I thought we were lovers."

"Well, yeah, that, too."

"Then why are we fighting?"

"I thought you were dumping me."

"No, Gus." Cydney cupped his face. Keep it light, she told herself. Make a joke out of it and maybe you'll survive. "I'm not dumping you until Saturday."

"Before or after the wedding?"

She laughed and Gus kissed her, slid his hands inside her sweatshirt and cupped her breasts, small, perfect little breasts he ached to feel in his mouth. He didn't believe she wanted to dump him any more than he believed her tears were happy. He hoped to God she was falling in love with him, because he was pretty sure he'd fallen in love with her.

"Since I'm supposed to be your date," she sighed when he let go of her mouth, "I guess I'll dump you after the wedding."

"Don't put yourself out. I'm sure Louella would accompany me."

"If she won't, Mamie will in a heartbeat."

"She wants me bad," Gus said, and they laughed, bumped foreheads and rubbed noses, until Cydney stiffened and frowned over the top of his head. "Uh-oh."

"Uh-oh what?"

"Louella's leaving. Looks like in a big hurry."

So was Mamie, Gus saw when he turned around. Sarah and Cloris and her sisters, too, in a gaggle of fluttering jackets and sweaters as they hurried down the porch steps. He could hear their voices, high and shrill, but he couldn't make out what they were saying.

"I don't like this, Gus," Cydney said worriedly. "Help me down."

He lifted her out of the Jeep and they ran toward the house. When Gus called to Louella, she turned away from her ambulance; Mamie stood with her, her hands on her hips. Sarah and Cloris and her sisters flocked around him and Cydney as they stopped in front of Louella.

"You're a right sweet gal, Cydney," Mamie said, shoving

her way forward. "Yer maw's a might pushy but she'll do, and I'm beginnin' t'take a real shine to the jackass. But your sis is a witch that starts with a *b*."

"What happened?" Cydney asked, her face pale.

"She ordered us outta Gussie's house is what happened!"

"*What?*" Gus shouted with Cydney.

"Now Mamie." Louella put an arm around her. "It wasn't that bad."

"The hell it wasn't!" Mamie shrugged her off and glared. "She called us the Mop and Broom Bumpkin Brigade!"

"I'll kill her," Cydney said, and wheeled toward the steps.

"Wait." Louella caught her arm. "Never mind what she said to us. Bebe's the one you best see to. Her mama took one look at all the pretty things we put up today and laughed. Country frump, she called it, and said it would not do for *Vogue* magazine. Clean broke Bebe's heart. Left your mama Mrs. Parrish flat speechless. Never thought I'd see that."

"Thanks." Cydney forced a smile past the spitfire snarl on her face. The fire in her eyes made Gus' pulse race and his imagination soar with visions of lavender lace. "I'll see all you ladies in the morning." She swept Mamie and Sarah and Cloris and her sisters into her glance. "We'll make the wedding cake we talked about at lunch. Okay?"

They all nodded, even Mamie, and Cydney launched herself up the porch steps. Gus caught her in the foyer and pulled her around to face him. Her face was flushed, her almond eyes narrowed into amber slits.

"Don't try to stop me, Gus. Sometimes you just can't ignore this strong a compulsion to kill somebody."

"I'm not going to stop you. I just want to flip a coin to see which one of us gets to drop-kick her off the porch."

"Be my guest. Just give me first shot at her."

"Go for it, babe."

And she did, like a heat-seeking missile following the trail of voices across the living room toward the dining room. All of them subdued, except for Gwen Parrish's throaty, Kathleen Turner contralto.

"Really, Mother, I think you're making entirely too much

of this. All I want is a few changes so I'm not the laughing-stock of *Vogue*."

Cydney burst through the doorway, skidding in her Keds on the bare floor at the edge of the Oriental carpet, her silver curls a tangled riot from the whip of the chopper blades. Her sister lifted an eyebrow at her, flicked the barest glance at Gus stopped in the doorway and smiled.

"Cydney. There you are."

Two of the pizza boxes lay open on the table. Gwen sat in the armchair at the end nearest the sideboard, Fletch and Georgette on her right, Domino and Herb and the Prince on her left.

"I spoke with the Mop and Broom Bumpkin Brigade, Gwen," Cydney said between her teeth.

"I offered to pay them and they took offense."

"You don't pay friends, Gwen. Of course, you wouldn't know that because you don't have any friends."

Gwen laughed. Georgette blanched and shot to her feet.

"Cydney," she said. "We're trying to have a civilized discussion—"

"Sit down and shut up, Mother. I'm running this show."

Georgette blinked and made a half-choked squawk.

"Sit down, George," Fletch said, tugging her into her chair.

"What show are you running, Cydney?" Gwen leaned her elbows on the table and her chin on her laced-together fingers. "The Rural Rubes of America Defense Fund?"

"No, Gwen. The Used and Abused Little Sisters of Big Bad Bitchy Sisters Club."

Gwen opened her mouth. She meant to laugh, Gus thought, until Cydney snatched the closest pizza off the table and smeared it in her perfect, flawless face.

Gwen shrieked and fell off her chair, flat on her ass on Aunt Phoebe's Oriental carpet.

chapter
twenty-seven

The pizza was a super supreme with everything, including anchovies that stuck to her eyebrows and melted cheese that gummed in her hair. Peppers, onions, pepperoni and black olives splattered the sideboard and the wainscoting. Tomato sauce oozed into everything. The Oriental rug was toast, but Gus didn't think Aunt Phoebe would mind.

He sure as hell didn't. He wished he had a camera so he could take a picture for Louella and Mamie and Sarah and Cloris and her sisters.

Domino screamed and flung herself away from the table. Straight into the arms of the Romanoff prince, who gallantly rose to catch her. He seemed to be doing his damnedest not to laugh at his fiancée struggling up on her hands to wipe pizza out of her eyes.

"*Cydney!*" Georgette screeched. "How could you! Oh, Gwen!" She started out of her chair, but Fletch yanked her back and shoved his nose in her face. "Butt out, George. This is between the girls."

Gwen plucked mushrooms off her eyelids and glared at him. "Well thank *you*, Dad!"

"See here, Parrish." Herb blustered to his feet. "I'll thank you not to speak to my fiancée that way."

"Be quiet, Herb. This doesn't have squat to do with you, either."

"Get up, Gwen!" Cydney scrambled around the table, shoved the armchair out of her way and stood over her sister with her feet spread. "There's another pizza up here and it's got your name on it!"

An extra large Canadian bacon. Cydney grabbed for it but couldn't quite reach it. She had one knee on the table, her arm stretched toward the box when Gus caught her around the waist and lifted her off her feet.

"That's enough, killer."

"The hell it is!" She twisted in his grasp, shooting him a furious, pizza-spattered glower over her shoulder. "I'm just getting started."

"Save some for me," he whispered in her ear, and she flushed.

Gus swung Cydney away from the table and offered Gwen a hand. She took it and pulled to her feet, wiped a hand down the front of her ruined apricot cashmere sweater, tried to toss her hair and smacked herself in the eye with a string of cheese.

"Thank you," she said stiffly.

"I'm Gus Munroe, warden of this asylum. If Bebe still wants you, you can stay. So long as you clean up this mess." Her jaw dropped and her eyes widened. Gus smiled. "I'd start with the carpet and club soda."

He looped both arms around Cydney's waist, turned away from the table, and carted her across the dining room.

"Nice touch," she said as he carried her up the back stairs. "Too bad my mother will end up scrubbing pizza out of the carpet."

"I don't think Fletch will let her."

She cocked her head at him over her shoulder, a curious arch in one tomato-caked brow. "What did you and my father talk about today?"

Gus smiled. "Oh this and that."

"Are you taking me to my bedroom?"

"Yep. You need a shower and I need to ravish you."

"Oh goody."

Gus put her down at the top of the stairs. She drew him into her bedroom, shut and locked the door and turned into his arms, wrapped hers around his waist and snuggled her head into his chest. He felt the shiver in her, the tremble of reaction in her muscles, buried his nose in her hair and smelled mozzarella and Windex, like he had last Monday night when he'd shown up unannounced at her house.

"I'm sorry about the rug, Gus."

"Forget it. I'd give every rug in this house to see that again."

"I don't know what came over me. No—yes, I do know. Every rotten, high-handed thing Gwen had ever done to me and Bebe and my mother. The wedding decorations and kicking Louella and Mamie and Sarah and Cloris and her sisters out of Tall Pines." She pressed her palms to her face, a triple-time adrenaline pulse beating in her throat. "I was so angry I could hardly breathe. The pizza was there and I just grabbed it and—" She blinked up at him. "Did I make a fool of myself?"

"You were magnificent. A real little Uzi. Got me pumped."

"Well, as long as you're pumped." She laughed, her eyes shining, stretched up and kissed his chin. "Get naked. I'll be right back."

She went into the bathroom and shut the door. When the shower cranked on, Gus sat down at the desk and laughed. My God, his life had been dreary. Maybe he'd been *de*-pressed, but he sure as hell wasn't now. As Aunt Phoebe used to say, he was having more fun than a barrel of monkeys. He had no intention of letting that end or letting Cydney go. He'd found her, he was keeping her and that's all there was to it.

She was smart and funny, adorable and sincere. She was a great cook, so he'd eat well. He grinned at that. She lived a sensible, prudent and well-planned life, except when her loony family upset her apple cart. A little bit of all the Parrishes together in one place went a long way, but he could live with that. He'd be nice to Bebe. He'd even try to like her. He'd sell Tall Pines if Cydney hated it. He'd knock it down and build her a palace in its place if that's what she wanted. He'd do anything.

"Cydney?" Fletch called, knocking on the door.

Gus got up, unlocked and opened the door.

"She okay?" Fletch asked.

"She's in the shower. When she gets out I'm going to make love to her, so if you could keep the rest of the inmates away from here for a while I'd appreciate it."

"Well, that was direct," Fletch said with a startled laugh.

"I've gone about this all wrong." Gus stepped into the hall, pulled the door shut and kept his voice low. "I took her to bed before I courted her, so I'm working on that. I'd call Elvin—he's a justice of the peace as well as the sheriff—and have him marry us as soon as Cydney gets out of the shower, but I want her to be the center of attention for something besides throwing a pizza in her sister's face. If she wants a big wedding, great. If she wants Elvin here in twenty, even better. Whatever she wants I intend to give her. I love her and if she'll have me, I'm keeping her."

"This is what I wanted to hear from you Sunday. When I didn't, I baited you. Cydney is one of the few good things I've done in my life. I've been a lousy father and I regret that, but this makes me very happy."

He offered his hand and Gus shook it.

"Take all the time you need. I'll see that you get it."

Gus stepped back in the bedroom and locked the door.

"Hey, old poop!" Cydney hollered. "Are you out there?"

"I'm here." Gus opened the bathroom door, leaned past it into the steam cloud fogging the mirror and saw Cydney, her wet head stuck past the partially open shower door. "Wanna wash my back?"

"You bet." Gus kicked the bathroom door shut behind him and peeled off his sweater. "Your front, too."

God she was lovely, sleek and glistening as a seal under the spray. His own precious little water nymph. Gus stepped into the shower, scooped his arms around her and lifted her against his naked chest to kiss her, a hot, deep, openmouthed kiss that made her whimper and wrap her legs around his waist. He groaned and gripped her bottom, backed her against the shower wall and took her hard and fast, catching the cry she made in his mouth. When he sagged against her, his arms trembling and hands spread on the wall, she sighed and stroked the wet back of his head with her fingers.

"I didn't mean to do that in here," he said, breathing raggedly in her ear. "I meant to take you to bed and take my time."

"You can still do that." She smiled when he drew away from her.

"It won't bother you that the rest of your family is downstairs?"

"My name will be mud for the rest of today. Maybe even tomorrow. It'll be a long time before anybody comes looking for me."

He considered telling her Fletch had stopped by, but she kissed him and he forgot. He washed her back and massaged her shoulders, felt the tension seep out of her and her muscles relax. He held her against him while he soaped her breasts and then her thighs, slid a finger inside her and teased until she moaned and he felt her bones melt.

Gus rinsed her and shut the water off, wrapped her in a towel, carried her to bed and told her how much he loved her with his mouth and his hands. The second the last Parrish but Cydney walked out of Tall Pines, he'd lock the front door, tell her he loved her and ask her to marry him. He wanted it to be just the two of them. He didn't want Georgette's nose in it or Bebe's nose or anybody else's nose.

How perfect, Cydney thought as she fell asleep on Gus' chest. The last time was the best time. She didn't feel the least bit sad. Just content and loved, even though she wasn't.

It was dark outside when she woke up with her face turned toward the window. A pool of light streamed over her shoulder. From the desk lamp, Cydney thought and yawned. She didn't realize Gus had gotten out of bed until she heard the tap of her laptop keys. She pushed up on her hands, peered over her suitcase and saw him sitting in the desk chair, his bare, smoothly muscled back gleaming in the lamplight.

"Hi there," she said, scratching her head groggily. Oh no. She'd fallen asleep with a wet head. Her hair was going to look like a Brillo pad run through the microwave. "What are you doing?"

"Shhh. Almost finished."

"Genius at work." She plumped her pillow against the headboard, sat up with the quilt around her and looped her arms around her knees.

"There. Done and save." Gus took off his glasses and straddled the chair to face her with his elbows folded on the back. He'd put on a pair of teal green boxers. "I left you a present."

"You wrote chapter six, didn't you?"

"And seven. Looked like you were shooting for my point of view in that chapter, too." He smiled and swept a hand through his hair. Eek. He'd done the same thing she had, gone to bed with a wet head. "I got bored watching you sleep so I snooped and gave you a hand. If you don't like what I wrote, delete it. Otherwise, it's yours with my blessing."

If he kept this up, she'd have to put his name on the book. Cydney Parrish Munroe. The name leapt unbidden into her head and sprang tears in her eyes. Cydney blinked them away, watched Gus smile at her and take another swipe at his hair.

"You should re-wet your hair and dry it." She leaned an elbow on her knee and her chin on her hand. "You look like a startled squirrel."

"Nice phrase." Gus laughed and pushed out of the chair. "Ever thought of being a writer?"

"A time or two." She smiled at him as he flopped down on the bed beside her and rubbed his nose in her hair.

"You should talk about *my* hair," he said, and she elbowed him in the ribs, then scooted over to share her pillow. Gus leaned against it and looped his arm around her shoulders. "Here's what your father and I talked about today. As Mamie would phrase it, there ain't a dang thing wrong with his patoot."

"I thought the word *patoot* refers to a horse's derriere."

"It does. Except when it comes out of Mamie's mouth."

"I don't even *want* to know how this came up in conversation."

"Careful. You'll get me excited." She wrinkled her nose

and he kissed it. "Seems the only time Fletch has trouble with his patoot is around Domino."

"Really? Boy." She shook her head. "Around Domino, I'd think most men would have the opposite problem."

"You'd think, wouldn't you?"

She cocked an eyebrow and tipped her head at him. "Do you?"

"No. My patoot is very happy where it is, thank you." He kissed her lightly and she smiled, almost but not quite purred in her throat. "I told your father I thought his patoot was trying to tell him something."

"I shudder to think what."

"I told you to watch that kind of talk. Clyde is getting very excited."

Cydney blinked at him. "Clyde?"

"My patoot. That's his name."

"*Clyde?*" She blinked again, then burst out laughing, so hard she shrieked and keeled over on her side, the quilt tangling around her.

"I don't think this is the least bit funny," Gus said, doing his best to sound indignant around the grin on his face. "Neither does Clyde."

"*Clyde!*" She howled, laughing so hard she gasped. She slapped a hand over her mouth and rolled toward him, spread her fingers and said, "Is that why Sheriff Cantwell calls you hoss?"

"Miss Parrish!"

"Oh my God, *it is!*" She shrieked again and doubled over, howling with laughter. "I don't want to know how that came up, either!"

"Come over here and I'll show you."

Gus dove at her, gnawing her ear with his whiskers, making her laugh until she cried and could hardly draw a breath. He settled down beside her then, chuckling and spooning her against his chest, her heart thudding beneath his hand cupped over her breast.

"Wonder if there's any pizza left." She sighed.

"Let's go find out." Gus slapped her rump and rolled to his feet.

When she came out of the bathroom in her green p.j.'s, her terry cloth robe and a pair of red socks, Gus had donned a Missouri Tigers T-shirt and navy sweatpants. Cydney stopped finger-combing her hair.

"Where'd you get the duds, bub?"

"I made a foray to my room while you were asleep."

"What time is it?"

"Almost ten-thirty." Gus turned away from her travel alarm, unlocked and opened the door. "After you, killer."

Stepping out into the alcove was like stepping into a tomb. It was eerily quiet. Cydney peered around the corner into the hall. The brass sconces on the walls, like the ones in the dining room, were lit, but she didn't hear a sound. Not a peep. Gus took her elbow as they went down the back stairs. She peered from the dining room into the living room, listened but heard nothing, frowned and followed Gus into the kitchen.

He was bent inside the fridge, then turned around as she hopped up on a stool at the island with a pizza box and two cans of Pepsi in his hands.

"Canadian bacon." He winked at her and flipped the lid back. "I knew it was wise to stop you. You want this hot or cold?"

"This is perfect." Cydney peeled a slice off the cardboard and munched. So did Gus, popping the tops on the Pepsis. When the grandfather clock by the R&R room doors chimed the half hour, she almost fell off her stool.

"You okay?" Gus asked around a mouthful.

"It's too quiet in here. Where the heck is everybody?"

"Dunno." Gus shrugged. "Wanna do a bed check?"

"No," Cydney said firmly. If her parents were doing something they shouldn't, she didn't want to know about it.

"When you smacked Gwen with the pizza, Domino jumped right into the arms of the prince." Gus wagged his eyebrows. "Wonder where his patoot is tonight."

"Gus." Cydney laughed at him and took a swig of Pepsi,

folded her wrists on the island and leaned toward him. "Mother told me today that Domino and Misha, that's the Prince's name, are old chums. He's a well-known photographer in Europe, did a lot of work in Paris before Domino married Dad. That's how Gwen met him. She went to Cannes for a weekend of R and R and there was Misha visiting Dad and Domino."

"Never mind." Gus slugged his Pepsi. "I know where his patoot is."

"For such an old poop, you have a really filthy mind."

"Honey, I write this stuff. Come to think of it, so does Fletch." Gus bit off a chunk of pizza and frowned as he chewed, swallowed and wiped his mouth and hopped off his stool. "Come on. We're doing a bed check."

"No." Cydney slapped her hand over his. "We are not."

"You aren't worried about Domino and the Prince, are you? You're worried about your mother and father."

Cydney winced. "Is it that obvious?"

"That they still got the hots for each other? Oh yeah."

"When I was fifteen, I cried myself to sleep praying Dad would come home." She slid her elbow on the island and her fingers into her hair, sighed and lifted a rueful smile to him. "My mother was just down the hall doing the same thing every night. It was awful."

"That was then, babe. This is now."

"He broke my mother's heart. If he does it again I'll kill him."

"Ooh, Uzi talk," he teased her. "You're making me hot."

She laughed a little, flattened her palms on the bar and pushed herself straight up on her stool. "It's none of my business, is it?"

"Nope." Gus stretched across the bar and kissed her. "Wanna sleep with me tonight?"

"Yes." Tonight and tomorrow night and every night for the rest of my life, Cydney thought. "But I'm going back to my room."

"Just don't sleep on the floor outside Georgette's door."

"I won't. I promise."

But she crept down the hall and pressed her ear to the door. Held her breath and listened until it was suck air into her lungs or turn blue and faint, but she didn't hear a thing. She thought about listening at her father's door, but she had no idea which room was his. She'd ask Gus.

Cydney brushed her teeth and went to bed, slept like a log and woke up with an aching bladder—Pepsi after 10 P.M.—and raced into the bathroom. Then she washed her hands and her face and brushed her teeth—avoiding the mirror for fear the sight of her hair would crack it—and stuck her head under the shower spray to wash her hair.

She'd just finished drying it and digging her last pair of jeans and her last sweatshirt out of her suitcase when someone knocked on her bedroom door. Gwen, she thought, her heart jumping. At least she had her underwear on. Cydney laid her towel on the bed and drew a breath.

"Come in," she called.

Bebe stepped into her room, shut the door and leaned against it.

"Did you really throw a pizza in my mother's face?" she asked.

"Yes, I did and I'm sorry. I plan to apologize, but—"

"Oh Aunt Cydney!" Bebe threw her arms around her and burst into tears. "Gramma said you did it because Mother laughed at the decorations I picked. You didn't laugh. You *never* laughed, even when I came back with that dopey Halloween stuff. Everything looks so pretty, I was so proud and she *laughed*. I wanted to die. Why did I want her here?"

"Whoa, Bebe, whoa." Cydney backed her out of her arms and sat her down on the blanket box, picked up her towel from the end of the bed and wiped Bebe's tears. "Your mother has very different taste—"

"Bullshit!" Bebe snatched the towel and glared. "Mother doesn't care about me or my wedding. She just wants to look good in *Vogue*!"

"You *are* a lot smarter than you've been letting on."

"I wish I wasn't. I wish I was dumb, stupid little Bebe. Poor Aldo thought it was a compliment when she laughed!"

She buried her face in the towel and sobbed. Cydney tugged the desk chair over and sat in front of her till Bebe dried her tears.

"What am I gonna do, Aunt Cydney?"

"It's your wedding, Bebe. What do you want to do?"

"I love everything just the way it is. I don't want to change so much as a single bow. It's perfect, just the way I imagined it."

"Do you want your wedding pictures in *Vogue*?"

"No!" Bebe balled the towel and threw it at the wall. "I want my wedding pictures in a nice little album I can put on the coffee table in our house so Aldo and I can look at them whenever we want and—and remember the *happiest day of our lives*!"

She wailed and buried her face in her hands. Cydney went into the bathroom for a cool facecloth. She brought it back to the bed, made Bebe lie down and pressed it over her swollen red eyes. She sat on the edge of the mattress and smoothed her forehead until the sob eased out of her breath. Then she got up and got dressed. She'd just tied on her Keds when Bebe took off the cloth and sat up, came to her where she sat in the desk chair and went down on her knees. Looped her arms around her waist and laid her head on her breast.

"I love you, Aunt Cydney. I wish you were my mother."

"Oh Bebe." Cydney cupped Bebe's head in her hands, her eyes full of tears, and kissed her hair. Bebe straightened and they hugged, rocking from side to side. "Your mother will come around."

"I want you to take my wedding pictures. I want somebody who loves me on the other end of the camera."

"I'd planned to take the pictures all along, whether Gwen likes it or not, so don't worry about that, okay?" Cydney smoothed Bebe's hair back and her niece nodded, her mouth trembling. "I wasn't there, but I can't believe your mother meant to hurt you. And she does love you."

"She called it *country frump*! Right in front of Louella and Mamie and Sarah and Cloris and her sisters. After they'd worked so hard to help, and we were all so happy with how

everything looked. You didn't see their faces, Aunt Cydney."
Bebe's voice spiraled toward shrill. "Such good, sweet women
and I already felt guilty because I hadn't helped as much as I
should and then my mother—"

"Stop, Bebe." Cydney gripped her shoulders. "Louella was
concerned about you, not Gwen's tacky comment. It's over
and you have to calm down. The ladies will be here this
morning to bake the wedding cake. Your mother can't keep
them away. Gus won't let her."

"Okay. Okay." Bebe rocked back on her heels, sniffling,
but trying to smile. "What a cool wedding cake this is gonna
be. All the different layers and different icings. Can I help?"

"You bet. Let's go grab some chow before they get here."

Cydney expected to find Georgette in the throes of making
breakfast, but the kitchen was empty. She'd left a note:

Every man for himself this morning. Fresh fruit, juice
and bagels in the fridge. Herbert is taking Fletch and the
French bimbo and Gwen and her Prince and me to Springfield for breakfast and a little shopping. Don't worry about
dinner. We'll bring it. Luck with the cake.

—G

"Hmmm," Cydney said. "This is very strange."

"Exceedingly," Bebe said. "Gramma never does a little
shopping."

"All six of them stuffed into Herb's Cadillac," Gus said behind them. "Oh to be a sardine in somebody's pocket."

Cydney laughed and glanced at him over her shoulder,
swinging onto a stool at the island with a grin on his face,
and Aldo, looking like a shorn but very handsome sheep, beside him.

"Why, Aldo, you cut your hair. It looks great. Very
becoming."

He swiped a hand at his bangs and flushed. "Thanks,
Uncle Cyd."

Louella and Mamie and Sarah and Cloris and her sisters
arrived in time for bagels and coffee. Hesitantly, when Gus

greeted them at the door, then with sighs of relief when he said Gwen wasn't there.

"Kicked her out on 'er fancy butt, eh, Gussie?" Mamie grinned, then frowned when he said she was only gone for the day.

While Mamie and Cloris and her sisters took charge of the cake, Louella and Sarah drafted Gus and Aldo to help clean house.

"I just paid a fortune to have this place cleaned," Gus argued, until Louella wiped a finger across one of the living room tables and it came up gray with dust. "How'd that get so dirty so quick?"

"Clean is a magnet for dirt," Louella said. "No one knows how or why. It's one of the great mysteries of the universe, Gus."

"Okay." He held up his hands. "Point me to a broom."

Louella pointed him to the vacuum cleaner and the carpeted staircases, the runner in the gallery hall and Aunt Phoebe's rug in the dining room. Most of the pizza stain was gone. What remained, Mamie said, would never be noticed from the back of a galloping horse.

Aldo mopped and waxed floors. Louella and Sarah tackled the bedrooms, changed sheets and towels, shook rugs and wiped floors. When Bebe went to help, Gus clutched his chest and faked a stagger. Cydney frowned, but her eyes twinkled.

By two o'clock, Tall Pines was spotless. Fresh beds and gleaming bathrooms upstairs. Sparkling glass, polished furniture and shiny waxed floors downstairs. They cleaned the R&R room, and made a final sweep of the great room, which Gus hadn't seen.

"Lovely," he said to Bebe, making good on his vow to be nice to her. Liking her would take a while. "If it makes you feel any better, I like it."

"Thank you, Mr. Munroe. So do Aldo and I. The great room stays exactly the way it is." She pulled the pocket doors shut with a firm click and Scotch-taped a sign to them that said: "To Whom It May Concern: Touch one thing in this room and die. Love—The Bride and Groom."

By three all the cake layers, a combination of yellow, white and chocolate, were baked and cool and ready to go into the freezer overnight. The butter-cream frosting roses and leaves and the tubs of different icings Cloris and her sisters made went in the fridge.

"We're clearin' out now, Gussie." Mamie offered him her cheek to kiss. "Before the witch that starts with a *b* shows up."

"Now, Mamie," Louella chided. "We'll come after lunch tomorrow, Cydney, put the cake together and do up the hors d'oeuvres."

"Thank you so much." Cydney hugged each one of them. "We couldn't have done all this without your help. You are wonderful."

"It's our joy to help," Cloris said in her chirpy little voice. "Weddings are so beautiful and special and—oh, just *so* happy."

She and her sisters dabbed their tiny noses with hankies. Louella and Cydney and Sarah sighed. Mamie dragged a sleeve over her eyes.

"If you're all so damn happy, why are you crying?" Gus asked, bewildered. "I don't get this."

"You're a man, Gussie, is why you don't get it," Mamie said.

"What does being a man have to do with it?" he asked Cydney, after he'd seen the ladies out to their cars and gone back into the kitchen.

"I don't know." She shrugged and wiped cake crumbs and icing drips off the island with a sponge. "You tell me."

I can't, damn it, Gus thought, not till your loony family clears out of here. He didn't like the look on her face. She seemed distracted.

"What's bothering you, Uncle Cyd?"

She shook her head, dumped the crumbs in her cupped hand in the sink and rinsed the sponge. "Nothing really. I just feel jumpy."

Gus went to her and slid his arms around her. She leaned the back of her head against his chest. He kissed her temple and she sighed.

"Will you drive me into Branson tomorrow? In the morning, since we'll be busy after lunch? I have to rent a car so I can get home."

"You don't have to leave on my account."

"I have to leave on *my* account." She turned and looped her arms around his waist. "I have clients, and a book to write, and so do you."

Don't leave. Stay. Marry me. All those things popped into Gus' head, but her nutball family could come through the door any second, so he didn't say them, just kissed a dab of icing off her nose.

"I could come see you sometime," he said. "Would you like that?"

"I'd love that." She smiled, but her heart wasn't in it. He could hear it in her voice, see it in the shadow in her eyes.

She didn't realize his heart was in it. That was the problem.

"If you think you can find Tall Pines on your own, you can come see me, you know."

"Signs!" She smacked her forehead and wheeled away from him. "I have got to make those signs!"

"What signs?" Gus followed her through the swinging door.

"Road signs—Bebe!" she hollered as she passed by the bar.

"Yes, Aunt Cydney?" Bebe and Aldo popped out of the R&R room.

"Where's the poster board and pens you found in Aldo's room?"

"Still there. I'll get 'em," Aldo said. "What are we doing?"

"Making road signs so the wedding guests can find Tall Pines," she said, and turned to face Gus. "If we make them now, you and I can stake them along the road on our way to Branson tomorrow."

So they made signs, in the R&R room on the Ping-Pong table. Most of them legit, but the funny ones Cydney came up with, "Leave a Trail of Bread Crumbs," and "Ignore the Buzzards Circling Overhead," had Gus and Aldo and Bebe laughing. He went to the garage for flat, plywood tomato stakes and a staple gun and put the signs together as Cydney lettered them and drew hearts and flowers, nosegays and little brides and grooms and a couple of vultures in the corners. Bebe and Aldo tied them with ribbons. Gus had just punched the last staple into the last sign when they heard the front door sweep open.

"Hey, Bebe-cakes!" Gwen called. "Where are you, sweetie?"

"Drowning myself in the lake," Bebe muttered.

"C'mon, Beebs." Aldo smacked a kiss on her mouth. "It'll be okay."

He took her hand and all but dragged her into the living room.

Gwen didn't so much as glance at Cydney when she stepped into the living room with Gus. She stood in front of the couch by the gallery stairs, her I'm-a-star-and-you're-not smile on her face, a long, blue silk bag with a zipper down the front thrown over the back of the sofa.

Cydney caught her mother's eye across the living room. She sat on the edge of the hearth between Herb and her father, an unhappy frown on her face. Cydney glanced at the dais, where Domino and the Prince stood with their heads together, murmuring in French, then back at her mother. Georgette shook her head no.

"I bought you a present." Gwen said to Bebe, sweeping her arm toward the blue silk bag. "Want to see?"

"That looks like a dress bag, Mother. What did you do?"

Gwen blinked. Thrown off stride, Cydney guessed, by the new, direct and perceptive Bebe. "I bought you a wedding gown."

"I already have my dress. Gramma bought it and I love it."

"I'm offering you a compromise, Bebe. I'm willing to let you keep your country cutesy theme if you'll wear this gown."

Gwen unzipped the bag and swept a long, ivory column of shimmering silk over her arm. Pointed over the wrist sleeves, high neckline, plunging back. Gorgeous, but it wasn't Bebe.

"I don't like it," she said. "I'm not wearing it."

"Yes you will." Gwen flung the gown on the sofa. "You'll

wear it long enough for me to take the photographs for *Vogue*."

"You aren't taking any photos, Mother. I asked Aunt Cydney to take my wedding pictures and she said she would. There won't be any pictures in *Vogue*, either. Not of *my* wedding."

"I made a commitment, Bebe."

"With *Vogue*, Mother, not with me. Never with me. You've always been too busy. You remember me now and then and call or send presents. That's not what I call being a mother. C'mon, Aldo. We're going for a walk."

Bebe held her hand out to Aldo. He slipped his fingers into hers and they walked away, up the steps toward the front door. Gwen spun after them, hands on her hips. Almost, but not quite, stamping her foot.

"Come back here, Beatrice. This is *not* settled!"

"Yes it is." Bebe turned around in the foyer. She had tears in her eyes and her mouth trembled, but she kept it together. "It was settled when you left me in Kansas City with Gramma George and Aunt Cydney. I didn't realize it until you swept in here and laughed at me. And Aldo and everyone else and everything we've done. Go be famous. I have two mothers. Gramma George and Aunt Cydney. I don't need you."

Aldo caught her in a hug as she spun away. Then he opened the door and escorted her through it like she was a queen.

Gwen just stood there, white-faced and staring at the foyer. The Prince and Domino looked at each other and crept away behind her, up the gallery stairs. Her father laid a hand on her mother's arm and gave Herb the high sign. He nodded and followed Fletch into the R&R room.

"Yell if you need me," Gus murmured in Cydney's ear. He caught her fingers from behind and gave them a squeeze.

When the R&R room doors slid shut, Gwen sat down on the oak and glass coffee table, bent her elbows on her knees and covered her face with her hands. Cydney looked at Georgette. She had tears in her eyes. Cydney hadn't seen her cry since Fletch left.

"Bebe's hurt, dear," Georgette said. "I'm sure she didn't mean—"

"Stop it, Mother. You can't put a lovely spin on everything." Gwen's chin shot up and she glared at Georgette. "She meant every word."

"No she didn't," Cydney said. "She's just hurt and angry."

"That was very well done." Gwen swung toward her, her eyes glazed with tears. "Even better than a pizza in the face."

"Now, you wait just a damn second—"

"I'm sorry." Gwen raised her hands. "As much as I'd like to accuse you of stealing my child, I can't. I gave her to you."

"Yes, you did. And by the way—thank you."

"Oh, you're welcome. Anytime." Gwen slapped her hands on her knees and stood up. "I guess I'll go pack."

"You aren't going anywhere." Cydney pointed a finger at her sister. "At four o'clock Saturday afternoon you're going to be sitting in the mother of the bride's chair with a big bright smile on your face. If I have to tie you in the damn chair, you're going to be there."

"Bebe has two mothers." She sighed. "She doesn't need three."

"Bebe has one mother, Gwen, and you are not bailing out on her. Not this time. I won't let you."

"Nor will I." Georgette rose from the hearth, a take-no-prisoners glint in her eyes. "Neither Cydney or I ever tried to take your place, and we refuse to now. The mother of the bride's chair is yours and you will be in it on Saturday, Gwen, come hell or high water."

Gwen sat down on the table again and raked her fingers through her hair. Of course it fell back into place perfectly—lousy, stinking, flawless hair—when she glanced up at her mother and Cydney.

"I had no idea I'd screwed this up so badly. The thought of trying to fix it just—paralyzes me. I don't know where to start, what to do."

"Do you honestly want to mend things with Bebe?" Cydney asked.

"Yes. I had no idea how much until she said she didn't need me."

"Need is one thing, Gwen." Cydney sat next to her and slung an arm around her. "But want is a whole 'nother ball game."

"What's this?" She raised an eyebrow at Cydney's arm on her shoulders. "Are you offering to help me win my daughter back?"

"Yes, I am. If you'll let me."

"Absolutely I'll let you. So long as you understand one thing." Gwen slid her a narrow-eyed smile and looped an arm around her. "If it's the last thing I ever do, I'll get even with you for that pizza."

chapter
twenty-eight

"Did Gwen say 'piece'?" Herb cupped his ear against the right-hand R&R room door. "Piece of what?"

"She said 'pizza.' " Fletch pressed his ear and the glass he'd grabbed from behind the bar against the door. If you're gonna snoop, he'd said, do it right or don't bother. "If you'd shut up we could probably hear."

"She said 'piece.' There's nothing wrong with my ears." Herb glared at Fletch. "Or my eyes, Parrish, and I don't like what I saw today between you and my fiancée."

Gus sat at the bar, grinning. This was *really* getting fun now.

"Don't get your shorts in a twist, Herb. George and I were married for eighteen years. We're old friends."

"Old friends don't suck each other's tonsils in J.C. Penney's shoe department when they think no one else is looking."

"A friendly little buss, Herb. Shut the hell up, will you?"

Herb opened his mouth just as Cydney shrieked. Gus bolted off the stool and knocked Herb and Fletch out of his way like bowling pins. She shrieked again as he flung open the pocket doors.

With laughter, Gus realized, when he saw her head stuck in the crook of her sister's arm and Gwen giving her a noogie, her knuckles scrubbing the top of Cydney's head like she was trying to start a fire. They were both laughing—Cydney struggling to free herself and Gwen to hang on to her. Georgette was laughing, too. Teary-eyed, but laughing.

"Ow!" Cydney wrenched herself out of Gwen's headlock and rubbed her head. "You would have to wreck my hair."

"Your hair's always a wreck." Gwen rumpled a hand in Cydney's curls. "I keep telling you to straighten it."

Over my dead body, Gus thought. He loved Cydney's hair. He loved Cydney. So much he could hardly wait to tell her.

"Let's have supper," Georgette said, heading for the dining room. "Vile, greasy and disgusting take-out chicken."

"Hubba-hubba." Fletch rubbed his hands together and followed her, his head cocked to one side to watch her walk into the dining room. "Nothing like a plump thigh and a well-turned ankle."

Georgette laughed at him over her shoulder. "Stop it, Fletch."

"Damn right, Fletch. Stop it," Herb growled, and stalked after them into the dining room.

"What in the hell was *that*?" Gwen said incredulously to Cydney.

"That was Dad flirting with Mother," she replied unhappily. "And Herb getting ready to punch him in the nose if he doesn't knock it off."

"This is wonderful!" Gwen gave a throaty laugh. "Maybe we won't end up being from a broken home after all."

"Bite your tongue, Gwen."

"Oh stop, Cyd. I think it's delightful. And way past time. You haven't been to Cannes. I have. I found a picture of Mother in Dad's office. I think he looks at it when he's in there writing. There's a suspiciously clean spot in the dust on his desk to suggest it."

"Dad is married to Domino, Gwen."

"So? I'm married to Misha." Cydney gaped, and Gwen laughed. "Marrying an American is still the easiest way to get out of Russia. We made up the engagement story for the papers here. In a year I'll divorce him. Dad will divorce Domino and she and Misha will move to Paris."

"The four of you cooked this up and you didn't *tell* me?"

"I couldn't. The Russians still get cranky about this sort of thing."

"There's a book in this somewhere," Gus said with a grin.

"Dad's already writing the fictionalized version. I've got dibs on the real story and the cover of *Time*," Gwen told him. "Where's Misha?"

"He and Domino slipped upstairs."

"I told them to be discreet. If Mother finds out about this it'll be on Dan Rather and then I'll have to kill her. Grab me a couple of wings, Cyd."

When she disappeared up the gallery steps and down the hall, Cydney plunked down on the table. "Nobody tells me anything."

She looked so waifish and woebegone Gus smiled. He sat down beside her, put an arm around her and a kiss between her eyebrows.

"Buck up, old poop. I've got something to tell you."

"Really?" Her almond-brown eyes brightened. "What?"

"Meet me on the back stairs at midnight. I'll tell you then."

"Ooh, a secret." Cydney rubbed her hands. "I love secrets."

Liar, her little voice said. *You hate secrets*. Which was true, but only because she sucked at keeping them from her mother.

It was just as well that Gwen hadn't told her. One tiny little arch in Georgette's eyebrow aimed at Cydney and she would've blabbed the whole story. She avoided her mother when she entered the dining room with Gus, kept her head down and sat at the far end of the table eating chicken and coleslaw and biscuits with honey.

When Bebe and Aldo came in from their walk, flushed and windblown, the only places left at the table lay directly opposite Gwen. Bebe balked, but Aldo sat down and pulled her into the chair next to his.

"Here you are, sweetie." Gwen offered Bebe her plate and the chicken wings Cydney had saved for her. "Your favorite."

"No thank you." She turned her nose up and dipped into the bucket for a leg. "I prefer dark meat."

Misha sat next to Bebe and Domino next to him. When he bent his head toward her and slid a French fry between her pursed lips, Domino cooed. Georgette glanced at them and up shot her eyebrows.

"Hey, George." Fletch reached across the table and caught her wrist. "Remember when the girls were little? We had to save for a week to afford a bucket of chicken this lousy."

"I remember." Her mother smiled at him. "One night a week I didn't have to cook. And you did the dishes."

"Those were the days, George."

"The days of dishpan hands and no money."

"You cried when I bought you a dishwasher for Christmas."

"Of course I cried. I wanted a mink."

They laughed at each other, their eyes shining. Herb glowered.

"I prefer your chicken, Georgie. This is greasy and undercooked."

"Then hie yourself to the fridge and see if there's any left, Herbert." Georgette flicked him an irritated frown and swung back to Fletch.

She missed the flicker of startled hurt behind Herb's glasses, but Cydney saw it. Gwen caught her eye and gave her a see-I-told-you smile, then poked Misha under the table and hissed, "This is *not* discreet."

It amazed Cydney to watch her father and Gwen play Cupid. For selfish reasons, of course. The cover of *Time* for Gwen, the material for his next book, the price of a new sable coat for her father. Even so, it was almost enough to make Cydney believe dreams could come true. The thought made her heart skip and her gaze leap across the table to Gus, happily chomping on a chicken leg.

He wouldn't say, "Meet me at midnight on the back stairs. I'll tell you then," and spout some drivel about chapter six, would he? Surely he had something private and momentous to say. If he didn't, she'd kill him.

If she had the guts to show up at midnight and hear what he had to say. Which Cydney decided at 11:35 she didn't. *Coward!* her little voice howled as she fled down the hall to Gwen's room and knocked.

"Hi," Cydney whispered when she opened the door. "I think we need a council of war about Bebe."

"What makes you say that?" Gwen replied. "The fact that she said, 'Suit yourself,' when I said I was staying for the wedding? Or the fact that she ignored me all evening? Even when we were Scrabble partners?"

"All of the above. Let me in and let's talk."

And Cydney did, nonstop, her heart jumping at every creak the house made—Was that Gus? Was he looking for her?—until 2:30, when Gwen kicked her out so she could get some sleep. Cydney tiptoed down the hall, her heart banging, and peeked around the corner at the stairs.

No Gus. Relief washed through her, then a clutch of dread. How long had he waited to tell her whatever he had to tell her? She'd never know now, would she? How could she sleep, wondering? The anxiety would kill her. Maybe he was still awake. Cydney slipped down the stairs. He could yell at her for standing him up, so long as he told her.

The dining room wall sconces were lit, their reflections shimmering on the polished tabletop. She'd crept halfway toward the living room when she heard moans and one of the leather couches creaking like someone—er, two someones—were rolling around on it. Well, nuts. Cydney turned toward the dining room swinging door, pushed it open and heard breathless, panting French coming from the kitchen. If Misha and Domino were in the kitchen, who the heck was in the living room?

Flip you for it, her little voice said. *Heads, it's your mother and father. Tails, it's your mother and Herb.*

"Oh shut up," Cydney muttered, and went back to her room.

Every little noise jerked her awake, sent her dashing to the door to see if it was Gus. She ventured once into the hall, peeked around the corner and caught a glimpse of a pale hem of nightgown slipping past a bedroom door. Whose nightgown and whose bedroom? She fretted about it all night and finally fell asleep with a sense of doom closing around her like the pillow she stuffed over her head to block out the house noises.

A little past eight Friday morning, she pushed through the dining room swinging door and heard something bang like a gong in the kitchen. Uh-oh. Cydney eased down the hall and peeked around the corner. Her mother stood at the stove. Her father sat at the island, hunched on his elbows and gazing morosely at her poker-straight back.

Gus sat catty-corner from him. When Cydney peered into the kitchen, he slid to his feet and started toward her.

"If we're going to Branson, we'd better get a move on." He caught her elbow and turned her around. "Get your purse and let's go," he said as he double-timed her down the hall. "Tell your sister and Bebe to stay the hell out of the kitchen. I'll tell Aldo and Herb."

"What's wrong?" Cydney asked. "What happened?"

"Beats me." Gus pushed her up the back stairs ahead of him. "Your mother was in the kitchen when I came down, all red and puffy-eyed. When your father came in she grabbed the skillet and smacked it on the stove. If I hadn't been there I think she would've used it on him."

"I knew it. I just *knew* it. Give me five minutes."

She ducked into her bedroom, Gus down the hall to Aldo's room. Cydney grabbed her purse and a red blazer, tugged it over her white ribbed top and jeans and dashed down the hall. Gwen came half-asleep to the door but snapped awake when Cydney told her that their parents were about to kill each other in the kitchen.

"Damn it, Dad. You were doing so well last night." Gwen sighed, then squeezed Cydney's arm. "Go get your rental car. I'll warn Bebe." A thin smile tugged her mouth. "She'll have to talk to me, won't she?"

Cydney went down the gallery stairs. Gus waited for her on the foyer, fumbling to gather the signs in the crook of his arm.

"Maybe we shouldn't go," Cydney said, taking half the signs from him. "Maybe we should stay."

"We're going." Gus took her elbow with his free hand, steered her out the door and down the porch steps. "You and I need to talk."

The sun was bright but brisk, the air chilly enough to vaporize Cydney's breath. "I'm sorry about last night. Gwen was upset and I—"

"My own house and I couldn't walk across the living room," Gus griped as he hustled her down the drive. "Somebody was going at it on the sofa and Misha had Domino spread-eagled on the kitchen island."

"I know, I heard them." Relief flooded Cydney that she hadn't stood Gus up. He hadn't been able to get to her any more than she'd been able to get to him. "Did you see who was in the living room?"

"It was too dark, but I'll tell you what." Gus passed her the signs, swung around to open the garage door and shot her a scowl. "I'm the warden of this asylum and I say tonight there's gonna be a lockdown."

He rolled the door up, tossed the signs and a hammer in the back of the truck, helped Cydney into the cab, got in behind the wheel, started the engine and kissed her hard on the mouth.

"Let's run away," he said, expelling a deep breath. "Pick a place."

"Outer Mongolia. Surely they can't find us there."

"Mongolia it is. We'll stake the signs on our way out."

Gus backed the truck out of the garage, cut the wheel to swing the nose toward the house and slammed on the brake. "Damn it!" he swore.

Cydney hooked her seat belt, looked up and saw her father running toward them, waving and tugging on his rally cap.

"Make a nice little hood ornament, wouldn't he?" Gus growled.

"After the wedding," Cydney agreed darkly. "Once he gives Bebe away we can have him stuffed and mounted if we want."

"Don't ask," Fletch snapped when she opened her door and scooted toward Gus to make room for him on the bench seat. "Just drive."

He didn't offer to help with the signs; Cydney held them

while Gus drove them into the partially frozen ground with the hammer. Fletch stayed in the truck, muttering and toying with an unlit cigarette. When they reached the car rental agency, he hopped out, lit up and paced the parking lot while Gus went inside with Cydney.

"I've got an idea." He opened the glass door and gave her a quick kiss. "We'll let your father drive the rental car to Tall Pines."

"You are astonishingly brilliant this morning."

"Desperation does that to a man. C'mon."

The only car available was a periwinkle-blue Ford Aspire, the size and shape of a goldfish bowl, with a standard transmission.

"I can't drive a stick," Fletch said. "Never learned."

So Cydney drove the Aspire, glaring at the back of her father's white head through the truck's back window all the way to Tall Pines. Halfway up the drive, they passed a flatbed tow truck on its way down with her mangled Jeep chained on the back.

"No!" Cydney cried. "My peach suit!"

Her shoes and the sweaters she'd bought, too. Cydney made a U-turn and chased the tow truck, laying on the horn and flashing her lights, all the way to Gib Elbert Senior's mailbox—not Junior's—before the driver saw the tiny little Aspire in his side mirror and pulled over.

Even with the signs, it took Cydney forty-five minutes to make her way to Tall Pines. She was so rattled she missed two of them and had to backtrack. She couldn't remember if she'd waved at Gus before she'd whipped the Aspire around in hot pursuit of her peach suit. What if she hadn't? What if Gus hadn't seen her? He could be worried about her.

How worried, Cydney wondered. Worried enough to call Sheriff Cantwell? Visions of search parties and APB's danced in her head. She could see Gus ripping her out of the car, crushing her in his arms and sobbing, "My darling! I thought you'd driven off the mountain. Be mine!"

When the Aspire topped the drive, she saw Gus' red pickup

by the porch steps and Crooked Possum's only cruiser parked behind it. Sheriff Cantwell stood in the grass circle with Gus, each of them pointing in a different direction. Cydney's heart did an oh-no-I-was-only-daydreaming flip as she slowed the car and rolled down her window.

"Here I am!" she shouted at Gus. "Call off the posse! I got lost!"

She didn't see the hatchet he held, the axe in Sheriff Cantwell's big hands or the fallen pine tree that had come down in the storm until she stopped the car by the fence enclosing the circle and Gus and the Sheriff swung around to look at her. Like she'd just fallen out of the sky.

The tree, Cydney realized. They weren't forming a posse to come look for her. They were trying to decide what to do with the tree.

"When did you get lost?" Gus asked her. "Where?"

"Um—no place special. Never mind."

Cydney hit the clutch and the gears and sent the Aspire scooting toward the garage. Past Sheriff Cantwell's cruiser, Gus' truck, Louella's ambulance and Sarah's station wagon. Gus hadn't missed her. No one had missed her. She was disappearing again. Right on schedule.

She almost kept her foot on the gas, almost kept going. Down the drive and headed for home. Surely someone would miss her if she didn't show up at the wedding to wash glasses in the scullery like Cinderella. But if she left, she might never find out what Gus wanted to tell her.

So she kept the Aspire pointed toward the garage, parked it inside, gathered her purse and her packages and started toward the house. The thwack-thwack of the axe Sheriff Cantwell swung at the shattered tree and the nick-nick of the hatchet Gus used to chip off small branches rang on the crisp air. He didn't look up. He didn't even see her. So much for breathless kisses and suggesting they run away together.

"Cydney," he called as she started up the porch steps.

She turned around and saw Gus waving her toward him. Her heart did another flip and she went to him, smiling. Her suit in its plastic bag draped over her left arm, the bags with her shoes and her sweaters in her right fist. Gus wiped sweat off his forehead with the back of his wrist and came up to the split-rail fence to meet her.

"Tell Aldo to get his butt out here and give us a hand, would you?"

"Oh," Cydney said flatly. "Sure." She sighed and turned away.

"Wait a sec." She looked back at him and he cocked his head at her. "Where did you go? I thought you were in the garage with the car."

"The garage," Cydney repeated. He'd thought she was in the damn garage. His garage, her garage. It didn't matter. "Why don't I just move my stuff out there?"

"Why would you want to do that?"

"Oh never mind!" Cydney spat at him, and spun away.

She should leave, just get in the car and go. If Gus wanted to tell her whatever he'd wanted to tell her last night, he could call her. Long distance. If he hadn't forgotten what he'd wanted to say. If he even remembered she was alive.

Oh shut up, her little voice snapped. *Go have some cheese with your whine, Bebe.*

"Bebe!" Cydney shrilled, coming to an indignant halt on the foyer.

"Yeah, Uncle Cyd. Have you seen her?" Aldo popped up behind the living room bar. "I've been looking all over for her."

"I haven't seen her, Aldo. I just got back from Branson. Gus and the Sheriff could use some help taking down the broken pine tree."

"Sure thing." Aldo stopped next to her in the foyer. "Would you find Beebs and talk to her? She had a big fight with her Grampa Fletch and nobody's seen her since."

"Oh no. What happened?"

"Don't ask." Aldo flushed and went outside.

The shutters on the pass-through were latched but the louvers were partially open. Cydney smelled onions and a ham baking, heard Cloris and her sisters' little bird chirps, Sarah's chatter, Mamie's drawl and Louella's laugh. She didn't hear

Georgette barking orders like a drill sergeant, but figured she had to be in the kitchen. Better find Bebe, Cydney decided, before her mother saw her and press-ganged her into K.P.

She hurried down the foyer steps, tripping over the suit bag that was slipping off her arm, made it to the closest couch and tossed her packages on the leather cushions. The sign Bebe had taped to the great room doors, TOUCH ONE THING IN THIS ROOM AND DIE. LOVE—THE BRIDE AND GROOM, was still there, but the doors were ajar. A thin sliver of light slid between them. Uh-oh. Someone was in the great room.

"Cydney." Georgette pushed through the swinging door with something crumpled in her right fist. "What the hell are you doing shopping?"

"I rescued this stuff from my Jeep, Mother." Cydney turned away from her packages. "Aldo said Bebe and Dad had a fight. What's wrong?"

"This, for starters." Georgette threw the crumpled wad in her hand. It was a paper napkin, cocktail-size, Cydney saw when she picked it up, unfolded it and read the gold lettering in one corner:

Bebe and Frodo Munroe, Saturday, November 10—

"Oh no." Cydney crushed the napkin. "This is awful."

"Your father thought it was the funniest thing he'd ever seen in his soon-to-be-over-with life. He opened the first box before the UPS driver had the other two in the house. He and Gwen laughed so hard they nearly hyperventilated. Bebe burst into tears. Aldo didn't get it. He's never read Tolkien. Bebe had to explain it to him."

"Let me guess. Dad laughed again and the fight started."

"Right." Georgette sighed and rubbed her forehead. "How dare he laugh at Aldo. How dare he call him stupid. Gwen defended Fletch. Herb defended Bebe. Gwen shouted at Herb. Bebe shouted at her mother and stormed off. No one's seen her since."

"Where's Dad?"

"I don't know and I don't care," Georgette snapped, but

her voice caught. "Gwen is upstairs e-mailing on her laptop and yakking on the cell phone I told *you* to take away from her. Herbert is sulking because I told him to butt out. The Prince and the French bimbo are in the hot tub, making a cuckold of your father. I'm on my way outside to borrow Sheriff Cantwell's axe and reenact *The Shining*."

This was her father's doing. The shrill in her mother's voice, the glitter in her eyes, still puffy from whatever Gus had walked in on in the kitchen.

"I've got a better idea." She put an arm around her mother and drew her toward the stairs. "Chocolate, a cup of tea and a long hot bath."

"There isn't time. Louella and Sarah—"

"Can manage without you. I'm here now. I'll take care of things."

"You always do." At the foot of the gallery stairs, Georgette caught Cydney's chin and gave her a teary kiss. "I think I'll lie down for a bit, too."

"Use your sleep mask and your earplugs," Cydney suggested.

"I'll do that." She held up a finger. "Good idea."

It was a brilliant idea. It would keep Georgette from hearing the screams when she killed Fletch. Gus said that whatever was or wasn't going on between her parents was none of her business, but what did he know? He'd thought she was in the garage with the car. The moron.

"Up you go." Cydney gave her mother a lift onto the stairs, waited till she heard her bedroom door shut, then wheeled toward the bar and pushed open the swinging door. "Hello, ladies." She smiled at Mamie and Louella, peeling potatoes at the sink, Sarah basting a ham and Cloris and her sisters assembling the wedding cake on the island. "Mother has a headache. I sent her upstairs to lie down. Everything okay?"

"Just fine." Louella wiped her hands as she came to the door and lowered her voice. "We can manage, Cydney. You tend to your family."

"Oh God." She sighed and winced. "How bad was it?"

"Awful loud and awful angry. Poor Bebe. Your father

laughed and her mama laughed and that just made it worse. It *was* funny. Bebe and Frodo." Louella's lip twitched. "But I can see why Bebe didn't think so."

"Aldo asked me to find her and talk to her."

"You do that. We'll take care of everything in here."

"You're the best, Louella. How can we ever thank you? All of you."

"Just give us seats up front where we can cry our eyes out," Louella said with a laugh. "And we'll be happy."

"You've got 'em. I'll be back as soon as I can."

Cydney crept across the living room, wedged her index fingers between the great room doors, held her breath and nudged them open. She peered through the crack and saw Bebe sitting on the dais, sniffling and wiping her teary eyes on a stack of Bebe and Frodo napkins.

I love you, Aunt Cydney. I wish you were my mother. Cydney pushed the doors open a bit more, started through them and stopped. She wasn't Bebe's mother. No matter how much her heart ached watching her unfold a napkin, stare at it and burst into fresh tears, it wasn't her place to comfort her. It was Gwen's. Time for Uncle Cyd to butt out and get a cat.

Gwen was slouched on her bed against a stack of pillows, her cell phone to her ear, her laptop on her knees when Cydney burst through the door without knocking. An ashtray with a half dozen or so cigarette butts sat on the corner of the nightstand. Fletch's brand, by the filters. Here was another beef Cydney had with her father. Contributing to the delinquency of a Type A personality.

"Gotta go." Gwen flipped the phone shut and tossed it aside. "Don't yell at me. I didn't mean to laugh, but it was the funniest damn thing—"

"Come on." Cydney pushed the laptop off her sister's knees, took Gwen's hand and yanked her off the bed. "You're gonna fix this."

She towed Gwen downstairs and across the living room, stopped outside the great room doors and laid her hands on her shoulders.

"Bebe's in there crying. Go tell her you're sorry. Tell her you love her. Ask her to please forgive you."

Gwen arched an eyebrow. "And that'll make everything all better?"

"What have you got to lose?"

"My daughter."

"I'm not fixing this, Gwen. I didn't break it. You did. You fix it."

"I can't. I don't know how."

"I just told you how. Get in there and do it." As Cydney reached for the pocket doors, Gwen caught her wrist. "Come with me."

"No. I'm sorry. I love you. Please forgive me."

"I've got that. You don't have to repeat it."

"I'm sorry about the pizza, Gwen. I love you. Please forgive me."

"You are not forgiven. But I love you, too." Gwen hooked an arm around her neck and hugged her. "What if Bebe yells at me again?"

"She won't. All she wants is her mother at her wedding."

"You'd better be right." Gwen let her go and sighed, her expression grim. "Okay. Open the doors before I chicken out."

Cydney did, then shut them and turned away after Gwen slipped through them. She didn't have time to eavesdrop. She had to find her father and kill him before her mother woke up from her nap.

I don't know why I bother, her little voice said. *But I'd like to remind you what happened the last time you—*

"Oh shut up," Cydney snapped, and raced up the gallery stairs.

Well, her little voice said indignantly, but at last, finally, it shut up.

She found her father's bedroom, but Fletch wasn't in it. He wasn't anywhere. The R&R room, the basement or the deck. She even checked to make sure he wasn't in the hot tub with Misha and Domino. If he wasn't in the house, then he had to be outside. Maybe in the woods. If she took a gun with her and Domino's sable coat, she could shoot him and claim she mistook him for a bear.

It was a long shot, but Cydney decided to check Gus' office on her way outside. Sure enough, there was Fletch, reading in Gus' overstuffed chair by the big window that faced the lake. He took off his reading glasses and moved his feet over as Cydney sat down on the ottoman.

"I want you to leave my mother alone," she told him firmly.

"Really?" Fletch laid the book he was reading on his chest and laced his fingers over the spine. "What does your mother want?"

"I don't know. I didn't ask her. I'm telling you what I want."

"Why should I care what you want?"

"You don't have to care. Just leave Mother alone."

"What am I doing to her that you don't like?"

"Oh stop it, Dad. You've been flirting with Mother since the minute she came through the door. You needle Herb—"

"Let's say I'm not flirting with her. Let's say I'm courting her."

"You're a married man, Dad. You have no right—"

"Neither do you, to march in here and give me orders. I'm not sticking my nose in your business. Keep yours out of mine."

"Mother is my business. You dumped her once and left me to pick up the pieces. I won't do it again. Keep leading her on and playing with her emotions and I'll be the one on Dan Rather blabbing the whole story about Domino and Misha."

"Oooh, threats." Fletch smiled, his eyes twinkling. "And here I thought you hadn't learned a damn thing from me."

"I learned plenty from you, Dad." Cydney stood up. "I learned I don't want to end up fifty-nine years old with a life like a train wreck."

"Maybe I'm trying to clean up the mess."

"Good for you. I hope you mean it." Cydney walked to the door and looked back at him. "Just don't strand my mother on the tracks."

chapter
twenty-nine

Her father paid no attention to a word Cydney said. He flirted and teased her mother all through dinner, until Georgette's cheeks flushed, her eyes sparkled, and Herb developed a tic at the corner of his left eye.

It was a lovely meal, prepared by the ladies of Crooked Possum. Ham with gravy and mashed potatoes, string beans and corn relish canned by Mamie. Sourdough rolls with butter and apple jelly.

Aldo ate like he had a tapeworm. Cydney hardly at all. Her father kept shooting her smug, I-dare-you glances that tied her stomach in knots. Why had she confronted him? She should've kept her mouth shut.

I tried to warn you, her little voice said. Cydney gritted her teeth.

When Georgette got up to serve dessert, floating starry-eyed toward the kitchen, Cydney shot out of her chair to follow her. Gus closed his hand on her arm as she pushed through the swinging door. She knew his touch and felt her heart tug as she turned around.

"I think Herb's about to pop your old man. Should I let him?"

"I'd like to say yes, but it'll only make things worse. This is my fault. I told Dad to stop flirting with Mother."

"Bad move, babe. See if you can talk some sense into Georgette. I know you won't quit till you try. I'll keep a lid on Herb." He put a kiss between her eyebrows. "You and me. Midnight. I'll come to your room."

Cydney was still miffed, still thought Gus was a moron for

thinking she was in the garage, but the simmer in his eyes made her pulse jump.

"I'll be there," she promised, and hurried down the hall past the bathroom and the pantry, the warmth of his fingers lingering on her arm.

"Darling." Georgette stood at the island, filling a tray with plates of sliced pineapple upside-down cake. "Wasn't that a wonderful meal? I've never mastered the art of ham gravy. I must ask Sarah her secret."

Cydney hied herself up on the rungs of a stool, spread her hands on the island and leaned into Georgette's face. "Snap out of it, Mother."

"Snap out of what?"

"The trance Dad has put you in."

"I'm not in the least bit entranced." A coy smile curved Georgette's mouth. "But I think your father is."

"What about Herb? He looks like he's about to blow a gasket."

"Of course he does. He thinks he has competition."

"Does he, Mother?"

"Cydney. You're making entirely too much of a harmless flirtation."

"I don't think it's harmless. I tried to tell you so yesterday, but you sent me upstairs to get Bebe. You wouldn't listen to me, so I told Dad."

Georgette's nostrils flared. "*What* did you tell him?"

"I told him to stop flirting with you."

"Obviously he chose to ignore you." Georgette picked up the tray and started around the island. "Which is precisely what I intend to do."

Cydney slid off the stool and stepped in front of Georgette. "Has it occurred to you that Dad's flirting with you just to annoy Herb?"

"Thank you, Cydney, for that lovely compliment."

"I love you, Mother. I don't want to see your heart broken again."

"My heart, my business." Georgette brushed past her. "Bring the coffee and keep your nose out of my affairs."

Nice job, her little voice said snidely. *Now Mumsy and Dadums are both pissed off at you.*

"Oh shut up," Cydney snarled, and snatched up the coffee carafe.

So what if she'd struck out with Fletch and Georgette? Gwen and Bebe were chatting like best friends when she came into the dining room. Two out of three wasn't bad. Especially for a peashooter.

"All right, everyone." Georgette tapped her knife on her water glass once dessert was over and most of the table cleared. "Time to rehearse the ceremony. To your places in the great room, please."

Bebe and Aldo and Fletch rose obediently. Cydney and Gus and Gwen and Herb remained seated.

"What do you think you're doing?" Georgette swept them all with a fiery eye. "You're the best man, Angus. Go with Aldo."

"Yes, ma'am." Gus saluted and followed his nephew.

"Herbert, you're the usher," Georgette ordered. "When I signal you from the piano, escort Gwen to the mother of the bride's chair."

"Right away, Georgie-girl." Herb offered Gwen his arm and squired her out of the dining room.

"Cydney, you—" Her mother's gaze swung toward her, then she blinked. "What *are* you supposed to do tomorrow?"

"Wash glasses in the scullery?" Cydney suggested.

"During the reception, perhaps. If need be. For now . . ." Georgette shrugged. "Pretend to be a guest."

"I think I'd make a much better fifth wheel."

"Oh don't be petulant," Georgette snapped, and spun out of the dining room. "Go sit somewhere and look weepy."

"That won't be tough," Cydney muttered.

And it wasn't. Her eyes filled the instant Gus took his place on the dais steps with Aldo. He looked s-o-o-o handsome. Even in a rumpled sweater and baggy jeans, even holding two fingers to the back of Aldo's head as he'd done to his brother Artie in one of the childhood snapshots she and Louella had taken off the piano and packed away in a box.

When Georgette played the opening chords of "The Wedding March," Cydney's throat closed. When Bebe came past her up the aisle on Fletch's arm, her heart swelled with joy for her niece and ached with sadness for herself. This time tomorrow, Bebe would be married. And Uncle Cyd would be on her way home to Kansas City to buy a cat.

"No, no, no!" Georgette banged a sour chord. "Measured steps, Fletch! Slow and measured!"

"If we go any slower George, we'll be crawling."

"Again," Georgette commanded.

Bebe and Fletch sighed and did it again. And again, and again.

"For crissake, George!" Fletch shouted. "At this rate, the kid'll be on Social Security before she gets up the aisle!"

"If you'd start on the same foot you'd stay in step!"

"What happened to slow and measured?"

"Slow and measured *and in step*!"

"It's not difficult." Herb swung out of his chair and into the aisle. "Here, Parrish. Let me show you."

"Sit down," Fletch barked. "Stick to trying to trip me on my way up the aisle like you did last time."

"I did *not* try to trip you!"

"Oh baloney! You'd love to see me fall and break my neck so you could give Bebe away tomorrow."

"What are you smoking in those cigarettes, Parrish?"

"Stop it!" Bebe spun angrily off her grandfather's arm, glared at him and then at Herb. "Stop arguing and picking at each other! I am *not* getting married in the middle of a war zone!"

"Sorry, honey." Fletch curved her hand around his arm. "Now look what you've done," he said to Herb. "You've upset Bebe."

"*I* upset her? You started this!"

"Herbert!" Georgette shouted. "Get up here and stand in for the clergyman. Cydney, what time will the minister be here?"

"I don't know, Mother. What time did you ask him to be here?"

"Cydney." Georgette paled. "The clergyman was on your list."

"My list?" Cydney's stomach clutched. "What list?"

"The one you snatched out of my hand at dinner."

"A week ago? That list?"

"Of course that list! Item one said 'Arrange clergyman.'"

"You made a copy. You did the shopping. I only glanced at the list."

"Oh forget the damn list." Gwen wheeled out of the mother of the bride's chair. "Which one of you called the minister?"

"Neither one of us, apparently," Georgette snapped.

"How could you do this?" Bebe howled at her grandmother. "How can Aldo and I get married without a minister?"

"It's all right, Bebe." Cydney pushed out of her chair and hurried toward her. "We'll find a minister by four o'clock tomorrow."

"Who, Uncle Cyd?" Bebe whirled on her, shaking and white-faced. "Who will you find?"

"Uh, well—"

"In a pinch I can call Elvin," Gus said, coming quickly down the dais steps. "He's a justice of the peace as well as the sheriff."

"I'm not a *convict*! I don't want to be married by the *sheriff*!" Bebe wailed, then burst into tears and raced for the pocket doors.

"Beebs!" Aldo shouted, and ran after her.

"Bebe!" Gwen called, dashing behind Aldo. "Wait, honey!"

Cydney didn't think she'd stop. She thought her niece would keep running. Out of the great room, out of the house. Her heart leaped, expecting it, but Bebe spun around in the doorway. She threw one arm around Gwen, the other around Aldo, and they bore her away, sobbing.

"Nicely done, Parrish." Herb glowered at Fletch. "That was even better than last night's Scrabble game."

"Oh, put a sock in it, Herb. You're just pissed 'cause I won."

"I'm pissed because you won on words like *pulchritude* and *fornicate* and the way you ogled my fiancée throughout the damn game."

"George was my wife long before she was your fiancée, Herb. I think that earns me ogling rights."

"If you don't knock it off, it's gonna earn you a fat lip!"

"That's enough, boys." Gus stepped between them and flung up his hands. "If you two can't get along, you can leave."

"Good idea." Herb turned toward Georgette. "Get your things, Georgie-girl. We're spending the night in Branson."

"I'm not going anywhere, Herbert. I'm staying right here."

"Me, too." Fletch dropped into a chair, crossed his arms and stuck his chin out at Herb. "But if you'd like to go, don't let us stop you."

"Fat chance I'd leave you alone with my fiancée, Parrish."

"She's my wife, Herb."

"Both of you stop it!" Georgette shot off the bench and spread her hands on the piano. "I am the mother of your children, Fletch, *not* your wife. You have one around here somewhere, if you can find her. I suggest you look in the hot tub. And how *dare* you, Herbert, imply that I can't be trusted with my ex-husband. I've never been so insulted."

"I didn't mean it that way, Georgie-girl. You know I—"

"And stop calling me Georgie-girl," Georgette snapped. "I hate it."

"Boy, so do I." Fletch made a face. "Yech."

"Stay out of this!" Georgette and Herb shouted at Fletch, then Herb swung toward him. "My fiancée is not spending another night under the same roof with you, Parrish."

"Your fiancée is spending the night wherever she damn pleases, Herbert," Georgette seethed. "Both of you stop pulling at me!"

"Great job, Herb. Now you've upset George."

"If you'd stayed in France where you belong—"

"*Knock it off!*" Gus thundered. Cydney jumped. Georgette blinked and Herb took a step back from the blistering scowl on Gus' face. "Okay, boys. I'm the warden, so here's the deal. No more fights or threatening to belt each other.

Next one who starts it gets tossed out on his ass. You two are not going to ruin Aldo and Bebe's wedding. If I see you within ten feet of each other tomorrow before Bebe walks down the aisle at four o'clock, I'll have Sheriff Cantwell lock you in the garage. Got it?"

"Got it," Fletch grumbled.

"Got it," Herb growled.

"Good. Anything you want to say, Georgette?"

"Yes, Angus. Thank you." She gave Fletch and Herb a scathing glare, her eyes glittering. "I've never been so mortified in my life. Don't either one of you dare speak to me. Not a single word."

"Okay, fellas. Thems the rules. Now let's find Bebe so you can shake hands and tell her you've settled your differences. Then I want you to go to your rooms and stay there until morning."

Gus thumbed toward the doors. Fletch slapped his hands on his knees and got up. Herb and Gus followed him down the aisle. Once they were gone, Georgette sat down on the piano bench and looked at Cydney.

"You were right about your father." She sighed. "And about Herb."

"Herb?" Cydney blinked at her. "What do you mean?"

"That was not a demonstration of undying love for me. That was a pissing contest," Georgette said bluntly. "A chest-beating show about male ego and ownership. If either one of those randy old goats truly loved me, they wouldn't have behaved that way."

"Maybe they both love you, Mother." Cydney hurried up on the dais, slid onto the piano bench and put an arm around her. "Maybe that's why they behaved that way."

"That's sweet of you to say, darling. Utter bullshit, but sweet nonetheless." Her mother smiled, but it was a weak effort. "I should practice some more. Will you turn the music for me?"

Georgette was still playing "The Wedding March" and Cydney was still turning the sheet music when Gus came into the great room with Gwen. They sat on the dais steps and waited till Georgette finished.

"Well, Warden Munroe?" She turned toward him on the bench.

"They were pretty convincing. I think Bebe bought it."

"I think so, too. Aldo believed Dad and Herb, so that helped." Gwen sighed. "Bebe's still awfully upset about the clergyman, though. What are we going to do about that?"

"I'll get on the phone and make some calls," Gus said.

"Thank you, Angus. I'll take Bebe a cup of tea and apologize."

"For what, Mother?" Gwen asked. "You didn't do anything."

"Yes I did." Georgette rose from the piano. "I let your charming old reprobate father turn my head. But never again."

Tears gleamed in her eyes as she walked toward the pocket doors. Gus sat on the steps with his elbows on his knees, a sympathetic smile curving his mouth as he watched Georgette walk down the aisle.

Cydney's heart broke for her mother. If you really loved someone you said so and did something about it. You didn't argue and fight. You didn't drop a rock on his foot and slam a door on his nose, either. And you didn't joke about who was going to dump whom and when.

"Crap." Gwen sighed. "We're still from a broken home."

"You'll like Herb," Cydney said. "He's a nice man."

"He's a colorless twerp."

"He treats Mother like a queen. He gives her anything she wants."

"Well no wonder she fell for Dad's malarkey. She's bored silly."

"She is not bored, Gwen. She's very happy with Herb."

"Oh please. Half the time Mother forgets Herb is in the room."

"Only when Dad's around."

"I just said that. Do you need a tree to fall on you, Cyd?"

She'd already had a tree fall on her—well, on her Jeep,

anyway—and still she'd let herself fall hopelessly in love with Gus.

"What we need to do is the dishes," Gus said. "And go to bed."

His eyes lit on Cydney, dark and smoldering. Her pulse jumped and her heart raced. She'd die if he came to her room and spouted some stupid drivel about chapter six. Right after she killed him.

"You need to get on the phone and find a minister." Gwen turned on the dais step and pointed at him. "Cyd and I will do the dishes."

Gus headed for the telephone in his office; Cydney and Gwen, for the kitchen. Gwen had just finished wiping off the countertops, and Cydney cranking on the dishwasher, when Gus pushed through the swinging door. She took one look at his face and said, "Uh-oh."

"Pastor Phipps and Reverend Marshall have gone hunting," Gus said. "Together. Cloris' brother is a Baptist minister in Springfield, but he has a wedding tomorrow at four o'clock. I think Elvin's our best bet."

"Swell," Cydney said unhappily. "Who's gonna tell Bebe?"

"Let's wait till morning," Gwen said. "Maybe she'll calm down."

"Morning it is. G'night, ladies." Gus slid Cydney a wink Gwen didn't see and pushed through the swinging door.

"I'm beat." Gwen yawned as she and Cydney climbed the back stairs. "If you get the urge to talk to me at 2 A.M. stuff a pillow over your head and smother yourself, will you?"

It was only 9:30 when Cydney shut her bedroom door. Two and a half hours till midnight. Oh God. What was she going to do?

If you really love someone, her little voice reminded her, *you say so and you do something about it.*

"Like what?" Cydney asked herself in the bathroom mirror. "Just blurt out, 'I love you, Gus. I want to marry you'?"

That's what an Uzi would do, but Cydney's peashooter heart quailed. What if she asked him and he said no?

But what if he says yes? her little voice countered.

"Then *you* ask him," Cydney snapped, and turned on the shower.

Her shoulders felt like iron, she was so tense. She stood under the hot spray until ten o'clock to loosen them, then dried off and put on her green-striped pajamas. At 10:30, she gave herself a facial. At 11:00, she did her nails. At 11:30 she had a panic attack.

On the stroke of midnight, Gus knocked softly on her door.

He smiled when Cydney opened it, his hair shower-damp, his jaw fresh-shaved and shiny. He wore gray sweatpants and one of his white pocket T-shirts. Under his left arm, he carried a rolled-up sleeping bag.

"Are we camping out?"

"Yep. Right here." He unrolled the navy blue sleeping bag on the floor of the alcove and unzipped it. "Your old man's a night owl. If he sticks one toe out of his room, the warden's gonna be here to nail him."

Cydney grinned. "I'll bring the pillows."

She grabbed two from her bed, tossed them on the sleeping bag and crawled into it with Gus. He zipped it around them, grunting and tugging at the teeth that kept snagging in the down-filled poplin.

"Need some help?" Cydney asked, sitting up.

"Nope." He yanked the zipper shut. "Got it."

They lay down side by side and snuggled together, Gus' cold, bare toes rubbing her warm feet, the hair on his ankles raising gooseflesh on her smooth calves. He slid his arm underneath her and turned his head toward her on the pillow. The hallway wall sconces he'd left on glowed in his eyes. Not quite like stars in a night sky, but close enough.

Cydney tipped her head up and kissed his chin, still slick and cool from his razor. "You have the best darned ideas."

Gus smiled and turned on his side, rolled her toward him and curved his arm around her shoulders. "Do I?"

"Oh yes." Cydney cuddled her cheek into the curve of his neck, drew a breath and inhaled soap and shaving cream.

"Glad you think so. I've got another one I'd like to discuss with you." He put a kiss on the top of her head, his voice a deep thrum in her ears. "I think it's the best darned idea I've ever had. Want to hear it?"

Cydney's heart clenched. "It isn't about chapter six, is it?"

"No." Gus propped himself up on his left arm. "This is about us."

"Us?" The heat in his eyes made her quiver. "You and me?"

"I planned to keep quiet till after the wedding, but—"

"Wait." Cydney pressed her fingers to his mouth. Her heart jumped into her throat, but it was now or never. Time to take her place in the Hall of Big Guns or forever remain a peashooter. "I have something I need to say to you."

"Okay." Gus slid down on his elbow, his head in his hand. "What?"

"I—" Cydney's voice squeaked. She snapped her mouth shut and bumped her forehead against his chin. She felt his heart beat, slow and steady, and so close to hers, she wanted to stay here forever. "I love you. I've loved you for ten years, since I read your first book. I don't want to dump you. I want to marry you and stay here at Tall Pines."

Cydney shut her eyes and held her breath, waiting for Gus to laugh or jump out of the sleeping bag and run screaming down the hall.

"Can I ask you something?" he said slowly. "Is that why you had pictures of me pinned up in the room above your garage?"

"Yes," Cydney confessed. "I fell asleep every night dreaming about you. I've got a catalog of Angus Munroe fantasies that would fill the Library of Congress."

"Really?" He was laughing at her—or trying not to. Cydney could hear it in his voice. "Did we ever make love in a sleeping bag?"

"No. I'm not much for the great outdoors."

"How 'bout a sleeping bag in front of a roaring fire?"

"No," Cydney said, wishing he'd laugh and be done with it.

"A sleeping bag in a hallway?"

"No. This is my first time in a sleeping bag."

"Then I guess I never proposed to you in one. In your dreams, I mean."

"No," Cydney said miserably. Just laugh and get it over with, will you? she wanted to say. Let me crawl back into my room and smother myself. "You never proposed to me in my dreams in a sleeping bag."

"Good. I want to be original." He slid a finger under her chin and tipped her head up. "Look at me, Cydney."

She cracked one eye. Gus wasn't laughing, he was smiling. Her pulse leaped and her heart pounded.

"Just so happens I love you, too," he said. "Will you marry me?"

chapter
thirty

"You love me?" I'm asleep, Cydney thought. Asleep and dreaming. Or I've died and gone to heaven. *"Really?"*

"I love you." Gus' smile widened and his eyes softened. "Really."

"And I'm not dreaming? You *did* ask me to marry you?"

"Since you asked me to marry you, it only seemed fair."

"Gus. Oh Gus." Cydney clutched his shoulders, felt warm skin and firm muscle under his T-shirt. She was awake. Gus was real and he loved her. He wanted to marry her. "What about my loony family?"

"To have you, I'll take them. Your mother doesn't scare me anymore. I must be getting used to her. Your old man can be a pompous pain in the ass sometimes, but so can I, so I figure you can put up with that. Your sister." He raised his right hand and tipped it from side to side. "As for Bebe. Well." He shrugged and smiled. "I'm trying, okay?"

"We've only known each other two weeks," Cydney worried out loud. "Are you *sure* you want to spend the rest of your life with me?"

"Positive." Gus grinned. "I've had more fun since I met you than I've had in all my thirty-five years. I'm counting on you to make the rest of our lives every bit as much fun."

"Boy, I don't know, bub. That's a pretty stiff order."

He grinned wider, caught her left hand and drew it inside the sleeping bag. "Speaking of stiff."

"Down, Clyde," she said sternly.

Gus threw his head back and laughed. Cydney covered his mouth and said, "Shhh!" He nipped her fingers and wrapped her in his arms. Cydney burrowed her cheek against his chest, smiled and felt tears in her eyes. He loved her. He wanted to marry her. Cydney the Nobody.

"I love you, Gus. I love you, I love you, I love you."

"I love you, too, babe. You haven't said yes yet."

"Yes," Cydney said, and sniffled.

"Are you crying *again*?"

"Happy tears, Gus. Goddamn happy tears." Cydney raised her head, her hands to his shoulders, and gave him a shake. "This is every wish, every dream, every fantasy I've ever had come true."

"I'd like to hear about those fantasies. Especially the kinky ones."

"Sorry. No kinky fantasies. A few X-rated, but mostly they're just schmaltzy, happily-ever-after dreams."

"Tell you what." He wagged his eyebrows. "We'll make our own kinky fantasies on our honeymoon. Where would you like to go?"

"Paris. The one in France, not Texas."

Gus laughed, softly so he wouldn't wake anyone. It was a tight squeeze, but he turned on his stomach and propped himself on his elbows. So did Cydney, the sleeping bag twisting around her. She kicked at it, gathered a pillow in her arms and tucked it under her chin.

"Here's what I think about *our* wedding," he said. "I want you to be the center of attention, so I think we should keep quiet till Aldo and Bebe are hitched. Maybe till your mother marries Herb, but that's your call."

"After tonight, I'm not sure Mother will marry him. Too bad. It would have been a lovely wedding," Cydney said wistfully. "A candlelight ceremony on Christmas Eve."

"We could do that. Or we could be married here at Tall Pines."

"I'd love to be married here." Cydney bent her elbow on her pillow and leaned her head on her hand. "But I don't want to copy Bebe."

"Okay. Got any hot wedding fantasies?"

"A zillion. Want to hear my most favorite?"

Gus grinned. "You bet."

"It's a church wedding. In Westminster Abbey, because you've been knighted for outstanding literary achievement."

Gus gave a shout of laughter and rolled on his back.

"You haven't heard the best part." Cydney clapped a hand over his mouth. "You win a Pulitzer and the Nobel Prize. For a wedding present, you buy me a castle in Scotland. On our honeymoon, we shear sheep."

Gus laughed till tears rolled down his cheeks. Cydney grinned, watching him, the deep rumble of his half-choked laughter against her hand humming in her bone marrow.

"God, that's funny." He kissed her palm, rolled toward her and wiped his eyes. "You should write a book about your fantasies."

"I *am* writing a book about my fantasies," she said, and kissed him.

A deep, openmouthed kiss that made Gus growl. His arms closed around her and pulled her against him, his lips—and Clyde—hard and eager. A giggle of sheer bliss bubbled up Cydney's throat.

Gus raised his head and sucked a breath. "What?"

"We can't have hot, wild sex in this sleeping bag."

"How d'you know? You've never done it in a sleeping bag."

Cydney laughed softly and wound her arms around his neck. Gus bent his head, took her mouth again and cupped her breast.

Around the corner in the hallway, something creaked. Gus pushed up on his hand and swung his head toward the sound. Cydney struggled to sit up beside him, the sleeping bag coiling around her like a snake. She heard a soft tap, then her mother hiss, "What do you want?"

"To apologize. I'm sorry I upset you and Bebe, George. I love you."

"Go away, Fletch. You're married."

"About Domino—"

"She's in the hot tub with Gwen's fiancé."

"Listen, George. I can explain Domino and Misha."

"Gwen will kill him." Cydney reached over Gus, grabbed the zipper tab and tugged. The teeth stuck.

"Let me." Gus fumbled the tab out of her fingers and gave it a pull. The teeth dug deeper into the down-filled poplin.

"I don't want to hear about your wife's love affair, Fletch."

"George, wait." Cydney heard a thump. Her father's hand against her mother's bedroom door, she guessed. "I love you. Leaving you was the biggest mistake I ever made. I want you back."

"Go to your room, Fletch, before Gus catches you."

"Gus can't catch *anybody*," he snarled between his teeth as he yanked on the zipper—"till he gets out of this *freaking* sleeping bag!"

"Too late!" Herb crowed triumphantly. "I've caught you, Parrish!"

"Go away, Herb," Fletch barked. "Wake Bebe and I'll deck you."

"Goddamn zipper." Gus jerked and wrenched but it was stuck tight. Cydney tried to help, but her fingers weren't strong enough. "Roll away from me. If I can wiggle out, maybe you'll have room."

Gus flopped on his back and rolled. Using her elbows and her knees, Cydney inched like a worm out of the down-filled cocoon.

"Both of you go to bed," Georgette said. "I'm not speaking to you."

"You were talking to *him*!" Herb accused.

"Well duh, Herb," Fletch said. "What does that tell you?"

"Why you—"

"*Herbert!*" Georgette gave a muffled scream.

Cydney heard a crunch, a thud and crawled faster, the sleeping bag winding around her ankles until Gus tugged it free. A door opened and she held her breath, afraid they'd wakened Bebe.

"Scram, you two!" Gwen threatened. "Or I'll call the warden."

"Call him," Herb challenged. "Parrish broke the rules."

"And you broke my goddamn nose!" Fletch howled.

"Dad!" Gwen cried softly. "You're bleeding!"

"You're an idiot, Herbert! You *both* broke the rules!"

"But Parrish broke them first!"

"Oh, go *away*, Herbert! Fletch, dear! Are you all right?"

"Made it." Cydney sprawled on her stomach, free at last, and scrambled around on her knees to help Gus out of the sleeping bag.

"Georgette!" Herb cried, stricken. "You're my fiancée!"

"Shut *up*!" Gwen hissed. "If you wake Bebe I'll—"

"*Oh no!*" Bebe wailed. "Not again!"

Cydney didn't hear her niece open her bedroom door, but she heard her slam it. People in Springfield probably heard her slam it.

"Well, that tears it," Gus spat, kicking the sleeping bag away.

"Goddamn it, Herb!" Gwen cried furiously. "Bebe, honey. It's me. Open the door, sweetie."

Cydney heard Gwen knock and another door bang open.

"Beebs!" Aldo cried. "What—Gramma George. Herb," he said bewilderedly. "Why are you bleeding, Grampa Fletch? Where's Uncle Gus?"

"I'm here, Aldo." Gus stood up, pulled Cydney to her feet and led her around the corner into the hallway.

Her father sat on the floor. Georgette knelt beside him, trying to pry his hand away from his nose. Gwen tapped on Bebe's door, her hand on the knob, Aldo beside her in a rumpled T-shirt and shorts. Herb stood, blinking forlornly without his glasses, in wrinkled blue pajamas.

"Do me a favor, pal," Gus said to Aldo. "Call Sheriff Cantwell."

"Never mind, Gus. I'm leaving," Herb said. "Are you coming with me, Georgette?"

"No, Herbert." She glanced him a gentle, too-bad smile. "I'm sorry."

"So am I," Herb said sadly, and tapped Aldo on the shoulder to turn him around. "Good luck to you and Bebe. I hope you'll be very happy."

"Thanks, Herb," Aldo said, and shook his hand.

"Bye-bye, kiddo." Herb gave Cydney a bleak smile and a wave.

"Bye, Herb." She smiled back at him and wagged her fingers.

He crossed the hall to his bedroom and shut the door.

"You still want me to call Elvin?" Aldo asked Gus.

"Depends." Gus folded his arms and scowled at Fletch.

"I broke the rules," he said, his voice muffled by his hand. His left eye was swelling, Cydney noticed, the bruise Gus' fist had left on his cheek purpling again. "Somebody get me an ice bag and I'll go."

"Not so fast." Her mother pushed Fletch down as he tried to stand. "You're still bleeding."

"Oh, for cryin' out loud." He brushed her off, pushed to his feet and wobbled. Cydney bit her lip at the blood smeared on his chin and the front of his yellow silk pajamas. "See, George? I'm fine."

"You are *not* fine." Her mother rose and faced Gus, drawing her pink silk wrapper around her. "Warden Munroe. May this old bounder have a reprieve until morning?"

"I don't need a reprieve," Fletch insisted. "I need a ride."

Herb's bedroom door sprang open. "I could use a copilot, Parrish, and the least I can do is give you a lift."

"Damn skippy it's the least you can do. I'll get my stuff."

"Grampa, wait!" Bebe yanked her bedroom door open. So abruptly she nearly pulled Gwen, who still had her hand on the knob, off her feet. She tripped and might've fallen, but Aldo caught the sleeve of her white bathrobe and kept her upright.

"I mean—" Bebe sucked a shuddery breath and turned toward Gus. "Can Grampa Fletch please stay? Just till he gives me away?"

Gus slid Cydney a sideways, whattaya-think glance. She arched a you're-the-warden, whatever-you-say eyebrow at him.

"Thumbs up, Fletch stays," Gus said. "Thumbs down, he goes."

Bebe and Gwen's thumbs went up. Then Aldo's, then

Georgette's. Cydney knew when she was beat, sighed and raised her thumb.

"Thank you, family," Fletch said humbly, his voice still muffled by the hand cupped over his nose. "And you, Gus."

"Don't make me regret it." Gus stepped toward him, took his arm and turned Fletch away from Georgette. "Let's have a look at you."

"I'd rather leave now, but I don't see well at night," Herb said. "On the highway, yes, on roads this dark, no. Could I stay till morning?"

"I can drive you as far as the highway," Bebe volunteered quickly. "Aldo can follow in Uncle Gus' truck and drive us back here." She looked at Gwen first, then Gus. "I mean, if that's okay."

Where Bebe's face wasn't pale it was red and blotched from crying. Her eyes were bright and wet with tears. And something else that made Cydney tip her head suspiciously, until Bebe wiped her eyes and she decided, no, it was just the light, just the sheen of tears on her lashes.

Gwen glanced at her. Cydney nodded. "Okay with me," she said.

"Me, too." Gwen smiled and curved Bebe's cheek in her palm. "I think the bride and groom could use some fresh air."

"Boy, could we." Bebe sighed and cupped her mother's hand.

"Can you find your way home, pal?" Gus asked Aldo.

"Heck, yeah." He grinned. "You put the signs up this morning."

"I'll get my things," Herb said, and darted into his bedroom.

"I'll get dressed," Bebe said, and slipped into her room.

"Me, too," Aldo said, and disappeared into his room.

"Your nose is a real mess, slugger." Gus tipped Fletch's chin up on his crooked index finger and frowned. "Put your pants on. You and I are paying a visit to the emergency room in Branson."

"Stop fussing, Gus. You're worse than George." Fletch shrugged out of his grasp and wove on his feet. "I'm fine."

"Don't be difficult, Fletch." Georgette took his arm. "You

can't walk Bebe down the aisle if you can't stand up. I'll help
you get dressed."

"Okay." Her father grinned happily.

Cydney winced as her mother swung him around and steered
him into his room. His nose *was* a bloody, swollen mess.

"I'll get some towels and an ice bag," Gwen said, hurrying away.

"There's one in the freezer," Gus called after her, then
grinned at Cydney. "The one you gave me for *my* nose when I
left Kansas City."

Cydney cringed, remembering. "And you still want to
marry me?"

"Hell yes." Gus laughed and put his arms around her,
holding her against him with his fingers laced together in the
small of her back. "As Aunt Phoebe used to say, this is more
fun than a barrel of monkeys."

"Seems like fun now, but it can get real old, real quick, bub."

"So what? We're gonna get old, too, babe. Together."

"Now *that* sounds like fun." Cydney sighed and kissed
his chin.

A door opened behind them. Gus let her go and Cydney
turned around. Bebe stepped into the hall in khaki shorts and
a sweatshirt.

"I love you, Uncle Cyd." She swept Cydney into a hug so
fierce she thought she'd cracked a rib. "Don't worry about
us. Aldo's a good driver."

"I'm not going to worry anymore, Bebe." She backed out
of her embrace and held her hands. "You're an almost married woman."

And so are you, her little voice said. Just thinking about it
gave Cydney a giddy little quiver.

Aldo popped out of his room in jeans and a sweater, swept
his palomino bangs out of his eyes and held his hand out to
Bebe. Herb appeared in his glasses, dressed, with his suitcase,
and shook Gus' hand.

"Thanks for the hospitality, Gus. No hard feelings."

"None here, Herb. Have a safe trip."

"I will, thanks. Ready, kids?"

"Ready." Bebe and Aldo followed him down the gallery stairs.

Gus laid his hands on Cydney's shoulders, turned her toward him and leered. "Wanna help me get dressed, little girl?"

"Undressed, yes." She leered back at him. "Maybe later."

He laughed and led her downstairs. Gwen met them in the living room with the ice bag and the towel, her eyes shimmering with tears.

"Gwen," Cydney said, startled. "You're crying."

"Of course I am," she sniffed. "Bebe hugged me and kissed me on her way out and told me she loved me."

"See?" Cydney knuckled her sister in the arm. "Told you so."

Gus went upstairs to get dressed. He came back a minute or two ahead of Georgette and Fletch. They were both dressed, Fletch leaning heavily on Georgette with his arm around her shoulders.

"If you don't mind, Angus," she said. "I'll tag along."

"Fine with me. I'll bring the car. I wouldn't wait up," he said to Cydney. "This could take a while."

Cydney and Gwen waved good-bye from the porch, then shivered inside, barefoot. Gwen shut the door and held out her hand.

"Bet me a pizza in the face Mother marries Dad on Christmas Eve."

"You're on." Cydney grinned and they shook on it. "I should warn you. Dad almost spilled the beans about Domino and Misha to Mother."

"Why am I not surprised? Where the hell are they, d'you suppose?"

"In the hot tub, last time Mother snooped."

"Let's kick 'em out. I have a bottle of brandy in my suitcase. We'll have a couple belts and a soak and sleep like babies."

Which Gwen did, for almost an hour in the hot tub. Cydney sat in bubbles up to her neck, watching Gwen snore with her mouth open and her head tipped back against the tub. Oh, to have her camera.

"My camera!" Cydney howled, smacking a hand to her forehead.

"What?" Gwen sloshed awake, spilling a tidal wave out of the tub.

"My camera is in my Jeep. How can I take the wedding pictures?"

"With mine. Come on." Gwen groped bleary-eyed for a towel. "Let's go get it before my bones turn to total mush."

They dripped inside and wove up the gallery stairs, half-lit from the megaproof brandy. Except for the grandfather clock ticking outside the R&R room, the house was still. At Bebe's bedroom door, Gwen paused.

"Did you hear Bebe and Aldo come in?" she whispered.

"I couldn't hear a thing over the bubbles and your snoring."

"Should we check on her? Make sure she's okay?"

"Bebe is sound asleep," Cydney said firmly, sticking to her resolve not to worry. "We are not snooping, Georgette Junior."

"Old poop." Gwen gave her the raspberry and hiccuped.

It was almost 3 A.M. when Cydney dumped Gwen's forty-pound bag of photo equipment on the blanket box in her room, rolled up the sleeping bag, tossed her pillows on her bed and fell onto them face first, asleep.

She woke up with her head buzzing from the brandy. Her travel alarm said 8:07. Why was she awake this early? Cydney dragged into the bathroom, brushed her teeth and took up a hair pick, braced herself and blinked in the mirror. For once, her hair didn't look like a fright wig.

It's an omen, she decided as she pulled on jeans and buttoned her oversized white shirt. A joyous portent for Bebe's wedding day.

And the sun was shining. She sat down in the wing chair by the window to tie her Keds, lifted the lace curtain and smiled at the blue sky. The puffy clouds and the happy-face sun thawing the frost on the grass.

That's when she heard Gwen scream.

Cydney leaped to her feet and ran. Out of her room and down the hall, nearly colliding with Gwen as she came tearing out of Bebe's bedroom. Cydney caught her by the shoulders and spun her around.

"Cyd! Oh God." Gwen clutched her arms in fingers like talons. "Bebe isn't in her bed. They must've had an accident. Call 911!"

"Did you look in Aldo's room?"

"Aldo's room!" Gwen wrenched free and raced across the hall.

Cydney wheeled after her, her stomach dropping like a stone when Gwen pushed the door open and she saw Aldo's rumpled but empty bed.

"Don't scream." Cydney clamped a hand over her sister's mouth. "Have you been downstairs?"

Gwen shook her head, sucking air between Cydney's fingers.

"They could be in the kitchen eating breakfast."

Gwen clawed Cydney's hand off her mouth. "Or stuck in a ditch somewhere, hurt and helpless."

"Bebe doesn't go to the bathroom without her cell phone, Gwen. Don't jump to conclusions. Where's Mother?"

"Asleep. I heard her around four give Dad a pain pill and tell him she was going to bed with her mask and her earplugs."

Thank God, Cydney thought. "Go look downstairs," she told Gwen, pushing her toward the gallery. "I'll wake Gus."

But first she went back to Bebe's room. She had no idea why, until she saw a white envelope tucked into the bottom of the dresser mirror.

"Oh no," she moaned, her heart sinking.

"Oh no, what?" Gus yawned behind her, his voice gravelly with sleep. "Did somebody scream or was I dreaming?"

"It was Gwen." Cydney looked at him, leaning puffy-eyed in the doorway in his sweats and T-shirt. "We can't find Bebe and Aldo."

"What's that stuck in the mirror?"

"I don't know. I'm afraid to look."

Gus shuffled past her and plucked the envelope out of the mirror. He raised it to his nose, peered at it and handed it to Cydney.

"It says, 'To Mother and Uncle Cyd.'"

"Oh no," she moaned again.

"We'd better find your sister."

Gwen was in the R&R room, hysterically flinging pillows off the couches just in case Bebe and Aldo were hiding under the cushions.

"I can't find them," she said tearfully. "Call 911."

"This was stuck in Bebe's mirror." Cydney held up the envelope. "It's addressed to you and me."

Gwen grabbed it and tore it open, took out a folded sheet of paper and froze. "I can't." She passed the note to Cydney. "You read it."

"I think you should sit down." Gus lowered Gwen onto the brown corduroy sofa and sat down on the oak table in front of her.

Cydney sat down beside him, her knees quivering. She thought she knew what was coming, unfolded the note and read aloud:

"Dear Mother and Uncle Cyd—If you're reading this, Aldo and I have eloped. I hope I can talk him into it once we get Herb off. I just can't take any more yelling and screaming and punching each other.

"I know none of you meant to fight like cats and dogs. I don't blame you, Uncle Cyd, for throwing pizza in Mother's face. You were defending me and Louella and Mamie. And I don't blame you, Mother, for wanting me to look beautiful and sophisticated in *Vogue*, but that's your world, not mine. I wish you'd been able to see that.

"Tell Grampa thank you for bawling me out for pretending to be stupid. Tell him I won't do it anymore. I just hope Aldo will still love me.

"Tell Gramma George it's okay to return the wedding

dress she bought me. And tell her I'll call her when we get back from Las Vegas.

"I think I can talk Aldo into this, if I tell him we can get married in one of the wedding chapels and then rent a car and go to Yellowstone. He'll get to climb rocks, so he'll like that.

"He won't like hurting Uncle Gus. Any more than I like hurting you, Mother, and you, Uncle Cyd, and Gramma and Grampa. Or disappointing Louella and Mamie and Sarah and Cloris and her sisters.

"Thank you all for working so hard to make everything so beautiful for the wedding. You deserve a party, so cut the cake and eat it and toast yourselves—and me and Aldo, if you aren't too mad at us—with that really expensive bottle of champagne Grampa brought from France.

"We love you all very much. Honest. Love, Bebe and Aldo."

"Shit!" Gwen flung one of Aunt Phoebe's cushions across the R&R room and sucked a calming breath. "They're okay. They're alive. That's the main thing. I can kill them when they get back from Las Vegas."

Cydney felt sick, glanced at Gus. He gave her a thin smile.

"I could kick myself for the pizza," she said to him miserably.

"You were provoked," he said, and glanced at Gwen. "No offense."

"None taken. I *should* be kicked for the wedding dress."

"I'll kick you," Cydney offered. "If you'll kick me."

"How about," Fletch said, "we take turns kicking each other?"

Cydney looked up at her parents standing in the doorway in their nightclothes, her father's arm around her mother. His left eye was black, his nose covered by a giant, flesh-colored Band-Aid. Georgette wore her hairnet, and her sleep mask on her forehead.

"I guess you heard me read Bebe's note," Cydney said dismally.

"Every word." Georgette crossed the room, sat down on the

couch next to Gwen and smiled weakly at Gus. "I'm so sorry, Angus. I'm afraid this is all the Parrish family's doing."

"Not quite, Georgette. I wrote the Grand Plan to Wreck the Wedding, remember, and I behaved like a total jerk in Kansas City. I think there's plenty of blame to go around."

"The only person who's lily-white in this is Aldo. Not the brightest crayon in the box, Gus, but he's a good kid." Fletch came around the back of the couch and sat down on Gwen's other side. "I hope this is the last trick my granddaughter pulls on him to get her way."

"Back off, Dad," Gwen snapped. "After last night's fist-fight I would've run out of here screaming, too."

"I feel fine, Gwen, thanks for asking," Fletch said, miffed. "My nose is cracked in three places and it hurts like a sonofabitch."

"Stop it, you two. Let's don't start again," Georgette said tiredly. "It's just eight-thirty. If we split the guest list and start calling, we should be able to reach everyone who's driving down from Kansas City."

"I'll help," Fletch volunteered. "Then I think we should do what Bebe said and throw one hell of a party for the Crooked Possum folks."

"I think we should stick to the original plan and have a wedding." Gus took Cydney's hand and smiled. "What do you think?"

"You mean our wedding?" She blinked at him, surprised. "You mean today? Here? This afternoon?"

"You said you wanted to be married at Tall Pines, but you didn't want to copy Bebe. That's not a problem now—Bebe bailed."

"Oh Gus, I'd love it." Cydney sighed. "But we don't have a license."

"So we'll get one on Monday and have a do-over."

"A do-over?" she laughed. "You mean two weddings?"

"Yeah. Two weddings." Gus grinned. "And two anniversaries. That way I'll have a shot at remembering at least one of them."

"Will Sheriff Cantwell marry us twice?"

"If I try to wiggle out of the second one, he'll lock me up and force-feed me Mamie's prickly pear jelly. What do you say?"

"Yes." Cydney kissed him and turned to face her family.

Her father grinned, then winced. Because it hurt, Cydney guessed. Her mother and Gwen simply stared, wide-eyed and openmouthed.

"Cydney," Georgette said dazedly. "When did this happen?"

"While you and Herb were in Arkansas, Mother."

"Don't blame Cydney, Georgette." Gus swung his arm around her and jostled her against him. "Blame it on strip Ping-Pong."

Fletch threw his head back and roared. Gwen gave a startled but delighted laugh. Her mother flushed, then smiled, took Cydney's face in her hands and smacked a kiss on her mouth.

"Will you play 'The Wedding March' for me, Mother?"

Georgette's eyes filled with tears. "Of course, darling."

"Dad? Will you give me away?"

"You bet, honey."

"Will you be my matron of honor, Gwen?"

"Nope." Her sister grinned. "But I'll shoot the wedding pictures."

"Quickly, everyone." Georgette rose and clapped her hands. "First to the phones to call Bebe's guests. Then breakfast."

"I'll get my cell phone." Cydney stood up, but her mother pushed her down beside Gus.

"You are the bride. You do nothing. Today, we are your slaves. Gwen. Start on the guest list. Fletch. Get on the phone and order us a limo. We're all clearing out of here after the ceremony so Cydney and Angus can spend their first wedding night alone in their own home."

Georgette swept them away and shut the pocket doors.

"My slaves." Cydney grinned at Gus. "I'm going to enjoy this."

"You deserve to, babe." Gus kissed her on the nose. "I need to have a word with your father and call Elvin before breakfast."

"You do?" She tipped her head at him curiously. "Why?"

"It's a secret. You aren't mad 'cause I blabbed ours, are you?"

"Let's see. I get two weddings, three slaves, and you for the rest of my life." She wrinkled her forehead thoughtfully, pursed her lips and then grinned. "Nope. I'm tickled pink."

Elvin said the same thing when Gus got him on the phone. "Why, I'd be tickled pink to marry you and Miss Parrish. Twice I'd be tickled pink, hoss. 'Gratulations. You're smarter'n I thought."

"Thanks, Elvin. Be here in half an hour."

Elvin made it in twenty minutes, which gave him time for French toast and coffee, but cut short Gus and Cydney's farewell till four o'clock.

"I'm about to be whisked upstairs for a day of extreme pampering. Gwen managed to pry Domino away from Misha to help." Cydney climbed on the bottom step of the foyer stairs and wound her arms around his neck. "I wonder if I can get Gwen to feed me grapes."

"Don't push your luck, babe. The honeymoon won't be near as much fun if you're in a body cast."

She laughed and kissed him. Gus collected Elvin and Fletch and set off in Elvin's cruiser with the lights flashing. Traffic gave way and they sailed into Springfield, where Gus bought Cydney a plain gold band—Fletch knew her size. Fletch bought a ring for Cydney to slip on Gus' finger.

"I told her it would look better in your nose," Fletch said.

He and Elvin laughed. Gus grinned and moved to the diamond case. He bought her a pair of 2-carat earrings and a 5-carat bridal set.

"For the do-over," he said to Fletch and a grinning Elvin.

When they returned to Tall Pines, the house was awash in women. Mamie grabbed Gus by the face, pulled his head down and kissed him.

"Your bride's cuter'n a bug's ear, Gussie. Her sis is still a witch that starts with a *b*, but I won't tell her so till you two is married."

Cloris and her sisters fluttered him into the kitchen. They

sat him down and fed him lunch, cut his sandwich, stirred his coffee and told him how beautiful Cydney looked already.

"The French girl gave her a facial," Cloris said in her chirpy little voice. "And a manicure she said was French, too."

"Do brides still do the something old, something new thing?"

"Oh my, *yes,* Gus. It's tradition."

"Would you take this to Cydney?" He reached in his pocket for the broach he'd slipped into it earlier, a small gold, openwork heart studded with seed pearls. "It was Aunt Phoebe's."

"I'll be right back." Cloris fluttered away and came back sniffling. "Miss Phoebe's pin is Cydney's something old. Her something new is what she's wearing for the wedding. Her something borrowed is Bebe's veil. Sarah fixed it up real pretty to match her outfit. Miz Parrish gave her something blue. A star sapphire on a gold chain." Cloris plucked a hankie from her cuff. "Mr. Parrish gave it to her on their wedding day."

Her sisters sighed. Mamie's bottom lip quavered.

Goddamn happy tears. Gus shook his head and took his dishes to the sink, pushed through the swinging door and saw the great room doors ajar. When he stepped into the room, he saw Louella fiddling with something on the piano and strolled toward her up the aisle, his hands in his pockets. "Hey, Louella. Need a hand?"

"I'm finished, thanks. Come see."

Gus climbed the dais steps and looked at Aunt Phoebe's grand piano. Four framed photographs sat next to the music stand. His parents' and Artie and Beth's wedding pictures, Aldo's high school graduation photo and a smiling snapshot of Aunt Phoebe.

"I thought," Louella said, "you might like to have your family at your wedding."

Gus felt his throat swell and tears well in his eyes. Goddamn happy tears, he thought, and smiled. At last, he got it. He climbed up on the piano bench on his knees, cupped Louella's face and kissed her on the lips.

"I couldn't have better friends, Louella, than you and Elvin."

"Oh, go on." She blushed and gave him a playful slap on the chest.

"Hey, bridegroom!" Fletch called from the pocket doors. "Get a move on. It's almost two o'clock!"

"Gotta go." Gus pecked Louella on the cheek, wheeled off the bench and trotted down the aisle to meet Fletch.

Two hours, he thought while he was in the shower. Two hours and Cydney will be mine, all mine. He shut the water off, knotted a towel around his waist and pushed open the glass door.

Fletch and Elvin were in the bathroom, already dressed in their tuxedos. Fletch sat on the toilet, the lid down, eyes closed and face upturned. Elvin leaned over him with a jar of cream foundation in one hand and a wedge-shaped sponge in the other.

"Ow!" Fletch howled. "Watch the nose!"

Elvin glowered. "You want me to send you back to Miz Parrish?"

"Hell no. This was her idea, so I wouldn't look fresh from a bar fight. Just be careful."

"You need a darker shade," Gus said, rubbing a towel through his hair. "I can still see bruises."

Fletch shot him a glare. "Butt out, Max Factor."

Gus dried his hair and shaved. Carefully, so he wouldn't nick himself, and turned out of the bathroom.

"Present from your bride on the bed!" Fletch called after him.

A pair of lavender silk boxer shorts with the name Clyde stitched in gold thread on the waistband. Gus felt his face scald and snatched them off the bed. Too late. A burst of raunchy, locker room laughter erupted behind him. He shot a blistering scowl at Elvin and Fletch, hanging through the bathroom doorway, grinning at him.

"You two did this. When?"

"While you were having Cydney's rings engraved," Fletch said.

Gus grabbed a pillow off the bed and threw it at them. The bathroom door slammed shut and the pillow bounced off it onto the floor. He laughed, quietly so Fletch and Elvin wouldn't hear him, pulled on the boxers and snapped the waistband. He hoped Cydney's color choice meant she was planning later to model the lavender lace lingerie he'd bought her.

Gus got into his tuxedo pants, shirt and studs by himself. Fletch helped him with the tie and the cummerbund. Elvin held his coat while he shrugged into it. At three o'clock, Gus led the way downstairs.

Everyone in Crooked Possum, all 162 citizens, filled his living room. A cheer went up when he appeared at the top of the foyer steps, led by Mayor Figgle, who was serving drinks behind the bar. Gus smiled and waved, so touched his throat closed and another wash of goddamn happy tears filled his eyes.

Fletch shook his hand. Elvin clapped him on the back and damn near knocked him over. Gus started down the steps, but Gwen waved him back, swung her camera forward by the strap around her neck and snapped at least a dozen rapid-fire pictures.

When she finished, she came toward him, an absolute knockout in jade-green silk, her hair swept up in a jeweled comb. She carried a single white rose, came up the foyer steps and bumped Gus down one. They stood eye to eye while she pinned the rose to his lapel.

"I love my baby sister," she said, low enough so no one else could hear. "Take care of her and you and I will get along just fine."

"Will do, sis." Gus grinned at her and she laughed.

At 3:45, Georgette rang one of Aunt Phoebe's bells.

"Seats, please! Seats, please! The bride is almost ready!"

Everyone shuffled into the great room. Gus and Elvin waited by the doors till they were seated. Fletch shook his hand and headed upstairs to collect Cydney. Georgette came to him, a corsage of white roses pinned to the jacket of her jade-green lace dress.

"I'll signal you from the piano, Angus, when I want you and Sheriff Cantwell to come up the aisle. All right?"

"Yes, Georgette." Gus nodded. "We'll wait for the signal."

"Excellent." She patted his arm, started away and turned back. "You do love Cydney, don't you, Angus?"

"Yes, Georgette." Gus smiled at her. "I do love Cydney."

"I thought so." She smiled, too, and blew him a kiss.

When she nodded to them from Aunt Phoebe's piano, Elvin laid a hand on his shoulder. "Here we go, hoss. Don't trip over your feet now."

"Thanks, Elvin," Gus muttered.

They walked up the aisle side by side and took their places. Elvin tall and solemn on the dais, Gus one step down on his left.

From the front row, Louella and Mamie waved at him, a box of Kleenex between them. Next to them sat Mayor Figgle and Cloris and her sisters, all in their little veiled church hats, their hankies at the ready.

Gus smiled at them, his hands folded in front of him. He felt calm as lake water on a still day until Georgette played the first chord of "The Wedding March" and the guests rose. His heart shot up his throat, he couldn't breathe and he felt himself start to weave.

"Steady, hoss," Elvin murmured.

He closed his eyes, opened them and saw Cydney coming up the aisle in slow, measured steps on Fletch's arm. A beam of soft autumn sun struck the runner at her feet. It bloomed into a pool of golden light as she stepped into it, looked up at him and smiled. The peach suit she wore glistened, her eyes shimmered beneath the halo of white tulle fluffed around her face.

Gus' heart stopped pounding and he could breathe again. He glanced at the piano, at Artie and Beth's wedding picture. His brother winked at him. He was sure of it this time. Absolutely positive.

When Elvin solemnly asked who gave this woman to be married to this man, Fletch said, "Her mother and I do." Gus came down a step, closed Cydney's left hand in his right and turned them to face Elvin.

"Are those tears in your eyes, bub?" she whispered.

"You bet." Gus squeezed her fingers. "Goddamn happy tears."

epilogue

Barnes & Noble Bookseller
Country Club Plaza, Kansas City
2 years, 7 months, 3 weeks, and 5 days later

Her wedding day—well, both of them, actually—were gloriously sunny and beautiful autumn days. So naturally, Cydney figured, it would rain on the day of her first book signing.

It was June and it was pouring. Barely 6:45 P.M. and the sky was nearly black. Thunder rattled the floor-to-ceiling windows overlooking the street. The rain spattering the glass glimmered like diamonds.

A real gully washer, Mamie would say. The jar of prickly pear jelly she'd given Cydney to commemorate this occasion sat on the tiny table the store had set up for her, next to the bouquet of pastel daylilies her mother insisted she *must* have. A teddy bear with *I Love You* stitched in red on its chest filled what little space remained.

"What am I going to do?" Cydney worried to Gus. "I don't have room for my books."

"For starters, pray somebody knocks the jelly off and breaks it."

Cydney frowned at him. He stood behind her, leaning against the Romance section with his arms folded. He wore jeans, a blue shirt and a navy twill blazer, his Ray-Bans and the ball cap she'd bought him to replace the one he'd crushed when he'd stepped through the wicket in her backyard. Cydney called it his I-am-NOT-a-famous-author disguise.

"Just a thought," he said, and grinned.

"It will break Mamie's heart if her jelly isn't on the table."

"I doubt Mamie and Louella will show up in this weather, babe."

Cydney doubted anyone would. "I promised, Gus."

"Okay. Lose the bear."

"Bebe and Aldo gave it to me for luck." She snatched up the teddy and hugged it. "And I'll lose my life if I lose the flowers."

"Cydney." He stepped away from the bay full of books and wrapped his hands on the back of her chair. "What is your purpose this evening?"

"Um. Point people to the bathroom and the Travel section?"

"No. Your purpose is to meet people, make nice, and sell books."

"Are you going to leave me here all by myself?"

"It's a rite of passage, babe. Trial by fire."

Served her right, Cydney supposed, for refusing to let Gus tinker with her manuscript. For saying, "Go write your own book," and slapping his hand every time he came near her laptop.

"Old poop." Cydney stuck out her tongue and crossed her eyes. "See if I buy your next book."

She didn't see the cart coming toward her until she uncrossed her eyes and blinked. Then she saw it, and the maybe twenty-year-old clerk pushing it, hovering behind Gus. The badge on his shirt said his name was Terence. The look on his face said he thought her name was Nuts.

"Oh—hello, Terence." She beamed a bright, I'm-a-professional, honest-I-am smile at him and thrust out her hand. "Cydney Munroe."

"Nice to meet you. Thanks for coming." He reached over the cart to shake her fingers and nodded at the crammed, matchbook-size table. "Where would you like me to put your books?"

"One second," Cydney said. Eeny-meany-miney-mo, she

thought, eyeing the flowers, the teddy bear and Mamie's jelly. "I'll clear a spot."

"Hi, Terence." Gus offered his hand. "I'm Gus Munroe."

"As in Angus?" His blue eyes lit up. "The mystery writer?"

"Sometimes. Tonight I'm just Gus. Cydney's husband."

"Dude." Terence knuckled him in the arm. "Max Stone rocks. We've got like a zillion copies of *Dead on Delivery*. Would you autograph one for me? And maybe a few for the store?"

"Uh—" Gus flipped up his sunglasses and slid a look at Cydney.

"Go." She smiled and shooed him away. "Sign."

Get writer's cramp, she thought glumly. At least one of us will.

"Glad to." He dropped his Ray-Bans on his nose. "Lead the way."

Terence pulled Gus toward Hardcover Fiction, flipping a wave over his shoulder to Cydney. "Be right back, Cindy."

"*Cydney,*" she said, and sat down on the hard wooden chair.

Well, wasn't this fun. For this she'd put on panty hose and the peach suit she'd been married in the first time. Where were the crowds? The press? Her legion of devoted fans?

In your fantasies, her little voice said. *Where they belong.*

Cydney spread her fingers in her lap, gazed at the gold ring on her left hand, the monster diamond with its matching band on her right, and drew a deep breath.

"Don't be a peashooter," she told herself firmly. "Be an Uzi."

Cydney stood up and went to the cart, picked up one of her books and smiled. Touched a finger to her name, Cydney Parrish Munroe, and the title scrolled above it in gold foil, *Mother of the Bride.*

When Gus came back at 6:55, she'd propped one of her books up against Mamie's jelly so people could see it. She'd moved the flowers to make room for a few more copies and sat with the teddy bear in her lap.

He stopped in front of the table, read the signs she'd made with a sheet of paper torn from the sketchpad in her purse— REST ROOMS, with an arrow pointing left, TRAVEL SECTION, with an arrow pointing right—and laughed.

"Show time, babe." He leaned over and kissed her. "Good luck."

Stay, *please,* Cydney wanted to beg, but she bit her lip instead till he'd strolled out of sight with his hands in his pockets. The only other human being, it seemed, in the entire section of the store.

Lightning flashed and thunder boomed. The windows rattled and the overhead fluorescent lights flickered.

I should've brought a candle, Cydney thought. "And a book to read," she said with a sigh.

"I can recommend this one." A middle-aged woman in brown slacks and a tan raincoat stepped in front of her and handed her a book. "I read it last week. It's very good."

"Uh—thanks," Cydney said, her voice stiff with nerves.

The woman leaned around the front of the table, read the signs and smiled. "How very nice to put a little help desk right here."

Two more customers asked if she worked here. When Cydney said no, they gave her a well-what-are-you-doing-here-then look and walked away, annoyed. A portly man with a handlebar mustache told her the whole Kansas City metropolitan area was under a Severe Thunderstorm Warning until midnight. The streets, he said, were flooding. Oh good, Cydney thought, I won't have far to go to drown myself when this is over.

She was doodling in her sketchpad, drawing a stick figure of Gus on his knees begging her for sex for, oh, say the next three years. The least he deserved for dumping her and prancing off, when a drop of rain plopped and smeared her pen strokes.

Wonderful. I'm sitting under the one single leak in this whole huge store, Cydney thought, until she glanced up and saw Louella and Mamie, standing in front of her sopping wet and smiling.

"Oh Louella! Oh Mamie!" She leaped up, around the table, and hugged them. "You made it!"

"Wouldn't a missed it!" Mamie said. "Even wore m'teeth."

"Look, Mamie." Cydney lifted her book. "Here's your jelly."

"Well ain't that clever." She smiled, flushing with pleasure. "I'll see to it you git a jar ever'time you do one o' these here things."

"You'd best sit down and get ready to write." Louella shrugged out of her raincoat and smiled. "There's plenty more comin' behind us."

Mayor Figgle and Cloris and her sisters. Roylee and Sarah Boyce. The Elks from the Lodge. Half of Crooked Possum at least. Cydney's throat closed at the sight of them lined up smiling in front of her table. Her eyes filled with tears. God-damn happy tears she had to keep blinking away so she could see to inscribe their books.

Louella filched a stool from Terence and sat next to her, handing her books as she needed them. Mamie trotted back and forth from the café, serving cappuccinos and lattes and a cup of Earl Grey to Cydney.

"Why don't I see your parents?" Louella whispered to her.

"I faxed Dad and left a message on Mother's machine here, but I'm not sure if they're fighting in Cannes this week or Kansas City."

"Are they married yet?"

"No. Domino and Misha are. Mother and Dad visited them in Paris."

"I can't believe your parents would miss your first book signing."

They didn't. In they swept at eight o'clock. Rain-soaked and craning their necks for a glimpse of Cydney. Georgette's hair was a sleek shade of silver to match Fletch's mane. "We *must* coordinate," she'd said.

"Darling!" Georgette kissed her over the table, tucked her hand in Fletch's arm and beamed. "Our daughter the author, Fletch."

He kissed Cydney and winked. "Thought we'd forget, didn't you?"

She didn't see Bebe and Aldo come in, but she heard them a few minutes later when eighteen-month-old Arthur Fletcher Munroe let out a squeal. Cydney peered through the crowd and saw him, clapping his plump little baby hands on Fletch's cheeks. Bebe caught Cydney's eye, smiled and waved at her with Little Artie's cap while she smoothed his blond hair.

The sight of the baby, the light of her life, made Cydney's heart swell. Who needed fantasies when reality was so sweet?

But fantasy walked into the Romance section at 8:17, all six feet and two inches of him, tall, dark and drop-dead handsome with an armful of long-stemmed peach roses. Gus went down on one knee beside her, laid the roses in her lap and grinned.

"How's this for dreams come true?"

"Perfect." Cydney sighed and wound her arms around his neck.

She yelped when Gus swept her to her feet, and laughed and clutched the roses as he bent her over his arm and kissed her. Mamie whooped, the Elks cheered, her parents applauded and Louella stuck two fingers in her mouth and whistled.

The loudest whistle Cydney had ever heard, so shrill she thought it was a siren. She turned her head toward the rain-speckled glass and realized it *was* a siren. She could see the flicker of rotating red lights on the rain-streaked glass.

"Look, Uncle Cyd!" Bebe pointed at the window. "It's Mother and Sheriff Cantwell!"

It was still raining pitchforks and little dogs, but Gwen's Armani trench coat was bone dry. She took her camera out of its case and looped it over her neck, her revoltingly perfect hair swinging precisely into place.

"Hold that pose," she said, and fired a dozen shots before she'd let Gus release Cydney and stand her up.

"That was some entrance, Elvin," he said to the Sheriff.

"Prob'ly gonna get chewed by the local boys, but what the hey," he said with a shrug. "I wasn't gonna miss this."

"I've got a list." Gwen swung her camera aside, came up to

the table and plucked a sheet of paper out of her pocket. "One for the Secretary of State, one for the Vice President, one for the King of Spain, one for the Prince—" Gwen stopped and frowned at her. "Close your mouth, Cydney. Sit down and start signing."

It took her till 8:45 to autograph books for all the people on Gwen's list. Terence brought two empty boxes, packed the books and followed Gwen, starry-eyed, to load them in Elvin's cruiser.

"See you at the restaurant, darling!" Georgette called from the far side of the room with Fletch. "Nine-fifteen sharp. We have a reservation."

"We'll be there, Mother." Cydney wagged her fingers at Georgette, swung around in her chair and faced Gus. "Did I pass my Trial by Fire?"

"With flying colors." He smiled and kissed her.

"How cool, Uncle Cyd!" Bebe gushed up to the table with Aldo, and Little Artie on her hip, his head on her shoulder, sound asleep. "The store guy said you sold *three hundred books*!"

"Way to go, babe!" Gus gave her a high five.

The smack woke Little Artie. He raised his head and blinked, his cheek red and wrinkled from Bebe's sweater, yawned at Gus and smiled.

"Give kisses and go to Daddy," Bebe cooed to the baby.

Little Artie opened his mouth and slobbered on Bebe's pursed lips. She laughed and passed the baby to Gus.

"Guess what, slugger?" He bent his head and rubbed noses with his son. "Mommy's a star."

Artie gurgled, laid his head on Gus' shoulder and smiled at Cydney, his long dark lashes drifting shut over his father's gray eyes.

"Mommy is pooped," she said, stretching on her toes to kiss Artie.

"Mommy has a congratulations party to go to," Gus said. "See you at the restaurant, darling!" he piped in the dead-on imitation of her mother he'd perfected over the last two years. "Nine-fifteen sharp!"

Artie giggled, rubbed his face in Gus' shoulder and went to sleep.

"We'll see you there, Uncle Cyd. You, too, Uncle Gus." Bebe and Aldo waved and headed for the door.

Cydney thanked Terence, who now thought her name was Goddess by the glow in his eyes, picked up her flowers, her purse and her jelly and limped out of the store with the baby snoring on Gus' chest.

"My feet hurt," she complained. "Why do my feet hurt?"

"Sitting too long." He cradled Artie with one hand and pushed the door open with the other.

The rain had stopped. The pavement gleamed in the late midsummer twilight. Cydney took a step and winced.

"I want to go home," she moaned. "Why can't I go home?"

"Because you only have one first book party," Gus said, as she slid past him through the door. "You can go home anytime."

Oh yeah, I can, Cydney thought with a smile, with the man of my dreams, the man who married me twice.

The Bunny Hop was an opening weekend tradition at the Belle Coeur Theatre. When the musical revue ended, the Bunny Hop music—"Da-de-da-de-da-de, Da-Da-Da, Da-de-da-de-da-da, HOP-HOP-HOP"—blared out of the speakers on the walls.

Lindsay Varner cheered with the rest of the audience as dancers costumed like 1950s bobby-soxers twirled onto the stage. They performed the steps so everyone could see them, then formed a line that danced off stage into the audience. The seats emptied as everyone joined in, Lindsay included, laughing and hopping between Aunt Dovey and Uncle Ezra.

Lindsay couldn't remember the last time she'd had so much fun in a theater. Certainly not since her mother, Vivienne, realized that Lindsay in her pink tutu and ballet slippers was her ticket out of Belle Coeur, Missouri, and a bad marriage.

The line threaded its way up the aisles and into the lobby where it ended in a crescendo of taped music, whistles and applause. Lindsay's sister, Jolie, creative director of the Belle Coeur Theatre, popped up the stairs onto the gallery overlooking the lobby. Her face shining and her eyes bright, she applauded the audience.

"Time now for the really big announcement I promised you!" Jolie called. "I'm so happy to tell you all that my sister, Lindsay, the delightful Jessie we all remember from that great

TV show, *Betwixt and Be Teen*, has agreed to grace the boards of the Belle Coeur Theatre this summer in a new play I've written. Ladies and gentlemen—*Lind-s-a-y Var-n-e-e-r!*"

Jolie sang her name out like a ring announcer at a boxing match and pointed at her, flushed and buried in the crowd of bunny-hoppers. Heads turned toward her, grins flashed and everyone applauded. Everyone but Lindsay. Jolie should have warned her.

"Go on, child." Aunt Dovey gave her a good hard poke that knocked her forward. "Get up there and take a bow."

Lindsay went, pasting a big bright smile on her face. She caught a glimpse of her sixteen-year-old son, Trey, in the crush, waved to him and blew him a kiss. He blew one back to her as she climbed the steps to the gallery and stood next to Jolie waving at the crowd.

"I'm going to kill you for this," Lindsay said between her teeth without a twitch or a flicker in her smile.

"You've gotta catch me first." Jolie slid away from her, batting her hands at the air to quiet the applause. "I can think of only one thing better than having Lindsay on stage again," she told the audience. "And that's having her *Betwixt and Be Teen* costar on stage with her. Ladies and gentlemen, please welcome to the Belle Coeur Theatre—" Jolie paused for effect and swept her arm toward the staircase that led from the gallery up to the second floor "—Noah Patrick!"

Hoots and whistles and thunderous applause erupted. An ice cold wave of shock rushed to the top of Lindsay's head then plunged to her toes. She hadn't seen Noah since her eighteenth birthday party. She'd never expected to see him again. And she'd hoped—oh, God, how she'd hoped—that she never would.

The crowd shifted, lifting their heads and their cheers toward the stairs on Lindsay's right. She could feel her smile, frozen in place on her face, her hands like ice, her fingers icicles wrapped around the gallery rail. *Look at him,* she told herself. *Just look at him and get it over with.*

The image stuck in Lindsay's head was Noah as she'd known him on *Betwixt and Be Teen*, blond, brash and beautiful. She turned her head and saw him coming down the stairs, a smile on his face as he waved to the crowd, and felt a head-spinning clash of memory and reality.

His blond hair was darker, cut to just brush the collar of the blue shirt he wore with two buttons open at the throat. His face was tanned, the Hollywood smile crinkling lines at his eyes and the corners of his mouth. He'd been slim and lean as Sam, Jessie's beloved. Now he carried more weight in his upper body. His chest and shoulders seemed a lot wider than Lindsay remembered, but he wasn't any taller. She'd always been able to look him in the eye.

Noah came off the last step onto the gallery, smiling and waving. He slid an arm around Jolie, scooped her against him, and touched his lips to her forehead. His gaze lifted past the top of her head and settled on Lindsay. He blinked, pulled away from Jolie and mouthed the word "Whoa."

"Hold it right there, young feller!" A furious voice bellowed up from the lobby floor. "Lucille would like a word with you about Sassy!"

"Oh, shit—Uncle Ezra," Jolie said to Noah out of the side of her mouth and gave him a push toward the stairs. "Get out of here. *Quick.*"

The shove didn't budge Noah, and he wasn't about to let it. After being out of the limelight for so many years, the applause swelling up from the lobby was heady stuff. So was looking at a beautiful woman. One who actually looked back at him. It had been a long damn time since that had happened.

Holy God, Lindsay Varner was gorgeous. Tall, willowy, elegantly beautiful. The pretty teenager he barely remembered from *BBT* had grown up to be Grace Kelly in *To Catch a Thief*. She was frowning at him, which meant she remembered *him*, all right, but he could work on that.

Starting right now, Noah decided, as he stepped around Jolie and headed toward Lindsay.

"You hang on to him, Jolie!" The angry voice roared out of the crowd again. "That's the no-good feller what lured my Sassy!"

Lindsay spun away from Noah, spread her hands on the

railing and peered over it. Noah followed her gaze and saw a tall, bony old fart pushing his way through the crowd toward the stairs with a doughy, white-haired woman wearing gold round-rimmed glasses—Robin Williams as Mrs. Doubtfire—pulling on his arm.

"Is that Lucille?" Noah asked Jolie.

"No. That's Aunt Dovey."

"Where's Lucille?" Noah scanned the crowd. "And who is Sassy?"

"My other aunt. The one who showed you up to my office."

"The scrawny little redhead who propositioned me?"

"That's Aunt Sassy. She's Uncle Ezra's wife, and he's the jealous type." Jolie clamped her hands on Noah's arm and yanked. He held his ground. "I mean it, Noah. You don't want to tangle with Uncle Ezra."

"What's he gonna do?" Noah snorted. "Shoot me?"

The old fart gave Mrs. Doubtfire a shove, reached the stairs and sprang up them, the angry scowl on his face fixed on Noah. Lindsay wheeled off the gallery to intercept him. Noah went after her, Jolie dragging at him like an anchor until he shrugged her off.

"*Lind-say!*" Jolie shouted.

Lindsay whipped around and saw Noah, glanced at Uncle Ezra, then at Noah again, and came up two steps to meet him.

"I'll handle this," she said, looking him in the chest, not the eye.

"Handle what?" Noah asked.

Over the top of Lindsay's head, he saw the old fart open his tweed coat and reach for— a shotgun. Jesus Christ. The crazy old coot had a shotgun in his coat. He pulled it out and kept coming up the stairs.

"Meet Lucille," Jolie said behind Noah.

The crowd was still cheering and clapping. Did they think this was part of the show? Or had Lindsay and Jolie's mother, Vivienne, the sneaky bitch, arranged all this just to get him shot?

Uncle Ezra stopped a few steps shy of the landing, raised Lucille to his shoulder and pointed her single barrel straight at Noah—and at Lindsay as she turned around to face him.

Noah flung himself at her, swept his arms around her and dragged her to the floor.

They hit the gallery with a thump. Nose to nose and out of breath with Lindsay partially on top of him. A happy accident that gave him a pulse-thudding feel of her curved-in-all-the-right-places body. Her eyes were a wonderful shade of blue, like the Pacific on a calm day. Wide-open and startled like her mouth.

What a mouth. Pink and lush. The most kissable mouth he'd been this close to in years, so he kissed her. Nothing fancy. Just a hi-there-long-time-no-remember brush of his lips. He expected her to recoil, but all she did was blink. Once, slowly. As if she shut her eyes and opened them again, he'd be gone. Like a bad dream.

"Noah," she said, her voice stunned and breathless. "What are you doing here?"

"Saving you from being shot by your lunatic uncle Ezra."

"Lucille isn't loaded." Lindsay's luscious pink mouth firmed into a frown. "She's never loaded."

"So much for being a hero." Noah flashed his best TV heartthrob smile. "Then I guess I stopped by to see if you'd care to pick up where we left off."

"Did you?" Linday's Pacific blue eyes darkened like a storm at sea, then she doubled her fist and punched him in the nose.